VICTORY

THE PAUL ISAAC VAMPIRE SERIES

JAMES GILLEN

Hydra
Publications

ISBN: 978-1-940466-69-9

Goshen, Kentucky 40026
www.hydrapublications.com

DEDICATION

To my parents, who have always been there for me through the good and the bad, the thick and the thin. To my loving wife, Valinda. Thank you for completing my life and endless smiles. To Samantha for being the daughter I find absolutely amazing. You make it fun to be a dad. To Peyton, my little dude. You allow me to be seven years old again and don't judge! And to Pursey, my beloved Bulldog. May you pursue life like you do cheeseburgers. To all the Paul Isaac fans, I thank you from the bottom of my heart and hope you enjoy the book.

1

THE WETNESS HIT me with pulverizing beads of precipitation as I picked up my pace across the Crowne Plaza parking lot. Cold wind pushed me back like an invisible bully. I lowered my head to keep the rain from blinding or drowning me. Goosebumps formed on my arms as I pulled the coat tight against my body, the cigar in the inner pocket pressed against my chest. I reached back inside the car and grabbed the black leather bag containing, among other things, an ax. The ax would be a necessity. The cigar, a luxury.

Through the rain and blinding lights, I surveyed the parking lot. I had hoped to spot Kansas' Explorer. He had been the reason I found myself down here tonight. Without his phone call, I would be warm and dry and at home.

The man had been spiraling downward at breakneck speed, but in the hardest part of my heart, I couldn't blame him. His wife and unborn son had been kidnapped by a twisted cockroach hell bent on taking over the city. A baby had been delivered dead in a gift box to him, while his wife remained in a hospital in a coma. Later tests had proven she had miscarried. Kansas, I feared, would never recover. In the few times I had seen him since, he appeared withdrawn, if not suicidal. I questioned his sanity.

Now he spent most of his time drowning his life in a bottle. I had wished worse things on him not long ago, and now every time I see him, I'm reminded of what a self-absorbed son of a bitch I am. One of these nights I plan on changing my ways, but this was not going to be that night.

The wind slapped the collar of my coat against my neck, cold with rain as I battled my way across the sea of puddles. As I made it to the sanctuary of the hotel entrance, I toyed with the idea of puffing on the cigar for a few minutes before going inside. I didn't feel like doing this tonight. Death had become as familiar to me as an old friend, but when it came into my life, usually it meant hunting down something vile, disgusting and ultimately evil. To make matters worse, it usually turned out to be hell bent on killing me as well. I had no reason to believe tonight's little visit would be any different. Like changing my ways, I had also promised myself that I would quit smoking the damn things, but again, this was not going to be that night. But against my better judgment, I decided to press on and get the inevitable over with.

Cold, stiff fingers grasped the handle to the glass door. I knew once I pulled it open, I couldn't go back. Even though I could clearly see inside, I shook with the unknown. Every crime scene left you thinking you had seen everything, and then it out does itself the very next time. Being cold and wet beat the hell out of whatever waited for me on the other side of the door.

I followed the trail of officers and paramedics into the lobby of the hotel. I began to scan the countless faces for Detective Ezekiel Kansas. All familiar faces, but none with the guts to look me in the eyes or acknowledge my existence. Nothing came easy for me. I consider it God's way of getting back at me for being such an over the top bastard.

Through the sea of endless faces, some I recalled and others I didn't, one stood out. One that made my world implode on impact. A part of my history I wasn't very proud of. My heart beat a little faster. Suddenly, I found myself far more scared of things other than monsters and victims. I wanted to turn and run, but before I could convince my stiff legs to do so, she saw me. Every part of my body instantly went cold.

"Paul?" A familiar voice broke my train of thought.

I did my best to act as though I hadn't seen her. In her eyes, I could tell she didn't buy it. "Ashley? What are you doing here?" I found myself at a standstill. Not sure whether I should shake hands, hug, or do nothing at all. I chose the safe option and did nothing at all.

By her body language, I could tell the awkwardness between us hadn't been just one sided. "You look great," Ashley said, giving me a fake smile as she wrapped her arms around me in a sincere hug. If it hadn't been for the bag in my hand, I would have hugged back. Instead I stood there like a bump on a log in awkward silence.

She let go and I took a deep breath and spoke, "You look overwhelmed." It had been eight years since I saw her last. She worked for the Paranormal Crime Scene Investigation Team back then. That's how we had met. I knew her ambition had been to be a detective in this field, but seeing her now made me realize just how fast time flew by. Different badge and credentials, but she looked the same. I took a quick look at her hand. No ring. I cursed under my breath. More proof of what a waste of space on the planet I turned out to be. "Detective Vaccarro, I see. I'm impressed."

A genuine smile this time. "Two years now."

My fake smile didn't win any awards either. Time to change the subject. "You still up in Jacksonville?" Small talk had never been a strong point for me, but with Ashley, or Detective Vaccarro, it had turned into something of a nightmare. I snagged quick glances over her small frame, hoping to see Kansas somewhere close by, but so far he had been a no-show. "What the hell are you doing here?"

She shook her head and pulled a strand of brown hair past her ear. I took in her girl-next-door beauty and reminisced the good times. "Yeah, with Price retiring and Detective Kansas on hiatus, the department brought me down to help out for a while." An awkward shrug. "Not sure my timing could have been any worse. They don't teach you things like this in the academy."

Truthfully, I wanted to get away as soon as possible. Seeing her had been a shock to my system and I needed time to process. Surprises like this need to be spoon fed to me. I felt light headed and queasy. I came here to stake a few hearts and instead had one driven through mine. "Speaking of Kansas, have you seen him?"

"No. I'm in charge of this one. He's still...out."

Out had been a nice way of saying it. "You heard what happened? His wife, the drinking." I trailed off from there.

"Yeah. That's what brought me down here. Truthfully, how's he doing?"

I thought it through before answering. "As good as someone can get when their loved ones have been destroyed by things that want to eat you. You know, the same things we made legal."

She looked around again. I followed her eyes to the bag in my hand, the ax in the other. "Officially, Paul, why are you here?"

I gave an honest answer. "A question I asked myself a hundred times as I swam across the parking lot tonight." She knew what I did for a living. We both were standing in the middle of a crime scene. I didn't find the dots that difficult to connect. "My job hasn't changed."

"Exactly my point. Is there something I can help you with?" Her response threw me a little.

"Kansas told me to come down here. That there had been a mass attack." I soaked in her green eyes and soft features. God, they sparkled like diamonds when she smiled. It seemed like a million years since I had last seen them. A melancholy storm fell over me. I no longer saw the love I had remembered from the past.

Ashley took a deep breath. "That's one way of putting it, but don't you still just kill vampires and victims of vampires? I mean, that's the point you wanted to get through to me, right?"

We had never seen eye to eye on vampire rights, so the statement didn't surprise me that much. Add in the tension between us, the niceties had to come to an end sometime sooner rather than later. "Look, I've told you over and over that I'm sorry. I know I'm the asshole of the century in all of this. Hurting you was never part of the plan. I'm not here to dig up old dirt." Why I chose now to confess, confused the living hell out of me. It had nothing to do with why I stood there. "God, Ashley, I'm sorry. It's just that I wasn't prepared to see you here tonight."

The smile on her face evaporated. "Understood. I've learned to live and move on. We both have our reasons for being what we are. I'm not here to confront you. If this hadn't been such a great opportunity for me, believe me, I wouldn't be standing here. I'll find the bad guy and stay out of your way. We will approach this as two professionals, nothing personal." She held out her hand. "Deal?"

I sat the bag on the floor, leaned the ax against the wall and shook her hand. I feared I would never let go. I started to ask for Kansas again when the vampire power trickled across my back. This night would go in the record books for one of the worst in my life. Gut feeling at this point, but my gut usually knew better than my brain.

Dieter Procnow sported a black rain coat still dripping with water. His hair mangled against his face. I might have been going to go out on a limb but I'd say it hadn't been washed since the first day he crawled out of a coffin. The combination of oil and water took him to a whole new level of greasy. He smelled like a living dead ash tray. Unlike most undead that use visual magic to mask their true decaying looks, Dieter really looked the part of a dead corpse. Pale, skinny, unpleasant. "What are you doing here?" His voice sounded low and gruff. A true element of surprise plastered across his face. Odd. He looked over to Ashley, damn, I kept forgetting, Detective Vaccarro. "Lady Vaccarro, so pleasant to see you." He lifted her hand and kissed it lightly. "Welcome home."

Detective Vaccarro smiled and looked to me. "Taking notes, Isaac?" Another genuine smile and a quick wink.

But my nightmare continued. Through the thick sea of people, I saw Quinn Rubio making his way toward us. Master vampire of the living dead, or *Dracul Morte'* in specific terms. Unlike Dieter, Quinn seemed well pressed, dapper as ever. He wore a black silk suit that fit so perfectly, you would have thought it grew on him like a second skin. A bright red shirt glowed under the black jacket as if made of neon. His long hair combed back in a ponytail, allowing us all to take in his pale dead face. Cologne wafted in the air and I did everything I could not to sneeze. His features were soft, almost feminine. His good looks usually got him farther than his power. Like a politician, he always knew exactly what to say, whom to say it to. He looked harmless, but I knew better. "I feel like I have just stepped into a macabre version of Abercrombie and Fitch," I added.

I could tell by the look on both blood suckers faces that neither had expected to see me. I didn't know why. Like it or not, I always got an invite when a victim had a set of fang marks in their skin. And from what Kansas told me, there were a lot of bodies with twice as many bite marks.

Luckily for me, Dieter moved away from me. "Again, I will ask you what are you doing here, Mr. Isaac? I do not know how things worked with you and Price or Kansas, but with Lady Vaccarro, you will not intimidate or take over as you see fit. Nor will you simply show up unannounced." He looked to Detective Vaccarro. "Showing up has never been your strong suit has it, Mr. Isaac?"

I faced Quinn and spoke in a controlled whisper. "And I don't know what they have told you about me, but when a human has lost his or her life to a blood lapper, it's my job to nip the disease in the bud. The fact that this crime scene is being run by you and your maggot freaks doesn't change a thing. I don't trust you. Conflict of interest if you will." He'd do anything he needed to do to keep his fellow coffin nappers from the business end of my weapons.

Quinn stared me down as if I had pissed in his cornflakes. "There are no vampire victims here, simply vampire...*victims*. There is nothing here that should concern you. Do yourself a favor and simply go home." He studied me. "Besides, if being a vampire is the conflict of interest, I could question you on the same terms, *Dracul Sang*."

A term I had heard a lot recently. An ancient title given to the master vampire of the pure-blooded coven in a city. Two types of vein lickers existed. Those born vampire (pure blood) and those that rose as vampires (commercial). The latter are the more popular among today's society. They are the ones that the world has fallen in love with. Beautiful, youthful and coveted among society.

"What does he mean by that, Paul?" Ashley asked.

Through a twist of vampire politics, I represented the *Dracul Sang* or master vampire of the pure blood coven of Orlando in the eyes of the coffin cockroaches. A status I didn't acknowledge. I had the roach virus running through my veins, and I had killed the last *Dracul Sang* of Orlando, Asa, some time ago. I hadn't come to terms with it. In fact, I hated it about as much as I hated the coffin monkey in front of me. We both knew it. Quinn enjoyed being an asshole. To Ashley, I simply said, "Nothing. Want to show me the bodies so we can both get on with our nights?"

"There is no need for such things here tonight. As I have said before, this is not a crime scene involving a vampire fugitive. You can go home. I am here on unrelated vampire business." Quinn looked at Dieter, then turned in the large hallway.

I didn't believe him. I also knew I wouldn't get any answers out of him. It didn't take a rocket scientist to figure out that Quinn didn't just arrive here at a roach crime scene to talk about unpaid parking tickets or other trivial "unrelated vampire business."

"Kansas?"

"I do not know, Mr. Isaac. I am not here to keep tabs on him." Quinn nodded to a bar to my right. "Try there, I happen to be dealing with something far more pressing. Now if you do not mind, I have business to attend to." He looked back to Ashley. "May we speak in private?"

I pulled a crucifix out of my pocket and let it dangle from the chain. I stood in front of Quinn, not allowing him past me. "Either we can stand here and swap old recipes and catch up on the good ole days, or you can take me to Kansas and keep your skin from peeling like cheap paint. You know as well as I do, that I will have this down your throat before you can get anyone over here to help you. Don't take a chance on it just to make my day."

Quinn watched the crucifix twist in the light, then turned and searched the crowd before addressing me. "Spoken like a true *Dracul Sang*."

Detective Vaccarro raced between us. I could tell by the look in her eyes, we were done catching up. The tense friendly conversations had come to an end. The eyes looking back at me were ones of authority.

"Stand down, Paul. Make no mistake, I am in charge. I will arrest you if I have to."

Seeing Ashley without warning had left me in an emotional freefall. Unlike me, she had moved on with her life, actually made something of herself. My best option simply to keep my mouth shut. I looked at the badge hanging from a lanyard around her neck. "Excuse me, Detective Vaccarro."

"Let's leave our pasts out of this, Paul. I've already told you, Detective Kansas is not here tonight. I am in charge. Unless you have a reason for being here, I will have to ask you to leave."

"If there has been a vampire attack here, Ashley, I have every right to be here." Controlling my anger grew harder and harder by the second.

"I agree, which is why I'm asking you to leave. There are no victims for you to behead."

I looked to Dieter. "Then mind telling me why Dieter's here?"

"Upon my request, Mr. Isaac," Quinn answered.

"And you are here because?"

"Picking up valuable…things, shall we say." He observed me for a moment. "You really do not know what has taken place here, do you, *Dracul Sang?*"

Out of the corner of my eyes, I could see Ashley's head snap to me. "*Dracul Sang?* Am I missing something here? That's the second time he's called you that."

Quinn nodded lightly. "I see the two of you have much to catch up on, Detective. Perhaps you can point me in the direction of Judge Lopes?"

"Lopes? What's he doing here?" I asked.

Quinn smiled. He had set the trap. "If Dieter shows you the bodies Mr. Isaac, and you see that there has been no vampire attack, will you do us all the favor and go home?"

Ashley spoke up. "I'll show him." She looked to me. "Then you are out of here. Do I make myself clear?" As I looked her in the eyes, my doubts were realized.

She was over me.

2

AHEAD OF ME, I could see a lot of the familiar faces, all with the same look of horror. Most human, sprinkled with a few blood lovers just to make things as complicated for me as possible. I could tell human from biter simply by who had a Styrofoam cup of coffee in their hand and who didn't. Each looked at me, then the ax against the wall. Those glances never ended in eye contact.

As I turned the corner that led to the convention room, I began to see the signs of something vicious. The doors to my left had been crushed in. Metal frames twisted into giant pretzels. Glass littered the floor. The carpet appeared stained with God knows what. In the air, I smelled the pungent odor of fresh blood. Metallic and warm. My mouth watered. First from the hunger caused by the virus in me, then in nausea as I thought about the source.

"Sure you have the stomach for this?" Ashley asked with a sinister grin as she moved past me.

I opened the door to the large room to see pieces and parts of bodies shredded and torn limb from limb. Blood drawn across the walls like a demonic Picasso painting. Most were no longer bodies, just the parts. Impossible to tell where one body ended and the next began, much less how many.

Red, white and blue helium balloons danced like ghosts in the air. The white ones speckled with crimson dots. Overturned tables and chairs confirmed the swift wave of violence. Plates of half eaten beef and chicken rested in chaotic patterns. A white cake sat at the front of the room untouched like a virgin bride.

I stopped just short of the madness, not wanting to contaminate the crime scene. I couldn't find a single square foot ahead of me where anyone could walk without stepping into a pool of blood or onto human flesh or organ.

A large roll of plastic had been taped down as a pathway that led in and out of the room. Puddles of blood seeped from under the carpet around it so thick you could hear it squirt out from under the footsteps of those walking along the pathway of death. Along the walls, I could make out the impressions of handprints. All trying to run from the death just before the monsters shredded them. My world bottled into a single word as I looked along the far wall. A word written in human blood. It stood there in full attention, daring me to ask the question. "What does 'VICTORY' mean?"

My world had suddenly been consumed by the one word. For a victim to write a word on the wall before dying, it had to be significant. For a killer to write it, profound. Why VICTORY?

"Why did Quinn call you *Dracul Sang*?" Ashley asked. Great way to break my concentration.

"Because he's an asshole."

She rolled her eyes. "Besides that?"

"I'll tell you over a drink sometime. Let's just get on to why I'm here."

"That's just it, Paul. No one seems to know why you're here. You say Detective Kansas sent you, but he's not on the task team, you say you're here to behead vampire victims, but there aren't any, so again... why are you here?" With no more fanfare than that, Detective Vaccaro exited the room. She seemed strangely agitated. Well more than normal.

I tried to answer, but couldn't. Unable to comprehend the amount of death staring back at me. I looked down at my feet. An eyeball gazed back at me. I took a step out of the room and swallowed hard. The smell of blood weighed heavy in the air mixed with a mixture of bile, shit, and room temperature meat. Again, I swallowed hard. "This was no roach attack. What the hell did this?"

I heard the throaty laugh. Dieter. "So as you can see, your services are not needed here, so if you do not mind, please go back to you pathetic life and allow us to do our job. If I find anything here salvage-able to cut the head off I will be sure to call upon your services. Now go throw up on your shoes and get out of my sight."

"Where's Kansas?" I asked again as I wiped the bead of sweat from my forehead. I thought I would pass out. The room spun like a top and voices were nothing more than vague sound in the distance.

"He is not here. I am sure I do not have to tell you, Detective Kansas is on leave for the time being on personal matters. Whomever sent for you, has done so with great error."

I grabbed him by the raincoat. "You heartless guano pile. You make it sound so innocent don't you. He wouldn't have personal matters if it hadn't been for you neck biters. Tell me where he is before I shove this crucifix so far up your ass that you'll be shitting Bible verses." Dieter was right about Kansas. He had been away from the day to day opera-tion in the Monster District. Taken time off to be at his wife's side at the hospital. From what I gathered, he used about as much of his time drowning in a bottle as well. Still, something kept me from moving. I knew Kansas had to be here somewhere. I had talked to him on the phone.

Dieter never attempted to free himself from my grasp. But his facial expression showed a great deal of composure. "My advice to you is leave before you make a fool out of Kansas and yourself. Both of you deny what you are. Pathetic has-beens that live in the past, talking about glory days that will never see life again."

I shoved Dieter free and turned to Detective Vaccaro. "What the hell is going on here, Detective?" I let the last word roll venomously from my tongue.

"Werewolf attack, or at least that's the consensus." She placed her hand on my chest and gently pushed me out of the room. "Seen enough?"

My eyes teetered back to the blood soaked area of the room, just feet from the hallway. "They were so close to getting out."

Detective Vaccarro shook her head. "Not really. They never had a chance. Making it out of the room and making it out alive were two different things here tonight." She took a step away from me and pushed her hair out of her face again. "My first solo case and I get this. Less experience than most here and being a woman in charge has left me with few friends on this. They all see me as the hot shot from Jacksonville coming down here and taking over. With those strikes against me, I feel...what was it you said, overwhelmed?" She stopped to watch a body being taken out on a stretcher. She ran a hand through her hair again, this time tying it up in a ponytail. Her eyes appeared glassy and tired. That's the dark side of working the freak district. The crime scene is usually the best part of the whole process. It's nothing more than spilt blood, dead bodies, and bad smells. Start digging from there and you find fangs, claws, evil, and psychopathic behavior. "It was supposed to be a fund raiser. Five hundred dollar a plate dinners."

"Shit." It seemed like the right thing to say. I didn't know why. Even with the campaign tapestry towering over the death below, I still refused to make that obvious connection. Funny how body parts make you look over the most obvious things in the room.

"My thoughts exactly. It was Dennis Peavey's election kickoff party. You know as well as I do that he's been thinking about running for Congress. Tonight, was supposed to be about shaking hands and kissing babies. From the word I hear, it would have been the most talked about election the city has ever seen, including the dirtiest."

"District Attorney Peavey?" I did my best to keep focused. A part of me smiled inside. Dennis Peavey made no bones about the fact of being anti-blood sucker. A part of me felt as though the battle to repeal the vampire laws had lost a big battle.

Ashley shook her head. "I don't know of any other Dennis Peaveys do you?" She gave out a sarcastic laugh followed by an emptiness like

I had never seen before. "Wife and two daughters were killed in there tonight too."

"Daughters?"

"Well, young ladies. Oldest twenty-five, youngest twenty, I think."

I looked back to the room again, still not believing what I saw. It appeared to be an endless sea of flesh and torn meat. More like a slaughterhouse than a black-tie event. "Why would werewolves do this? Shifter attacks on humans are not that common unless provoked. They prefer the taste of wild animals to human flesh." I tried to grasp my mind around it. "Victory? Victory for what?"

She looked at me as if I knew nothing. "Don't tell me it doesn't ring a bell with you."

I shrugged.

"My initial hunch is that it's for the Victory Party. The pro-vampire party."

"Makes no sense." I said to myself more than anything.

An officer handed her a coffee. She waited for him to leave before answering me. "You know vampire politics like I do. They don't play by the same set of rules, rarely agree on anything, so it could be another branch of the party hoping to regain lost ground. Or could be a way to gain either a sympathy vote or a power play against the pro-wolf candidates out there." She stuttered and regained her train of thought. "We don't even know if the two things are related, just that it is more than just a little bit of a coincidence."

I let it soak in for a moment. "You really think they would go to this extreme? And to leave their mark on the wall like that?" Two men carried another body bag past us. "I've seen my share of political mudslinging, but nothing like this." Then it hit me, "Isn't Judge Lopes running for Congress too?"

"I think so, not sure. I'm still trying to catch up on things around here. From what I've heard, Lopes and Peavey differed on two big issues, or at least they did when I lived here. Peavey wanted to repeal legalization of all vampires, Lopes planned to expand the rights to all vampires risen after the law was in place. Of course, there's the other little issue."

"And the other issue?"

Detective Vaccarro blushed. "Legalization of necro-porn. You know, sex with a vampire and a human." She took a deep breath. I could tell she searched for the right words in her head. "Feeding on the human. Until they die. Lopes and the Victory party wanted it legalized, while Peavey wanted it all squashed when it came to vampire sex."

"I know what necro-porn is, Ashely."

That caught her attention. "Really. Do tell."

My look must have been enough. She smiled and moved on.

"The elections next year will be very heated on both vampire and wolf expansions in the cities. Just like when the vampires gained rights, there will be fanatics coming out of the woodworks for what they believe in. I'm afraid this might be the tip of the iceberg."

"Who has the most to gain by Peavey being dead?" I asked it as a rhetorical question.

"The wolves and vampires I suppose. But why kill this many people? It doesn't fit any of the scenarios. Lopes possibly."

"We're dealing with monsters. They don't fit any scenarios. And my money is on Lopes. He's nothing but a puppet for Quinn anyway. If he gained control of this city, we're all doomed. I think in the long run, he has the most to gain by Peavey's death."

We walked down a hallway out of the way of the circus around us and into the small bar at the far side of the lobby. Compared to the rest of the floor, the bar had been spared. A few overturned chairs, but nothing significant. The television in the corner of the room still played at low volume. Some sort of sports show from what I could tell. Other than Ashley and myself, the place looked deserted. She checked again, in all directions before she spoke. "What could have done this, Paul? To be honest, the pieces don't seem to fit."

"It's not a roach attack. I agree. No vampire could have done something like that. I don't think this is the work of some political party either. Fanatical yes, but not like this. They know they have too much to lose by doing something like this. Personally, I think it was an assassination."

"Could werewolves do something like this?" Ashley whispered.

I thought about it. "Maybe. Seems unlikely. Why would they care which politician wins. They will get screwed either way."

"Maybe they were promised something in return."

Made sense. "You mean like, kill our rival and we'll help you expand your territory?"

"Well, one thing's for sure, Kasey's dumb enough to fall for it."

"Could just one do it?"

"No."

"Damn."

"I'm assuming you only have one suspect. Wolf?" Before she could answer I asked another question. "What about surveillance cameras?"

"Got a couple of people working on it. Seems as though all were blacked out just before the attack." A familiar squint of thought. A look I remembered. It brought back too many memories. I had to convince myself all over again I had done the right thing. "Whomever did this, planned ahead."

I thought about what I had seen. "How many were in there?"

She shook his head. "Don't know for sure until we get a hold of the guest list. I'm guessing 200 at least. Every news van in the country is out there in the parking lot right now. They will be looking for answers." She gave me another half-smile. "Your time is up. You have to go. I've let you see what I'm dealing with tonight. No naughty vampires."

Before I could answer, I received a text from Kansas.

'Now that you know, meet me at the pub across the street.'

3

As I stood to leave, a shadow fell across the doorway. Judge Lopes looked at me with equaled surprise. Short and overweight, he looked more like a bowling ball than anything else. Gray curls surrounded his Latino face along with a mustache that made him appear older than the truth. We knew each other well. He reluctantly signed off on death warrants for the vein weasels I hunted. In truth, he had become nothing more than a pathetic puppet, played by the Cockroach Nation. He made my duty of separating heads from bodies nearly impossible. Legally, anyway. He had been in Quinn's back pocket since the vampire laws came into effect. I could tell by the political smile this was going to be something I didn't like. "Paul Isaac? What are you doing here?"

I looked at Detective Vaccarro. "My God, who's running the city tonight? Every creepy crawly is here. Now I'm really curious." To Lopes, "Mind telling me who the hell you have hiding in custody?"

Quinn interrupted with a wide smile. "Please bring her in here for a moment. I would hate for Mr. Isaac to be left in the dark. After all, he is dying to know what is going on."

Angie appeared in the doorway, pale and distant. If she recognized me, it didn't show. She looked ragged and torn. By her standards, very overdressed in a black tank top that barely covered her more than adequate breasts and faded jeans. Her hair shined jet black and tangled so thick I couldn't see her face clearly. Dried blood painted her normally caramel skin.

"Angie are you okay?" I asked. Fear and confusion setting in.

I tried to move toward her, only to be stopped by dead hands. "She's fine for now, Mr. Isaac. Simply sedated. Fortunately, the blood is not hers." Quinn's eyes took in her body. "Then again, it could be her demise."

"You son of a bitch!" I felt my rage beginning to take over. I raced forward and had the roach by the throat. My momentum pushed us both to the doorway, nearly knocking Angie to the floor.

"Is this what I think it is? You bastards think she did all that? She's the one you said you had in custody?"

"You know her?" Ashley asked.

"Sort of," I responded, releasing Quinn. I didn't want it to go further than that.

Ashley spoke. "We found her passed out in the hotel, covered in blood. Appears to be flesh under her nails. We think she may have changed tonight, did something stupid. We will be looking into DNA under her nails, cameras, the whole nine yards, but for now, yes, she is in our custody."

"As you know, Mr. Isaac, Angela has not been following shifter protocol and changing under the full moon. I do not have to tell you of the dangers in that. It is well documented that in such events as this, the shifter can go mad and kill everything in its sight once they have succumbed to the need. We have no other choice in this matter. I assure you I hope to find her just as innocent as you do. I will do all I can to protect her against all costs. Looks as though my wolf might have gotten a bit carried away tonight." Quinn looked back at Angie.

"Your wolf?" I felt my body go numb.

Quinn's face became the most animated I had ever seen. "That's right, you haven't heard the good news have you? When you refused to make Angela your wolf, she came to me. Appears she is tired of the games Kasey and you play. She has had her fill of boys."

"To you?" I gripped the butt end of the wooden stake on my hip.

"Paul?" I heard Ashely in the distance.

"Yes. She has been living with me for weeks now. I've been trying to get her to change and be herself, but as you know, *Dracul Sang*, she doesn't change easily. For you or me." He looked back out to the lobby. "I must admit I had tried to force her to change for her own good. Now I fear she has done something very lethal."

"Liar!" I withdrew the wooden stake and swung it at Quinn's head. The roach moved just in time, sending me out into the lobby before I could catch my momentum.

Quinn laughed. "I assure you, it is very true. Now the authorities feel as though Angela has gone and done something very, very bad. I am in a strange predicament. Seems as though several of the guests were vampires which means whoever is responsible must come before a Vampire Council." He looked to Lopes. "Not to mention what she did to the humans. There will be an outcry for justice. I promise you, I will do everything I can to make sure she is saved. But I can offer no guarantees." He looked to Lopes, but continued to talk to me. "My loyalty must be with the vampires. Blood before lust. You should know that."

I started to come back on Quinn when dead hands grabbed me. Dieter pushed me against the far wall, but my attention remained on his master. "I hope you still feel that way when I stake you for all of your actions, Quinn."

"There is nothing here to talk about, Mr. Isaac. These matters do not pertain to you." Lopes looked past me to Quinn. "You've had your fun. Now get her out of here. I have a press conference on all of this in fifteen minutes. I want you to answer a few questions for the cameras as well. As I have said, it'll be good for the vampire community and human trust."

I moved toward Lopes. "Tell me the truth, Lopes. Do you really buy all this? That one wolf could do all of that or is this just another diversion for you and your bloodsuckers?"

Quinn spoke. "Always the skeptic are you not, Mr. Isaac? You think it is always my kind that kills and eats the things in this city. It is no secret that Commissioner Peavey and the wolves were not the best of friends. Chances are, that more than one wolf may have been involved. We will get to the bottom of this crime. Kasey and others are not innocent of things either. But we must deal with one thing at a time."

"Meaning you paid him off? Hope you at least got a hand job for all your trouble."

Quinn simply smiled and shrugged. "The victims consisted of many of my coven. Now dead. Since some of my own have been brutally murdered, I am within my rights to ask for custody of those responsible. Tonight, human law has given me that right." He looked over to Lopes as he pulled Angie closer to him. If the dead bastard pulled her any closer, I planned to break his arm. "As I have stated, Angela has been with me and there is no explanation for her being here. It is my obligation to bring Angela before the Council." He kissed Angie on the forehead. "Perhaps with a good word from me, they will allow leniency. Without my influence, there is a great possibility that the Council will kill her. Which is why I have bound her to me. It is the only possibility of saving her life."

My eyes immediately went to Angie. "Oh hell no!" This time, I pushed free of Dieter. With all the energy I had, I went to Angie. It took me a few seconds to find it. Then my world imploded. The son of a bitch had bitten her. Two small marks on her right shoulder, already in the process of healing before my eyes. She had been bound to him as lover, slave, blood source, whatever Quinn wished under the rules roaches lived by.

I tried to stay in as much control as I could. It took all my self-control not to blow Quinn's head across the hall, but I knew I had to remain calm. Doing something stupid and getting myself locked up wouldn't help Angie at all. There would simply be another set of fangs in her before sunrise. I turned to meet Quinn, eye to eye. Dangerous, yes, but I did it anyway. "I won't let you take her out of here. Ashley, do something."

I heard Ashley's voice. "But it seems as though deals have been made behind my back. Money goes a long way in a campaign year." She looked back at Quinn with something I had never seen in Kansas. Backbone. "And why the hell would any of your vampires be at this rally? Peavey was not your candidate for the office. Makes no sense. No pun intended, but they wouldn't have been caught dead here."

Lopes spoke. "This isn't about a campaign, Detective. This is about making all of this go away and go away fast. Inside our human court, this could take years to come to an end and we don't have time for that. We are a tourist city. The tourists stop coming, we don't eat. We all know the whore's guilty as hell anyway. If you men would stop thinking with your dicks you'd see that already." Lopes looked to me. "Just because it has tits doesn't make it any less dangerous."

I stepped toward Lopes until our noses nearly touched. Truthfully, I didn't know if I would be able to restrain myself. Dieter started to move, Quinn lifted a finger to stop him. "You miserable slime ball. There's no way I'll let you get away with this. If Quinn bit her without her consent, you have more problems on your hands than you thought possible. The two of you will go down for this. All of it."

"Will someone tell me what's going on?" Ashley asked. We all ignored her.

"It's not for you to decide, Mr. Isaac. You should know by now that the masses are easily influenced by what they see and read. In a day or two, they'll be demanding her death. Children died in that attack. Due process or not. Someone has to die for this. Who is not important. You should know that by now."

Quinn placed his hand in the small of Angie's back and began to move back out the door. Once out in the hallway, he turned and looked back at me.

I moved past Dieter and Quinn. I grabbed Angie by the arm, but couldn't free her from the cockroach. In the process, my fingernails raked across his dead skin in a wild swing. "You son of a bitch. Don't you ever touch her again. You and your Council harm one hair on her head and I'll burn Bat Town to the ground. I promise you that."

Quinn ran a finger across his lip and wiped away the bead of blood. I think deep in his twisted mind, he enjoyed the pain. And if that's the case I plan to bring him all the pleasure he can handle. "See it as you will, Avenger, but the truth remains that I have arranged for her safe keeping. As long as she is my lover and blood let, I control her fate. I would ask you to pray that I can convince the Councils that death is not necessary." His voice slithered into my head. *"Do not fret, Avenger. Once I grow bored with her blood and body, I shall feed her to the Council. Trash in, trash out, I think the saying is."*

I tried to move closer to Angie, only to be stopped by two unknown officers. This time I found myself forced a lot harder to the tile floor. I was afraid my right eye might pop out and roll under the desk. "Get your hands off of me! Angie! Look at me! Tell me this isn't true!" I pushed free of one of the officer's grip and looked up to Ashley. "Do something."

Lopes spoke. "It's out of either of your hands. She had skin under her nails, blood from the victims on her body, and the fact that she hasn't changed for months now. Deep inside, I think you know that the little bitch did it. Don't fight us on this, Mr. Isaac. There are a lot of families that lost a lot more than a love crush tonight. I am obligated to make things right for them."

"The only thing you're obligated to is the vampire standing right next to you. You're not looking for justice, you're looking to make all this go away. I'll never let you get away with this."

"We already have. By the time you get anyone to listen to you, she'll be dead. Even the most liberal of humans will not find sympathy for her and her kind. It's about time you are a team player and learn your boundaries. Accidents can happen. If anyone knows that, it should be you," Lopes spat out.

A light went on. I pointed my finger in the international 'a-ha' sign. "She couldn't have done it."

"Why?" all said in unison.

"Look at her. She's still dressed. If she had gone mad and turned all furry, her clothes would have been ripped to shreds. And as you can see, she's still dressed. There's your proof. Sorry Quinn, but no free dinner tonight. You got the wrong monster."

I had said it before I could stop it. Monster. I still thought of her as a monster. I wanted to scream at my actions but it was too late. Even Angie gave a slow turn to me. I could see the hatred for me in her eyes. Seeing her as a monster is what had started all of this. She believed if she could control the change, I wouldn't see her as a werewolf and she would win my heart. Wrong. It wasn't her. I had come to terms with that a long time ago. My insecurities had put us in this predicament. I wouldn't allow her to get close to me even if she were the most human of all God's creatures. I had become a hard ball of hatred and despicable anger. Now I looked at Angie and saw what my actions could do. What they had done. I prayed a silent prayer that she couldn't have done all that damage and caused all that death. If it took pounding a square peg into a round hole to make her innocent, so be it. Truth be told, I grew more scared of her being with Quinn than being guilty.

Quinn swayed to me. The smile on his face allowed me to know he caught the slip of the tongue. "The *monster* you refer to was found naked. We have already told you this. Do you not think I might have brought her clothing when I came? After all, I simply had to go to the chest of drawers in my bedroom to find them." He started to leave once again. "My blood lets want for nothing. I anticipate their every need."

I stood between Quinn and Angie. "Over my dead body will you take her out of here." I turned to Lopes. "She has to be taken into custody of the human courts first. You of all people should know that."

Quinn nodded ever so slightly. "Technically speaking, you do have the first part right. And that is quite a thought provoking comment." His face perked up with a dangerous smile. He lifted his finger. "I may have a solution to our dilemma."

I could already feel the rug being pulled out from under me. "And what might that be?"

"As I am sure you know, a powerful vampire can in some instances force a change on a wolf. I find myself far too involved in this tragedy to do so, but you could report to the Council as being the one responsible for turning her. You have been known to try such things with her in the past. In doing so, you could save her life." He allowed his words to trail off.

"Paul, what the hell is the problem here?" Ashley requested again.

"You son of a bitch. You want me to confess to being a master roach in order to save her life?"

"In accordance with vampire law, is it not true? After all, that is why Olivia wanted you dead. And I do not think it such a secret that you indeed killed Asa. Surely if this wolf means as much to you as you are acting, this truth should not be so hard to admit to. I am more than willing to give up my claim to you in exchange for your accolades."

"What the hell's he talking about, Paul?" I heard Ashely ask. God, I wished there had been a way to get her out of the room.

I stood here trying to keep my skeletons in the closet. I could admit to the Council that I accepted my role as a master roach and save Angie from Quinn, or deny it and hope that I could prove she had nothing to do with the killings. "I'm not admitting anything to you or the Council. She belongs to the pack first, the human law second and Quinn and the rest of you maggot heads third," I answered. "She should at least be handed off to Kasey before any of us. Master fang head or not."

Out of the corner of my eye, I could see Angie look over to me. If she still believed in me or felt anything other than vengeance and hate, it didn't show in her eyes. I had no doubt that if she had the strength, she would have ripped my throat out.

"I will not allow her to be released to the wolves. There is too much at risk to do so," Lopes answered as he gave me a quick glance. "They will not abide by the laws that must be enforced. The bottom line is justice must be carried out." He looked to Angie. "Besides, we don't think she's the only wolf that did this. They will all go down for this if I have anything to do with it."

"Well, Avenger, what will it be? Master Vampire or not? It all seems very simple to me. You admit what you are, you get the girl, I go away. It all ends tonight if and when you can prove her innocence." He ran his long fingers through Angie's hair. "I have great influence on this city, *Dracul Sang*. Admit your guilt and the wolf will not be arrested until you face the Council."

I looked to Lopes. "I can trust you on that?"

He shook his head.

I looked back to Angie. She slowly raised her middle finger in protest. I felt her hatred toward me, but something in her eyes still lured me in. Power that the fang heads could never produce. Still, my pride hung in the balance. I could say I was doing it for Angie, but all it would really go down to nothing more than Quinn's little game of putting it on record that I confessed to being a roach. I knew I could save her my way. I always had. She could hate me as much as I hated myself. It wouldn't change a damn thing. I kept my eyes on her as I spoke. "Tell the Council to come get me."

4

I LOOKED at my watch as I drove the 'Cuda across the street in search of the mystery pub. Still about five hours of darkness. Time steadily slipped away. If I planned to have the upper hand when daylight broke, I'd need all the help I could get. As luck would have it, my help rested in a relapsed alcoholic in a bar. Beside me, the envelope from Powers Attorney at Law. Unopened. And would stay that way for now.

The rain had finally stopped, washing everything in neon glow and puddles. Smoking the cigar to calm my nerves, I thought about everything I just saw and the pieces that just didn't fit. I came to the realization that it hadn't been the murders that had me so wound up. She had returned to my life like an albatross around the neck. Time hadn't healed my wounds. I slammed the steering wheel. Distraction, more than likely, would get me killed.

I parked the car along the sidewalk just short of Bailey's Bar and Grill. The Grill part consisted of grilled cheese sandwiches which were far more dangerous than any of the night crawlers hiding in the shadows. I shut the engine off. With a glance, I took in the small bar as I opened the door.

I stood next to the car and continued thinking as I finished the cigar. I checked my weapons, just in case as I took a deep breath and counted to ten. Why did she have to come back?

I stepped inside the small bar and allowed my eyes to adjust to the dim lighting. No matter what bar you find yourself in, it smells the same. Stale beer and cigarettes from generations long ago still lingered in the air like old ghosts.

The bar had six small round tables with four wooden chairs around each, all to the right of the bar, topped off with a small juke box that looked like it had seen better days. To the left was a pool table with a glowing Budweiser lamp above it. Two men were engaged in a game. The one shooting looked up at me from his hunched position, then returned to the little white ball in front of him.

In the far corner stood a poor excuse of a Christmas tree with sparse ornaments and one strand of multi-colored lights. It seemed to be begging me to shoot it and put it out of its misery.

At the front of the space stood a tall bar with four stools. Three of wood with brown cushions and one chrome with a red cushion. Kansas sat with his back to me, partially slumped over as if being held up by the bar itself.

The bartender, which I assumed to be Bailey, looked at me as he wiped the water from a clean glass. He was tall with a lanky build, graying hair, pulled back into a ponytail. No smile or emotion on his face. Skin like old leather, worn and littered with character. Blue eyes shined out of the darkness like beaming lights. To him, I probably looked like nothing more than another all-night drinker, coming in to drown away my sorrows of women and money.

I pulled the stool closest to Kansas and looked over to see the empty beaten face that used to be a great detective. He hadn't shaven in about three days, his shirt covered in unknown stains and his hair, or what remained of it, was in need of shampoo. A great contrast to the Kansas I once knew. The man that I would swear ironed his underwear. Shoes you could see your reflection in.

"Wha'd'ya have?" Bailey asked.

I ordered a bottle of Bud and stood next to Kansas trying to think of what I should say and how I should say it. He showed no signs of me being here. His eyes continued to look down into the glass before him, as if he had been caught in the gaze of a dirt napper.

"How's Stephanie?" I asked as I took the beer from Bailey.

Kansas blinked as if it had brought him to. He turned his head and faced me with a growing drunk smile. "Paul? What are you doing here? Merry freaking Christmas." I stayed still for a few seconds, allowing him to focus on me as he gave me a big hug. He swayed just enough that it was a possibility that if he shifted his weight just right, we could end up on the floor. Kansas took a deep breath and turned to his drink. He picked it up, sloshed it around in the glass a couple of times and finished it off. He raised his index finger and pointed it at me. "You were right, Pauly, I should have listened to you. You told me those sons of bitches were nothing but trouble, but did I listen? No. Now they took my family from me."

"She'll come out of it." What else could I say to a grieving man whose wife remained in a coma?"Doctors ain't so sure about that. They ain't doing nothing but taking blood and running tests and still nothing. She's no better than the day she got there. I don't think any of them have a clue what's wrong." He raised his glass to the bartender as the man sat my bottle next to me. "Even if she does make a full recovery, they still took my son. Ain't nothing ever gonna change that." He turned back to me, eyes glassy with alcohol. "This was going to be his first Christmas, Pauly. And you know what the sad thing is?"

I remained silent.

"I ain't bought a damned thing for him. I've given up. If someone walked into this bar today holding him in their arms, I ain't got nothing to give him for Christmas." He looked back to the bartender and lifted the glass again. "And all the bills. Jesus Christ. My insurance ain't going to pay for all that. I can't pay for all of that."

The bartender looked at me and I agreed. "I think you've had enough."

He looked at me with glassy eyes. "You know how much they charged me for those blood tests. And she still ain't no better than she was when she came in. I tell you, Pauly, I'm gonna get even with those sons a bitches. Kill them all. Every last one of them." He started to cry. "God, I'm so sorry for what I did to you."

"We're cool," I reluctantly answered as he put his arm around me.

"Remember how I almost got you killed over all of this? I used to think you were just some psycho son a bitch that had a chip on his shoulder. Used to believe in live and let live, but no more Pauly, no more. Turning over a new leaf. Like you, I'm gonna kill 'em all. One by one. And you know who's gonna be the first to go? Quinn." He slammed his glass on the wooden bar. "Another drink!"

I patted him on the back. "I think you've had enough."

"That's just it, Pauly, no matter how much I drink, it's never enough." He wiped his eyes and tried to keep the tears from falling. "Did I ever tell you how we met?"

I took a swig of beer. "No."

"September twenty-third, ten years ago. It was a blind date. We met at an Italian restaurant on Orange. I was so scared. I think I threw up three times before I ever got there." He gave a quick exhale. "She was wearing this little pink top and jeans. I stared at her through the window for about an hour before I got the nerve up to go inside. I thought she was the most beautiful woman I had ever seen in my life. My knees were knocking. I nearly dropped the roses I had. She looked up at me and I just knew, she was the one. I was in love and I didn't even know her. Nothing about her. I promised I would love and protect her for the rest of her life. I vowed to give her everything her heart desired." More tears. "Now look what I've done. She's in a fucking hospital with tubes coming out of her, unable to speak or even open her eyes. I've failed at everything I ever promised her."

I wasn't sure what to say. Or even if I should say anything at all. There were no right answers and nothing I said would change the truth. We could kill every cockroach in this city and it wouldn't guarantee that Stephanie would ever open her eyes again. I felt helpless, but the anxiety in knowing time was wasting was making things worse. "Zeke, you called me to come down to the Plaza tonight. Why?"

He stopped and looked at me. "Paul, I know we've had our differences in the past, but you need to listen and trust me on something." I could feel the cold matter-of-fact voice slam me.

"I'm listening."

"I brought you into this as soon as I could." He took a deep breath. "God, I don't even know where to begin." He wiped his eyes. "Paul, you gotta trust me and not over react. You know Lopes and Quinn are going to distance themselves from all of this as much as they can. Lopes and Quinn are both there, which means there's a cover up. Just promise me you won't overreact."

Me? Over react? Who did he think he was talking to? "Okay," I said with great apprehension.

"They have a suspect already in custody on this. You're gonna go fucking ape shit when I tell you everything, but you have to believe me, this one is out of my hands. I'm going to be sucked into all the red tape and protocol of this. I'm counting on you to, you know, do what needs to be done." His eyes shot back at me with a looming storm inside them. "I didn't call you tonight because we thought it was a vampire attack. You saw what they're dealing with over there."

"Angie, I know." I gathered my thoughts. "How did you even know about it?"

He gave me a mischievous laugh. "I was sitting right here when the first sirens went off." He whispered in my ear. I held my breath. Something nasty lurked inside his mouth. "They don't know it, but I got a scanner. I heard the whole thing. Went over there and the sons a bitches told me to leave." Another smile. "And guess who I saw?"

"Ashley."

"No, Ashley. You know the one who…"

I stopped him. "Yeah, I know. Now what can you tell me about all of this. Quinn and Lopes seemed to be joined at the hip on this one, which leads me to believe they know more than what they are letting on to."

"Is Angie okay?"

I shrugged. "For now. They'll kill her to save their own asses. I have to get to her fast." I did my best to keep my voice down. "When you heard everything happen earlier, did you see or hear anything? See any werewolves, possibly, maybe?"

Another laugh. "Bet it was fun seeing you there with Angie and Ashley together. Cat fight city."

I grew defensive. "Can you just tell me what you know about all of this? They want to blame it all on the wolves, but something just doesn't sit right with me. I think Lopes had everyone murdered because he feared Peavey might win the election. Now he's got the killer and possibly a sympathy vote from the voters."

"Just pulling your chain, Paully. You shouldn't have let that one get away."

"What did you see or hear, Zeke?"

He grew serious. "Can't believe everything you hear."

"What's that supposed to mean?" I grew agitated.

He leaned in. "Talk among those in the inner circle is that all this was caused by zombies."

I opened my mouth, but nothing came out. I had heard of zombies attacking in remote areas of the world, but never in Orlando. I had never seen a zombie before. I knew vampires could raise them, but I couldn't wrap my mind around it. "Zombies, as in raised from the dead by blood suckers? Isn't that a Cardinal Sin among the coffin weasels?"

Kansas shrugged. "Don't know. If you ask me, anything that involves the Council involves death. A vampire jaywalks, what does the Council recommend, death. Stay up too late, death."

I thought of my own situation and the Council. It gave me chills. Kansas hit the nail on the head. Chances were real good that I would be six feet under when it was all said and done. Innocence and guilt rarely made a difference. "You don't seem so optimistic that zombies are the answer."

Kansas grew preoccupied with peeling the label off of the beer bottle in front of him. "What do I think, Paully? I think Peavey's dead because he hates vampires."

God, he was drunk. "Hates vampires? Jesus, Kansas, the man's the most in bed with the vampires politician out there. That's why this doesn't make sense to me. I think Quinn had Kasey and the wolves do something here and now Angie's their scapegoat."

He shook his head in disagreement. "Nope. About two months ago, Peavey came in yelling and screaming about how his daughter was dating some vampire and he wanted him arrested. He wanted me to shut the whole district until we found him. Problem was, Peavey's daughter was of age. Wanted a search warrant, but you know as well as I do that Lopes wasn't going to sign anything for him. Political rivals or not, they've never been civil to one another." He belched. "The whole sex thing is where it's at for those two. One sees an opportunity to make a lot of money and the other wants it limited. Follow the money, Paully and you've got your guy. Lopes and Kincaid had financed all the vampire legalization from that money. Partners in crime. I think Peavey was getting too close to their investment. A billion dollar business, Paully. We should think about getting our share of the pie. Seems simple to me. Peavey stepped out of line and they got him."

"Did the vampire have a name?"

Kansas struggled to think. "Domino Z or something like that. Worked at one of the necro-porn companies according to Peavey." He stared into space. "Let's at least have one drink in honor of the vampires that were killed tonight. Got to find a silver lining in something."

I patted him on the back, reluctantly. "Let's get you home, Zeke. You're drunk."

5

IT HAD BEEN twenty four hours since I left the Crowne Plaza and in that time, Lopes and Quinn had done a great job of damage control, as well as planted a seed of hate. The city had turned against the werewolf community in violent fashion. Since the early days of the vampire rights movement, I hadn't seen the city so polarized. Radio talk shows were already knee deep in the killings and the after effects.

The thing that puzzled me the most continued to be why all the effort in separating themselves from the murders. I had seen it first-hand. It hadn't been by cockroach means. It only made me suspect them more though. Peavey had been the one politician willing to stand up against vampire rights and expansion. It all tied in together some-how. What I had seen might not have been a direct killing by Quinn and his fang heads, but the blood remained on their hands and I'd die proving it.

I thought back about all the things I knew concerning Angie. She didn't look well. She still hadn't changed, or at least not enough. I remembered the night I tried to change her from human to wolf and the bruises it caused me. I pushed the doubts further down in my mind. No matter how sick or weak Angie got, she or any of her pack could have done the horror I saw. But if Quinn had been able to change her along with a few others, the possibilities grew endless.

I drove along a two lane road that only a generation ago had been nothing more than orange groves. I realized that like the citrus industry, I had become nothing more than a reminder of the past. No matter how many times I rehearsed my tired lines to those that were so far up the roaches' asses, things were not going to change for the good. They would overlook the death and blood stains and trade it in for a common cause of equality among the demographics of the earth. They would pat themselves on the back in the name of humanity, while selling their own species down the river. No, it hadn't been that at all. It boiled down to money, profit, and greed. The poor humans I vowed to protect couldn't see the truth beyond their bank accounts.

I tried to justify everything that I had done tonight, but fell short on every attempt. By trying to be human, I had become a much bigger monster than anything I hunted. Still, I couldn't come to terms with accepting my role as a master roach. How could I? They had killed my parents, Father Garcia, countless other faceless people around me and now I had to become one of them just to save those fragmented pieces of life I still cared about? Still, if I had simply acknowledged my role in roach politics, Angie would be by my side safe. Pissed off to hell, but safe.

In the distance, I saw the flashing amber lights of a car on the side of the road. I gripped the steering wheel a little tighter. Being broken down in the dark left you way too vulnerable to things that went bump in the night. Sprinkle it with rogue coffin munchers just waiting for such things made it a flirtation with death. Knowing something had turned people into the consistency of hamburger meat, made it inhumane to drive by without helping. Changes in my life needed to start now. Think about someone other than myself, no matter what it cost me. Just your friendly roadside master vampire at your service.

Then there are those times when you should have simply picked a different road. This was one of those times.

As I pulled in behind the white Mercedes, I could tell between the strobes of amber that the vehicle had a flat on the left rear. The flashes of light lit up the wet road like spilled paint. I opened the door to the 'Cuda and began to walk toward the car, leaving the headlights on so I could see. The air remained damp and humid, but the rain had finally stopped.

I saw the door to the car open and realized my nightmare had taken on a new kind of twisted fate. "Need some help?" I said before I could stop the words. Dr. Lydia Petty, or as I call her Dr. Feelgood. My therapist.

"Speak of the devil and he shall arrive," Dr. Feelgood said. "Thank God. I've been trying to call everyone I know. I think the storm has played havoc with my reception somehow." I could already see that cynical smile on her lips. "Keeps saying I don't have service." She placed her phone back in her pocketbook, still on her shoulder. "After what I've heard on the radio, I'm glad you're here to help."

I couldn't think of anyone I'd rather *not* see tonight. Yet my nemesis stood before me. "Nope. You'll be lucky if I hold the flash-light while you change the tire. I just stopped to laugh at you." I looked down at the tire, or what was left of it. "How long did you drive it like this?"

"Long enough that I made sure I got all the air out of it." She gave a nervous smile. By the looks of her, she had just left the office. Feelgood sported a plaid skirt of different colors of brown and a beige blouse, buttoned up to the top button. Any more conservative and she would have exploded. Her glasses caught the flashes of the hazard lights on her Mercedes, giving her face an unreal illusion of no eyes.

I smiled as I squatted next to the shredded piece of rubber. The tire and I had a lot in common. Worn out, useless, and frayed. Not to mention beyond the point of repair.

She paced. "I have AAA. I'll have them come in the morning. No need to have you out here all night on this road. It's too dangerous. Do you mind just taking me back to my office?"

"Shouldn't you buy me drinks and a steak first?"

"As hot as I am do you really think I would have to buy dinner?" She gave me a genuine smile. It felt good. Not just the smile, but the fact that we were actually being nice to one another. After what I had done tonight, nice was going a very long way.

I fought the smile inside me best I could. "Won't take but a few minutes. Pop the trunk. Unless you have a body for one of your patients to munch on later."

"And I wonder why you're still single." We had, without saying a word, called a truce, even if just for the night. She hit a button on the key fob and the truck sprung open with a thump. I should have known better, but I expected the trunk to be as cluttered as mine, filled with everything from forgotten laundry to magazines not proper to have around the house in mixed company. But it appeared as pristine as the day she bought it. Under the thin layer of carpet, I found everything I'd need.

"So where were you on such a lovely evening?" I couldn't help the sarcasm. Every thought now consumed with Angie and the things I had witnessed, a good verbal fight seemed apropos. Thanks to tonight's storm, I found it difficult not to find my feet in standing water or mud. This gentleman thing sucked.

"I had an appointment with Veronica Powers. She's handling some legal issues for me. She said for you to give her a call if I saw you. It was very important." She grew silent.

There's a name I could have gone all night without hearing. A vampire lawyer, cold and vicious, but dear God, had a playground for a body.

I used the lug wrench to loosen the lugs and placed the jack under the car. I fought the urge to bang my head against the back fender of the Mercedes. The envelope still sat in the passenger's seat. Unopened. "Ms. Powers. And how is our lovely attorney to the vein drainers?"

She bent down next to me, avoiding the small lake at her feet. "Great. She's helping me on my next big adventure. I'm taking on a partner."

"About time you get laid," I joked.

Another genuine smile and a playful slap on my back. "I'm talking about my practice. That's what I met with her about. She's taking care of all the paperwork for me."

"Wow, guess you'll be able to get in the head of twice as many roaches now."

She let out air in protest. "I've asked you time and time again not to use that terminology around me. It's…disgusting. Dr. Yancey will be helping me out on certain days. Seems a few vampires wish to speak to one of their own on certain issues. They don't trust the living completely yet." A long pause. "Dr. Yancey has been a big help though."

"Dr. Yancey?" She said it as if I should know the name. I didn't. Not that it mattered. I started to repeat my question, but Feelgood continued.

"Victor. He was a psychologist before he became a vampire, you know. With the new laws opening doors for vampires, I think he might revisit that occupation again soon enough. It's fascinating to hear everything from his studies on the industry. Another reason vampires are such a valuable part of our community. We have living text books right in front of us."

Never knew the coffin sleeper's last name. I fought against the anger that washed over me. The son of a bitch tried to kill me. A cold blooded assassin of my kind. "Yeah, but text books don't kill you if you look the other way." I looked at her hard. "You do know what he does now, don't you?"

"From what I'm told, he was quite a doctor for his time. A miracle worker some would say. I find it a great opportunity. I hope to learn a lot from him."

I could feel my heart beat against my chest. I looked up at the doctor. "He's a killer. I don't give a damn what he did when he was human. His role as a roach is to hunt those like me and kill them. Dr. Yancey, as you call him, will die by my hands. I promise you that. He's an assassin of our kind. I hope to God you don't plan on letting him talk to humans alone."

I could hear her steps as they moved across the sand and pavement at the shoulder of the road. I continued to work on the tire, but could see her feet stop next to me. "I don't want to fight with you tonight. I'm not even going to say that you're wrong. Let's just drop the subject." Silence for a moment. "Where were you headed tonight?"

"Just coming back from one of the most fucked up murder scenes I've ever come across."

I looked up at her. She must have seen it in my eyes. "You were there?"

"Yeah, false alarm for me I guess." Images of bodies and the blood returned to my memories. "Feelgood, you don't want to go down there. It's not pretty." I looked at my watch. 3 A.M. "Shouldn't all little neck biters be getting ready for bed?"

A roll of the eyes. "I will be talking to those that can come and see me and if time allows go to those that can't. Not all of my patients are vampires. Unlike some people, I don't discriminate."

"I hope that's what you tell your patients that have lost a loved one to those things. Sorry for your loss, but look on the bright side, they don't discriminate on who they suck."

She raised her hand in defeat. "Let's agree to disagree." I watched as she searched for something to say. "In all honesty, how have you been these days?" I could only see fragments of her shadow in the flashing lights. "Why haven't you made an appointment lately?" I heard her say. With the trunk open, I couldn't see her, but I knew her eyes were dead on me.

I stood and walked in her direction, picking up the spare and jack and closed the lid. A thousand excuses ran through my head, but none that I thought she would believe. "Been selling Tootsie Rolls at the airport. They say if I sell enough, I get to go to camp this summer."

"All the summer camps in the world couldn't help you, Mr. Isaac. But since I have you here, I think I'll use this as your therapy time." A girlish giggle escaped. "After all, if I can't talk about you behind your back, as a doctor, I should be able to offer you treatment to your face."

I rolled my eyes just out of sight. "Does HMO cover me all the way out here?" I redirected my question.

"Are you doing okay?" Things suddenly got serious. I could hear it in her voice.

I placed the doughnut tire on the car and tried to think. "I go out every night and kill dirt nappers just for the hell of it. I hang pink helium balloons to their testicles and fill their necks with candy. It doesn't make the pain go away, but it doesn't make it any worse either."

Feelgood rolled her eyes. That alone made me happy. "The last time we talked you were dealing with the deaths of Father Garcia and of Josh Price, Detective Frank Price's grandson. That's a lot for anyone to deal with. If you keep bottling it up inside, it will never go away." We were face to face. "Talk to me. As a friend, not a doctor."

I started to cry. Did everything I could to stop it, but damn it if it didn't beat me. I looked away as I took a deep breath. "You know, I feel more guilt with the death of Price's grandson than I do with Father Garcia. And for the longest time I didn't know why. It ate at me like some kind of cancer."

"You remember killing Joshua. You feel more responsible. It's actually a normal thought."

I paced with nervous energy. "No. That's not it. With Father Garcia, it was almost an unspoken thought that we might one day be killed by these things you get in the head of. Death just happened to be part of the job. But with Josh, there was something more. Something more real. He didn't deserve to die. Unlike Father Garcia and I, to a point Josh never poked a stick at them." The night ran through my memory like a movie. "I remember having to kill him. The screams and cries of Frank Price. I couldn't look at him. No matter how hard I tried, I couldn't look him in the eyes. I haven't talked to him. Haven't asked for his forgiveness. Don't have the balls to do it. Jesus, what am I supposed to say, sorry about your grandson but the law is the law."

"Perhaps that's the first step in your healing." I felt her arms around me. I didn't want her to let go.

"That's just it. I'm so ashamed of what I did, of what I am. It's the first time it hit this close to home. I've killed victims that I knew in the past, but not one that had this much of an emotional chain attached to it. The twisted part is that I didn't even know Josh, never even knew he existed until the night Frank showed up on my doorstep. Now, he's about all I see when I come face to face with any of them. And now I'm one of them."

"And what are you, Paul?"

"God!" I shouted as I tried to keep it all together. "That's the thing I don't know. I don't know what the hell I am. Where I stand in all of this. I feel I'm being pulled in a million directions and I don't feel comfortable in any of them." I pulled away from her and grabbed her by the shoulders. "Do you want to hear what I did tonight?"

"Tell me you didn't have anything to do with that."

I could have pushed her into the middle of the road for that. "No, I didn't have anything to do with the murders at the Crowne. Given the option though, I would have rather that be the case. No, I confessed to Quinn and his little band of misfits that I was not only the new *Dracul Sang*, but also turned a wolf into a violent killing machine."

"Why would you do that?"

"It was Angie and I did it to save her life. Something I should have done a long time ago, but as we both know, I'm far too stupid to make any credible decisions on my own." I balled my fists to keep from saying or doing something stupid that I would regret. "Tire's fixed, doctor. Have a good night." I slammed the trunk lid. "This is goodbye for us. I won't be in therapy again. Call whoever you need to. Chances are I'll have a gun in my mouth long before they come for me."

Feelgood leaned against her car, arms crossed, and looked at the ground. "I can have you Baker Acted for saying that, Paul." She moved against me. "I don't care what you think of me or of what I do, but you have to remember one thing, as your therapist, I will do whatever I have to, to keep you safe from even yourself. Please don't shut me out. I don't pretend to have all the right answers, but you need to talk to someone."

I started to take a step toward the 'Cuda when Feelgood grabbed me by the arm. "What do you plan to do?"

I allowed her to keep her grasp. I spoke with playful sarcasm. "Whatever the hell I want. I'm *Dracul Sang*, bitch." All of a sudden, I loved roadside therapy.

6

My cell phone rang at five in the afternoon the next day, waking me from a dead sleep. Visions of the death I had seen at the Crowne Plaza came rushing back, causing me to jump. In the fog of trying to regain consciousness, I recognized Kasey's voice on the voice message, the alpha male of the werewolves in the city. It didn't take long to realize why he had called. Angie's life hung in the balance and he wanted to meet with me.

Looking at my missed messages, I also had six from Kansas. I didn't listen to them. Something in the back of my mind told me to call him back, but I didn't. I had to talk with Kasey about what I knew. Chances were good that he would be the only ally I would have in, not only keeping Angie safe, but possibly the entire pack. I didn't like or trust Kasey or any of the other furballs, but they were still better than the vein suckers and I had to somehow make myself believe they felt the same way about me.

I arrived from a small side street off Hughey Street in an area where the Bat District ended and the fur ball community began. The long shadows around me warned of the limited daylight left. An edge of cold bit the air. Unlike the roaches, the furballs had no issue with the sunlight, making my being here all the more dangerous.

For me, there were no friends down here. The wolves had just as much reason I might not be able to stop what ate me, but I would see it coming. I thought about what I had seen at the Crowne Plaza and double checked the 9mm, just in case. These things could very well have been the culprits and I had been stupid enough to be their next chew toy.

The neglected parking lot moved with countless pieces of trash. Cans and liquor bottles dotted the pavement like landmines. The street light above me already buzzed in the waning winter light. Moths and other insects danced in the warm glow. Knee high weeds had taken over islands of the pavement. A green dumpster rested to my left, trash and debris scattered along its base.

The building sat parallel to the rail road tracks running behind it. Built of red brick, yellowed by sulfur water, neglected by time. Black graffiti words and colorful artwork gave it new found character. In the front of the building, a large concrete ramp ran up to twin somewhat white oversized doors where I assumed large trucks at one time had delivered goods. Along the top of the warehouse were large windows, dirty and aged, one with a sizable hole in it. A large chain linked fence with barbed wire surrounded the area, faded and twisted.

In the distance, I saw the large buildings of the downtown area, looming over the skyline like gothic creatures. Bat Town sat at their feet just out of view. The interstate roared in the background.

Something told me to start the car back up and never look back. Whatever Kasey wanted couldn't be good. We weren't friends or allies. We simply had a common cause in our love/lust for Angie and that would never be enough for either of us to trust the other. Yet, here I sat.

I hadn't seen him since the night we killed Olivia and Judas, so I knew things would be awkward at best. Secrets were told that night that put Kasey at a great disadvantage at winning Angie's heart. He had been the one that looked the other way when Piel killed her brother. All of this played through my head as I looked around from inside the car. I had a better chance of leaving here in a body bag in the back of a hearse than any other form of transportation. And I willingly came here. Alone. Note to self: You're an idiot.

From the side of the building, I saw a figure walking my way. I stiffened with anxiety. I glanced in all directions for others that might be hidden in the shadows. Checked the rear view mirror. Nothing else moved.

As she grew closer to me, I recognized a female form. Tall. Very tall. Hair shaved close to her head, dark eyes encased in heavy makeup, thin lips, porcelain pure skin. She looked unreal and flawless. Young, maybe twenty or so.

Gothic vibe sprinkled with attitude. Thigh high black boots over faded and shredded blue jeans, mesh top that outlined everything underneath. She looked tough and vulnerable at the same time.

"You here alone?" she asked, stopping short of my door.

I remained put. "See anybody else?"

"Don't screw with me. I don't play games. It's all I can do not to pull you out of the car myself and shove your head up your behind. Now, I will ask you again and this time you will respond with a yes or a no. Are we clear?"

I liked my head where it was. "Crystal."

"Are you alone?"

"Yes."

She didn't seem convinced. Almond sized eyes searched the desolate area before coming back to me. "Does anyone know you're here?"

"No." My fingers inched closer to the 9mm, just in case. Like the wolf before me, I searched the area for pretty much the same reasons.

"Get out."

I took a deep breath and tried to gain as much bravery as I could muster and opened the door. "You are?" I asked as I stood and shut the door to the 'Cuda behind me.

"The one that will eat you and crap you in the woods if you double cross us. Move."

She motioned me toward the warehouse and I had no intentions of doing anything other than that. I found myself oddly turned on and scared at the same time. Kind of liked it. "Is Kasey here?" No response. I knew she had heard me, no need to ask again.

We walked another thirty feet or so across what was left of the parking lot. She stopped at the concrete ramp and looked around again. "I told you, I came alone."

At the top of the ramp, we came to the smaller entrance door. Apparently it had been unlocked. We simply walked in. She turned on the lights to the narrow hallway and I stopped. Not from anything I saw, but from what I smelled. Stale blood and sour meat.

With my new-found viruses, I had become very sensitive to those two things. As familiar a smell to me as bacon. And if I didn't control it, just as appetizing.

My guide gave me a pathetic smile as if she took pity on me. "It's okay. They're already dead."

Not the most exciting thing I had heard tonight and in my line of work, just because it was dead, didn't mean it couldn't kill or eat you. "What the hell is this place?"

She continued to walk ahead of me, never turning. "A murder scene if you make one wrong move."

We came to another small door painted white, neglected, faded by time and dirt. The hallway, just wide enough that we could walk normally down it, just tall enough that the wolf in front of me didn't need to duck. A small reception area to my left and two doors to the right, which I guessed at one time or another had been used as office space. I tried not to glance at the wonderland of flesh in front of me, but lost the battle. She never made note of it, but I knew she was aware of my quick takes.

We went through the second door, which opened into the main warehouse. A smooth concrete floor, industrial shelving that towered twenty feet high. Mostly empty except for a few large boxes here and there. Bright industrial lights shined on us with blinding intensity.

I felt him before I saw him. Kasey stood in front of me in a black t-shirt and jeans. Kasey's dirty blonde hair had been cut short, resting above his collar. He had about two weeks growth on his face. Everything about him looked tired. Almost defeated.

"Wasn't sure if you'd show up or not," Kasey said, his arms folded across his chest. The woman moved to his side, staring back at me. "This is Tanya."

"We've met, what do you want?"

From behind the shadows of the large building I could see twenty or more wolves moving toward us. Right now, in human form. My eyes instantly scanned the building for escape routes while my fingers reached for the 9mm with silver nitrate bullets. I knew I didn't have enough for everyone, but I'd take out as many as I could before they got to me.

"What did you do to her?" Kasey balled and released his fists several times. I knew him well enough to know it meant trouble for me. I instinctively took a step backwards.

"Nothing. Believe it or not, I'm trying to save all of you from being exterminated." I looked around. "Is this your secret hideout?"

Kasey didn't seem to be amused at the joke. "That's not what I've heard." Before I could react, he grabbed me by the shirt and pushed me backwards. "After she saved your pitiful life, you do this to her!" My momentum stopped when my back hit the wall. Otherwise I had no idea how far we would have gone. I didn't have the strength to stop him. "They will still kill her. You have to know that."

I continued to watch the other wolves around us. I didn't need them to join in the fun. As a last resort, I pulled the 9mm on Kasey. The barrel rested against his chest. "Let me go or I swear, I'll leave you bleeding right here."

"You turned her didn't you?" Tanya added. Behind her, the others started to close around us, ready to attack at any moment.

"Tell your little puppies to back off or I swear to God, I'll kill you in front of them." Everyone froze. I bought only a fraction of time, but I'd take it.

"According to the news on the street, you turned her and caused all the deaths. I don't think you did it. I don't think you could, but now you've endangered all of us and I want to know why!" Kasey's spit hit me in the face. I did everything I could not to shiver with disgust. "I want to hear it from you that you had nothing to do with it."

"If I hadn't said I turned her, they were going to kill her. I am trying to save her life, Kasey. Something that I don't see any of your pack trying to do. Powerful vamps can turn furballs from human to animal. We both know I can't. I've tried."

"By you admitting that you turned her makes her and all of us guilty by association. You did nothing to help us. If anything you led us to slaughter by Lopes and Quinn. By now, when it came to those two, I would have thought you'd learn to think past your penis!"

I kept my anger under control. "I did the best I could." I pushed the barrel of the gun into his chest a little harder. "Now that we've both successfully threatened each other's life, can we talk about this a little more civilized?"

"Do you think shooting me will make your problems go away, *Dracul Sang*?" He released me and started to pace the floor in front of me. "If you had only done what she said, none of this would be happening right now." He shook his head as he thought. "And for what? Now, you've admitted to the authorities that you were the vampire that turned her. A lot of other people are put in the cross hairs by your denial of what you are." He moved back on me again. "Tell me you didn't do anything that night to put her in harm's way. Tell me you didn't turn her just to piss Quinn off."

I lowered the 9mm for now, but made sure it remained in plain sight. "I told you, I didn't turn her. I got a call from Kansas to come down to the Plaza after the fact. They already had Angie in semi-custody. Nobody there believed she did it, but they used her to get me to admit I was the *Dracul Sang*." I took a deep breath. "You've seen what I can do, or better yet, can't do. I couldn't change her if I wanted to. Not her or anyone else here. I'm not a blood sucker. I needed to buy Angie some time. You know I wouldn't have admitted something like that if it hadn't been for Angie."

"I think you went there with the mentality that if you couldn't have her, no one could. She chose Quinn over you and you turned her out of spite," Tanya said as she moved next to Kasey. "You turned her out of revenge."

The cell phone in my pocket buzzed. I jumped. "So is this the flavor of the week, Kasey? Seems to be way more devoted to you than Angie. Perhaps she will be the one that will do all you're dirty work for you. We all know you're capable of killing anyone." Truthfully, I had become scared and angry and all I had to counter was deflection from what they thought I had done. Hopefully, it would buy me enough time to get myself out of here alive.

Kasey gave a half smile. "You mean the lies about Angie's brother and how I set him up to be killed."

He took the bait. "Well you did, didn't you?"

The alpha wolf looked back at those around him. "I don't know what you're talking about *Dracul Sang*, but what I do know is that you've admitted to turning one of my wolves into a killing machine and according to popular opinion, turned the city against us." He licked his lips. "And in our laws, I have every right to gut you right here." He smiled. "You know now that you've admitted to turning Angie, they are going to kill you too don't you?"

"Not if I get to them first. Better me be arrested than Angie."

Kasey laughed loud. "Arrested? You've admitted to being *Dracul Sang* and turning her. There is no protection for pure bloods in this city. You will be killed. Lopes knew that, Quinn knew that. If you're going to be the top vampire in this city, you better learn vampire politics. Or should I say, you should have."

"What about Angie?"

Kasey shrugged. "What about her? You've already admitted to turning her. Stopping the vampire that killed all those people just might turn the public opinion of all of us."

"I didn't turn her." My anger rose. I pulled the 9mm up again. I had no doubt this had the potential to turn very ugly. My nose continued to smell something dead. Not coffin bait, but something truly dead.

"Doesn't matter at this point if you turned her or not. You admitted you did. The public will demand you pay for all those deaths." Those deep animalistic eyes pierced through me. The wolf inside him now just below the surface. Like the rest of them, they needed the moonlight to change, but even in human form they were far stronger than anything without the virus. "You say you didn't, but isn't it true that you were able to channel Olivia at the church?"

Cold chills shot through me. The nightmare of that event rushed back into my mind. With little effort, I would be puking on the floor in front of me. I wanted desperately to deny everything he insinuated to, but I couldn't. I had channeled the vampire into the church the night Father Garcia died. For a quick moment I thought about the possibility of channeling through Angie. Impossible, but the seed had been sown. "I did not change her." Each word escaped with growing anger. Each word a statement all to itself.

"I don't care. You being dead solves so many of my problems. My little secret goes to the grave." He caressed Tanya's arm. "Angie being dead gains me more than it hurts me. After what she's slept with now, I have no use for her. In a matter of time you both will be out of my life forever."

I looked to Tanya. She would be my ace in the hole. Bringing Angie back to the pack didn't seem like one of her top priorities. If I could get her to doubt her role in all of this and turn just a little against Kasey, I stood a shot of getting out alive. "You're lying, Kasey. We both know you can't just sit around and watch Quinn kill her. Eventually, you will have to make a move or you'll be the roaches bitch forever. You're alpha male. You'll have to go get her. What happens to Tanya when Angie returns? Does she get swept to the side?"

Tanya moved closer to me. "Won't matter once you're dead."

Kasey placed his fingers in his mouth and whistled. "White, come here."

A large man walked toward Kasey. He looked to be of European decent. Short blonde hair almost colorless, cut military style, which I assumed was how he had gotten his nickname. A little over six foot tall, bulging muscles and assassin eyes. White stopped next to Tanya with his arms folded across his chest. He looked at me with deadly intentions.

A knowing smile rose on Kasey's lips. "White, tell Mr. Isaac your theory of what happened at the Plaza last night."

"Zombie."

I expected a more descriptive answer, but it hit hard on its own. My mouth opened and shut several times as I gathered my words. "Zombie?"

Tanya spoke up. "Have you ever seen a zombie attack, know anything about them?" She said it as if she already knew the answer. In slow steps, she moved to me.

"Enlighten me."

She looked to White. He gave her approval. "You will have to excuse White. He's not well versed with the English language. From Germany. He moved here after the wall came down."

"Welcome," I said with all the sarcasm I could muster. "In all that time, zombie is the only word he's learned?"

Tanya ignored the comment. "White saw what happened that night and it wasn't caused by Angie or the pack. If his story checks out, a vampire is behind it. Maybe you."

"Convenient," I added, baiting for more information.

Tanya grabbed my jaws and pinched them together so tightly I expected the skin to break. "Shut up and listen." Eyes bulged from sockets as she quivered in anger. "Pack rules or not, I will chew your throat out if you give me any reason to. Don't underestimate me." Fingers released me with a violent pull. Kasey and White did their best to hide the grins on their faces. "He counted four, maybe five zombies coming out of the lobby that night."

"Is that all there was, or is that as high as he could count?" Being scared made me very stupid.

"You see, if in fact, the murders at the Crowne Plaza were caused by zombies, we have a sweet little vampire to kill."

"I don't follow," I grunted.

"Zombies can only be raised by certain vampires. Sort of a talent if you will. Something that not all vampires can do, which gives us a big break. We need to find out which one of the vampires in our city can raise the dead." Her foot released my throat. "Which leads us to you."

"Me?" Didn't see that coming.

"You, Paul." This from Kasey. He reached down and grabbed me by the arm and lifted me back to my feet, or as close as I was able to get at this point.

Pain shot through my groin area as I fought off another urge to throw up. "Why me?"

"Seems as though you have a lot of skills that the vampires have including channeling. Not that farfetched that you could raise the dead as well."

"I wasn't even there that night. I told you, Kansas called me to come down there because of Angie. I didn't change or raise anything."

Kasey put his arm around Tanya and pulled her to him. With a dominate motion, he kissed her cheek. "Let me tell you what I know, Paul."

7

THROUGH THE LARGE windows that lined the top of the warehouse, I could see the nighttime sky had eaten away at the sunlight. The skyline reflected in the dirty glass with grotesque colors and shapes. Stars danced on the canvas of blackness, awakening the monsters that lived under the bed. I cringed with anxiety. Every bone in my body told me to run.

Kasey approached me, leaving Tanya in the sea of fur balls gathering at a safe distance. I could see the confidence and courage growing in their body language. Not a good sign for me. Again, my bones urged me away from here, but I ignored them.

"I just had to hear it for myself that you hadn't really killed all those people that night. Didn't sound like you. The killing, yes, but to kill a politician that thought as narrowly as you do? Bit of a stretch. Then again, there are rumors that the new *Dracul Sang* is also a vampire executioner. Times are changing in the district."

"Peavey never had a soft spot for the furries either, Kasey. Maybe you had more to do with those deaths than I originally thought. With Peavey dead, your chances of gaining more power and land for development still lives. A bit convenient if you ask me." I didn't think he had anything to do with the murders, but getting under his skin made me enjoy the visit a little more. "As far as the *Dracul Sang* reference, perhaps I can adopt a little puppy from your pack like Quinn did."

Kasey gave me the "I really hate you" look. "Right about now, Judge Lopes is signing a warrant for your arrest in connections with the murders at the Crowne Plaza. This time you'll not slip through the fingers of justice. Detective Kansas will not be able to save you, with or without therapy. Within an hour, your name and face will be plastered on every channel, local and nationwide. As a human, you might have had a chance, but you won't be charged as a human this time. Pure blooded vampires are not under the same protection as the commercial ones." Kasey strutted with sickening confidence. "Only one thing in your future, *Dracul Sang*." He ran his forefinger across his neck.

In hindsight, I should have seen that coming. Kasey happened to be right. Someone would have to be the scapegoat and Quinn and Lopes knew Angie would be the perfect bait. Something I questioned from the beginning. I just hadn't thought it through the way I should have. When you don't consider yourself a blood sucker, you don't think like one.

Didn't really matter though. I would have done the same thing either way. "So what is it that you want from me? Save me? Offer me some sort of alliance?"

He laughed. "You happen to be the most optimistic pessimist I know, Paul." Kasey grew serious. "As we both touched on earlier, you know a thing or two about me that I would, let's say, like to remain secret. Now, you say you won't ever say anything to Angie, but we both know it still hangs around my neck like an albatross. That little detail will come back to haunt me at some time. We both know that. You have lycan virus running through your veins which makes you a risk to me, like it or not. You are the new *Dracul Sang*, which makes us enemies even if the other things weren't an issue." He shook his head. "No, Paul, you are not here so that we can work together. In fact, distancing myself from you based on what I know is the only logical option."

"So you plan to kill me? Shocker. We know how that turned out the last time."

"In a few minutes when the public finds out that you are responsible for all the fun things that happened at the Plaza, what do you think their reaction will be? An anti-vampire rights politician killed by a zombie raising vampire? If I were you, I'd hope the Council gets to you before the angry mob. This is one scenario I think it might be for the best."

"That's why finding the real killer is so important. Don't kid yourself into thinking that they won't kill Angie as well. I'm trying to save one of your own. Killing me won't bring her back. You still have a necromancer out there and your wolf in the hands of the undead. Is that what you want?"

"I've thought about all of this really hard over the last few hours. Revenge on my wolves has been frightening to say the least. Hunted because of something they didn't do. How could I as Alpha male regain the public trust, win them over?" He reached back for Tanya's hand and pulled her next to him. "All in the timing, Paul."

I started searching for exit routes and things I could use as weapons and distractions. In a very short period of time, the pack would overpower me. "What the hell are you talking about? Even with me dead, she's not going to come back to you. Chances are, Quinn will still kill her."

Tanya giggled, but Kasey spoke. "You think that's what all this is about? Angie?"

I shrugged. "Always has been in the past."

Kasey shook his head. "Not this time. She's betrayed everything. I'm planning on Quinn and Lopes killing her." He ran his hand along Tanya's body. "I have a new toy now. No, this is what I've planned. I help the police capture you, give them Angie as my peace offering from the pack and gain all the good graces of the police, community, and vampire district. It all works out well for me and no ones the wiser." He looked back to the others that still stood, ready to attack. "This is our day. A new day. If there's one thing I've learned from you, it's not to allow your heart to get in the way. It compromises you, weakens you, distracts you. Something that you forgot about when you claimed to be *Dracul Sang*. All for the love of a woman that no longer loves you. We both should have come to that conclusion a long time ago."

I pulled the 9mm back up. Kill Kasey and hope the others hesitated long enough that I could make a run for it. Simple idea, full of holes, but all I had. "Something you're not thinking about."

His attention seemed to be far more focused on Tanya than me. Things had a way of working out. "And what would that be?"

"The necromancer vampire that did all those wonderful things is still out there. I don't expect him to just go away. He's going to know you're still a risk to him. What happens when he comes looking for you?"

Now his attention turned back to me. "Now that's where you're wrong. The vampire in question raised the zombies to kill Peavey and his family that night. Any further actions to be taken will be on Quinn. Personally, I don't care one way or the other. You'll be dead, the pack will be vindicated and I will be absolute ruler of the wolves." He stared at the 9mm, still on him. "Killing me won't get you very far. All the wheels are already in motion. Besides, if it makes you feel better, I, nor any other wolf here, plan to harm a hair on your head. You are free to go any time you wish."

Didn't make sense, but I started to take a step backwards anyway. Cautious and trembling. "The truth will come out. All of it. Killing me will only delay everything for you."

Kasey laughed. "I told you, I'm not the one that's going to kill you. My hands will be clean of all of this." He raised his hands. "By the way, how did you like the package delivered to you?"

I stopped in confusion. "What package?"

"The one with your dead girlfriend's head in it."

I nearly fell to the floor. "Isabella?"

With psychotic laughter, Kasey clapped his hands and looked back at me. "Yes, that was her name! Thank you. God, I couldn't remember her name. Hand delivered it to you that night. I don't even have to ask if you still have it. I know you do. What will the cops and the people you serve think when they look through your house and find it? God, Paul, you better run like your life depends on it. I'd hate to be you right now."

"You son of a bitch! Why would you give me her head? What did you do?"

Kasey shook his head. "That's where you're wrong. I had nothing to do with her death. Just helping out with a little delivery. Something I was more than happy to do."

More of the wolves joined in the laughter. I became equally scared and angry. Tanya spoke. "Do you hear them?"

The laughter died into silence. I continued to back up. I didn't hear anything.

Kasey added, "You're right, Tanya. I hear them too." He looked back to me. "I think the warrant has been signed, Paul. Last thing you want is for the cops to find that head in your house. Better tie up as many lose ends as you can." The vibe in the room began to change. Animalistic sounds began to gurgle in their throats. A musky smell rose. Human eyes now took on a canine look.

In the distance, my ears began to pick up on the sound as well. Sirens. I stopped and looked back to Kasey. "That's why I'm here? So they can arrest me?"

A wolf-like grin reformed. "I've already told you, Paul. It's about public perception. Nothing will build trust with the community like bringing a killer to justice. As for the real necromancer, we're pretty sure we know who it is. Don't worry, I'm a patient man. I'll take care of things. As for Angie, I'll make sure it's quick and painless. I may even shed a tear."

The sounds grew louder. My heart beat faster. Time evaporated. I had no choice but to run for my life.

8

MY FEET no more than hit the pavement of the parking lot outside the warehouse when extremely long fingers reached out and grabbed me by the arm. A fearful noise escaped before I could stop it. The best way to tell a pure blood vein sucker from the commercial ones is that the pure bloods were living creatures. They had been birthed and they would die, although most lived about four hundred years or so. Pale white skin, so thin you could see the blue veins below the surface. By touch, they were warm blooded, breathed air and had a heartbeat. But the most visual contrast fell with those large black eyes. No whites at all. So deep in color you could sink into them and never find your way out.

"I apologize if I have alarmed you," Aelfric said as he loosened his grip on me. Behind him, I could see one male and one female. The male I knew as Camuel de Belatucadros and the female as Ella Selene.

The three stood before me like an impregnable wall, but something told me I wasn't in danger. My fingers reached for the Magnum, unimpressed with my gut feeling. Unlike the commercial brand of these things, the pure bloods were more scarce and rarely seen in public. Which led to another bag of questions.

"There will be no need for weapons," Ella Selene said as her eyes fixated on the Magnum.

"I'll determine that," I replied. Nothing more than an act. My fingers instantly let go of the weapon. I looked back to the warehouse, then to the 'Cuda, a good twenty yards from me. No matter where I went, I found myself face to face with things wanting to bite or chew on me. And that relied on me being able to get to either destination.

"We come in peace," Aelfric tried again.

"You do know that there are wolves in there don't you?" I asked, pointing behind me.

Aelfric smiled. "Their presence is of no value to me. If they wish to confront us, I shall deal with them promptly."

I saw Camuel de Belatucadros whisper in Aelfric's ear. Camuel outdated the other two by a good century. By human form, he looked to be about seventy or so, but in vampire years, I had no idea. He had no hair on his head. I had no way of knowing if it had been by choice or if these things had male pattern baldness. Either way, he looked like a large onion. From what I had gathered in limited dealings with him he didn't speak a word of English. He saw it as nothing more than a primitive language. Most of the pure bloods still spoke a version of the lost language, which for argument sake combined a version of pre-Latin and what sounded to be some sort of Slavic slang. It had given birth to the words *Dracul Sang* and *Dracul Morte'* among others. Loosely translating into blood of the living and blood of the dead.

Aelfric spoke again. "He wishes to know the truth. I apologize in advance for his impatience and our intrusion on this evening."

I looked at the younger male. Six foot tall, thin and large pointed ears. Black hair contrasted against his albino skin, giving his overall look that of a young boy, innocent and shy. But I knew better. The three monsters before me were the real deal. They lusted for blood and power among their own kind and nothing more. Holding on to tradition and seeing all things in either black or white.

I promised myself to watch my tongue. They wouldn't think twice of killing me in front of any number of witnesses. Human law didn't include them. Defying authority never even registered as a priority among them.

"What truth is that?"

"It has come to our attention that last night you confirmed yourself to be *Dracul Sang* of the city. Is this truth?" Ella Selene asked. Her appearance resembled that of an elf. Small to the point of almost being delicate. Like Aelfric, her features were childlike. Long black hair reached her hips, decorated with glass beads of infinite colors. Like the other two, she dressed in solid white. Among the things I knew of her, she had the worst reputation of the three when it came to power and violence. Father Garcia once told me she could rip your throat out without moving or touching you. I didn't plan on testing that rumor.

I weighed my options carefully, not knowing what the outcome of any of them might be. In my opinion, none of them would turn out so great for me. Vampire politics never gave you much wiggle room when it came to options. One, I tell them no, they see me as nothing more than a threat and kill me for no other reason than they had nothing better to do, two, I say yes, they kill me to become the new *Dracul Sang* and disappear into the blackness of the night with no more fanfare than that. Either way, my outcome remained consistent.

Damn.

Behind me, I heard the door to the warehouse open. By the power trickling down my skin, I knew who stood there. "Your idea, Kasey?"

"No, but it will still get the results I want. Aelfric, so nice to see you."

Ella Selene focused in his direction. "Wolf, these are matters that do not concern you. I ask that you leave us to our business." I found it amazing how she could sound so sweet and innocent, yet I knew well enough that each word had been wrapped in barbed wire.

"This is our territory." Another voice added into the mix. The female roach looked in his direction. An apologetic smile formed her lips. The wind lightly played with her black hair, glass beads clicked together as a chime. But under it all, I could feel her darkness rise and slither to the surface. "Your name?"

"Gaine," the wolf replied.

"Shut up!" I heard Kasey snap at his wolf. I feared it had been too late.

Ella Selene continued to smile as she studied him from the distance. "Please except my apologies, Gaine. We wish not to outgrow our welcome here." She held out her hand in his direction. "I ask you to come and take my hand in a gesture of peace."

Something didn't feel right. Ella Selene spoke the right words, but something still lurked just out of reach. Inside, I begged the wolf on the loading dock not to make the trek down to where we stood. But out of the corner of my eye, I could see a figure make its way to us.

"Gaine, get back here," Kasey commanded. Still, the figure advanced until the man stood next to me.

Compared to Ella Selene's small frame of barely five foot, Gaine's six foot plus frame became exaggerated. His wide shoulders towered over the vampire. Arms as big as her torso reached in her direction. Gaine threatened, "Shake and get the hell out of here you blood sucking bitch."

In my own defense, I side stepped another few feet from Gaine. If any of the three before us saw me move, they made no mention of it. All three sets of ancient eyes looked at the lone wolf without emotion.

A few seconds later, Kasey stood next to Gaine. "Forgive him, Ella. He's nothing more than a mouth in need of training. I ask of you to take care of your business and move on. Please." The urgency in his voice rang clear. He knew the danger his wolf had put himself in.

The thin smile on Ella Selene's lips grew wider. "I have no issue with your wolf. Youth is brief and wasted on petty things. I thank you for allowing us to trespass without your consideration. We will not be long. I assure you."

Kasey stood there waiting for something to happen. Hell, I did the same. Gaine had looked into the mouth of death and lived to tell about it. I breathed for the first time in minutes as the two wolves moved toward the warehouse again.

"Gaine?" Ella Selene called out. Barely louder than a whisper. Her hand still extended. "It is customary for all digressions to be solidified in peace with the shaking of hands."

The wolf looked back. His eyes wide. Quick glances to Kasey, but the alpha made no attempt to move or speak. Gaine stood lifeless.

"Please. It is all formal, I assure you." Ella Selene's hand remained outstretched.

Time seemed to stop as Gaine built the courage to take the first step. But then he began to move in reluctant form. Never stopping until he came face to face with Elle Selene. He looked at her hand for another few moments. Beads of sweat trickled down his face. "I'm so sorry. Forgive me." His words nothing more than vibrating terror.

"You are forgiven."

Gaine's hand shook with spasms as it grasped Ella Selene's. His hand so large, Ella Selene's completely disappeared. The two stood there for a moment. Nothing happened. Nothing. Sound had disappeared around us. Time had stopped. The vampire looked into Gaines face, that sweet smile still dominating her features.

She looked to me. Those large orbs of blackness covering me in screams of souls hundreds of years old. Her tiny hand still inside Gaines. Both motionless.

Both of the wolf's eyes shot forward from his head. Jelly-like matter splattered on Elle Selene's dress. Gaine screamed in agony, his hands quickly covering the sockets in his head. I watched as the veins and arteries in his head filled with blood and punched through the skin walls of his temples and cheeks. Bone began to crush. His face now red with pressure. Loud screams filled my ears to the point it hurt. Power rose over me and pushed me to the ground.

Gaines head exploded in large pieces. Bone and matter sprayed across the parking lot. The metallic smell of blood filled the air. The wolf's body fell to the pavement in a solid thump. Fluids escaped from the open neck.

Ella Selene turned and looked back to me. Her questions very matter-of-fact. "Is there truth in the words? Have you accepted your role?"

My mouth moved, but nothing came out. Surely I hadn't been the only one that just saw that! I pushed myself upward again and tried not to vomit. "If you plan to kill me, please do it now."

Aelfric gave a spark of laughter. "Kill you, why would we do such things?"

"I have admitted to being *Dracul Sang*." I looked at the three and took a giant step toward the 'Cuda. I wouldn't make it, but it gave me false hope. "If any of you want it, please feel free to take it. I only said it to protect someone."

"The wolf?" Aelfric replied.

"Yes."

A puzzled look dominated his face. "And why would you do such a thing?"

"They were going to kill her."

Ella Selene stared back at me. "But she is a wolf?"

"Are you going to kill me or not. God knows you can so get it over with if that's what you came to do."

The young male shook his head. "We are here to protect you. You are now our *Dracul Sang* as well. Though not by our choosing. Nor are we pleasured by the situation, we must follow vampire protocol."

Camuel de Belatucadros spoke to Aelfric in ancient language. "He wants to know when the Council seeks to judge you for the actions against the wolf?"

I shrugged. "I don't know."

My answer was conveyed to the elder and he seemed unhappy with the answer. Again he spoke in the ancient language. I looked to Aelfric for the translation. "He wants to know what should be done with the human woman?"

"What?"

A fourth vampire appeared out of the shadows. He pulled a figure to us, washing her in the street lamp above.

"Ashley?"

9

THE VAMPIRE LED Ashley to me, his eyes never leaving mine. Black orbs of death consumed my attention. I tried to read his face, but found nothing. Emotionless even in his methodical walk, he stopped just short of me, lining up with the other three ancient creatures. He looked down at what remained of Gaine, then back to me. His expression never changed. I had guessed things of this nature probably were not all that uncommon in his world.

"Is everything well, *Dracul Sang*?" he asked. Like the other three, he dressed in all white, had pale skin, black hair, cut short. They resembled a religious cult in some ways. A cross between an alien and something that lived under the bed.

"I really wish you all wouldn't call me that," I said more under my breath than anything.

The vampire looked at me with a puzzled look. "But this is what you are. Against my better judgment, against all I believe in, but it is the way. For now."

"For now? Is that some sort of threat?" My fingers went for the butt of the Magnum again.

He raised his hand as if to stop me. "I only say this because our predicament is so unusual and unprecedented. I mean you no disrespect, but until you have been judged by the Vampire Council, your fate as *Dracul Sang* and as a living and free being is subjective." He looked back to Ashley, "In the meantime, I have brought you a gift."

From what I could tell, Ashley had not been harmed. Scared shitless, but other than that, in good shape. Her hair, like yesterday had been pulled back in a ponytail. Dressed in a dark blue or black uniform with the bright yellow letters, PDA, or Paranormal Detective Agency. She looked good in her official uniform. A bit small for the equipment, but handled it well.

I ran through my mind of all the scenarios that might have led her to the grasp of blood feeders and I didn't like any of the conclusions. Smart, talented, beautiful, but possibly a bit too ambitious. As I had learned the hard way, when dealing with these things, one had to be very careful and do whatever it took to possess any advantage necessary. She had been crying. Black mascara ran down her cheeks, eyes red with irritation, but so far untouched.

"Mind telling me what the hell is going on, Paul?" Her voice shook. Anger and fear had created something that looked back at me with unforgiving hatred.

Something told me she might have gotten too close to the roach that had been responsible for the murders at the Crowne. Kansas and the wolves had used the term zombie, which meant somewhere down the road, a vampire had to be pulling the strings. I looked at the four next to her. Could one of them be the one that had raised the zombies? I had no doubt they were powerful enough, but it just didn't make sense. None of them could care less about Peavey or politics. Not their style. They would have found that sort of death as exciting as a kid in a ball pit. We would have found them still basking in their enjoyment if it had been them.

"Not sure myself," I said in a low voice. I looked to Aelfric. "What's this about?"

The young vampire looked to me, but never moved his head. "We have been informed that she might be here to arrest or kill you." His demeanor remained very matter-of-fact as most of his type were known for. Only torture brought out more than what I saw right now. I played it safe and considered that a good sign.

Camuel de Belatucadros spoke in Aelfric's ear. "He wishes to be the one that opens her throat."

I looked back to Ashley. "Are you alright?"

Ashley's attention fell on Aelfric. "After what he said, that's your question, Paul?" Eyes on me. "What the hell is going on here? Is this some sort of joke?"

"*Dracul Sang?*" Aelfric asked.

"She is not to be harmed," I answered.

"You need to tell me what's going on. Why do they all call you *Dracul Sang*? Where's Asa? When did you start hanging out with the vampires?"

The woman looking back at me held so much of my heart, yet I stood with nothing to say. It was too much, too soon. I hadn't prepared for her to return to my life. Not now of all times. "Why did you really come back?"

Confusion covered her face. "It wasn't for you if that's what you're thinking."

"Perhaps I should break her neck?" Ella Selene asked with little fanfare. I couldn't get past her concoction of innocence and evil. Solid black eyes shined in the moonlight. Pale pink lips, thin and full of youth. I had never felt power like that she possessed. It alone, could be lethal, I had no doubt. "A true *Dracul Sang* would have no issue with it. A true test as to whom you protect."

Before she moved, I spoke. "No. She is not to be harmed."

"But…" Ella Selene started.

"I said no!"

Ella Selene acted as though I had taken away her favorite toy. Only one dead body. Far too slow a night for the little killer. She bent her head low, refusing to look to me. Could she really be pouting?

I had to tread lightly here. Ella Selene might be under control for now, but I had no doubt that she could crush my skull just as easily as she did Gaine's. I found myself face to face with the most dangerous ninety pounds on earth. If she chose to kill Ashley, I feared there would be nothing I could do to stop her. That alone sent shivers down my spine.

Aelfric looked to the vampire holding Ashley's wrist. "Ivan, let her go." And he did.

"Where's Asa?" Ashley asked again. "I'll take an answer from any of you, since Paul seems to be suffering from selective hearing." She rubbed her wrist where Ivan had held her. "Paul, I'll ask again. What's going on?"

I weighed my options. I could lie, but I knew she would see right through them. I didn't even believe the truth. Based on our history it would not go over well. "I killed him."

"Not that hard to believe." Ashley took it all in. I could see her trying to process it all. "Why do they call you *Dracul Sang*? Unless I'm mixing something up here, that means Master Vampire, right? Last time we talked, you were a human and wanted me out of your life because of them, now this."

Talking about it still brought up too many anger issues. Best thing to do is put her back on the defensive. She hadn't come back here to help solve a case. We had unfinished business. I had been okay with that, but obviously, she hadn't. "Do you really think I left you to hurt you? I was trying to protect you. You should never have come back here. For God's sake not now."

"You proposed to me." I caught her balling her fists and stomping. A classic move of hers. Living together for almost two years, I had learned a lot about her body language.

Four words that could have been a bullet. Dumbest thing I had ever done in my life. Not for her actions. Eight years ago, Ashley consumed my world. I knew it was the wrong thing to say as soon as I said it that night. Already I knew I would never be able to go through with it. "I did it to protect you. I told you that. Nothing has changed. Just because you're some hot shot detective now doesn't make you invincible. As you have seen, they will still find you and they will still kill you. It's all they know."

More tears fell across her face, not out of fear, but something far more emotional. "Protect me from what? You seem to be part of their little club now. What else were you hiding from me?" She looked at four vampires that stood between us. "I loved you. I was willing to give up everything for you. I never pressured you into marriage. Not once. You were the one that proposed to me. I simply loved you. That was enough for me. You're the one that took it the next step. I was okay with living in sin. I only wanted you. I didn't need the picket fence and two and a half kids."

Now I felt my own anger coming out. "You don't think I know that?" I began to walk to her. "This is why I let you go. If you had married me, you would have been in constant danger. I kill these things for a living. We would never see them eye to eye. You were part of the movement to get them legalized and I was part of the movement to cut their heads off. Eventually, that alone would have destroyed us."

"Do you realize the embarrassment you caused me?"

I did. "I'm sorry."

"Sorry? You left me the day before our wedding. All my family and friends were in town. Everything in my world ended with one apology? And you think I'm supposed to be alright with it?"

"I thought yesterday you said everything was good between us. Why are you bringing all this up now?"

Ashley looked to the vampires to my right. All four stood at attention like stone statues. "This is why! I've been kidnapped and my life hangs in the balance while you play master vampire."

"I simply thought you would be better off without me. I don't know why we have to talk about all of this now."

She slapped me. "I'm a woman! Do you really think I was okay with being left on my own, hours before the biggest moment of my life? Do you want to know just how bad I want to hate you? And you did it all to protect me? Look around. Do I look safe to you?"

I grabbed her by the shoulders. Everything rushed back. I remembered the touch of her skin, the smile in her voice, the endlessness in her eyes, her smell. Yes, I loved her, but that had nothing to do with me anymore. "If you hadn't come back, you would be. Just like I told you.

Anything associated with me dies sooner or later. I loved you enough to see that and make the decision for the both of us. Do you really think I would propose to you just to break your heart? "

Her hands pushed me away. Eyes scanned me. She looked at the vampires again. "But I don't understand. How can you be the *Dracul Sang*? You're not a vampire."

"You seem to be the only one that thinks that. Seems as though my mother had the vampire virus, passed it along to me. When I killed Asa, I technically became the *Dracul Sang*. Until the incident at the Plaza, to be honest, I had ignored it. Truth is I don't care what happens to these blood lovers. Between you and me, I still plan to kill as many as I can."

She took a step back. For the first time, she saw me as something other than human. I could see it in her eyes. "You're a vampire?"

Out of all of that, that happened to be the only things she heard? Again, I grabbed her by the shoulders. "No. I'm still the same person I've always been. Just a technical glitch. You have to believe me."

"Why were you really there that night?"

"At the Plaza? I told you. Kansas called me and told me to meet him there."

"Let me tell you what I know, Mr. Isaac."

Oh, Mr. Isaac. This would not be good.

"According to our findings, the woman you are desperately trying to protect had been turned by a vampire and killed those people. We both know you pretty much confessed to Quinn of the same thing, and now this? Rumor has it that the woman in question, Angie, I think it is, used to be your girlfriend."

"We were never dating. Friends at best."

"Friends at best? Seems like you're going to an awful lot of trouble to save someone that's only friends at best."

"I owe her my life."

She gave me a look I had seen far too many times. "How?"

"Not long ago, she had been kidnapped by another vampire coven and bitten. That same vampire tried to kill me, Angie killed it before that happened. When they fed from Angie, they left her weak and vulnerable to all roaches. She tried to get me to feed off her and bind her to me. I refused and now she's a servant of Quinn's."

A genuine laugh. "Are you listening to what you're saying? You can feed off of people, yet you don't claim to be a vampire? And let me tell you something else, she didn't seem to be with Quinn out of some sort of binding. I think it's her choice. You're just too blinded to see it."

"I'm not a vampire," I repeated.

"Then stop acting like one. Because all of this seems to contradict everything you're lying to yourself about."

"This?"

She waved her hand in the vampires' direction. "All of this. You playing master vampire after saying that we could never be husband and wife because of them. That you hated monsters and now you are willing to give up your own life for a werewolf? My God, Paul, who are you? Really?"

I had no answer.

"Tell me you didn't do it?"

"No. I didn't kill anyone. I confessed to save Angie's life."

"She's very pretty."

I had no intentions of following that. "Why were you looking for me?"

"I was talking to a couple of people at the precinct about Price and your name came up. They say you killed his grandson and Father Garcia. Is that true?"

She had hollowed me out with that one. "I don't know what to say to you?"

"You did it didn't you?"

"What the hell do you want me to say, Ashley? Price's grandson was a vampire. He attacked me and Price. I had to do what I had to do. Truth is, Price actually killed him, but I took the blame. Father Garcia…I don't know what happened. Honestly, I don't."

Fear swelled in those big eyes. She no longer looked at me as lost love. Evaporated in one evening, one conversation. "Tell me you didn't do that to Kansas and his family."

It had been unthinkable that she would say that. I shut down. "Think what you want, Ashley. If you came here to punish me, go ahead. I deserve it. I really do. I'm everything they told you about me, but I had nothing to do with Kansas and his wife and son. I've been placed in this living hell because of my own actions. I get that. Everything is spinning out of control and I deserve every evil thing that comes my way. Losing you is something I'll never get over, but I'd do it all over again if I had to. Anything near me is in constant danger because of what I do. I'm a miserable and horrible person that will never get well. I wish you well in all you do, but you're out of my life. We're two totally different people that'll never have a future together. I'd hate knowing I had kids that would grow up without parents, become an orphan because of me. I beg you to pull your gun out right now and blow my brains away. I wish someone would do me the favor. Do something I don't have the guts to do myself."

She wiped away the tears from her cheek, leaving a thick black trail of mascara. "I wanted to ask your opinion on something I found out today. That's why I was looking for you. A lie. An excuse really. Truth is I wanted to see you, but I did want to ask your opinion on something work related."

"Which is what?" I questioned if she had heard anything I said. I knew Ashley better than anyone. She had heard me. She would process it for days, re-process it some more, then learn to hate me like everything else in this city.

"Seems as though one of the cameras caught a glimpse of something shortly before the attack and before they were turned off. Do you know of a vampire called Inderia?"

I didn't need a mirror to know my face blushed. Sweat hit me hard. Another tricky answer and question bout. "Yes, she's a...an...umm."

"Porn star?"

I simply shook my head.

"Why would a necro-porn star be at the convention center the night of Peavey's big party? Do you know where I could find her?"

"I have an idea. Let me talk to her."

"Damn it, Paul! You can't keep treating me like some little helpless creature. I know what I'm doing. And more importantly, I'm the agent on this, not you. If anything you're an accessory to murder at the moment. An hour ago, I would have said that was insane to think, but looking around now, I'm not so sure."

I looked to Aelfric. "Let her go. She's not to be harmed. Get her somewhere safe."

Without hesitation, all four vampires took a swift step back, away from Ashley. Perhaps I could use these little minions more than I originally thought.

"That's it?" Ashley asked.

I began to walk toward the 'Cuda. "What else would you like, Ashley?"

I could hear her stop behind me. "I could shoot you, you know."

Still, I walked, never turning around. I pulled a cigar from my shirt pocket, a lighter from my pants pocket and lit the sucker. "Then shoot me."

"You are under arrest for the murders of those at the Crowne Plaza, Paul Isaac. Stop or I'll shoot!"

I opened the door to the 'Cuda. "Do it now, Ashley. Beats where I'm going."

Footsteps in my direction. Moving fast. "Wait. I'll go with you. You'll get killed on your own."

"Probably." I started the car. Ashley moved to the opposite side of the car and tried to get in. The door remained locked. She pulled on the handle a few times, then banged her palm against the window.

"You son of a bitch!"

I couldn't take the chance of getting us both killed. I worked better alone. Especially when it came to killing things. Less loose ends to follow through on.

One minute nothing, the next Ella Selene stood next to my door, looking into the open window. "Does this mean we do not get to kill her, *Dracul Sang*?" Her voice flooded with disappointment. I almost felt sorry for her.

I put the 'Cuda in gear. "That's exactly what that means, Ella Selene."

"You trust them?" Ashley asked through the window glass on the opposite side of the 'Cuda.

I blew the first lung full of cigar smoke free of my lungs. "I'm *Dracul Sang*. You'll be fine."

10

I NEVER QUITE MADE IT to South Street, when I saw and heard the chaos. Screams filled the air. Figures ran toward me. The ground crawled as the mass fanned out across the lawn and parking area ahead of me.

I slammed on the brakes just as a man slid across the hood of the 'Cuda. In an instant, I found myself surrounded by a sea of panicked faces, all pounding their fists at the windows, begging to be let in. "What the hell is going on?" The 'Cuda rocked as more gathered around it, pulling against the locked doors. A woman screamed in fear. Others screamed in pain.

I grabbed the Magnum, checked it for fire power, placed the 9mm in the hip holster and pushed my way out of the driver's side of the car. Instincts told me to run in the opposite direction of the crowd and I'd find the monster. So far, I had never been proven wrong.

As I cleared the gathered crowd by the 'Cuda, I caught a glimpse of Kasey in wolf form. Believe it or not, it gave me hope. He would be stronger and better than the naked human version.

Through an opening along the street, I saw the culprit of the pandemonium. I stopped in disbelief. Creatures moved across the ground in sweeping fashion, taking down those within an arm's length. Dead, emotionless faces. Not human. Not fang head. What the hell were they? Zombies!

I moved toward one of the creatures as it pursued a man, no more than thirty yards from me. I found it impossible to get a clear shot. People ran in and out of the line of fire. Somewhere within the few steps I took, I had aimed and lowered the Magnum several times.

The creature moved with great strength and speed and quickly overpowered the man. From behind, it took its victim to the ground just as I fired. Flesh flew into the air as the bullet hit it in between the shoulder and neck. Black ooze slowly leaked from the wound like molasses, while the monster bit into the man's throat. It lifted its head, holding a large piece of flesh between blood stained teeth, chewing it. Dark red liquid spread across its already rotten face. Small fragments of the skin fell back to the ground through a hole in its cheek. Its victim twitched with involuntary movement as a fountain of red death shot into the air.

I took a step back as the monster looked at me. These were not the eyes of a cockroach, but something every bit as sinister. I took another aim at it as a woman rushed by. I lifted the muzzle just in time, then re-aimed on my nightmare. I took the shot, catching it in the left thigh.

The monster grabbed the head of its victim and smashed it hard onto the concrete of the sidewalk. Fingers reached inside the split skull and scooped brain matter and placed them to its lips. A black tongue twisted from its mouth as an earthworm slithered on the ground. I stood and stared in horror. I had never in my darkest nightmares seen anything like this.

It held the remaining pieces of the brain in its hand like a large apple as it rose back to a standing position. Those demon-like eyes remained on me, though I didn't see much thought going on behind them.

I pulled the Magnum back up. Fired again. The bullet struck it in the chest. More body matter sprayed the ground. The monster fell back a few steps, more from the momentum of the bullet than anything. I saw the shadows of those running away through peripheral vision, but I couldn't unlock my eyes from the creature before me.

I looked to my left and caught a glimpse of Kasey as he attacked another of the monsters from behind. Even with the power and strength that he had in animal form, the creature threw him clear. The ground grew littered with half eaten bodies, chunks of flesh, twitching corpses that died so quickly that life still moved in them. More wolves gathered in the streets, each trying to chew their way past the monsters.

Lips parted in a half growl, followed by a full tilt run towards me. These things were powerful. Fast. Out of sheer desperation, I fired again as my feet began to back pedal from the monster. Again, I hit my mark. I caught the thing on the side of the face. Bone and rotten flesh flurried through the air. Only half of the head remained, but still it came. Nothing killed this flesh eater.

I pushed clear of another soon-to-be-eaten-victim as I turned. Human instincts kicked in, but my mind already knew it was futile to think I could save myself, much less any of the others in harm's way.

Gray, bloated fingers touched my shoulder with enough power that it felt as though my spine snapped. My body twisted to the ground, while the grip never released. The monster fell with me. Rancid breath shrouded my head as the open mouth targeted my face.

My Magnum fired one last time instinctively. Heat. Lots of it. Flashes of light. Burning flesh. Maggots and beetles escaped through opening pores of the monster. The grip loosened. More heat. Fire. Flesh disappearing. Bone exposed. The smell. I pushed free of the burning body on top of me. Heat and fire bit at my own flesh. Stings of pain on exposed skin as pieces of flesh landed on my arm. I fanned the small orange flame out with multiple slaps of my hand.

Above me, stood a man with some sort of flame thrower. Yes. A freaking genuine flame thrower. Where did this night end? Kansas held out his hand to me as he perched the flame thrower against his shoulder.

I hesitated grabbing his hand. I needed a few seconds to collect my thoughts. My eyes searched the ground next to me for the burning corpse that now resembled a black marshmallow more than anything.

"I can't kill them all by myself. Take my hand, get up and help me save some lives." Without further hesitation, I did as he commanded. If

I were to be his next victim, he would have already toasted me. *Save a few of them?* I thought. We were outnumbered and out powered. "Here," Kansas answered as he handed me a smaller version of the flame thrower he killed the thing with.

I know I must have looked at him like a cow looking at a new gate, because it reflected in his stare. My fingers reached for the fire power then retreated. For some stupid reason, I tried to rationalize what had happened. My comfort zone had narrowed.

"Zombies. Living dead. Flesh Eaters. Start killing or be eaten. Choice is yours." He slammed the flame thrower into my chest and began to move away, targeting another monster some thirty yards ahead of us. I looked at the flame thrower in my hands, not sure exactly how to use it, but if it killed these brain eaters, I'd be a quick learner.

In the streets and along the lawn of Town Hall, I could see several other officers using the flame throwers. They were in full-on riot gear, looking like something out of a science fiction movie. Even from the distance they were, I could feel the flashes of heat. Sirens screamed in all directions. Blue and red lights flashed against the architecture. The smell of propane burned my nostrils.

An officer barbecued the zombie battling Kasey. The wolf fell to the ground next to the monster either from exhaustion or injury. From this distance I couldn't be real sure.

Kansas shot another flame on the zombie he had targeted. It sped away, glowing with a tail flame of oranges and blues before finally falling to the ground and becoming extra crispy.

There were other zombies still out there, but now had retreated down dark streets and disappeared into the chaotic crowd. Within seconds they vanished. After seeing what they were capable of, it left me with no doubt that there would still be a trail of dead bodies leading us back to them. I hesitated in chasing them. I didn't use my brain much, but I liked it where it was.

The streets looked like a battle zone. Dead bodies littered the ground in all directions. A total of four burning zombies lit the darkness with illuminated death. We simply stood in silent survivor's remorse.

The stench brought me back to the Crowne Plaza. Burning bodies, opened flesh, heat. I threw up. A lot. I had little doubt now as to what killed those people in the hotel. Which left me with one objective.

Kill the necromancer responsible for this hell.

11

Overhead I heard the helicopters thunder by. Search lights illumi-nated the starless night in search of the creatures that had for the second time in a week left pieces of flesh scattered in their path. Each flash of light reminded me of the horror that had taken place. Strobes of light and piercing sounds approached from the distance as word of the carnage hit the streets. The living cried and huddled together with little chance that consoling words would make things better. We were all left with the hard fact that death had invaded with a vengeance.

I turned back to Kansas, who looked up, tracking the path of the chopper with his eyes. As his attention came back down, he turned to me with a cold and heartless glare. The flamethrower rested in his hand, still smoking from the last use. I could see policemen move in shadows. We all had the same look and more than likely, the same questions. I had hunted and killed roaches since the day I was able. I had even killed a few fur balls and shifters in my time, but never in my life had I even come across a zombie.

Kansas stopped a few feet from me. He started to speak, but I inter-rupted him. "What the hell were those things?" Before he could repeat himself, I threw my hands up. "I know, you said they were zombies, but I need a little more information than that." I looked at the flamethrower again. God that thing was intimidating and impressive. "You seemed to have come a bit too prepared not to have some sort of inside information on them."

He shook his head slowly. "Ever answer your goddamned phone?" He looked at the Magnum in my shoulder holster. "Your weapons won't work on them." More cursing. "I tried to call you all evening. Lopes and the police are looking for you. Gonna pin you for the murders at the Crowne Plaza. I tried to warn you." He studied me. "You got my messages didn't you?" I didn't answer. "Where the hell have you been?" I started to speak when I noticed a Glock pointed at my chest. Before I could speak, he continued. "For God's sake, Paul, tell me you're not considering being one of them."

"A zombie?"

He shook his head, the Glock still on me. "A vampire."

Now I felt confused. "Why would I be a vampire?"

"The other night at the Crowne, you said you would go before the Council and be known as the master vampire. It's all over the department gossip. That you turned Angie. Tell me you're not really going to do that. For Stephanie's sake, tell me it's a lie." I couldn't tell if he was scared or angry.

"I said those things to keep Angie alive and give us more time to find out what really happened. I didn't have a choice in the matter. We both know they will use it against us, but you have to believe me, I'm still one of the good guys. Now if you don't mind, please take that gun off me."

Kansas lowered the Glock and nearly crumbled to the ground. "I'm going crazy, Paul. I can't take this much more. All I want to do is put this gun to my head and pull the trigger." He looked back up to me. "I don't even know who I am anymore. Why won't she just wake up? What did those bastards do to her?"

My attention remained on the flamethrower as the skeptic in me began to come out. "How did you know what kind of weapon to bring? A flamethrower isn't exactly a common weapon to have on you. Somehow I think you knew what you were going to be up against."

"I still have a scanner and heard the call. They don't know I still have it, I guess. Maybe they don't care. Like it or not, I'm still a part of this force. I'm looked at as a liability. But I now know a vampire is responsible for both attacks." I started to ask the big question when Kansas snuffed it out. "Zombies do not exist without the power of a vampire. Your wolf didn't raise the zombies, but that doesn't mean that she's not involved. I'm going through data banks of information on which vampires might be necromancers. Most keep that sort of thing a secret, but some can't help it." He began to move past me, but I flanked him step for step. Yeah, I know answering my questions weren't the highest on his to do list, but when something tries to eat me, I tend to have a few questions that need to be answered. "You need to get out of here. If they find you, they'll arrest you. They were coming for you when all this broke out."

"Found anybody yet? On that data thing, I mean?"

"Three possibilities. Dieter happens to be one of them."

"Let's go talk to him."

Kansas stopped my first step. "You know you can't. Let me see what I can find out. You were supposed to be dead by now. Stop and count your blessings. We don't want him to know we're looking in his direction on this. If I can prove it, trust me, you'll be interrogating him from his pile of ash." He looked at the flamethrower in his hand. "I owe him and the rest of those worm eaten bastards a little something."

"Is that why all those lovely sirens were going off. Just to get little ole me? In Lopes' situation, all guns blazing and sirens blaring makes good TV.'"

Kansas shook his head. "No, you were supposed to be picked up nice and easy at a location just out of town here. The zombies were the ones that got all the attention. Started off of Kaley. Two buildings on fire that I know of." He looked around. "Look, I ain't got a lot of time here, obviously. I just need you to lie low for a while." A nervous laugh. "God, I thought you'd be dead by now. One in a million chance I'd find you down here. Don't go home, they're watching your place." He pushed me. "And answer your phone!"

"Jesus," I said under my breath.

"This might have been the best thing that could have happened to you. They weren't going to tell the public about the zombies. Just that you and Angie killed all those people. Not until you were dead, that is. From what I make out of it, the zombies were supposed to be your doing and they just happened to kill you along with everybody else. Ties up a lot of loose ends. If they find you in time, they can still work all that in." He put his hands on his hips. "Guess the cat's out of the bag now, huh?"

"That's why I'm not worried about being arrested and given a fair trial."

"Paul, why did she go to him?"

I grew defensive. "Angie had nothing to do with those deaths and you know it."

He continued to stand there, waiting on a real answer.

I caved. "When we killed Olivia and Judas, because they fed off her, it made her vulnerable to just about any vampire out there. She wanted me to bite and feed off her to keep her safe, but I didn't."

He rolled his eyes. "Your wolf is in this deep. The real question is, is she a willing participant or not. Let's not forget the fact they found her unconscious at the scene of the crime. According to the local newspapers, Quinn and Peavey were at odds on expansion of the vampire district. You and I both know that Quinn is strong enough to be a possible necromancer, but he's too smart for that. He never does anything himself. Which means we have another son of a bitch out there strong enough to raise the dead." He stopped, gathered his thoughts and swallowed hard. "Off the record, I'm looking into any accounts of any vampires that have done this type of thing before, or any that have the reputation of doing it. It has to be someone close enough and under the control of Quinn. He wouldn't just trust anyone to do that kind of stuff."

"Why tonight? Do you really think the vampire responsible for all of this raised them again just to kill me?"

Kansas looked as though he hadn't thought of that question. "What?"

"I get why Quinn did it the other night. It, in a twisted way, makes sense. He needed Peavey out of the way, but tonight? It makes no sense at all, or am I missing something?"

The detective shrugged. "I'm sure we're missing something. Just not sure what yet. Remember, I'm not on this one, so information comes to me a lot slower." He ran his fingers through his thinning hair. "Make no bones about it, Isaac, I will kill those things." He wiped away a tear. "Not because of this either. Just visited Steph in the hospital and each time I do, I want to kill them a little more. Every time I see her, I see them. I can do the time if need be, but mark my words, I will get every one of them one of these days."

If there happened to be one thing I never claimed to be good at, it had to be talking people out of killing daisy pushers. I separated those that were for vampire rights and those that opposed them into two categories; the ones that were pro-fang hadn't lost someone to them and the anti-fangers were the ones that had. To me it remained very simple.

Kansas teetered on that edge of hatred that had seduced me years ago. In myself, I saw purpose and plausibility in my actions, but in Kansas I saw the ugliness and the danger. I feared his actions. I could empathize with him, but never wanted to see it turn into cold blooded murder and that continued to grow into a real possibility. "Talked to Feelgood last night."

"Really? Thought you would have killed and buried her in your backyard by now." He tried to smile, but it never quite blossomed.

"Well, I say that because of something I found a bit strange." I gathered my words carefully. "You remember the word on the wall the other night?"

He shook his head. "Yeah, VICTORY."

"At first, I thought it could have been something to do with the Victory Party that caused all of that, but a little bird told me something that has me thinking."

"Bad idea, but go ahead."

I gave him the middle finger. "Inderia was at the Crowne the night of the murders. She's on video. Now in my line of work, I know things. Things I wish I didn't. But one of the things I do know is that Inderia is a stripper and necro-porn star that is the leading bitch for those wanting to keep necro-porn alive and well in the good ole USA. Her group is a branch of the Undead Victory movement to allow full feedings in the name of pornography. We all know that if it succeeds, there is a lot of money to be made. Killing Peavey is a step in the right direction as far as they are concerned. I'm sure you've heard of them."

A grin sprouted. "In fact, I have. A bit radical if you want to know the truth. A growing group for the legalization of necro-porn and porn in general I guess. Burned the house of a known ex-porn director turned evangelist in Coral Gables about a year back. Another incident where they allegedly killed a star's dog after she spoke out against the behind the scene secrets."

"Could they have been behind the murders at the Crowne?"

"Because of the word on the wall, you mean?"

"Exactly."

Kansas thought about it. "Not out of the realm of possibility. But I think the waters are a little deeper than an angry porn star. Before things got…well you know, I had been working on an investigation of the Victory Political Party. Seems as though they are a dummy party to launder illegal monies. The people that pull the strings for the Victory Party also have connections with Necro Pussy. If we play our cards right, there might be a link to all of this. When I got too close, that's when Stephanie was kidnapped. I don't think it was random at all. They were sending me a message that I had gotten too close. They have worked really hard to ruin the credibility of both you and me. It's us or them."

"We are looking for a necromancer, which according to my knowledge on the subject, has to be a vampire. Inderia is a vampire. Inderia's group is called Undead Victory. I think it's time to shake a few trees and see what falls out."

"You think you'll be any more welcomed at Quinn's little stripper joint? I'll look into it."

I smiled. "You're married. I'll go." I patted him on the shoulder. "You owe me one."

In return, I got a genuine smile. The first from Kansas in a very long time. "You're such a giver."

12

Everything told me to wait, but patience betrayed me. Being a wanted man, I no longer possessed the luxury of time. If Inderia could raise the dead, I needed to stop her quickly. Something I knew would be easier said than done.

Quinn always came to mind when things got twisted and ugly. When it came to things like this, the first thing you have to ask yourself is, "Who will the deaths benefit the most?" And my answers continued to lead me to Quinn. Sometimes I forced them to lead me there, but I eventually got there.

Two white limos sat in front of the club. A large fountain of concrete lions sprayed water in complicated patterns on the lawn. Bright lights illuminated everything in a wash of overkill. Music moved from muffled to loud, depending on whether someone entered or exited the large doors ahead.

I could feel the power leaking from the Risen Sins Gentleman's Club long before I stepped under the red canopy lined with bright white lights. A thick red carpet led me to the main doors of the hell hole I planned to enter. Tinsel and garland with large red bows were placed everywhere. A nine foot tree stood to the left of the entrance, wrapped in bright red ribbons and twinkling white lights. Against the far wall, I saw a picture of Santa with fangs in a sleigh, being pulled by eight bats. Nothing said Merry Christmas like fangs and a mistletoe. In front of me, a large wooden counter. Eye candy gyrated behind the bar to the beat of industrial music.

Humans with incredible amounts of expendable income and lack of common sense, found the place irresistible. Far more than the average strip club, Risen Sins had a reputation as the most exotic club in the south, catering to the most privileged of clientele. Overpriced drinks and nothing short of blatant prostitution. According to information I had heard, Tortured Skin still operated out of here on a more discrete level. One of the clubs Peavey had targeted over the past few months. And more than likely one of the reasons he was dead.

No matter what type of monster I pursued, no matter how I tried to avoid it, I always seemed to end up at a place like this. No surprise there. Quinn represented the vacuum of evil and everything eventually got sucked in here. Selling skin and sex remained just as profitable for the undead as the living.

From behind the podium, I came face to face with two roaches I knew well. Even though I didn't like them any more than any other coffin sucker, I found them tolerable. I didn't consider any blood leech harmless, but I did catch myself easing my own tension just a bit. I kicked myself as I caught it. Mistakes like that, would get me killed a lot quicker than I wanted to believe. They were cockroaches, plain and simple, which meant they drank human blood to survive. None of them fed from animals like in the romantic novels most women drool over. These were the real deal. Predators and nothing more.

Everyone ignored the danger inches from their throats. I wondered if they had even heard of the attacks just a few miles from here. Or could it be that the lust and sex sold here outweighed their own safety?

"Hello, Benny, Fernando," I said to them. They hadn't appeared to be aggressive, but tonight, I approached everything with caution. Both roaches before me were of some sort of Asian descent. Filipino, I think they said, but I'm not sure of it. I had always thought it odd to have Spanish names while being from the other side of the world. Benny busily wiped his hands on a white hand towel and seemed preoccupied with nervous glances.

"Good evening, may I help you?" Fernando said with a pleasant smile. He had a slender frame and spoke softly. Shiny black hair reflected the light like a mirror. I didn't know much about him, but there seemed to be a lot of loss and sorrow behind those dead eyes. Too bad I didn't care enough to ask. In the distance, I could see other coffin critters as well as humans coming in and out of the shadows. Like Benny and Fernando, nothing aggressive, simply curious. At this point anyway.

"He is not to be disturbed. Quinn always catches Angie's last show, then escorts her home." The neck licker speaking, Benito, was shorter and heavier. Large ears flanked either side of his head. His personality and voice carried far more confidence than Fernando. A nervousness in his voice made me doubt the answer.

I balled my fists to keep from grabbing Benito. "He has Angie stripping here?" I looked through the opening that led into the main play area as the door swung open and three drunk young men exited. This time searching for Angie. "In a goddamned vampire sex club?"

Another voice interrupted us. "Women of Angela's beauty and charm should never walk these streets alone. You never know what you might run into." I felt my body tense a little more as I saw her approach. Veronica Powers, Quinn's lawyer and part time lover. She stood nearly six-feet-tall, beautiful from head to toe with glowing golden hair, but unlike most of the other women in this district, skin wasn't her trade of choice. She towered before me in a neck hugging blouse and matching skirt of burgundy. Heeled shoes with just enough lift to make things interesting from behind. A large black leather brief-case clutched tightly against her chest. "She's the reason everyone comes here." He gave me a dirty smile that made me want to stake him where he stood.

"I know enough that a woman with Angie's integrity wouldn't be caught dead alone with a blood leech like Quinn." I took a step forward, stopping Veronica in her tracks. "And what could possibly bring something like you to a place like this? Don't tell me Quinn has you working here too?"

"Integrity? What would you know of the word." Veronica never changed emotions as she spoke. "Did you receive the information packet I sent you?"

I remembered the envelope on the passenger's side of the car. "What information packet?"

She smirked. "Perhaps you should look into it instead of blatantly lying. As a representative of Mr. Kincaid's estate, I would like to have everything taken care of immediately." She looked to Benny and Fernando. "If you will excuse me, I am famished. I have a date with a very special blood let. Please have Quinn sign the paperwork I left on his desk. I will be in his bed if he needs me. At his beck and call." She looked back to me. "Ignoring it, will not make it go away."

"What's in that envelope that has your panties in such a twist? It couldn't be more than some bleeding-heart cockroach trying to ad to my demise." Her face never changed. It bothered me enough to ask another question. "And what could Albert Kincaid's estate have to do with me? You have no proof that the prick was my father. Nothing more than more coffin lies."

"I would think you would want it to be more of a private matter than something to be discussed here. Just read it and get back with me." Veronica moved a strand of hair from her face. A waft of perfume filled the air, but to me it still stunk of death. "As for the truth about your father, I personally do not care, Mr. Isaac. I am not here to prove it one way of the other, just to tie up loose ends on his matters of business."

"We're all friends here, Veronica. And whatever Kincaid has left for me can be buried up his ass for all I care. His gift to me was seeing him without his head. Like with all of you, I found him to be nothing more than walking manure in an expensive suit."

She wet her lips with her tongue. Nothing erotic. Just a nervous action. "Seems as though you are the beneficiary of his death and business assets. He has left you the family business. Out of obligation I am sure, but it is yours all the same. Congratulations, Mr. Isaac, you have inherited the empire of law suits and legal actions against a multitude of necro-films."

"Necro-films?" I repeated.

"Pornographic movies containing at least one vampire and one human. In the truest sense, a pornographic movie in which the vampire feed from the human until dead while having relations. I find it surprising you do not know that, Mr. Isaac. The very thing that Commissioner Peavey planned to stop. How convenient that he is now dead." She moved closer to my ear. "You have gone on record to say that you caused the wolf to change at the Crowne Plaza, you inherit Albert Kincaid's pornography business, Commissioner Peavey is dead. I am sure it is all coincidence."

Fernando and Benny looked to the floor. Something told me they already knew. The phrase necro-films already sent shock waves through me. It was a growing problem in the sex trade industry and my so-called biological father had been the king of the industry.

"Sure you want me to continue, Mr. Isaac?" Veronica's eyes dug deep into me. I couldn't look directly into them, but I could feel them challenging me to ask more questions. She loved this. I imploded from the filth and horror of it all, while she basked in its simplicity.

"The son of a bitch left me his necro porn business?" Even from the grave the bastard attacked me and his fellow humans. I tried not to add fuel to the fire by showing any sort of emotions. "Well played, sweetheart."

Another blood sucker entered behind Veronica. Victor licked his lips as he looked me up and down. He towered in front of me, dressed in black leather and fringe. Muscular and standing nearly as tall as I, he had proven to be a lethal foe. Long flowing black hair gave way to blue highlights along the left side of his head, while the right had been shaven smooth to the skin. "That's right. He has left you the estate of NecroPussy and all its holdings. DVD's, merchandise, titties, twats, and dicks. Not only are you the spawn of a vampire, but also the seed of pornography. Seems as though the apple truly does not fall far from the tree. Welcome to the world of necrophilia profits. With Peavey dead you stand to be the king of the world. If you live through the Council's investigation among other issues."

"You look like a French whore, Victor." We had a very bad history. In the time before the laws came in effect, Victor had been the opposite of me. He sought out the vampire hunters and killed them. We were so different, yet so much alike. My Magnum pointed to him before I had time to think. He scared me more than any of the other neck biters in this city. Given the chance, he would kill Angie just to spite me. I spun into sensory overload. "I hear you're opening shop with Dr. Petty. So good to see you turning your life around." Yes, sarcasm.

A naked female roach followed Victor out the door and commanded attention. Strikingly beautiful. Long black hair, lust filled eyes twinkled behind the dark makeup. She smiled at me and even though I knew it all played on vampire magic, I turned to mush like a shy little boy. "Ah, *Dracul Sang*, I didn't expect to see you here tonight. Can I get you a drink?" She looked to be no more than twenty. Her voice soft and mischievous. "Perhaps more?"

"I'm not here for the drinks, honey."

She gave a schoolgirl giggle. "Of course not. Who is, right?" With that, she smiled, shook and turned for me to take her all in. I obliged. "Come inside with me. I'll make sure you get what you came for."

"I don't think so."

"Kandi, please leave Mr. Isaac alone. Go back inside and entertain the paying customers."

"But he's one of us now. Vampire. *Dracul Sang*." She looked me up and down with wanting eyes. "Is it true that you now own Necro-Pussy, *Dracul Sang*?"

Victor's composure never changed. "Now." With that, Kandi disappeared deeper into the room in search of an unoccupied pole. Passing by me, she blew me a kiss and said some rather naughty things with those eyes.

"Kandi?" I blurted.

"Better than her real name of Margaret. What do you want?" Victor never had been one for small talk. Didn't blame him, this had been the longest conversation we had ever had.

"Where's Quinn?" I kept a hand on the butt of the Magnum as I looked around the large room. "I know about the little game he and Inderia are playing."

Dead eyes rolled ever so slowly to me. "Whatever are you talking about?"

"Don't even act like you don't know. He and Inderia have been raising the dead. Zombies. To kill Peavey. To frame me." I lowered my voice. Why, I didn't know. "And they've attacked again. Just a few miles from here."

Victor looked to Benito and Fernando, then back to me. "Zombies?"

"That's right roach boy. We are on to him. Either you can tell him I'm here, or I can find him myself." Victor grabbed me by the shoulder. "Careful, dead head. I'm the new *Dracul Sang*. Actions like this could get you into a lot of trouble with the pure bloods."

The vampire released me with a quick jolt.

"Where the fuck is Angie!" My voice echoed in the open air, reminding me I had yelled louder than I thought. I looked back to Veronica. "I know she's here. Don't get yourself killed over something like this. I know Quinn's out there turning dead things into killing machines and I'm here to deal with it." I pushed the Magnum under her nose and moved her back a step. "Now I'll ask you one more time, where is she?" I said as slow and methodical as I could. I tried to keep what little cool I still had intact, while intimidating at the same time. A hard double standard to keep. I could feel Quinn's power close by. As distinct as a fingerprint.

"In Quinn's Room of Blood and Decadence," Victor added.

I started to turn the Magnum on him when his hand grabbed my wrist. "No need for that now, Avenger. Believe me, death is coming soon enough. Before this conversation is complete, I predict you might want to save that bullet for your own head." Victor smiled and let go of my hand. His eyes remained on me as he spoke in my head. I avoided being caught in them for now. *"Raise it on me again, and I will not hesitate to break your wrist and kill you with your own weapon. It would be such a waste to kill you without the pain and suffering first. I want you to see me kill Angie before you die."* I pulled it down, but I sure as hell wasn't about to put it away just yet. This fucker had tried to kill me numerous times and I had no doubt tonight would be the same old song and dance if it were up to him.

"Leave, sign the papers and have a great life," Veronica added. Somehow, I don't think she said it with sincerity. "If things continue on their current path, this may be the last time we have to talk."

I refused to listen any more. "First and foremost, the man's not my father. Not on my terms anyway. He was nothing more than a manipulative, perverted man that led the way to cockroaches being legal in this town so he could gain power in the necro-erotic industry. Nothing personal, but he didn't give a damn about cockroach fucking rights. The only thing he cared about was lining his own pockets. He used you. All of you, and you're too dumb to know it." Albert Kincaid being associated with me had grown as annoying as having gum on the bottom of a new pair of shoes. No matter how hard I tried to get it off, it stuck and spread into something far nastier. "Go to hell. All of you." To Veronica specifically. "You can take those papers and shove them. I ain't signing nothing from that bastard."

Veronica smiled. "Gentlemen, please excuse me." She stopped at my ear. "All the death and lawsuits belong to you now as well. Welcome to the nightmare, Avenger. We will take you down and never expose a fang." With that, she slipped a set of keys in my pocket. "I cannot think of a better piece of shit to hand this all too. And as for your wolf, I plan to do things to her that will scar the most jaded of whores." She picked up the briefcase and moved down the red carpeted runway and disappeared through a door. We all enjoyed watching her leave. Time stood still until she faded from sight, then someone hit the play button on life again.

13

VICTOR MOVED TOWARD THE DOOR, almost walking on air. "I have to admit, Avenger, I understand your anxiety. Quinn has said Angie is the fuck of the world. Men go mad when she steps into the room. Must be a bitch to have lost her so easily." He moved closer to me. "Perhaps she could be new talent for your inheritance. Sometimes, I can hear her scream from out here. Just not sure if it is pleasure or pain."

"I'm not leaving here without Angie. When the police realize what Quinn did tonight, he's going to be dead anyway. Best thing you can do is let me get what I came for and get out." I pushed past Benny and Fernando, but stopped by Victor. "Perhaps you are forgetting a very important thing."

From behind, I could hear Fernando telling me I had to leave my weapons and religious artifacts outside. I never slowed my step.

Victor's undead power poured through me in waves of electrical shocks. "Such as?"

"Angie doesn't want to be with you and as long as Quinn is alive, she is his to possess. Even if you could take her from here, she would only come back at her first opportunity. Like it or not, there is nothing you can do about it. Please do not take away my pleasure by having to kill you before I kill her."

"Quinn is already a dead man. I know what he did tonight; I know what he did at the Crowne Plaza. It's only a matter of time before the police come crashing through that door."

"What is it that you think Quinn has done?" I could tell by the way he said it, he already knew the answer. He knew about the zombies, he knew about all the fun and games. I didn't plan to get caught up in his web of lies. Remain focused, Isaac, get what you came here for.

I knew Quinn wouldn't simply come out of hiding and allow me to take Angie. If I wanted her, I would have to go into the abyss and pull her out. How twisted my life had become. I had to go into the pit of the darkest monsters I had ever faced to save a werewolf that would probably try to kill me anyway. We had parted on less than good terms. Note to self: Make funeral arrangements for myself.

I pushed past Victor, opened the oversized door and started down a side hallway where I felt the most power. Lush red carpet fell under my feet, incense flowed in the air, a small candelabra swayed in the invisible current around me. Ahead of me, I saw two doors to my right, two to the left and one straight ahead. A faint smell of blood and animal gathered. My heart pounded faster. Fear and hope collided. My legs shook with uncertainty.

Victor growled with laughter. "I've been waiting to kill you. Waiting a very long time." I turned to face him. He filled the hallway behind me. I had no way out if I needed one. With methodical care, I continued to move toward the door at the end of the hallway. Something hid just out of sight. "Vampire executioner, *Dracul Sang*. It doesn't matter what you call yourself. I've made a living killing things like you for more than two centuries. No need to stop now." He turned out the lights.

My heart beat against my chest with growing intensity as the light around me became a distant memory. Darkness had swallowed me whole. Even the outline of my hand disappeared. My ears strained to pull in the sounds around me. Some real. Some imaginary. Breathing. Mine, I hoped.

I could hear the shuffling of footsteps. I pulled the Magnum out of the holster and searched. And I had good reason. Something else lurked in the darkness with us, staying just out of reach. I could feel it. Power. Lots of it. And close.

Losing my grip on what little bravery I had, I turned and ran toward the door somewhere ahead of me. I didn't have time to defend myself against Victor, no time to think. I could only run like hell, even if it had been in total darkness down a short hallway.

My body hit the door. Victor slammed into me. Bones that I didn't know I had popped out of socket. Dead hands reached out to me.

The first bite pierced me in the back of the neck like a thousand bee stings. I fell against the door frame as skin ripped from my face. Fingers scratched at my throat as undead fell from the ceiling. A chorus of demonic sounds filled the narrow passage. Fangs pierced deep into my shoulder as I brought the Magnum around to meet their owner. I never hesitated as I pulled the trigger. Hot ash covered me as sulfur hung in the air. The ground crawled with them. The more I brushed away the more landed on me. I became buried alive in coffin crispies.

Something slammed against me with the force of a bus. I had very little room to give as I hit the door with my back for the second time. A fist hit me with repeated fury. I shot blindly in its direction, but as the blows continued to come, I missed.

In the flash of my Magnum I saw another vein biter move on me. With my left hand I ripped a wooden stake free and drove it up through his sternum. I could feel and hear the bones and muscles give way until that wonderful popping sound of his heart being punctured. Cold, dead blood ran over me as the monster fell between me and the door.

I could feel the rush of speed and power as Victor bore down on me again. I shot wildly into the dark. Followed by another. I hit fang heads with every shot, but with as many as there were, I'd never get them all. Again, I pulled the trigger, only hearing a click.

Victor's weight crushed me against the wall. My legs buckled under the force of Victor's attack, sending me to the floor. I grabbed what I could find of Victor and slammed back. We rolled along the floor, neither willing to give up any ground. My muscles ached as I fought to stay alive.

His mouth wrapped around my arm and bit down. I felt the tendons dance in pain. I screamed. I took the butt of the Magnum and slammed it against his temple. My hands squeezed the sides of his head and tried to lift him off of me. Liquid oozed through my fingers. Sticky and cold, as if picking up lose hamburger. I screamed again, this time as my imagination played gross images through my brain.

Above me, I could see the flicker of candles as the door gave way. I panicked as I took in the face that still hung onto my forearm. I could only catch pieces of his dead face as the tingles ran through me like electricity.

My fingers pierced him in the eyes and flesh gathered under my nails. Pellets of liquid sprayed me as those fangs set me free. Blood and saliva shot from his mouth as his hands reached his eyes. He rolled over with screaming pain.

I pulled free.

Momentum carried me past Victor. I stood as quickly as I had fallen. I had stepped into something far more evil.

14

STANDING BEFORE ME, I took in one of the most beautiful women I had ever seen. Inderia's skin was the color of light coffee, her eyes round like almonds, with flawless straight black hair that fell to her waist. Large black tribal tattoos started at her neck and snaked to her feet. She looked to be a mix of Haitian and Aztec decent. Her nude body shimmered in the afterglow of countless candles that lit up the room. Thigh high leather boots, the only thing covering her perfect skin. She worked the lust shows along Church Street and had a reputation of being an erotic feeder, which simply meant she sucked blood from wealthy clients, while they paid her for the act and called it sex.

These men never saw the vampires as walking corpses. They only saw what they wanted to see. Vampire magic made beauty an illusion human eyes couldn't see through. Nothing more than a thin façade on the face of death.

The room danced in flickering candlelight. I felt warm and smelled blood. I could feel a distinct dampness around me. Panic filled me as my eyes fought to adjust to the shadows and darkness. The room illuminated in deep colors of reds and blues, satin sheets wadded up on a large bed in the background. The floor a white tile, shining against the colors and lights. Various sexual toys, or weapons, depending on how you look at it, hung along the walls ready to be played with.

I took a step back as Inderia entered the glow of the soft light. Her chin, breasts and belly covered in a thick paste of blood as if she had recently bathed in it. From what I knew of the underworld, the decorations were intentional. A cockroach of her stature could drain a body dry and not spill a drop if she wanted. This looked like a product of torture. Whoever the blood belonged to couldn't have survived this. This fantasy got out of hand. Something told me to run, but I held still.

Victor and others stood at the doorway, daring me to try and escape. Looking back, he had made it too easy to rush down the hallway. I had done exactly what he wanted me to. Whatever hell I walked in on, I found myself committed. I planned on using my time wisely and started to pull the clip out of the Magnum and reload.

"There will be no need for that, *Dracul Sang*." Inderia spoke with such a soothing and hypnotic voice. My mind pushed forward trying to continue the task, but my fingers refused to move. I could feel her curling up in my brain like a kitten, playing with my thoughts, searching for all the skeletons that I had hidden away in dark places. She would use my weaknesses and fears against me. "Please put your weapon down. Indulge in my world of pleasure and pain. I assure you, lust is far more satisfying than violence. There is no need for fear. Not for the true *Dracul Sang*." Those viper-like eyes remained on me like a caged rat.

"Who's the dead man you're wearing?"

She looked at the blood on her chest, back to me and smiled. "This old thing? Just something I had hidden in the back of my closet. Not to worry, we both had a good time." Another step towards me. "Now, please put away your weapons. I mean you no harm. After all, you came to me, not the other way around."

"You killed them all didn't you?"

She looked at me and smiled. "You think I raised the zombies?"

"Peavey told on you and you don't even know it." I grew with confidence.

"And how is that, *Dracul Sang*?"

"Before he died, he wrote the name of your little man haters group on the wall. Been to any club meetings lately?"

Her smile broke. "You think my organization has something to do with the murders? *Dracul Sang*, I assure you I had nothing to do with such things. Peavey vowed to help end all the disgusting things that keep women in bondage to men."

"Well at least you are leading by example aren't you?"

"You know nothing about me. Who better to enlighten the world than those that live it. I manipulate and do the twisted things to punish and devour those like you. I'm not a slave but a hunter in the lusts of men. Dying is the pleasant side of things I can do."

The Magnum dropped from my fingers as if invisible hands had forced them open. I struggled to regain control of any of my bodily functions, only to find her constrict me tighter each time I rebelled. My body ached with invisible pleasure. I fought against it. Animalistic feelings washed over me as I looked back at her. Rage and lust mixed into something that began to take control of me.

"That's right, Dracul Sang. Feel my pleasure warm your veins. Ache with desire. Indulge in the decadence of blood. Use me for every-thing you crave. Abuse my skin, molest my soul, fill your mouth with me and drink of my body. I will deny none of your secrets."

"I am sorry for the intrusion, Inderia. I will take care of things," Victor said as he moved further into the room. "Been waiting a long time to drain this one."

Inderia smiled with seduction and waved him off. She walked towards me as if gliding. Her Caribbean accent melted in my ears as I caught wind of the fresh blood painted on her skin. She caught me looking and giggled like a schoolgirl. She ran her finger along the crimson liquid on her belly and held it to my mouth. "Would you like to lick me, *Dracul Sang*? Perhaps from other places?" She stuck the bloody finger in her own mouth, then placed her lips on mine. Her tongue massaged me in small erotic licks. Unbearable heat radiated off of her body.

The scent of blood caused my mouth to water. Her power tingled within me with pleasure and intolerable pain. "That's it, lover. Lust for me. I feel your desire begging to be set free."

"Where's Angie?" I struggled to think. I couldn't take my mind off of the blood. Forget skin. Forget sex. I wanted the blood.

Her expression changed as I spoke. No longer the soft spoken diva. I could see sparks of jealousy running along her ancient face. Still, she smiled as she ran a fingernail along my cheek. "You choose the taste of an animal when I offer you the drink of eternal life? She is nothing more than a trinket. A quick desire. I am infinite pleasure." Another long kiss. Her hands worked along my body, feeding my skin. Her fingers massaged sensitive things on my body.

"Where is she?" I gasped. Her silhouette shimmered like a specter. I pulled away from her spell.

I knew Inderia well. Dangerous and willing to kill just to gain the pleasure from it. In fact, it motivated her. She enjoyed the hunt far more than the kill. She used her beauty as bait. But under all the erotic skin hid a lethal hook. Sharp and unforgiving.

She smiled as she walked around me. Undead eyes took me in. The Magnum remained at my feet and I knew damned well that I would never be able to grab it and have it on her before she killed me. We had started a very risky game, and I had become prey. "Quinn will be along shortly. *In the meantime I wish to have a little fun with you.*" Another brush of her nails along my cheek. *"At your expense of course."* A playful giggle.

"Do not get yourself killed over sex games. All I want is the wolf and I'm out of here."

The sultry creature stopped and looked back at me. "Getting myself killed? You should have used better judgment. You come here threatening to take away Quinn's blood let and think that things will go smoothly for you? How sweet. Under the lethal shell lies a school boy wishing to carry his crush away." Her laughter filled the room as she cocked her head back. "Tell me you are not so naive as to think that he will just allow you to take her and all will be forgiven." She lit large candles that illuminated a room I never saw. Light hollowed out one of the walls. "I, on the other hand, may be able to save both lives. Yours and the wolf's."

I saw several men bound at the wrists and hanging from large ropes, nude and blindfolded. All decorated with erections. A stream of blood ran from each throat. "What is this place?" I said more to myself than anything.

Inderia followed my stare to the hanging men. She smiled as she turned back to me. "Sorry, *Dracul Sang*, I mix dinner with pleasure. Fear not, the poor, pathetic creatures are not dead. In fact, they've never felt more alive. They pay to be dominated. Presidents of companies, CEO's, politicians. Powerful men in need of a little discipline. I give them a release from that world. Here in my sanctuary, there are no board meetings, no time clocks, no rules, no limits, no thoughts." She licked her lips. "Even our dear Peavey has been here."

"Guessing that's why he had to die?"

She shook her head. "Disgusting is it not? But they pay for me to blood let them in a way that no other woman can satisfy them. Their human desires and fetish pleasures have brought them here as willing participants. And tomorrow night there will be others. An endless supply of both blood and pleasure, all waiting to be tasted upon my lips and at my disposal. They only see and feel the magic. Willing to sacrifice what they know is real for something in their minds."

"Cut them down. They're too stupid to know what they're doing." I kept my eye on the men, but thought about the Magnum at my feet. I knew I would need it.

Inderia shrugged. Those large round eyes never left me. "I told you, they are fine. Just a little dazed in the afterglow. It is all legal I assure you. Naughty. Perverted. But legal all the same. How long have we known one another? Ten, fifteen years now. Have I ever broken a human law?"

"Give me Angie and you can go back to your pathetic game," I said bluntly. "What you do with them does not concern me. I'll be back to kill you for the zombie attacks."

She jumped as if he had shocked her, followed by a mischievous smile. "I do wish to ask a favor of you. Allow me to taste you while you taste me." She ran her fingers between her legs and moaned with animated pleasure. Now painted with blood and other fluids, she returned the finger to her mouth. "As for zombies, I know nothing of which you speak. Now, relax and enjoy."

With her eyes closed, I began to crouch to my knees. In my head I planned the extra distance would gain me speed in picking up the Magnum. Deadly orbs opened and snapped to attention. *"Not so fast, my deadly one. Pick it up and it will be your throat I taste,"* she said as she wrapped around me "I know your fears, *Dracul Sang.* Afraid to love, so instead you chose to hate. It has consumed you to the point that you do not know your own feelings or capabilities. You are *Dracul Sang.* You are a god. You do not ask for anything. Take what is already yours. I can free your mind of the wolf you seek. Show you things you cannot even imagine. There is no need for death tonight. Not yours or Quinn's. Indulge in what is already yours."

I cleared my head of any thoughts and dove to the floor with as much speed and power as I could. Inderia's magic fell strong on me, but I didn't think she planned on me actually trying anything.

As I rose back to my feet, I placed the Magnum against her temple. I pulled the trigger, yet she stood before me smiling. Nothing happened. I pulled the trigger again, expecting to see her brain matter splatter across the room. Nothing. Not a damn thing. She began to laugh hard. I looked at the Magnum, only to find my fore finger extended and thumb up in the shape of a weapon.

"Looking for this, *Dracul Sang,*" Victor said as he held my Magnum in his hand.

Inderia grew excited with the situation, which made things more deadly for me. Entertain the psychopath in order to buy more time. "I love it when boys fight over the girl. Something primal about the games to the death. Kill him, *Dracul Sang.* Make it messy. Violent. Do it for me." She laughed with excitement. "Please. Take what is yours. Victor's life or my body. Which will you choose?"

I could feel her power rise as it danced on my skin. Far more powerful than it had been a few minutes ago. *"You do not know the power of a sensuous bloodletting do you? Never felt the caress of its magic. Its addiction.* She worked her arms around my neck. Throaty songs of lust filled my ears. I breathed deep, taking in her scent. The scent of the blood. *"We both can gain so much from it master vampire. I crave the taste of power in the blood I smell in you. Kill him and we will fuck the wolf together. You can leave here with us both."*

I heard Victor scream, but didn't know why. Everything pushed to the back of my mind. If the Magnum remained on me, I had no idea.

"Allow me to show you what I can do, Dracul Sang. I will give you my body, my soul." She slithered her hands along my chest. Lips now against my ear. *"My life."* I felt her tongue touch my cheek. *"My lips and mouth will give you pleasure no flea bitten bitch can."*

I tried to push her away, but she gripped tighter. She wrapped around me through invisible hands like a constrictor. Her eyes grabbed me. I couldn't look away. I fell into a black abyss of terror as my mind became her possession. I could see the fangs, feel the puncture, but found it impossible to move.

To my surprise, I didn't feel the pain that I had felt from bites in my past. Instead, I felt a warm, welcoming feeling move through me. A thousand fingers ran along my body, filling me with euphoric pleasure. Soft touches all over my skin as if explored by velvet gloves. I no longer had a desire to escape. In fact, I wanted it to last as long as possible. Deadly or not, I wanted it to continue. A rush of pleasure poured through me with such power that I began to ache with orgasmic desire.

Flashes of Inderia filled my mind. I could see her above me. Her soft, smooth skin against me like a warm blanket. Her ample breasts formed against my chest. My hands moved along her body, taking her nipples in my fingers and feeling them instantly grow erect. Small beads of sweat trickled along her curves. Her nude flesh formed against me with addicting sensations. I traced her length until I reached her ass. I kneaded the flesh like dough as she rose above me, allowing me to fill inside her. She moved with piston-like pulsation above me. Her fingernails drove into my chest. Her mounds of flesh bounced with each peak of motion. Those hypnotic eyes rolled into the back of her head as she gasped in desire. Moans filled the air as she grew closer to her own completion.

I looked into her face and saw the seduction multiplying as I grabbed her waist and dictated our speed. With each thrust, the movement grew more intense. My body ached to complete the act, but I fed off of the pleasure with such conviction, I refused my body's needs.

My hands cupped her breasts as we moved as one machine. Dark hand prints formed along my touch with warm moist solution. I looked at my hands as they slid to her waist. Crimson tracks of dark red finger painted my touch with slippery trails of sweetness. I brought my hands to my face and sniffed the darkness that fit them like liquid leather gloves. My tongue curled around one of the digits and tasted the syrup. Sweet and seductive to my mouth and nose, like candy. I sucked the finger clean, then moved to the next. With each taste, it grew more intense. I feared I would eat my own hand.

"That's right my love, taste it for me," Inderia spoke as she continued to move above me. Her hands smeared the marks I had made on her skin and brought the taste to her own lips. I watched with anxiety, afraid she would lick it all before I had a chance to dip my hands into the lust again.

I had lost interest in the act of our bodies and the pleasure it produced. No longer needed her nor wanted her. My world had been reduced to the shiny thick liquid that seemed to cascade around me. Hunger turned into a new lust as I shifted her off of me. The floor around me had turned into a pool of the aphrodisiac-like fluid.

I cupped it in my hands and filled my mouth as quick as I could. My throat swallowed it with so much force, I nearly choked. Still, it didn't stop me. My thirst insatiable. I brought my lips to the liquid and lapped it like a dog.

"Do you like it, my *Dracul Sang*?" Inderia spoke somewhere in the distance. She looked different. Her flesh fell away from her frame like melting ice. Chunks of meat leaving the bones. Rotting odor filled my nostrils. Still, I lapped the liquid. Dead eyes looked back at me, rolling in a blood stained skull. Crawling flesh, alive with maggots and worms now replaced the coffee skin. Still I drank.

I merely shook my head, almost annoyed that she would speak to me. My lust for her had vanquished. My fears stripped from my thoughts. Only the taste remained. I drank.

"It is the blood of our ancestors. Nectar of immortality."

I heard the words. The convulsions stirred in my mind, but I remained helpless to stop it. I saw my world spin out of control. Heard the voices in my head beg me to lift my head, but truthfully, I didn't want to. I would taste it all before I quit.

"My beautiful son."

My eyes shifted up to see my mother standing just out of reach. She wore a white flowing gown, but somehow the blood never stained it. Her long flowing curls danced in an unseen breeze as I continued to drink. Even the vision of my mother couldn't break the spell. I grew angry with her. She was here to take away my blood. MY BLOOD! I wanted to speak but the sanguine taste continued to flow into my mouth at such a rate that I couldn't form words.

"Give in to the urge, son." In the darkness, another form appeared. Albert Kincaid. He stopped next to my mother and placed his arm around her as he smiled at me. He watched me lap up the blood. He appeared younger than he had been when he lost his head. Literally. Even in death, though, the sleaze factor within him spilled over. The thought of he and my mother being together sent shivers down my spine, but still I drank. "Give in to the victory, my son."

Son? Any other time, I would have been at his throat for saying such a thing. I would never acknowledge him as my father. Cockroach lies, made to make me a fool. I refused to believe the slander against my mother. Refused to see her as a monster. Never in a million years would I allow it to be truth. Still, the taste consumed me.

The word victory stuck in my head. The same word I saw written on the wall at the Crowne Plaza. Victory? From what? For who? I wanted to ask the questions, but my need and desire for the blood over ran the thoughts with justified lies.

Inderia stood next to them and the three watched as I continued to gorge myself on the blood. I felt the growl in my throat as I surveyed the room. They were not here to help me. They were here to take away my blood. MY BLOOD!

From a crouched position I attacked with all the strength I had. Razor like fangs jutted from incisors inside my mouth. Power juiced me with super-human strength. My jaws reached my mother and clamped down. Not out of hunger, but of anger. I would protect the blood with my life.

I could taste her flesh in my mouth. Bits of skin floated across my tongue as I swallowed with aggressive power. I ripped and shook my head with vengeance. Hands reached to pull me free. I fought them off. I would kill them in time as well. They would all die for being here. I no longer loved my mother or hated Albert Kincaid. They were simply interference in my world now. I saw them as competition for the blood at my feet.

My mother's blood rushed down my throat as I swallowed. Powerful and sweet. I wanted nothing more than their deaths. My mind told me they were already dead, but I had fallen too far to reason with reality. I felt sick inside as I grew more and more aware of my actions, but still unable to stop the act. Better yet, refused to stop.

More hands grabbed me. I continued fight against their pull. This was my blood. MY BLOOD!

"Paul!"

"My blood!"

"Paul!" A little louder this time. A little more…real?

"My blood!" I screamed as I felt a hand pull me free of the flesh. The best way I could describe what happened next would be like drowning in water, nearing death, then a hand pulls your nostrils above the water. I gasped and spat. I fought against the hand. "My blood!"

"Paul!"

Laughter filled the room as I opened my eyes. I lay on the floor gasping air. My lungs burned as if on fire. I vomited blood. I tried to move away from it, but found it impossible. I screamed.

"Paul, you okay?"

Above me, I saw Kansas. His eyes the size of golf balls. I wanted to speak, but couldn't. I couldn't do anything other than try to force as much air into my lungs as I could. Disoriented, unable to tell the difference between fact and fiction. I wanted to go home. I wanted to move. Wanted...

My tongue raced across my teeth in search of fangs. Nothing. My eyes searched the room again as they fought to adjust to the light. "What..." I started.

More laughter. I rolled my head to the right and saw Inderia above me. She giggled with unexplained excitement. Her right hand held the side of her neck. Dark red fluid raced between her fingers and mixed with the dried blood from her earlier letting.

I turned away. The blood that only seconds ago I craved, now repulsed me to the point that I puked a second time. I grew cold. Very cold. Shivering. Couldn't stand. Movement took every ounce of energy I had. Run. I had to run. Far away. Now. "What..." I tried again.

"You dirty boy," Inderia teased.

Kansas lifted me up into a sitting position. He began to drag me away from the vomit that now oozed around me. I was thankful for that. Things began to look up. "It's alright. We have to get you out of here. Now." I could tell by his voice, he was scare shitless. And I couldn't blame him. I didn't know what happened and I found myself in the same state of scared shitlessness.

"What..." I tried for the third time as I fought the urge to puke again. I swallowed it back down. I had just been dragged away from the last pool, no need to make another.

"What happened?" Inderia asked as she pranced around me. "You were feeding off of me like a real vampire. Sucked me until I had to have them drag you off of me. Such a stud."

I looked at Kansas for confirmation. He looked away. Confirmation granted. I tried to stand. I fought the fear that grew inside me. He shifted next to me, but never spoke. He kept his eyes on Inderia. I wanted to believe he still had my back, sort of, but at the time, I couldn't make up my mind which side I found myself on, much less anyone else. Again, I tried to stand. Power grew in the room.

"No need to leave, Avenger. The party has just begun," Quinn said as he gallantly floated across the cold air.

15

QUINN STOOD BEFORE ME. He glowed in the candlelight. In all my fun, I hadn't felt him enter the room. His pale skin flickered in the flashes of gold, reflecting his body in multiple shadows on the wall behind him. It gave the room the illusion of more dirt nappers than weren't really there. I had never seen him this under-dressed before. Minus the dapper pin stripped suit and perfectly combed black hair. The monster before me appeared wrapped in a neon blue silk robe with Asian dragons of silver thread. His hair fell across his face as if he had suddenly been woken from a long nap. A silver cross hung around his neck in defiance. See, the trick is, it has to be a crucifix blessed by a priest to make them sizzle. A simple cross held nothing more than the metal it had been crafted from. We both knew that, but the novice guests that met him were immediately impressed by the bling. I, on the other hand, saw it for what it was. Nothing more than a trick of light. "Merry Christmas, *Dracul Sang*. Looks as though my gift has come early."

"I didn't know the undead celebrated."

His stare turned to ice. Behind those ancient dead eyes, I could see him calculate the dilemma. "On the contrary, my friend. According to news at the moment, you are a wanted man. A vampire capable of

turning wolves and raising the dead. Killing you would be well justified in the eyes of the human laws. You entered my establishment with
weapon in hand and I defended myself. Rather cut and dry."

Inderia moved closer to him. She took quick glances into his eyes
from time to time. Like with Victor, she wanted this to end bloody. I
don't think she really cared which of us survived. The fight for life and
death turned her on. Her power jumped through the air with excitement. It pulsed along my skin in erotic waves. "Where's Angie?"

Deadly fingers had me by the throat before I could react. I never
even saw him move. Ten feet away one second, fingers digging into
skin the next. I felt the momentum build as he threw me against the
door we had entered earlier. My back slammed against the frame, split
the wood and spilt me across the floor, pounding in pain. I hadn't
recovered from the bloodletting experience, so each little throb magnified the one before it. I only saw blurs of speed followed by bone
jarring pain. The process repeated several times, only growing in intensity and severity. "No one comes here and takes what is mine! Especially not you!"

Before I rolled to a stop, his foot crushed into my rib cage, tearing
muscle from bone. My lungs rattled against my chest as his power and
strength abused me. I wanted to scream, but the pain kept it from
escaping.

"My father was a very brutal man. A drunk. He used to beat my
mother, my brother and myself almost every night. I lived in fear of
him. He took my childhood, my security, my esteem. I made a vow as I
grew older that I would kill him one day and never allow anyone to
hurt me or the ones I loved again." He drew closer. "And I kept that
vow, Mr. Isaac. I became a vampire in 1652 in the Virginia Colonies. A
willing participant. I killed my father and everyone that knew him
shortly after turning. I will do the same with you." A more aggressive
step towards me. "In time I grew that hate for the living until I became
a master vampire. If I will kill my own kind, I most definitely will kill
your kind." He grew within ten feet of me.

I pulled the 9mm from the holster and shot. The bullet raced just
below the rib cage and exploded out the back. Kidney and muscle scat-

tered across the floor as the master roach fell to his knees. Quinn held the wound as blood and bile began to flow. His eyes showed the terror of my shot. Pale skin turned crimson. Groans of pain escaped his throat. He spat blood. Eyes of vengeance looked back up to me.

I hadn't tried to kill him. If he died too soon, I might never find Angie or get her out alive. On second thought, as I looked into those eyes of hell, I knew I used the wrong weapon with the wrong bullets. Silver nitrate would slow him down, but not kill him.

Kansas moved toward me. Inderia drove him to the floor. With invisible power she flipped him against the far wall, where he hung in midair, screaming with pain. Black shadows raced across his body as invisible undead began their torture. I still wasn't sure which side Kansas would, but I knew I had to get out of my current situation. I took a step toward the door.

Victor crushed the side of my face with a swift kick. He looked at me with merciless anger. I had no doubt that if I didn't get to the Magnum now, I would be a dead man. Simply shooting him? Bad idea. Very, very bad idea. I found myself scooting back with controlled speed. He moved toward Quinn and helped the master roach to his feet.

Inderia grabbed Kansas by the hair on his head and pulled him toward Victor and Quinn. He struggled, but said nothing. "We kill them both. A reminder to their kind that we are not to be tampered with. Human or otherwise, we send an example that this type of behavior will not be tolerated."

Kansas pulled his gun on Inderia. His hands shook with indecisive jolts as he looked up at her. I could see the wheels turning in his head. If he shot Inderia, I knew Victor would kill him. If he didn't, it would be Inderia that took his life. "I'm here for the necromancer that raised all the zombies tonight, Quinn. We both know you're behind it all. I swear, I'll put a bullet in all your heads if you don't do what I say." From the floor, Kansas didn't look all that intimidating, but he had the gun. I told myself it had to be some sort of advantage. He came to his knees.

"Pull a gun on us and think I will let you live? You will die just like your pathetic friend." With a twist of his wrist, Victor forced the gun from Kansas's hand and drove him back to the stone floor. Dead magic infested his body. Kansas screamed in pain.

Inderia turned to me. I could tell by her body language, she didn't fear me. She had no hesitation in that evil walk. Pushing things as far as they would go lit her up. "My, my, all my boys are here and playing so nicely together. A minute ago, you were indulging me, now you wish to kill me? I love the excitement, *Dracul Sang*. But what you have done now is unforgivable."

Victor pitched Kansas's gun to the floor, then held Inderia back as the gape in his lips showed the lethal fangs. He watched Quinn with careful eyes. Something about that look told me that the two weren't as close of friends as they wanted me to believe. I just happened to be more of an enemy at the moment than Quinn. Victor had made no bones about it. He wanted to be *Dracul Sang* of the living dead. I would use it to my advantage if possible.

"You come here to kill me, *Dracul Sang*? It will take more than trickery and bullets." Quinn walked towards me in a visibly painful limp. The silver cross twisted in the light, painted in the hues of his blood. He shook globs of matter from his hands. His twisted black hair fell across his face in matted knots. "Not even the maggots will find enough to feed from either of you."

I wanted to run, but I couldn't. I froze with fatigue and fear. I crab crawled to the best of my ability, but he made the ground up without any effort at all. Power forced me closer to the cold tile floor.

Pale, warm hands had me by the throat again. I could see the muscles and bone already knitting back together through the opening in his robe. It surprised me. The silver should have made things at least difficult for him.

The fingers on his left hand punched pain through my chest. Boney appendages laced in impregnable madness. The right hand now clutched my balls with just enough intensity that I held my breath. Infectious nails broke skin. It already ran through my head I would be separated from some very personal property. My mind filled with unimaginable pain. "You think you can come here and take Angela from me?" He turned to look at Kansas again. "A pathetic drunk with no hope of ever being more than what you are right now. Do you really think you can drink it all away. You've lost your son and your wife already, why risk the life of another vampire like Paul Isaac?" He gave a disgusted huff. "Are you even sure the baby was yours?"

Kansas screamed and tried to move toward Quinn, but the power locked him to the floor. I could hear him cursing and screaming. I couldn't allow Kansas to be a deterrent for my being here. He could deal with the zombies. I came for Angie and couldn't care less who else ended up in a body bag.

"What happened tonight can't be covered up, Quinn. You've taken this too far. People will want answers. I've done my part, give me Angie and we all walk away to hate another day."

Quinn's eyes glowed. "Really? Is that why I have a bullet hole in my side?" He picked me up by my sternum. His fingers tightened to the point I yelped. Piercing deep into my flesh. Then without warning he freed his fingers and licked the blood on them. I began to hope Kansas would shut his mouth soon. It appeared to be costing me a lot of unnecessary punishment. "Seems as though you might be a bit inadequate at protecting the things you are loyal too."

The master night walker patted the muscle and tissue around the exit wound on his side, more out of curiosity than anything. I could see the wheels turning. He wanted to kill me, but something caused some hesitation. For that I said another thank you prayer. I gasped for air, but the jabbing sensations overrode the effort.

I kept an eye on Kansas too. His gun had silver nitrate bullets as well, and unlike me, he would have no problem putting one in me or Angie. If we walked out of here alive it would be on my shoulders.

It touched me as if alive. Wolf power and close. "Angie?" I gasped. Blood worked down my front like invisible fingers as it flowed from the holes in my chest. Small red dots decorated the floor under me.

"I'm right here, shithead."

I could smell the vanilla before actually seeing her. With the remaining strength I had, I raised my head and looked in her direction. Naked and as beautiful as I had ever seen her. Caramel skin wet with droplets of water. By looking at her, she had just stepped out of the shower. Her large breasts bounced with each step as she drew closer to me. Long black hair clung to her like passionate fingers, catching the fire from the candles. Her lips painted in dark red colors as if dipped in rubies. "Do I look like I need fucking rescued? Last I knew you were feeding me to these things. Now, you come in here wanting to play hero."

"I didn't feed you to shit, Angie. Kasey is the one that led Judas to you that night. If you want to stay here and screw corpses, that's up to you." I looked over to Kansas, "but that son of a bitch over there is here to kill you and all your bed buddies. And I don't think your lover boy will save you when push comes to shove." As healthy as she looked, I had no doubt that she had started changing again, which gave me hope that she hadn't gone mad and really killed all those people. "The only reason he has you here is to piss me off. You know, the same reason you're here."

Her lips formed a pout as she moved within inches of me. "Thank you for caring. If you wanted to save me, you could have done so. You chose not to didn't you? And don't give yourself so much credit. I don't think of you enough to think about pissing you off." Parts of her touched me. Even in the valley of the shadow of death, couldn't help but to lean into her just a bit.

Quinn looked at us. Jealousy replaced anger. His pulled her away from me. "Angela, my dear, please put something on. You're far too radiant for our guests." His eyes turned to me. I kept my focus on the wolf. By doing so, not only did I get a bowl full of eye candy, but it pissed Quinn off just a bit more. Angie was a hell of a distraction fully clothed. Naked she melted your eyes. Quinn spoke the truth. She was far too radiant.

She turned to her dead lover and saw the new hole I had put in him. "You're bleeding!" Unfortunately, I could feel the genuine concern in her voice. I thought I would throw up. My mind told me that she did it to get at me, but it still made me want to bullet in something. She started to touch the wound when Quinn stopped her.

"Silver nitrate. Do not touch it. I will be fine." God, he played the role of victim like a song.

Angie spun back to me. Beauty and beast became one. "You really are a miserable bastard aren't you?"

"Guilty," I said with a light shrug. "Now that we are all here and acquainted. Who's the zombie puppeteer?"

Quinn waved her off with his free hand. "Angela, darling it is merely a flesh wound. Do not trouble yourself with such matters." He looked to me and smiled as he kissed her cheek. "Like you, they are not leaving here." His dead hands traced along her breasts. "After they are dead, you may kiss it and make it better."

I rolled my eyes to keep from throwing up. "If I knew you were going to do this, I'd never stopped Judas from tea bagging you," I added as a final insult. Bad idea.

The sting of the slap hit me, knocking my head back. I knew there would be more pain to come and began to rethink my being here. Let the bitch die. I took it back as soon as I thought it. I had lost enough in my life to these shit suckers. I'd be damned if I allowed them to kill her too. Even if it meant having to fight her to death myself. I know, it made no sense, but welcome to my world.

"Was your precious reputation more important that saving me from the things you've always told me were pure evil? Deny what you are all you want, Paul, but you're just as much of a monster as the rest of us. Your father was a porn king, your mother a vampire, and now you have confessed to being *Dracul Sang*." She grabbed my chin and looked in my eyes. "Now that I think of it, you are the most legitimate monster in all of Bat Town. But don't worry; at least your reputation is still intact."

"Keeping screwing cockroaches and so will yours. You don't really think they will let you live do you?"

Her face touched mine. I could feel her incredible power. "I didn't kill those people at the hotel and I don't need you to save me. You died tonight for being stupid. I'm growing very tired of everyone treating me like I'm some precious little breakable figurine. I don't need you, Kasey, or Quinn to protect me. I will choose who I sleep with, who I align myself with, and if you or anyone else in this God forsaken city doesn't like it, they can go to hell."

Quinn laughed. "That's my girl. Tonight, we kill a master vampire and a detective that whores himself out to the humans. Afterwards, we will celebrate by making love until the sun goes down." He moved to my ear. "Unless you want to watch before you die."

Before I could respond, Inderia slipped behind Kansas as he made a move for the gun only a few feet away. I wanted to warn him of the approaching danger, but nothing escaped my mouth but a soft whimper. She nearly ripped him in two. He bowed at the spine, his eyes bulging from his head. The gun spun from his hand and rested in the shadows just out of my view. "Allow me to kill him for you, darling." Other fang heads moved into view and took Kansas captive. The bitch roach walked behind Quinn, resting her hand across his healing wound.

Angie snapped Inderia's hand. She would have broken it, if it hadn't been for Quinn grabbing the wolf's wrist. "Enough with the dramatics, Inderia." Quinn continued to heal. I could hear the skin meshing together as the blood that once poured from the wound, now nothing more than a scar. He used the time to gather his strength and I couldn't do a bloody thing about it. "I have brought you the master vampire of the pure bloods. What more do you want? Feed from him my precious and we will discuss such matters later."

Inderia picked up Kansas's gun and held it at her side. I grew anxious. I had no doubt that the bitch planned on killing her competition. I wanted to say something, but when you can't scream in pain, warning of any danger nearby wasn't going to be an option. "A real vampire eliminates its competition, no matter how beautiful."

"A..Ang…Angie." I prayed to God that she would follow my eyes to Inderia. If she hesitated at all, she would be dying of silver poisoning if not dead on the spot.

Victor moved in the distance. I felt my heart skip a beat. He had always been one unpredictable monster. I had no doubt he would allow Inderia to kill Angie in front of me just to put one more twist on my balls. He looked at me and smiled. Out of all the monsters in the room, he had the most to gain.

Inderia aimed the gun on Angie. Quinn turned to see the action taking place behind him. The wolf dove behind a large trunk on the floor. I flew through the air, landing underneath the string of naked men Inderia had been playing with. My chest exploded with more pain, other parts of me retracted in relief. Quinn grabbed Inderia by the arm just as the gun fired. I could smell the silver nitrate fill the air.

Quinn wrestled Inderia to the ground. She screamed in defeat. Victor ripped the gun free with such force, I wondered if there weren't a few fingers still attached to the trigger. I looked to Angie, who for the first time had a look of terror in her eyes. I started to move toward her, only to see her show her teeth like some sort of rabid dog. I did the right thing and backed off. Kansas tried to move against the other blood heads in the room, only to find the odds well against him.

Victor and Quinn stood, while Inderia remained hunkered on the floor, whimpering and defeated. Ten or so vampires lurked in the shadows behind them.

Angie's situation had vastly improved. Mine, on the other hand, hadn't gained any ground. My chest throbbed like a strobe light. I searched for my Magnum, but chances were, even if I found it, I wouldn't be able to get to it in time to save my skin.

A drop of blood hit me in the face. I looked up, seeing what I would call nothing more than hanging cockroach meat. They swung from the ropes that bound their hands. Alive and twitched against their bindings. Muffled screams escaped the gag balls in their mouths. I could only imagine their fear, as they swung blindly. At the moment, I didn't care. I had landed on the floor and I still had two of everything I should have two of.

Victor struck me. He clawed my skin and lifted me to a vacant rope next to Inderia's blood bunnies. I fought the move with everything I had, but found myself powerless against his madness. I tried to kick, but things below were so sore I couldn't really fight. Jolts of pain washed up through my testicles and belly each time I tried to move. I felt my hands being tied above my head. Muscles pulled until my arms threatened to separate from the sockets.

"Quinn!" I screamed.

"Yes, *Dracul Sang?*"

I felt my body lighten as I elevated from the floor. I kicked at

Victor, but being levitated, left me with no strength. Five finger holes in my sternum and busted balls didn't help. "You'll not get away with this. The Council already knows what you did." From my new vantage point I could see the room filled with cockroaches. The floor crawled with undead life. The smell of blood grew in the room. My heart pounded against my chest so hard I feared it would explode.

I couldn't catch my breath. The large ropes didn't allow me to expand my chest. Being scared beyond my darkest nightmares didn't helping much either. "The zombies. They know you did it. You can kill us, but there will be more coming for you. Stop this now and you might make it out alive." I looked over to Angie, who stood in front of me with her arms folded. She made no effort to help me. "Angie, if you don't help me bring him down, they'll kill you too. He's set you up for all of this!"

"You had your chance, vampire man. You turned your back on me, remember. If you think saving me now will save your ass in return, you're sadly mistaken. At least with the vampires, I know who I am and where I stand."

"He raised the zombies, Angie! Even if you let them kill me, know that much. You owe yourself that much."

Quinn floated next to Angie and wrapped his arms around her. He kissed her, then looked back to me. "We know nothing of these zombies you speak of. Perhaps you should look at those closest to you for those answers."

I hung in mid-air, in the coven of vein weasels. My imagination played games with me. I could feel them move around me. Fingers lightly touching my skin. The room seemed much colder than it had been minutes ago. My own breathing began to amplify in my ears. I swallowed the saliva in my mouth as it turned into cotton.

Victor laughed as he picked up a long whip from the near wall. He whipped it once, sounding with a loud crack. "Oh, Avenger. You have been played so many times by us that it is growing to be no challenge at all."

I started to scream when the death rolled through the door. God help if we lived through the night.

16

FOUR WEREWOLVES CRASHED through the door and flooded into the room. They didn't appear picky on whether their victims were human or blood licker. I had to use that to my advantage. One carried an arm that still twitched with the afterglow of undead life. Screams filled the room. I pulled on the material that bound me. The knots grew tighter. I twisted like a fish on a hook, helpless to stop or escape the approaching madness.

Tanya moved on a neck biter in the corner, ripping away his throat in a single bite. Before he could fall to the floor, another wolf scooped a handful of guts from the dead head's stomach in its mouth and chewed on intestine. A second wolf fell on the body and pulled away the left rib cage. He bit down on the bone with a loud crunch. I swallowed my horror as I searched the room for Angie.

Victor and another roach threw Kansas forward, toward the furballs and retreated into the blackness of the room. Tanya tried to grab him as he fell, but wrapped her arms too high and Kansas wrestled free. Kansas lunged forward and grabbed a sheet off of a nearby bed and wrapped it around some sort of pipe. He lit the sheet with a candle and rushed toward the nearest furball, setting it on fire.

"You know what makes them attack more than anything, *Dracul*

Sang?" Inderia asked as she gave me a toothy grin and touched the five blood holes in my chest. "Blood. That's why they have come here. They smell the blood." She sliced my throat with her fingernails. Nothing life threatening, just enough to allow the blood to stream across my skin. I had simply become furball chum.

Inderia moved in front of me. Not to protect me in any way, but instead darted back and forth in an attempt to avoid the uninvited guests. With a single kick, I rolled Inderia toward one of the approaching wolves. Together, they rolled into a ball of panic. Kansas pushed the wolf toward its burning friend and now, two flesh eaters were in flames.

Inderia moved with roach speed. She grabbed Kansas' gun and turned toward Angie. She stopped in a state of panic. Like the rest of us, she remained trapped. Heat and light grew intense. Smoke made things difficult to see. Burning flesh smothered the room.

"Angie!" I screamed as Inderia fired the gun. I kicked in helpless action. Unable to free myself.

Angie's eyes turned to me as the bullet pierced the bed post behind her. She dove to the far side of the bed. Inderia shot twice more.

Tanya grabbed one of the hanging men next to me and chewed a large hole in his stomach. If there had been any bloodletting magic that still ran through him at the time, it evaporated when dead teeth bit into living flesh. Thick solution rolled from the opening. I could smell the bile from his stomach. Strong and putrid. I gagged.

The two remaining werewolves began to focus on the hanging men next to me. No need to chase food when it hung in front of them, helpless to run. This gave me more motivation to break free.

I watched as the chaos built around me. I swung and twisted, cursing in my own dilemma. Roaches continued to move by me, desperate to find some sanctuary from the creatures that had invaded their secret horror room. Some climbed the walls hung from the ceiling like rotten fruit.

Kansas made his way through the bloodshed and held off the wolves from personal attack with a large flame at the end of a stick. A third wolf started to burn and fell to the floor. Everything had become shadows as the smoke built. I couldn't breathe. My eyes burned.

Many of the cockroaches made their way out of the room through the long dark hallway I had entered. They returned moments later with wide eyes with terror. It took me a few seconds to figure it out, but then it hit me. The morning sun had risen. They were trapped like fish in a barrel. I looked at Quinn and Victor and smiled. A few minutes ago, I had been destined to be furball shit, but so were my little fang head friends. They had taken away my option for survival, but the rays of the sun had returned the favor. And like me, they were aware of it.

Angie turned to face me from the far side of the bed. With quick snaps of the neck, she kept her eyes on Inderia as she hunted her down through the chaos. I had lost track of whether Inderia had reloaded the gun or not, but it remained in her right hand, the fire stick in his left.

The fire alarms sounded. Sprinklers went off, adding to the chaos around me.

Tanya turned to me and gave a toothy smile as bile and blood dripped from her chin. Decayed skin moved loosely from his face as he chewed on the last of the meat in his mouth. A halo of flies circled his head. I closed my eyes as Tanya began to move on me.

I waited in darkness for the first mouthful of pain only to have the stench of death replaced with the sweet smell of vanilla. I opened my eyes to see Angie only inches away. No smile. No emotion at all. I had no reason to believe that she wouldn't kill me herself. Given the choices before me, I hoped she would. Better to die by a scorned naked woman than a decaying ugly fang puppet.

In half wolf form, Angie drew lethal claws. I shut my eyes again and awaited the deadly nails to separate my skin. Instead, she cut the binds above me and in one flash of power I had been freed. My knees buckled as I hit the floor, followed by the weight of one of the zombies. I tried to lift myself, but the quick snaps of jaws compromised my ability to accomplish the act.

I could see and hear the trampling above me as the vein lickers continued to try and find safety along the ceiling. A head rolled next to me, still screaming. Arteries squirting blood. Eyes blinking. I shoved it away as I made a lunge toward the Magnum, kicked in a corner of the room.

I jumped to my feet. Angie stood only feet away. She remained suspended between wolf and woman. "Thank you," I said. It seemed melodramatic, but sure as hell heart felt. "You have to get out of here, Kasey's here to kill you!"

"Kiss my ass, Paul." With the alarms, I could see her mouth it, but not hear it. Things were looking up.

Tanya moved on her, sending her crashing to the floor next to me. Powerful jaws opened as she attempted to take a bite out of Angie's back. I shot Tanya expecting to save the day. Unlike the others, I noticed a custom made Kevlar vest. She had come here far more prepared than me.

I shot a second time, but a shadow moved above Angie. Inderia landed on top of her. Angie screamed as she tried to pull free. Inderia wrestled her to the floor and struck her again and again in the head with the butt of the gun. Blood trickled from Angie's forehead as she fought for her life. A distant look filled his eyes. A look of lust and hunger.

Water filled my eyes. I couldn't focus. The room remained thick with black smoke. The alarms the only sound.

Anger washed over me as I witnessed the beating. I pulled the Magnum on her and started to shoot just as Angie lifted Inderia off of her. They moved too fast for me to get a clean shot. I put the Magnum back in the shoulder holster and pulled a wooden stake free. This fight would be decided by hand to hand combat. And knowing how Angie felt about me, it might cost me my life, but I planned to kick a lot of ass and take a lot of names and make it as violent as I could.

I moved with as much speed as possible, allowing my body to ram into Inderia with all my weight. Our heads hit first. I felt her body shift against my attack. We landed face to face, me on top. Her deadly fangs snapped at me in surprised anger. My knees shifted to her chest to allow me the leverage I needed to bring the stake down on her sternum. I wanted enough power that the point would be embedded in the floor on the other side. Sweat filled my wounds and stung like hell.

She struck me with the butt of her gun. I saw birds and heard bells, but stayed on the attack. I knew the longer I had to fight with her, the greater the chance the zombies would have at finishing their meal. And even if they had their fill of flesh, I had Quinn and his bat heads to worry about. But it didn't matter at the time. All I wanted was blood and violence.

Staking her with one clean shot would be too easy. She'd never feel the pain or see the joy in my eyes. I wanted her to beg for me to finish it. I wanted this brutal attack to last as long as possible. I knew prolonging the affair only gambled with my own life, but willing to take the chance.

I held the wooden stake with both hands and brought the weapon across her head, smashing jawbone with the blow. The grasp on me weakened with each swipe of the attack. Her pale face of white grew more and more red as the dead blood in her found the open wounds.

The stake snapped in my hands like a brittle twig. Her face resembled a puzzle. Then she turned the tables. The barrel of her Glock moved toward my chest. I heard the shot go off above the sound of the alarms. Saw the flash. Even felt the heat, but my adrenalin blazed so high. If she shot me, I didn't feel it. I didn't care. If I bled to death, so be it. None of these daisy pushers would strike Angie, much less kill her. A deadly flood broke through the dam of my emotions and Inderia just so happened to be the recipient.

I grabbed the wrist that held the gun with my right hand and the elbow with my left. With the remaining strength in me, I broke the arm across my knee like a stick. I heard the scream escape from the dead mouth below me. Droplets of blood caught in the air. Inderia screamed in my face. Bone ripped through living dead skin in jagged pieces. The gun fell to the floor.

Rage ran at an all-time high. I grabbed the Magnum from the shoulder holster and put it to her head. Angie pulled me off of her just before my fingers could do the walking. "Enough! Get the hell out of here!" Her face showed a tint of rage.

My ignorant rampage turned personal toward the wolf. "Are you saying that for my benefit or hers?" She glared at me. I nodded. "Just what I thought. You sleep with one cockroach you sleep with them all, is that it?"

"Stand in my way, Paul, and I swear, I'll rip more than your heart out."

I stood above Inderia and kicked the gun free of her grasp just for good measure. I reached for Angie's wrist. I gave quick glances upwards making sure none of the hanging undead planned to drop in on our party. "If you're willing to spread your legs for them, why not kill for them too."

"Go to hell." I could see the storm grow in her eyes. I took a step backwards.

"Meet you there honey, but why else would you give a damn about keeping Inderia alive? I would think killing her would be priority number one." I paused for effect. "Unless she's the one pulling your strings, not Quinn. Makes sense why she wants you dead so bad. Dead dogs tell no tales."

She pulled free. "I'd rather die by vampire than live like you." She moved toward me. I took another step back. "To you and Kasey, I'm nothing more than a possession. A prize. And both of you are too stubborn and ignorant to admit it. At least with Quinn I know where I stand. With him it's about power and lust and neither of us expect anything more. I don't need him or love him so save yourself the aggravation of playing the jealous boyfriend. Being with him pisses you off and that's all I want out of life right now."

I pointed to the door. "The sun is up. There's nothing either of us can do to save any of them, even if we wanted to. Look at putting a bullet in their heads as the humane thing to do." I looked down at Inderia, who rolled across the floor in pain. "You stay here, and that bitch is going to kill you and I'm not going to let that happen." "Kasey sent them here to kill you, me, and Quinn. I don't care what he does to your boyfriend, but you won't die on my watch. I have too much invested in you now."

I grabbed the 9mm I had used on Quinn and pointed it at Angie. "You're coming with me."

She never moved. Animal eyes stared back at me with ultimate defiance. "No."

With the alarms and sprinklers going off, conversation became nearly impossible. The smoke still lingered, but the sex shop would survive the fire. Talking grew cumbersome, my breathing shallow and labored.

I tried to move her, but just as I thought, she never budged. "Shoot me if you want, but I'm not going anywhere with you. My place is here. If the police or the Council find me guilty, so be it. Go home and play house with your old girlfriend."

Behind me, I felt the power raise the hair on my arms. I turned to find Quinn looking at Angie with sad eyes. "Go."

"What?" Angie asked.

"You heard me. Go. Paul is right. For now you are safer with him than with me. The police will be here soon and they will arrest you."

"You said you would protect me from the police and the Council."

Quinn looked at the gun still pointed at Angie. "Please, Paul, I ask you to keep her safe." To Angie, "I will protect you and I am. Under the present circumstances you are in danger here. I feel the attack tonight was meant for you. You will return to me at sunset, but for now, go." He kissed her cheek gently and turned away. Vicious eyes turned back to me. "Anything happens to her and I'll eat you alive."

17

ON OUR WAY out of Risen Sins, I had Angie put on a blouse and skirt, left by one of the employees I had found in a small break room. We needed to stay off of as many radars as possible. Angie had the beauty that would stop a bus and draw a crowd while in a burlap sack. Lead her out into the streets nude would be like putting a beacon on us. Trust me, someone would notice and remember seeing us.

I could think of only one place to go with a werewolf wanted by every living and dead thing in the city. Not the greatest idea I had come up with, but then again, options were limited. I pulled the set of keys out of my jeans pocket and slowly exited the car. In my mind, opening this door solidified that this skin trade hell hole really belonged to me. Hours ago, I saw it as an albatross around my neck, and now it had become the best sanctuary I had.

"If you wanted to make a porno with me, Paul, you really should have just asked. No one's ever had to keep a gun on me to have sex," Angie said as I moved to her side of the car and opened the door. Long golden legs slid out the door, shining in the sunlight. A light breeze pushed her scent into my breath. It sounded innocent, but I could hear the bite just below the surface.

"So you know this place?"

"I know if you have a problem with nudity and freak shows, you're in for a big surprise. This is the NecroPussy studios. It's owned, or was, by Albert Kincaid." Her eyes glistened with mischievous thoughts, followed by a powerful lust filled grin. "Question for you is, why are we here?"

I moved past her without answering her. With a twist of the key, I opened the trunk to the 'Cuda and withdrew a hammer and the four crucifixes I had. I needed more, but then again, I never planned on things going this way.

The sun beat down on me and sweat sprouted across my brow. Even in December some days grew warmer than I liked it. I looked and listened around me. It was quiet. Too Quiet. As if we were the only two on the planet.

Yellow tape surrounded the place. Blood stains could be seen against the white paint along the bottom of the building. The front door had been caved in. In fact, the whole place looked like a hurricane had passed through. I took it all in as I thought. The zombie attack from last night had started here.

It didn't make sense yet. Why would Quinn and Inderia start the zombie walk from here when Kasey had me cornered across town? Closing my eyes, I dismissed it all. Trying to make sense out of monsters usually left you with more questions than answers.

A shadow fell across my vision. Instinct and nerves reacted. I pulled the 9mm on Angie before I could even stop the move. Her eyes grew wide. She never moved. A large smile sprouted on her face. "Gonna use that big gun on me, Daddy?" She gave me a very sarcastic smile and moved past me, entering first. "Put that thing away. You know you're not going to shoot me, even if I tried to kill you. I've played along with the whole hostage thing long enough this morning for you. You're like all the other guys around this town. You think with your penis and it gives me all the advantage I need."

I swallowed what little pride I still had and followed. My only moral victory, I continued to hold onto the 9mm. Out of protest more than anything.

"What the hell happened here?" Angie said as she looked at the carnage.

It looked as though the monsters had entered the building. Everything looked trashed or broken. Shadows concealed a lot, but from what I could see, the place had been attacked. Glass littered the floor, chairs and other furniture, nothing more than twisted metal, holes in the walls.

"Zombies."

My fingers fished for a light switch. Being a playground for dirt nappers, the place didn't have windows, which meant no light entered. Angie could see without issues, but I froze in the pitch, until finding my little friend electricity. And being my first time here, I had no idea what waited in the room and where. Something told me my shins were about to take a beating.

"Why are we here?" Angie continued to look around, picking up small broken objects and examining them.

Light gave me a virgin view of the lobby area, complete with jungle print wallpaper and a female roach bitch crawled on her hands and knees, naked. To the twisted and sick, she appeared to be seductive. I saw death with a boob job.

I thanked God that at least at first sight, we were alone. I allowed my senses to grow to full tilt, in search of any powers or energies in the rooms ahead of me. A vein sucker could be stalking in the darkness just outside the reach of light. I cursed as I placed the 9mm back in the hip holster and pulled out the Magnum. Kind of stupid. I had a wolf in the room with me and I put away the nitrate bullets. I had no reason to believe a blood leech hid in the room, yet I held a weapon filled with ultra violet.

"Do you bring all of your kidnapping victims here?" Angie asked as she circled the room. She appeared to be far more comfortable here than me. For good reason I suppose.

I volleyed all the lies in my mind. Telling her the truth would open nothing but more cans of worms. Right now, I had all the open cans I could stand. I took a deep breath and came back to reality. I never had been a very good liar and nothing I could think of wouldn't be picked apart by Angie . My head dropped in defeat. New strategy. Answer the question and do not elaborate. "Hiding out from your boyfriends."

"Why here? My boyfriends aren't afraid of battery operated toys and handcuffs. This is where we would go to hide from you." Another full on grin. Again, I ignored it.

I continued to look around the room. Decent in size, roughly a hundred foot square, with a large receptionist desk at the left end with the company logo of fangs nestled in plump lips being licked by a tongue, all in shiny gold on the front. The words NecroPussy Inc. sat under it all like a foundation. Three black leather chairs with gold rivets butted against the far wall. A leafy plant sat in the corner like a punished child. Thick maroon carpet spread out like a blood soaked sea. A large oriental rug covered the floor of another naked woman with her hands hiding all the necessary parts. Modest domed lighting illuminated the room with soft colors. In the air, I could smell the combination of a thousand perfumes, all fighting to be the most obnoxious. I looked at the door just to the left of the desk and knew a circus of uncountable fetishes waited on me. I took a deep breath as I stood and stared at it just short of forever. I would have stared longer if it hadn't been for that annoying little voice behind me. "I asked you a question. Why are we here?"

"They won't think of looking here. Not the humans anyway." I reached for the handle to the door as if it were a thousand degrees. My nerves jolted on edge, more than when facing the most evil of the neck biters and I didn't know why. I pushed the handle down. "It's locked," I said more to myself than anything.

"I'll bet one of those little handy dandy keys in your hand will open it. How did you get keys to this place? Little optimistic to be taking me here on a first date, don't you think?" The answers and questions came from than non-stop mouth like a machine gun.

I pushed the key into the lock and it gave way. I felt relieved and frightened at the same time. The relief came from feeling safer the further into the suite we burrowed. The fear hadn't been because of all the penises and vaginas I might come across, but all the penises and vaginas I expected to see belonged to me. Legally speaking anyway.

"Have you suddenly lost your hearing or are you deliberately ignoring me?"

I looked back to her. I had to smile at her sudden anger. "Deliberately ignoring you."

She didn't smile back. "And how has that worked out for you so far?"

Again, I didn't answer. I pushed the door open and moved inside. Like with the lobby, the area was black as pitch. My hands reluctantly searched for a light. My imagination played with my insecurities. I expected a set of claws reached out and grabbed my hand. My body never relaxed until I found the light switch.

The room filled with bright light. Much brighter than the soft feel of the lobby. A large studio area divided into three sets, each with a king size bed, camera and complete sound stages. Too my far left, a sleigh bed, rustic looking walls, much like in a log cabin, a fake fireplace, and a pair of snow skis. The floor had been covered with something to represent snow.

The middle set, the most seductive in every way imaginable. Victorian wallpaper framed the facade, taking the eyes back in time before the Civil War. A large canopy bed, lined with a thin white sheet, allowing only shadows to be seen when pulled tight. The foundation a deep red carpet, thick and rich in color and quality. Hundreds of unlit candles filled the room. Dozens of fake red roses stood on guard just out of reach of the fake flames.

And then door number three. A coffin shaped bed made of hard black leather with more straps than I could count dangled off the sides. The bed looked like a large dead bug. The room carried a darkness all its own. Even unoccupied, I could feel the energy coming from it. It left little to the imagination, that this was the fetish room. If only those walls could talk. Most visitors would sense the sex and fantasies of this place, I felt the souls of the humans that had died either by choice or otherwise in the crimson films this place was famous for. They were illegal, but the cockroaches and the perverts didn't seem to get that memo.

I stood in the center of the room and stared at the sets, while Angie ran from room to room in giddy amusement. I wanted to tell her not to touch anything, but knew she would attack my insecurities. Although she didn't pick up on it, her actions caused my anxieties to grow to immeasurable heights.

Taking a much needed breath, I put the Magnum away and started to reluctantly explore my new surroundings. I cursed Albert Kincaid in my mind. I could see his face laughing at me as I looked around. Most fathers left their sons, homes, cars or money, mine a porn empire. His last fist to the gut to me. The proverbial middle finger to who I had been to him and who he had been to me. I didn't see this place as a business with profits. I saw it as lawsuits and death from those that wanted justice.

Other than the sounds of Angie's footsteps, nothing made a sound. I needed quiet to think, but the silence fell so thick it distracted my every thought.

"You gonna tell me why we're here, or do I have to beat it out of you?"

So much for the silence. I looked over to Angie who sat on the middle bed with her left leg crossed over the right. I smiled. The glance reminded me nothing hid under the waitress skirt.

"What do you remember about that night? The night before the killings."

That playful demeanor changed as if I had slapped her. "Nothing. I was working at the Risen Sins, then woke up at the Crowne Plaza covered in blood with Dieter looking down on me. Perv."

"Where was Quinn?"

"He had a banquet at the Coffin that night. Investors for the district. He wasn't there."

How convenient, I thought. Maybe I had been trying to hammer a square peg into a round hole, but he looked as guilty as hell. Inderia might have been the scapegoat, but Quinn pulled the strings. "And you don't remember leaving the club?"

"No. I did my last show, talked with a few people, had a couple of drinks and woke up in a very bad place. I can still see all those dead bodies and being dragged out of there like some kind of killer."

"Who did you talk to?"

She tried a fake smile. An attempt to change the subject. "Aren't you Mr. Detective this morning?"

"Angie, this is serious. You need to focus. The Vampire Council will kill you in order to make the district look good for the fang heads. We only have a few hours to get you out of here. Now think. What do you remember? Who did you talk to?"

"No one in particular. I just mingled with the people at the club. I didn't commit anything to memory. Didn't know I'd be waking up with a hotel room full of dead people."

"Were any of them cockroaches?"

"Other than the other entertainers I'm assuming?" A gentle shrug. "No." Her eyes lit up. "Wait! The two vampires that were found dead at the Crowne Plaza! I remember seeing them. They were talking to me and Inderia right before I passed out. "

"Did you drink what they gave you?"

She knew where I was going. Her hands went to her head as if trying to crush her skull. "Yeah, I know, I shouldn't have, but I was with Inderia. I knew she couldn't drink, so I thought I was safe. Seemed harmless at the time. It's the last thing I remember." Her hands came away from her head and she looked at me as her black hair draped into her face. "You think they drugged me don't you?"

"Possibly."

"And you think Quinn had something to do with it, don't you?"

"After tonight, I'm not sure who isn't involved. I had never seen wolves attack like that. In a room full of innocent humans, maybe they could have been involved."

Angie shook her head. "Kasey wouldn't have done anything like that. Yeah, he hated the ground Peavey walked on, but he's smart enough to know not to draw that kind of attention. He's smarter than you give him credit for."

I cringed as she moved toward me. Thank God, she stopped short of killing me. "Your boy Kasey's wolves didn't seem to have a problem with attention tonight. Killing you is high on his list. Perhaps you were supposed to be dead that night instead of just passed out. It would have worked out really convenient for Kasey."

"Why would Kasey want me dead?"

I froze. The truth would be so simple, but I knew it would incriminate me as well. I did the only thing I could. I lied. "You're sleeping with a coffin lover. You alive threatens his manhood and alpha status. Can't be all that fun to look the other furries in the eyes knowing they know what you're doing."

"I'm sure Tanya will keep him occupied."

If she only knew all the people I had talked to tonight. "Doesn't matter. It's the principal. He lost you to a blood sucker. His ego is at stake here. It's not a wolf thing, not a roach thing, it's a man thing."

"Oh, you mean it's stupidity?"

I kept my mouth shut.

18

"WHY DID YOU DO IT?" Her voice fell soft and innocent on my ears.

"What?"

"Confess to be the master vampire, to tell Quinn and the Council that you turned me?"

"To save your life." I faced her. "I know you think it's all prejudiced on my part, but Quinn is using you. By having you in his bed, he can preoccupy me and Kasey at the same time. It's a power move. At least with me saying I caused you to do those things, it might give you an out with the Council calls on me, not to mention the human laws."

"But they'll kill you. If not the Council, most definitely your girlfriend and her posse."

"She's not my girlfriend. If anything she's an inconvenience right now. A distraction."

"From who, me?" I caught the playfulness in her voice as she nudged me with her elbow.

I laughed in discomfort. "No, she's nothing like…"

For the first time I looked at her. I mean *really* looked at her. Visually, stunning and even that had been an understatement. She would stand out in any room like a blossoming rose, but as I looked into her eyes I saw something…real. I thought about my mild change and began to see more than fur and claws. Call it an epiphany but I saw something other than monster. I saw a human being. A tough exterior to her, but a vulnerable softness as well. I couldn't put my finger on it just yet, but I saw hurt inside those big eyes, camouflaged by the confident, yet annoying mouth just below them.

In the new light, I saw the deep bruise and scab on her forehead caused by Inderia at the club. I ran my finger across it lightly. I couldn't imagine anyone hurting her like that. Under all the façade hid a vulnerable body that damaged as easily as mine. I realized how fragile she truly was. "She hits like a son of a bitch," she said with a smile as she backed away from my finger with a slight cringe.

"How did it happen?" I asked. My body quaked as I dove into unknown waters. Rip currents to be more exact.

"What?"

I opened and shut my mouth twice, then re-gathered my thoughts. "You know, you. What you are."

Her face grew serious. That hurt filled her eyes and at the moment, I didn't know why. "That's just it, Paul. I don't know what I am to you to answer that question." She shrugged. "Half the time, I'm not sure what I am to me."

I stood just out of reach as I looked down on her. Though I'd never admit it to anyone, especially her, I came to the realization that I would protect her with my life. As sad as it had been for me to come to terms with, she remained the only friend I had. "No. I mean, becoming a..a…" I circled my hands, trying to get the words to break free from my thick tongue.

"A werewolf?"

I shook my head. My body grew numb. I tried to avoid putting her on the defensive, but I knew with our past history, that it could very well happen. I had told her again and again that all I saw was the monster and to bring it up almost felt taboo. I remained quiet and hoped for a sign that I hadn't offended her.

She leaned back on her elbows and looked up at the ceiling and gathered her thoughts. When her face came back up to meet mine, a glossed look filled those eyes. I had somehow punctured a wall that had been impregnable. I wanted to apologize, but I waited.

"I was fifteen. I lived with my mom just south of Cocoa in a small apartment. My dad ran out on us long ago and mom worked three jobs at times, just to keep food on the table and clothes on me and my brother's backs. I was often left alone to fend for myself. A latch key kid." She wiped her eyes. Her voice shook. "I became a problem child. Angry at the world. Rebellious. Even to the ones that loved me the most. I began to hang out with the wrong crowds, partying into the morning. I grew up way too fast.

His name was Jimmy. Long hair, leather, hung out with the much older boys. I was infatuated with them all for who I thought they were. Mysterious. Free. In control.

Jimmy started talking to me one night when we were all hanging out in a parking lot close to the beach. I was a silly girl that thought his interest in me was love. The attention made me feel warm and alive and I fell head over heels for him. I didn't know what I was getting into, but I knew it had to be better than the life I had.

I lost my virginity to him. Stole for him. Got high with him. Sold stuff for him. Shit, on occasion I sold myself for him. I would have done anything he wanted in return for the attention and what I thought was love.

I moved in with him not long after that and that's when things began to change. He grew darker, more distant. His friends would come over and they would talk about things in code, disappear for hours, returning naked, sweaty, bloody. I would ask what was going on, but he never gave me a straight answer.

He grew abusive when he drank. There were times when I thought he just might kill me. He would hold a gun to my head and tell me he would pull the trigger if I didn't do what he told me, which always ended up being selling drugs or stealing something or sex. If I ran away he would hunt me down, kill me, my mother and brother.

It went on for months and I could feel my freedom slipping further and further away as he grew more controlling. The violence grew each day. I was so scared." She wiped away a tear that mixed with the thick black mascara and stood. Her hand traced the pattern on the bed spread as she walked around the room. For a moment she turned away from me.

I walked to her and tried to give her an awkward hug. I had heard of this thing called compassion, but hadn't experienced it until now. "It's okay."

"No!" She sprung from my grip with a violent tug. I waited for the wrath to come, but instead she walked a few feet away and stopped, but didn't turn to face me. I didn't know what to expect next. I heard a soft sniff and a clearing of the throat. "I need to tell you this. I haven't told anyone since it happened. I was so ashamed of it. For many years I even thought I deserved it." She faced me. "I tried to run. I ran as hard as I could, but somehow he found me so easily. He and his band of friends took me back to the apartment where my mother and brother lived. Told me he was going to teach me a lesson. I begged him not to hurt them, but there was a presence about him and the others that told me things were going to be bad."

"He killed them," I whispered. I wanted her to stop telling the story. It hit a little too close to home. The last thing I wanted were similarities between us and our losses. Such things would make me look really bad for the way I act and handle things.

"Jimmy cut my mother's throat in front of us. He told me it was to punish me for being disobedient. I still remember my brother screaming and crying while I died inside. It had been my fault those thugs were in the apartment. *My fault*." She began to cry. Her hands balled into fists. I made a deal with myself not to go to her again. She wasn't ready.

"We didn't know it, but it had been the good part of the night. Jimmy and his friends began to howl at the sight of my dead mother. I felt the power sweep into the room as they tore her apart and ate her in front of us. They changed into these…things. Wolves. I ran from the room as fast as I could go. I was so scared. I heard them behind me as I ran across the parking lot outside the apartment. I ran faster, but I could still hear them coming. I never looked back. I left my baby brother there to die.

The first canines hit me in the shoulder. They pulled me down. I slid across the pavement. I felt the sting, but nothing compared to the fear I had. Above me, yellow eyes and white fangs of this monster that was half human and half wolf. It was Jimmy. I could just tell. He bit me in the throat. I couldn't breathe. Couldn't scream. Just so cold. It felt like a dream. Not real.

I woke up about three weeks later in the hospital with all these IV's hanging from my arms. I was told, very matter-of-fact, that I had been attacked by a werewolf and that I had contracted the virus. I knew enough about the virus to know that it wasn't illegal to have it, but we were separated from society like lepers. Forced to live in slums and hunted by the ignorant people that saw only the animal.

The police came by, asked a few questions, but I could tell they just saw me as a drugged out runaway. Like everyone now, they didn't believe me to be all that innocent either. I knew my life was going to be in juvenile centers or at best foster homes and I couldn't face that. So I snuck out one night and never looked back. I accepted the truth. I had become a freak. A monster. A werewolf."

"And your brother too." I concluded.

She shook her head. "Yeah. Him too. He lived in foster homes until one night he got into more trouble and they cast him out on the street. When my brother found me, he was so angry and distrusting. I couldn't blame him. He used that pinned up anger to rise to the top of the pack and soon became the leader until he was killed by Piel. He never really forgave me for leaving him that night, but then again, neither did I."

"Did the authorities ever find Jimmy?"

"No," Angie said as she walked back toward me. The defiance in her face returned. "But I did."

"You killed him."

She shook her head again. "You could say that." Angie sat on the bed again. "So as you can see, I'm a menace to society. A monster as you call me. I deserve everything the Council does to me. Everything Quinn does to me."

"I'm sorry." I said it more for me than her.

"No need to be. I have felt this way since that night. Not because of the virus but because of what I did to my family. You don't need to have fangs or change shapes to be a monster, Paul." Those eyes looked into mine. "And now I'm going to be killed by the Vampire Council for something I don't remember doing. Fate has finally caught up with me. But believe me, if I'm able to watch my mother die and leave my brother to suffer the same fate as me, I'm capable of doing everything they say I did."

"No you're not. That's why I came to get you. I'm not going to let them use you as their scapegoat. You didn't do it. Inderia and Quinn are behind this."

She touched my cheek with her finger and gave a melancholy smile. "You're so sweet. But you know as well as I do that I'm capable of doing it. I'm sleeping with the master vampire of the city and I refused to change for four months. I'm capable of anything and we both know it."

"Capable yes. Guilty of it, no."

"You say it, but you know in your heart, you don't know if I'm innocent or not. I *am* capable of being a willing participant in helping the vampire that raised the zombies. You don't trust me in so many ways it's not funny. You see a monster, a killer, a vampire freak, even beautiful, but you don't see innocent. You wanted me away from Quinn because he had me, not because you believed in me." She shook her head in disgust. "Like all those years ago, I was left on the outside looking in. No one wanted me for me. Everyone had strings attached. I had nowhere else to go, so I went to Quinn for protection. A wolf on her own is very vulnerable. Trust me, I know."

"And you don't think being with Quinn has strings attached?"

She looked at me, but said nothing. Those hazel eyes lowered away from me, leaving me with my answer.

"I wouldn't have risked everything to get you out of there if I didn't believe in your innocence."

She snapped back up from the bed. "Come on, Paul. You pulled a gun on me for touching you a few minutes ago. And you didn't bring me here because you think I'm innocent. You brought me here to keep me alive and away from Quinn. Big difference."

She was right. "And until a few minutes ago, I thought you would try to kill me just for being me." I tried to smile, but stopped it. "We haven't been on the best of terms lately if you remember and back at the club I had no reason to think that had changed. And to clear the record, I didn't give you to Judas and his fang heads that night. I let Kasey convince me that meeting with you and breaking off all communication would be the only way to save you. I would do anything for you."

Her eyes grabbed me as she slowly returned to the bed. Hands moved along my skin, causing shivers and goose bumps. Power filled the room as the palm of her hand ran across my chest. "Prove it," she purred as those incredible lips melted on mine.

My first reaction had been to resist, but I didn't. I allowed that luscious tongue to explore along my mouth and lips. I felt the heat rise in me as she slowly licked like a small kitten with a dish of warm milk. Inside, my heart thumped like it had never done before. Sweat began to form along my brow as I took in her smells like a secret garden of exotic flowers.

She pulled away from me and looked into my eyes with an animalistic stare. Inhibitions were discarded as she let out a small pocket of air, much like a purr. She leaned back and unbuttoned her top with care, exposing more and more skin with each move. I had obviously seen her naked before, but knowing that look as I did, it allowed me to see her for the first time all over again. "Trust me?"

I shook my head yes, but inside I screamed no. Sex and heavy petting didn't make anyone innocent. If that were the case, our prisons would be empty shells of concrete.

"Liar," Angie added as she popped off the bed and grabbed two sets of handcuffs, which in the NecroPussy sound stages seemed to be a dime a dozen. She returned with a naughty smile. The waitress shirt still dangled on her body, but with each move she made, I got quick glances of her breasts in teases that quickly drove me crazy.

With precision and care she planted the cuffs on the bed beside her. I looked at them with both excitement and fear. Her hands reached for my trench coat and pulled it free of my shoulders. I stood and allowed it to fall to the floor. Fingers moved under my shirt, pulling it upward and off of my body in a continuous motion.

Although it seemed like hours, in minutes, I stood before her with nothing on but my jeans. My boots kicked off, my coat thrown across the floor, my shirt...missing. I trembled with emotions and feelings that I had never experienced before. At any moment, I honestly thought I might pass out. I'm sure I had the same look and thoughts running through my head that Angie had. Raw need. Something about this place and all the sexual tension that lingered did something to us, or at least I allowed that to be my story. The wolf with me would no doubt be more in tune with the sights and smells than yours truly.

She leaned against me, completely free of her clothing. The touch of her soft skin against me made me ache with pleasure. My hands wrapped around her, lifting her to me as I cradled her ass in my palms. I could feel those tits against me, but no matter how close I pulled her, it wasn't enough. My fingers cupped as much flesh in them as they could, but still I tried for more. Her ass soft, yet muscular, twitching with intensity.

Again, she licked me with power, while her hands explored my face and body with growing desire. Legs twined around me as her lust grew. Passionate kisses grew more and more intense as she worked along my neck, biting the lose skin with her teeth. It stung with pain, but drove my urgency for her with each snap.

She loosened her attack and pulled away from my hands and touched the floor again with the balls of her feet. Lips returned to mine as her fingers frantically worked on the button on my jeans. I felt them give way, followed by the quick sound of the zipper parting. Instantly, they fell to the floor, followed by my underwear.

I found myself completely naked against her. Even if I wanted to, I couldn't turn away. Killer or not, I wanted to be a willing participant. There were worst ways to die.

I thought briefly of her and Quinn and knew it couldn't possibly be like this. Raw need took over every sense, fear and insecurity. In a sick and twisted way, I saw this as a way of getting back at not only Quinn, but every damn daisy pusher in the land.

Angie licked along my neck as her hands began to move along my manhood, which throbbed and begged to go. I had to think of furry bunnies just to keep things from progressing a little too quickly. Her teasing bites and licks began to move south along my chest in a slippery trail of destruction stopping briefly at my nipples. She sucked and licked them with perfection, while my own hands began to work her breasts with massaging care. I pinched her nipples in my fingers with just enough force that I heard her moan and stiffen.

She slowed her onslaught and looked up at me with eyes that seemed to be filled with an infinite supply of cravings. Angie carefully touched a scar along my stomach I received from a neck biter years earlier, then traced it with a gentle lick on her way to my shaft.

I had to grab the nearest bedpost as her warm lips descended on me. I could do nothing short of rock in place to the rhythm she created. My fingers played in her hair as she mercilessly continued her act. Her free hand moved in synchronized motion with her mouth.

When I could take no more, I pulled her back up to me and picked her up again. I twisted just enough that I could lay her on the bed with force and care all at the same time. Her hand never let me go, while her mouth quickly found mine again. She refused with a quick grunt and grabbed the cuffs just to her right. "Tonight, it's about you and trusting me."

I felt the cold metal around my wrists before I had the time to react. Behind my head, I heard the unemotional snap and a victorious giggle from Angie. I swallowed hard and prayed that things were not going to go really bad at this point. Being paranoid and bound at the same time isn't the best of combinations, but I shook with uncontrollable need that it didn't matter and the anxiety was quickly vanquished.

She straddled me like a goddess on a perch in heaven. Her tanned skin flawless other than the bruise on her forehead and felt more like cashmere than flesh. Long black hair poured from her head and onto my skin like a sensual waterfall. I pulled at the cuffs. I didn't fear for my life, but instead, begged to touch the things I saw.

She shook her head no as she bent and kissed me softly. "Does it feel good?"

I couldn't answer.

Angie began to grind on my penis with playful movement, not allowing me inside her. I could tell by the moans, she found ways of relieving her frustrations, while I remained little more than a puddle of need. "What do you want, baby?" she asked in a little voice.

I couldn't respond verbally. I only hunched with my hips in a frantic gesture. I did everything I could to find my way inside her, but she positioned herself too high for the act. "Please," I finally gasped.

Angie moved her hips higher, allowing me to slip inside her. I groaned in ecstasy. The wolf above me moved in a hypnotic groove while her hands now pushed against my chest, allowing her body more leverage. With each pulse, I could feel myself overloading with pleasure.

She grit her teeth, fighting back her own completion. Her breasts heaved up and down in waves as my hands fought against the restraints. I wanted them in my hands and mouth as we moved together. Every sense in my body screamed to touch her and be touched by her.

My hips began to shift and rock harder as she leaned backwards, her hands now gripping my ankles. Her body glowed with sweat and need as I heard her cry out. Again, she shifted forward and raked my skin with her nails. Red trenches of blood formed, followed by a sting of pain. Still, my hips moved against her with violent thrusts. "Don't let me hurt you," I managed to say.

"Hurt me!" she replied as she grabbed her breasts and played with the nipples. Deeper sounds poured from her throat as she howled again. This time I couldn't stop my own act. My body grew as stiff as a board as I finished. My breath seemed to never come as I pulled so hard on the cuffs, my right one came free.

We both screamed in pure heat. I felt her tighten against me so hard, I feared she would snap me in two. My free hand now touched her manually for one final climax. Within only a few seconds she had become my personal addiction and like a junkie, I couldn't stop my habit no matter the cost or destruction behind it. Intervention would never work on me now.

Angie melted against my chest in heaving breaths of exhaustion and afterglow. I brushed away the hair from her face and kissed those relentless lips again. I could feel her soft breath tickle my skin. The smell of vanilla now a scent on me as well. With what little strength I had left, I pulled her down on me, melting into as much of her as I could.

19

I REDRESSED in the same clothes I had entered the room with, while Angie found things that were more her speed. I had to agree, a conservative waitress outfit just looked so out of place on her. She looked far more comfortable in a black fishnet bodysuit. It left absolutely nothing to the imagination. She turned several times in front of a full length mirror along one of the walls in several seductive poses. I watched with erotic amusement. "You know you can't leave here wearing that. Anything within a mile of here will remember seeing you. Might as well go back to being naked."

She simply answered, "We're in a paranormal porno studio. Anyone seeing us come out won't even bat an eye. Naked women and men coming out of here all the time. Chill out and enjoy the fact that you just got laid by a beautiful woman and didn't have to pay for it." She laid a soft wet kiss on me that lingered far after the lips had receded. Had to give it to her, she had a point.

In my mind, I kicked myself for our playful romp. Like with words, I couldn't take it back. And for me, I had trouble looking Angie in the eyes. Things were different now. No matter how I defended it, we were no longer just two monsters with issues. We had become two monsters with issues and a sexual past. I cursed my penis.

Beyond that, getting past the fact that I had slept with the commercial master vampire's left overs, left me with a sick feeling in the pit of my stomach. Shivered danced along my spine. Suddenly, I needed a hot shower.

Angie and I both heard the lock on the door spring open. We froze like two little kids that had just been caught doing something wrong. We didn't have time to hide. Whatever came through that door would see us.

A young man entered the room and jumped. His eyes grew large as he saw me. He fumbled with a small hand gun as he slammed into the wall behind him. He turned as white as a ghost. He had been just as surprised to see us as we were of him.

He quickly regained his wits and placed the gun on us. "Who are you? Who sent you?" His eyes wide with fear. He shook as he looked around the room. "Where are they?"

I didn't move. Angie did the same. "Take it easy, no one's here to hurt you."

"Those things, where are they?" He continued to act insane, waving the gun in all directions. I had little doubt he was on something. As jumpy as he appeared, getting shot remained a high possibility. "Those monsters, did you see them?" By watching him, we were nothing more than a distraction for something far more menacing. I didn't like that. "Tell me I wasn't tripping."

I gathered he had seen the zombies march through here. "They're gone. No one here but us." I extended my hands to show him I had no weapons. Gaining his trust and doing it quickly might keep us out of the emergency room or worse. "Who are you?"

"Skippy." He finally seemed to land on Angie. "You two here for filming? Who sent you, 'cause those things really messed stuff up. Won't be able to do anything for a few days." Again, he looked in all directions with the gun pointing at nothing and everything at the same time. "Which one of you's the vampire?" He fixated on Angie. In the time it took him to really take her in, I knew something with him had to be really off. No red blooded man missed her in a crowd. "Damn, tell me it's you."

"We're not here to have sex," Angie said as she smiled and looked up to me. I blushed.

Skippy had on a bright yellow Hawaiian shirt and khaki shorts. His long dirty blond hair in corn rows down his back and stopped just short of his ass. His face looked boyish with stubble on his cheeks about three days old. Goatee stretched to his chest. Tall but stringy. He held out his hand to Angie. "Skippy Malibu, nice to meet you."

"Skippy?" she giggled as she placed her hand in his.

"Myron. No one in this business is going to be legit with the name Myron. Skippy was Kincaid's idea." He shrugged. "To be in porn, you need a porn name. What do you think?"

"Fitting," was all I could say without breaking out in pure laughter.

I walked toward them and held out my hand. "I'm…"

Skippy shook my hand with excitement and gave a big smile. "God, they say you're a dick, but have to say without sounding like an ass kisser, I disagree. Dude, I know who you are. You're the bad ass vampire killer. Not to mention my new Yoda."

"Welcome to my adobe, compadre'." He looked at me, then back to Angie. "Dog, don't tell me you two…" He sniffed near Angie. "Bitchin'!" I honestly looked for a rock to hide under. "God, tell me you got it on film. It will be better than any fang bang film." He didn't seem to be able to contain his enthusiasm. He slapped my hand. "Righteous."

"Yeah, Paul, righteous." Angie did her best not to smile.

I looked around the large sound stage area. Everything here reminded me of Kincaid and that alone made me want to puke. I didn't find the business as ugly as the man behind it. According to Veronica Powers, I owned this place now. Even in death, Kincaid was spreading his disease.

Skippy looked Angie up and down. "You gotta come in and do a movie for us." I felt a bit of jealousy grow, but couldn't really blame him. She had everything any man thinks of when thinking of a sexual diva. Besides, we weren't anything more than friends with benefits. Leaving here hand in hand and skipping was still a far-fetched act. Skippy gave her yet another hug. He moved past us and placed the gun down on one of the carts behind the hovering cameras. "I'm willing to sacrifice this perfect body as your co-star," he added, touching along his tan chest. He pulled a bottle of Jack Daniels out of a drawer and twisted the top off. "Open invitation for you, Betty."

"Well, I've already had my audition for the day." She gave a lick of her lips as she winked at me. I blushed and pretended to be looking at one of the cameras, but on the inside, I high fived myself.

He took a long swig from the bottle, grimacing as the burn entered his throat. "You guys scared the shit out of me. Thought you were another psycho coming in here to either trash the place or turn me into maggot chow." He looked around the room as if there still might be another monster in hiding. "Been hiding in here since last night, Bro. God, I could go for a burrito right about now." He studied us for a moment. "God, dude, I thought Inderia had killed you."

That brought me back out of my day dream of naked werewolves. "What's that?"

"Burrito, could go for one."

"No, what about Inderia?"

"Something about the new ownership of NecroPussy and your name kept coming up. She talked about you having to go down." Another drink. "Tell me you killed that psycho. She's out of control."

The conversation with Veronica rang true in my head. Made sense if Inderia already knew who I had inherited this hell hole. I had fallen right into the commercial vampires' web. Confess to being the master mind behind the murders at the Crowne Plaza, have the Council kill me for it, and things go back to the dirty little secrets that she and Quinn shared. They killed me without lifting a finger. "How do you know that?"

"Inderia does a lot of movies here. Conversations happen, I over-hear more than I should, I guess. Not happy about Peavey biting the big one. When these chicks make the kind of money that they do, they don't want anything messing up their little trick. Trust me, any of them would kill to keep the dead presidents rolling into their accounts. You can trace every dollar on Bat Street to this place."

"I would think that she would be more than happy with Peavey out of the picture. He planned on stopping all vampire activity that hadn't become law. With this being Inderia's bread and butter, having Peavey out of the way would be a dream come true for her."

Malibu laughed as he listened. "Dude, you don't know Jack about that homeboy. Biggest perv this side of the Mississippi. Secretly kept this party rolling."

"Peavey?" Angie asked. Back to me, "Other than the obvious, why would she want you dead?"

I played dumb. Simply shrugged the question off.

Skippy broke the silence. "Yeah, used to send us young girls all the time from the runaway centers he managed. Little or no paper trail. Made big jack doing it too. Trust me, the man's not the saint you think. Came in here all the time and paid for a little bump and grind. Dude was into some freaky stuff from what the ladies told me afterwards."

I looked to Angie. "Sounds like Peavey and Lopes weren't so different after all." I thought about the bloody word at the scene. "Still doesn't mean someone in the Victory Party couldn't do this. Just because both men wanted to see this business keep producing money doesn't mean they weren't enemies."

Skippy spoke. "Man if you only knew. This place is funding the Victory Party. Paying like a gazillion dollars to their candidates." He pulled a Lopes for Congress window sign out of a drawer. "In fact, the Victory Party Headquarters is here in NecroPussy office space. And as for Peavey and Lopes being enemies, all for Hollywood, baby. They're in the same bed."

"Makes no sense," I said.

"Quinn's master plan, dude. The two candidates go against each other in the election, one will win. Guaranteed. They work for the same boss. Or did."

"Genius," I said more to myself than anything. Refocusing, I looked to Angie again. "Well, all of my theories are a notch lower. I don't have a motive for Inderia or Lopes for killing Peavey and his friends."

Angie shrugged. "Too many chiefs trying to run the same pow-wow. Power is the driving force here. Like Skippy, said, one of the two were guaranteed to win, but one of the two were guaranteed to lose too. We don't know if that played into this. The party might be happy with the outcome, but one of the two candidates would have to go out and get a real job after the elections. Lopes could have seen that coming."

Skippy perked up. "They two weren't all that close, baby. Worked for the same party under the radar, but Peavey had his issues over the last couple of weeks here. Threatened to kill Lopes, threatened to kill everyone here, burn the place down."

"Why?" Angie asked.

"He came in here threatening to blow the place up if I didn't hand over a DVD of his little princess doing the nasty with a certain vampire. Messed the place up. Had a gun, put it to as many heads as he could. The dude had lost it. Found out about his daughter making her skin debut. Thought Lopes had put her up to it."

"Peavey's daughter was in a necro-porn movie?" He now had my attention.

Skippy clapped his hands as he laughed. "One fucked up bitch, dude. Came in here high on some shit and begged one of our vamps to do a movie with her. Seems from the conversation they more than just knew each other if you know what I mean. Promised the director a blow job too if he would film it. Told us her dad had ruined her life and would pay. Then something about finding her boyfriend in bed with some other skank. Wanted to send a copy to both of the men in her life."

"I'm assuming you filmed it."

"I didn't film it, but yeah it was on film. She ended up polishing everything in here. We kept giving her blow and she kept giving us blow." He howled with more laughter. "A lover's quarrel never felt so good. I can only imagine what they would've done to make up. A few days later, Peavey came in here and did what I told you. Didn't think any of us would make it out alive." Another swallow from the bottle.

"Men," Angie huffed. I could tell by her demeanor, she wasn't a bit offended by the story, just the kiss and tell part.

Skippy blew her a kiss. "Jealous."

"So you filmed the movie and daddy found out about it and wanted it destroyed," I summarized.

He nodded. "Yeah, we all knew we had something when she came in here. She told us who she was. Things like this just don't fall in your lap every day. We were going to be millionaires off of it at election time. Skid Row was about to be a thing of the past. We gave her a copy of the movie and she told us she planned to give it to daddy for his viewing pleasure."

"I'm guessing you didn't give Peavey the original file?"

He waved me off. "Are you crazy? We knew what we had. He had too much to lose. Saved a copy to a thumb drive. But about two days later, someone broke in here, looking for the files. Totally trashed the safe. Twisted it as if it was made of paper. Wasn't no politician that did that." He looked back to Angie. "He sent someone here to rattle our cages. I thought you guys were the next wave of file hunters."

"Did they get the file?" she asked.

"Yeah, someone got it." I could hear the disappointment in his voice. "The thumb drive anyway. They destroyed the computers in here, including the one with the original file. Toasted everything."

"Who are the vampires you keep talking about that were in the movie and filmed it?"

"Dominic and Z."

A name that rang a bell. Kansas had been close. We weren't looking for one vamp, we were looking for two. "Wait," I started. "It's two vampires, not Dominic Z, correct?"

"You know 'em dude?" He high fived me. "Yeah they were two dudes. Both vampires. Z handled the camera, produced, shit like that. He knew how to slice and dice the filming on the computer and made it real. Dom had the goods between the legs if you know what I mean. Done about thirty movies and just tore it up, dude."

"This dude, Dominic, had a 12 inch dick and she took it all. Craziest shit you ever saw. Word is, someone might have gotten to them. Can't say for sure. Someone out there wants everyone associated with this movie dead. Now that Peavey's dead, i thought all this would settle down. I mean, they already got the file, what else can they want?"

I looked at the campaign poster again. "Same thing they always want. Blood."

20

THE PROBLEM with winter had been a truth I had known since child-hood and my fear of the things that hid under my bed. Daylight never really gained a foothold. Even the brightest of winter days had a shadow to it. A grayness that never allowed you to truly bask in the rays of the sun.

Today had gone by in a flash. Shadows once again grew long, a coldness in the air. Everything around me looked dead. Even my own life had no positive outlooks. Everyone and everything had suddenly reminded me of just how alone I had become. Darkness had become my only constant companion.

Things had out of control inside my head as I returned to the 'Cuda. My hands shook with such vigor that I dropped my keys several times before I got the driver's side door opened. I could taste the bitter bile biting inside my throat. None of it had anything to do with vampires that wanted to kill me and zombies that wanted to eat me. As soon as the sun dipped below the horizon, I knew Angie would be out of my life again. Another bitter taste in my mouth of who I had become.

Ashley's words echoed in my mind. *"There are no vampire victims here. There is nothing here that should concern you. Do yourself a favor and simply go home."* The best advice anyone had ever given me and I ignored it. Looked past the truth and tried to find the lies. I tossed in limbo between worlds I knew nothing about. I had overstepped the boundaries of the human laws, confronted and attacked the nucleolus of the undead world and had butted heads with the fur balls of the city. I had finally alienated myself from every living and living dead thing as far as the eye could see.

I plopped down in the seat and closed my eyes. Scenarios ran through my head like a series of bad movies. With as much diligence as I could muster, I began to dissect what I knew and didn't know. Inderia planned on killing me. Not because I represented human interests or the interests of the pure blooded vampires, but because I had reluctantly become the owner of a necro porn business. With everything I knew about the Victory Political party, Peavey and Lopes, I still had nothing to lead me to the true killer I sought. Quinn and Inderia remained at the top of the list, but I needed more than that to stop them and clear my name.

A wiser man would have cashed his chips in, allowed Kansas and the police to hunt down the killer and hope for the best. But I had never been that wise of a man. Even if I backed off now, I had stirred too much up to quietly disappear. It became all too clear that finding the cockroach responsible would be the least of my nightmares.

My thoughts were rudely interrupted by the scent of vanilla. Angie leaned inside the open window and kissed me on the cheek. Nothing sensual or erotic. More of a mixture of sympathy and apathy. She brushed away the lipstick smear and gave me a fake smile. "Where are you going?"

Maybe not now, maybe not tonight, but at some point, if I lived long enough, I knew I would have to face Quinn in all of this. The reality of it hit me hard. All my life I had wanted to put a wooden stake through his heart and now I had to compromise my actions. As I looked at her, I could tell she thought the same things. Neither of us had the guts to say it or much less talk about it.

It had been three nights since claiming to be *Dracul Sang* and turning Angie into a killer animal. The Council would be calling soon.

Odds were against me to survive their inquiry and that at least gave me an out. Perhaps I would cheat the vampires out of sucking me dry after all.

Angie took a deep breath and stood next to the car. My eyes traced her body, as I reminisced every second it had been in my hands. Saliva filled my mouth as if I had just smelled a well done steak. I watched as her long hair danced in the breeze, and caught the last bits of sunlight like fireflies in a jar. I wanted to touch her and bring her back inside the car, but instead, I remained still. "What happened?" She gave a slow shrug of her shoulders. "None of my business, I know."

"What do you mean?"

"The woman detective. Ashley? She's human."

"It's complicated." I shrugged. "If I can screw something up, you know I'll do it." I refused to look at her.

"It's just that you told me that you couldn't love me because I was a werewolf. I didn't know what she did to drive you away."

I laughed at myself. "She didn't drive me away. Actually the opposite. We were young, barely in our twenties. Started out as pure enemies. Back when vampire rights were just starting to become headline news. She and her army of fanatics actually picketed our church." Strange, but the memory of that day made me smile. "I saw her in the crowd and thought, this is the most insane and stupid woman I have ever seen in my life."

Angie laughed. "Until you met me?"

No way I planned to answer her. "We had a heated argument right there in the courtyard of the church. I threatened to throw her in the fountains and she threatened to castrate me. That's when I knew she was the one for me." I could almost reach out and touch the memory. "We lost touch for about three months, even though I knew every rally she went to. Not because I cared about her, but because I needed to do surveillance."

"Liar," Angie softly answered.

"As fate would have it, she became a cop in the Bat District. To protect them. Our hatred for one another grew to a new level. I did everything I could to make her life a living hell. I would wait until she arrived before doing what I had to do, just to watch her turn away. Not much after that, I learned her sister died of Leukemia and saw her break down. Never in my life had I seen someone cry so hard. It tore a hole in my soul. We talked, had coffee, went on a non-date and ended up liking one another." I stopped again. My voice quivered. "Things moved along nicely, we became more than friends, moved in together. But not everyone saw our relationship as something good."

"Her parents," Angie replied.

"I wish. Father Garcia."

"What!"

"He couldn't get the things that killed my parents out of his head. Couldn't see past the things that had shaped him, couldn't get past the things that he had lost."

"Sounds familiar."

"As we became more and more serious, he would grow angry with me, telling me Ashley would destroy everything I had worked for. At the time, I didn't know about my mother being anything other than a mother. No one had the balls to tell me that my mother had been a vampire and my father a vampire killer. All I knew was that Father Garcia and the elders in the church continued to put pressure on me to leave Ashley. When I proposed, I thought Father Garcia would have a stroke. He refused to even look at me for about a month. People began to talk behind my back about how could I be a vampire assassin and love a vampire lover. This was before the laws were in place and being political incorrect towards them was common." I looked to Angie.

She smiled. "Go on."

"We came home one night about a month before we were to be married and someone had written vampire lover in red paint on our apartment door. I had such mixed feelings. At first, ashamed that anyone thought of me that way. I remember being ashamed of taking Ashley anywhere because of her beliefs. On the other hand, I felt sorry for her. I loved her and didn't want anything to happen to her. Not like this. But like two idiots in love, we pressed on. Believing that we could overcome our differences and take on the world. It seemed so simple at first. Probably for the best that we didn't get married."

"What stopped you?"

It took a while before I could continue. "About a week before we were to get married there had been an attack on the family of another vampire assassin. They had killed his entire family, even the dog. Blood everywhere, people protesting, hating each other, depending which side of the fence they were on. And I remember Father Garcia pulling me aside and telling me that if I went through with the wedding to Ashley, the same thing would happen to me. That I was selfish for thinking that I could be what I had grown up to be and also be the husband to a woman that didn't see things the same way I did. He took me to the morgue and showed me the little boy and what had happened to him. Kept asking me if that's what I wanted for my son. Told me that was what the body of my own mother and father looked like after they were killed. I would never be welcome in his sanctuary again if I married her.

I grew angry after seeing what those things did to that family and tried to separate them from how I felt about Ashley, but I couldn't. I could feel my hatred for everything exploding inside. The night before our wedding, I went out looking for the vampire responsible for killing that family. I had a good lead on who it had been. About three in the morning, I found him hiding at his mother's home. He hadn't been a vampire for very long. I kicked the door in. Screams. Begging. I still can see his mother's face, pleading with me not to kill her son. Two smaller children were in the home as well. I remember turning and grabbing the mother and telling her she couldn't be a good mother by allowing a vampire to be in the home with children.

My anger over my own parents' deaths and the tension in my own relationship had hit a boiling point. To me, I planned to teach them all a lesson on what these monsters really were. They were so scared. The kids had these wide eyes, full of tears, crying in terror. I closed them out and pulled the vampire out from under the bed. In front of them all, I drove a stake through his heart. Told them he had killed an innocent family and deserved to die. I stabbed him again and again. The youngest boy, maybe ten, I will never forget the look on his face. People began to ask how men of God could do something like that."

"That's why they called you the Saint Avengers?"

I dug my nails into the steering wheel. Betrayal rose in my chest. "Father Garcia wasn't there that night. I had gone out on my own to kill the vampire. Turns out that the victims of the vampire attack were those of human vigilantes, not vampires."

"Oh, God, Paul, I'm sorry."

"Father Garcia knew it. He told me the lie to make me hate vampires enough that I would hate Ashely. He covered for me in the killings and we were cleared of federal charges, but I'm still guilty of everything. The only saving grace is that the laws of protection were not in place yet.

He told me that I wouldn't ever be able to protect my family if I continued to be who I was. I wanted to please everyone and did the exact opposite. I told Ashley I couldn't do it and be honest with myself. I have tried for eight years to tell myself I had done the right thing and I haven't convinced myself." I placed my hand on Angie's. "I don't hate you because you're a wolf. Never really did. I hated you because you couldn't see the real me. I wanted to be hated. And now look what I've done to you."

"What is it that you think you've done to me?"

Her voice never gave away her emotions. "I pushed you into the arms of Quinn. Once again I thought I had done the right thing, only to put someone in greater danger than I planned to rescue them from."

"I'm not in danger. I can take care of myself."

"He doesn't love you."

"I know that. I don't love him either."

"Then why are you there?"

"To get away from Kasey. I know what he's capable of and I know what he's done to my family. If I don't stay away, I know he will either kill me or I will kill him. It's just better to be where I am."

"What do you mean by what he's done to your family?" I grew scared.

"I know the secret the two of you have been trying to keep from me."

I started to speak, but Angie continued. "Don't lie to me right now,

Paul. I know it's true. I remember it all from the night we killed Olivia. I'm not stupid. I just thought you might care about me enough to tell me." She started to walk away.

"You can't be out here at night alone. You know that." I believed it to be true, but if I had been honest with myself it was just a poor excuse to get her inside the car.

That grin that I loved to hate rose on her again. Mischief behind every fiber in her being. "You want the girl, kill Kasey, not Quinn."

I looked up at her. "You're going back to that murderous bastard aren't you?"

With her eyes set on mine she lowered herself back even with me. "Who I see and where I go has nothing to do with you. We had sex. We both needed it at the time. That's all it was for me. That's all it is for me with him. And never think that it's your place to tell me where to go or how to live my life." Angie stood back up and began to cross the street. "You've seen what Kasey plans to do. Next move is up to you."

I wanted to say something, but I held back. She was right. Right about every last word. I had assumed that it had been more than sex in some sort of way. Not love, but something more selfish. I wanted to keep her from being with Quinn. I still didn't have control over her. Hell, I didn't even have control over my own life. But it went deeper than that and she and I both were too hard headed to meet in the middle. I saw her running back to Quinn as running into the jaws of death and she saw it as keeping control over her own life versus surrendering it to me. A deadly concoction that had very serious consequences. "Sad. You're dead and you don't even know it yet," I finally yelled out.

She turned back to me and stood in the street, her arms folded across her chest as if waiting for me to continue to stick my foot in my mouth. Her eyebrows lifted with Latin attitude. "Are you done?"

I simply stared back, happy that I at least had the car door between us. "Get in. At least let me drop you off somewhere. If you're going to go running into fang boy's arms you won't want to be too tired to feed his desires."

Angie continued to stand in the street. I caught myself looking for oncoming traffic for her. Still hadn't decided what I planned to do if a bus rounded the corner. Part of me would want to save her, part of me wanted it to smash her flat. "What is it with you and Quinn and Kasey...men in general that think that I need to be rescued and controlled all the time?"

I counted to ten and then spoke. "I'm not trying to rescue you. Just trying to keep you from having to walk when I have a perfectly good form of transportation to take you where you want to go. But I know you. I know you won't do it because you will see it as being weak, giving in, losing yourself, whatever your latest edition of Cosmo calls it. If you want to be too stubborn or too stupid to accept a ride, don't. None of those things are going to matter after he sells you to the Council. The sad part is, if something out there kills you before you make it back to fangs-r-us headquarters, it would be doing you a favor."

She walked back to me with that stripper-like sway that made me uncomfortable. I could smell her as she slinked back to my window. Caramelized skin peeked through the fishnet bodysuit. My heart beat a little faster. "Tell me something, Paul, and be honest." Her voice was soft and peppered with lust. Like velvet caressing my ears.

Angie pulled my chin up. I hadn't realized that I had been staring at things just behind the mesh, but I had been caught in eyes brighter than diamonds. "What?"

"If I wasn't sleeping with Quinn and if Kasey didn't have such a hard on for me, would you really give a damn if I walked out of your life tonight?"

"Of course I would." I looked away, trying to analyze the truth in my head. I wanted to believe it so bad. Wanted to believe that I would care. Did care. There had to be more to my miserable life than coveting the master roach's mistress to our relationship. But underneath it all, I came to terms with the fact that until I found out that she was messing around with Quinn, I rarely thought of her. True, she proved to be royally pissed at me at the time, but still, I continued to be so self-absorbed as a human being that nothing mattered. I hadn't really even thought of Father Garcia that much since his death. Life for me had become an endless series of meaningless days. I pulled away from her.

"You had your chance to save me. To win me, and you refused to look beyond your own selfishness. Denying that you have vampire blood running through you, that your mother was part vampire, that you're not a master vampire, none of this will make it go away. Now you're about to see the only woman with enough balls to love you, turn and walk away. Not because I don't love you, but because you can't love yourself.""So instead you find it spiteful to sleep with the fang head of the month." I gave a disgusted laugh. "Well I can't say he doesn't love himself, so I guess you made the right choice."

She took a step back and gave a melancholy smile. "See, that's why it can't ever be more than what it is with you. You have your agendas in Bat Town, and I have mine, and sometimes those two worlds collide. I've given my heart out to men before and it comes back abused, crushed and neglected. Trouble is, I've learned from my mistakes. I can't say the same for you."

"Angie," I started.

The wolf held her hand up. "Save the bullshit that you're about to spit out." She gathered her thoughts and spoke again. "I step back and look at my life and the way it is right now. And you know what? I like it, so why would I want to ruin it with complicated shit like love and devotion when I can have lust and desire and walk away from it all with my heart still intact and freedom at my feet. When you cut through it all, we're the same. I've traded love for lust and desire. You've traded it for death and violence." She gave me another light kiss on the cheek. "Don't take this too personally Paul Isaac, but you're just not worth the drama." I watched as her figure flashed in the headlights of the cars as they moved up and down the street. Horns blew and cat calls littered the air. Angie remained fixed on me.

I watched as she crossed the street, just as the bus I had been watching for drove by. I started the car as she disappeared into the growing night, not sure if I would ever see her alive again.

21

THE SUN DISAPPEARED below the horizon less than half an hour and I already felt the effects of my own paranoia. The night closed in around me in an invisible death trap. No matter what I did, it would find me and eat me alive. A full moon glowed above me, brighter than anything I had ever seen before.

My joints ached. Pain throbbed through me to the point that I almost pulled over. I hadn't eaten or slept well in days. Fatigue set in, attacking me from every angle and with the intensity that couldn't be ignored.

I doubled over as the burning of muscles continued to rip me apart. Unable to hold back the howling scream that followed. I swerved into the oncoming traffic. Horns blew. Lights flashed. Sounds filled my head, not from the outside world, but from within. I pulled hard on the wheel to regain control. My hands gripped a little tighter. I focused a little harder. I tried to overcome the discomfort. I felt my body give in to the pain again and found myself staring into the headlights of oncoming vehicles again and again.

My chest tightened. I pushed against it with my fist, trying to do anything that would ease the torture that demanded attention. I couldn't breathe. My mouth opened and closed like a fish out of water, only to find me gasping on nothingness. Heart burn? Ulcer? Tumor? Whatever the source, I couldn't take anymore.

Everything from that outside world seemed to melt away and become more and more distant as the thing inside me pushed to get out. Take that back. Clawed to get out.

I knew I wouldn't make it to the hospital before my muscles gave birth to something evil from within. I had no other choice but to stop the car in a nearby parking lot and confront the growing intensity inside me. It wouldn't be a coffin biter that killed me, it would be a bad diet and chronic fatigue.

My muscles tightened. I found it nearly impossible to turn the steering wheel enough to get the car off the road. More horns blared. This time behind me. I heard the distant echo of shouts and profanity as my car drifted to a stop just inside a parking lot off of Garland Street. During the day, the lot would be full of employees and customers of a nearby business, but as night fell, most of those had left for the day. I only remembered seeing a handful still abandoned around me.

I howled in pain again. My left foot slipped off of the clutch, causing the car to lurch forward, the back tires to bark, and the engine to come to a sudden and violent stop. The jolt of the car caused my forehead to meet with the horn in a comical yet violent end of my forward motion.

My stomach tried to regurgitate, but the convulsions grew so intense that nothing could enter or leave my body. I wasn't sure if that was a good or bad thing. Either way, my situation grew worse second by endless second.

I opened the door and basically fell out of the car onto the unfor-giving pavement. My back landed on a bed of large gravel, adding to the already unbearable pain. With the strength I had, I rolled away and came face to face with a slick of oil that had leaked out of the last car parked here. I balled my hands into fists and felt the cuts and warm blood.

Tears of pain filled my eyes. Streams of crimson run across my palms. "Oh, God!" I shouted as the pain and illusions painted a horrifying picture before me. My fingers grew short and stubby, while my hands elongated into something resembling a paw. Nails had turned into claws.

I rolled over on my back, unable to hold still. Above me, I saw the large glow of the moon shining down on me like a beacon of death. And much like me, clouds gathered around, changing shape without consent.

Unable to stop the cramps in my muscles, I rolled again, and tried to get to my feet. I refused to look at my hands again. Refused to believe what my eyes saw. I felt my own power race out of me. A deep growl gurgled in my throat as I tried to stand only to roll into the side of the car and slide back to the pavement.

My hands felt as though they had been turned inside out. Pressure built as my muscles swelled. I cried out as the merciless pain from my muscles tightened to the point that the bones in my right hand broke and shattered inside my skin. The left mimicked the right, followed by cascading breaks along both forearms and splintering up through my shoulders.

Sight, nothing more than quick flashes of light, unable to truly focus on anything. I could hear the blood run through my veins and my lungs fight for air as if amplified. Nostrils flared wide. I discovered scents that I had never smelled before and with the intensity that made me second guess my attempts as a full breath. While they were larger than life, they weren't at all pleasant.

I could hear footsteps. I called out to them for help. Warning. I wasn't sure. I needed something to stop the pain. My muscles continued to contract and stretch. Bones became brittle and broke, changing and then reforming inside me. My pelvis shattered, causing me to scream with non-human force. My claws dug into the side of the 'Cuda and I ripped the metal like wet paper. Somehow, my body began to turn into animal form.

The footsteps grew closer. Surely they heard me. Even if they didn't help me, I had to believe that they would report it. I didn't care if it was friend or foe as long as they had a bucket load of morphine.

I didn't think I could stop the change at this point or not, but I put every bit of effort I could into staying as human as possible. But I found the act impossible to stop. I tried to steady myself and repeated how impossible this was inside my mind. The cockroach virus has teased me from time to time at the sight and smell of blood, but until this week, I had had no symptoms of the were-virus in me. Question was, why now, and what did it mean for me in the future.

I lay as still as I could with my head to its side on the pavement and fought the urge to tighten my muscles. As I looked under the car, I could see feet. Panic took on several forms inside me. Being furry the obvious, but now I had a very real threat of a blood sucker just out of biting distance. And now, just for kicks and giggles, it could be an insane dirt napper with the power to raise zombies to eat anything that moved.

"Eeeewwwalll!" I screamed. Translated into *who's there*, but I remained confident that whatever or whoever stood on the other side wouldn't be able to speak *spaz-pain-fur ball*.

As the sounds fell out of my mouth, I saw the feet begin to move toward the front of the car. I rolled, to the best of my ability, towards the approaching figures and tried to reach for the Magnum, only to be horrified. I no longer had opposable thumbs! Only padded paws and curved claws. I had made it about half way through a change. I could still see the human skin just below the growing fur. Flesh broke free of my clothing, but with each passing moment, the human side of me grew more distant.

I howled in terror.

Above me stood the towering framework of Kasey. With my elbows propped up best I could, I began to drag myself away from him. But with every bone in my body broken or breaking, movement becomes a carnival of pain. Running away or fighting my way out failed to be an option. I found myself at his mercy and we both knew it.

"Kasey…" I spat out. I thanked God that I could even speak.

Kasey stood above me glittering in new sweat. He had that *just changed* look about him, dripping in a film of slime. A wet dog smell overpowered my sense of smell. Fur still stuck in the droplets on his naked chest. As my eyes adjusted, the real horror filled in the blanks. The large man-wolf above me was full monty.

22

HE LIFTED me until we were face to face. Like me, he showed signs of the animal in him. Amber eyes looked back at me, wild and dangerous. Nothing human about them. His large chest heaved in and out as if he had been running before finding me. I wanted to defend myself, wanted to feel the fear, but instead, I succumbed to the relentless pain that throbbed through every cell of my body. It consumed everything about me, nothing else existed.

"Kill me," I grunted. My body tangled into a grotesque mess. All my clothing had been tattered and clung to the sweat on my body. Being nude never hurt so bad.

"That can be arranged." Kasey smiled with gleaming canines. He had plenty of his own hang-ups, but there was no mistaking the fact that he was a lethal machine, capable of slicing me in half if he chose. "I knew one day the virus would take effect. If I didn't have a legiti-mate reason to kill you before, I definitely do now."

With all the effort I could muster, I tried to break free of the large arms that held me prisoner, only to feel the slightest of twitches. Move-ment became only a memory to me now. The voluntary kind anyway. Inside, my muscles and bones continued to shift and twist somewhere between human and beast. Both fighting to be set free.

Kasey dragged me away from the parking lot and threw me into a dark alley behind me. Not a good sign if you have any thoughts of staying out of harm's way. The wolf had the strength to pick me up and carry me if he had wanted to. Being treated like a rag doll just added to the darkness in his motives.

My face landed in a small puddle of water. Around me, I could smell the decaying stench of garbage wafting from a large green dumpster and something really dead. My grunts echoed between the two walls on either side of me. Above me, I could see the glowing sphere responsible for the start of my troubles.

In slow motion, I looked to my left. I saw the fur ball standing between me and the only way out of the alley. With the light behind him, I made out his large silhouette of death. His shadow stretched out across my body in domination.

He stepped toward me in slow, methodical steps. Light from a nearby street lamp illuminated his expressionless face. He breathed in controlled gasps, his hands balling into fists, then stretching out straight. Stopping just short of stepping on me, he bent low and looked at me for a moment. Large hands grabbed me by the shoulders.

"Where is she, Paul?"

Kasey threw me hard against the wall to my back. Long fingers wrapped around my throat before I had time to hit the ground. If he planned on choking me, he needed to work faster. I had trouble breathing long before his paws grabbed me. But I could see the vengeance and merciless anger in his face. His hands shook with it.

"How dare you touch her."

Ah, we were back to this were we? Funny how almost all the blood and scars we had caused one another led back to caramel skin. I gasped for breath in between the shards of pain, trying to gather enough strength to speak. "I...don't...know," I got out in spastic speech. "...talking about."

A second slam into the wall. Even if he broke me in half, my bones would be sacrificed. Most were splintered before the inquisition.

I could feel the heat coming off of him. Long black hair slithered from his wide shoulders like a large spider. "I'm not playing games with you tonight, Paul. I know she was with you." He sniffed the air. "I can smell her on you." The look of revolt moved across his face. "This would have all been over by now if you hadn't stuck your nose into things you shouldn't be a part of. The thought of the two of you together is nothing short of disgusting."

"...weren't so disgusting..." I reminisced.

He shook me again. "It won't matter in a few minutes. Once and for all, you will be out of our lives. The threat to me will die with you. No longer having to cover my tracks and secrets, no longer having to worry about the vampires. Mark my words, Paul, I will kill her."

Knowing that I had been further with Angie than he would ever get, was now going to be used against me. He had always been jealous of the fact that the she-wolf had the hots for me, but now that we had sealed the deal, I definitely had been axed from his Christmas card list. I did the best I could to shake my head. "With...Quinn." I tried to catch what little breath I could. Either the pain was leveling off or I was getting used to it. I didn't particularly like either scenario. "...happening...me?"

"You don't know?"

I stared back at him but refused to waste the energy in answering. We both knew the answer. Given a second opportunity to ask my question it would have been, "How do I stop this?"

"Surely you're aware of the were-virus in you, Paul. Problem is, unlike the rest of us that can compete the change from human to wolf, you have a vampire virus in you as well. You won't be able to complete the transition." Another jolt against the wall. "Lucky for you, it's going to be all pain and no gain." I felt the swift kick to my balls and instantly doubled over. I had thought I had experienced the greatest pain I could ever endure, but Kasey proved me wrong.

I fell into a pathetic lump on the ground, trying my best to breathe through the pain and find my happy place. I was naked, in agony, unable to defend myself and had little hope that things were about to get any better. Sweat dripped from the tip of my nose. I alternated between hot and cold. My body grew weak and dehydrated. If Kasey chose to kill me, I had no way to defend myself. I had become nothing more than trembling pain.

A female wolf crouched low enough to look into my eyes. "Remember me? I'm the one that promised to kill you." I was blindsided by a kick to the face. All I could see were stars as the blood formed instantly. I struggled to breathe. Damned if I moved, damned if I didn't.

Tanya had survived.

I never saw her sneak up on us. But I remembered her. I knew better than to answer or give another unneeded comeback. Instead I laid still and hoped that whatever they were about to do to me would be swift. "Where can we find her, Paul?"

"Not in Kasey's bed..." I grunted.

Kasey added several more kicks to my face and body. I remained motionless, simply to make sure that he had it all out of his system before I uncoiled from the fetal position. Plus, I knew Kasey well enough to know that the less I fought back the more it would piss him off.

With the little strength I had left, I looked up again through the thick solution of blood and sweat. Kasey pulled me back up to my feet, unaffected by my screams of pain. "I have to give the credit to Quinn whether I like it or not. He knew what would have us at each other's throats. Nothing like a dog in heat to make the alphas blood thirsty. It's the reason he took her in and made her his own. He knew one of us would kill the other trying to get her back. One thing he didn't count on happens to be me wanting her back. Unlike you, I don't take sloppy seconds from a vampire." He studied me. "Much less two."

"She knows about you." I tried. For some reason, Kasey couldn't get it through his thick head that Angie would never be his sweetheart and that I had no interest in sweeping her off of her feet. But now with Angie's, as Kasey poetically put it, scent on me, convincing him of that was really going to be a problem. I thought about what Angie told me. Kasey had been her biggest threat, not Quinn. I still couldn't wrap my head around that one.

Kasey shook his head. "In just a few hours you and Angie will both be dead. You by the Council and Angie by my wolves. But have no fear, I'll make her suffer for the things she did." Another kick to my ribs. "To think you two thought you could kill me and take my place."

Though in excruciating pain, I had to laugh. "You think I want to be king of the fur balls?" I continued to watch the female move in the distance. Though I knew I wouldn't have a choice in the matter, I wanted to try and keep her from getting behind me. It gave me a false sense of control.

"It's not what I think you want, but what the possibilities are. And it is possible that you could rise up and challenge me as the alpha male and I will not allow that to happen." He moved in on me. I could feel the breath snort from his nostrils. "You didn't plan on being a master vampire but you are. Just like Angie's brother. You don't wait until the problem is too big or don't solve it because it might not be a problem. You squash it before it can be a problem."

I did my best to read him, but there wasn't enough putty to make anything out of it. "Lies." I struggled to get the one word out. "If you kill me...murder."

Kasey gave me a toothy grin. "Not anymore. You've confessed to being the *Dracul Sang*, which took away any rights you have as a human being. But those you now represent will be the very ones that kill you. I won't have to do it. I walk away with clean hands. They will find Angie guilty even if I don't get to her. We both know Quinn is only using her to get to us and if there is no us, he won't think twice about giving her to the police." He bent down close to me and whispered in my ear. "And I'll be there to watch you both die."

I looked back at Kasey and tried to ask the question, but my strength was fading. My muscles continued to twitch with the weight of the full moon on them. Pain had been replaced with constant pressure as the bones and muscles refused to stretch any further. I remained neither human or wolf and the internal organs, muscles and bones of my body paid the price for it. "Should...have...killed...you."

Another quick kick to my ribs. "Yeah, I guess you should have." And with that, the wolf howled in perceived victory, as another figure stood in the distance. And she oozed with undead power.

23

KASEY PROVED to exceed my vision of a coward and cold blooded killer. Unlike the undead, which have no issues in confessing to be what they were, Kasey hid behind lies and strength. Trusting him had proven again and again to be harmful to my health. I made a mental note of it for later action.

I pulled myself to the side of the building as much as I could. I tried to control my breathing and remain calm, but I didn't have the strength to fight for my life. I remained somewhere between man and beast. Muscles and bone unsure of their roles. Naked and weak, I could see my weapons lying next to my leather trench coat. I didn't have the opposable thumb to use any of them.

Hard steps echoed in the alley. Heavy sounds of boots with methodical cadence. The figure moved toward me. By the shape, I could make out a female form. And not just any female. Before the light hit her face, I knew tonight would end badly.

Dressed in a black laced corset tied with a bright red ribbon that lifted her assets in a way that they absorbed all the light from the full moon, Inderia loomed over me. The colorful tattoos that inked her body glowed in contrast to the rich colored skin around them. Thigh high black boots with stiletto-like heels showcased her legs and buttocks. Her long black hair draped over her dead skin, eyes hidden behind dark sunglasses. Lips redder than anything I had ever witnessed before. S&M never felt so deadly.

The power shocked me as she moved close enough that I could touch her. My body trembled with lust and hunger. But even with those odds against me, I couldn't keep my mouth from going off. "Good to see..escaped being dog food, Inderia."

"Shut up and listen. You're my bitch now." Couldn't argue so far. She glanced back out to the parking lot. Somehow I think she planned on us being alone. "You need to make a choice and make it now. Do you want the slut to live or die?"

She slunk next to me and smiled as if she had won something. The see through mesh of the costume she wore left little to my imagination as to what she looked like naked. Sharp red fingernails traced along my skin. Dark purrs filled her throat. "I see what all the fuss about you has been, *Dracul Sang*. I came here to see you die, now, I am not so sure of things. Perhaps there can be other uses for such things." My naked skin shivered with cold and fear.

I could tell by Inderia's smirk that I wouldn't have to ask many questions. Her mouth gaped open, exposing razor sharp tools, I only imagined would be in me soon. "Before you die, there are things we need to discuss and I think you know what those are."

"You...raised..."

A shake of the head. "No, I had nothing to do with any of that. Simply found opportunity knocking. I'm talking about something far more valuable than who wins an election. I'm talking about control of the necro porn business. At the moment, you control it, like it or not. Veronica has tried on several occasions to get you to sign the papers and you have refused. Now we can do this quickly or make it fun for me. I have all night, darling, but make no mistake, you will sign the paperwork."

"I won't let you gain control of it. You're done. You and the rest of the roaches."

Now a full on laugh. "Let's look at things as they really are, Saint Avenger. You are technically a human until the Council arrives. If you sign now, everything will be binding as a human. After the Council meets with you and you become the *Dracul Sang*, free and clear, you will not be able to own NecroPussy Incorporated since pure blooded vampires do not have the same rights as commercial vampires. The business will be taken away from you. Veronica has had the papers drawn up so that she is the power of attorney on the business. Once you are dead, I will buy it for pennies on the dollar and gain all the controlling interest."

"Your brand of sex is still illegal right now," I answered.

Inderia's power pushed at my change. I could feel the pain ease and by the looks of my paw-like hands, they became ever so slightly human again. I had to focus on my breathing. The more controlled I made it, the less the change seemed to twist inside me.

The blood sucker's mouth opened wide enough that I could see the lethal fangs. "Presently, it is legal as long as the human does not die. The two can have sex, the vampire can feed, the act can be filmed. The sticky part is the full feed and death of the human." She kissed my cheek. "Once Lopes wins the election next year, it will all be legal. We both know it is only a matter of time. There is too much money to be made to be ignored. Just as it had been when the legalization of vampires started."

I closed my eyes and tried to reverse the shift a little more. The use of my hands would be the difference between life and death for me. Like a long distant friend I looked at the holster that held the Magnum. Without it, I was no threat at all to Inderia, even if I became a full on wolf. "Won't sign it."

"Oh, I think you will. I've invested way too much time into this for you to stop me. Even if you die, I win. You do know who had the most shares of interest in NecroPussy don't you?"

Now it was my turn to shake my head. "No."

She moved like a cat as she toyed with me. The left boot kicked the holster with the Magnum a little farther away. "Peavey. He had been in the pocket of Kincaid since the beginning. Owned over a million dollars in shares of NecroPussy, but the night before his death, he, for some reason, just handed all those little shares over to me. Change of heart I'm guessing."

"Blackmail?"

She grinned wide enough that I could see those lethal fangs. "I am in the business of power, *Dracul Sang*. And I know how to get it. Peavey had far too many secrets and vices to put up much of a fight." She bent over me, allowing me to see the tops of her perfectly round breasts. "Give him skin and the brain will follow. All the time I was digging his grave." Kasey handed her the stack of papers and an ink pen. "Now, please sign the paperwork and I will make sure Angie dies quickly. You've seen my playroom. Don't let her end up there without an upper hand."

"So kill me. Get it over with. I'm not signing anything. I know you killed all those people at the Plaza. They'll prove it. I saw what you did at NecroPussy. I know about Peavey's daughter. Kansas will find you and you will have nothing but a death warrant to show for it." And I meant every word.

The vixen strutted around me, studying her prey. She pulled her sunglasses low on the bridge of her nose as she eyed me. "The great vampire executioner naked and shivering. Begging for death." She grabbed me by the neck and pulled me to the side of the building behind us. My back hit with a solid thump. The papers fell in my lap. "You're already a dead man. Don't let Angie take the fall for all of this. Even if you don't give a damn about yourself, think of her. You know I can kill her."

I had enough hang-ups without responding to that. I continued to eye the Magnum and knew I had little chance of killing Inderia. I was no match for her, unless I could regain control of my body. "Joke's on you, Inderia. The vampires that answer to me will find you."

Her laugh echoed off of the side of the building. "You think those things are going to be loyal to you? The only reason they haven't killed you yet is that they are so into tradition that it's their weakness. They don't respect you. Once you're dead, the only thing on their minds will be becoming the next *Dracul Sang* of the city. You will rot, forgotten. There will be no retribution from them. They will see your death as the answer to a problem. Solved by your Council more than likely. You don't see them coming after you because of the death of Asa do you? And he was far more respected than you."

"Asa's not dead. No one has... proof of it. So even though you might be able...to kill me, it won't make you anything other than a murderous bloodsucker. I'm a human...they will hunt you down...kill you."

Inderia stuck a heel in my chest, pushing me flat on the ground. She seemed ten foot tall from my perspective. I pulled back as she gave a throaty laugh. "And you base all of this on the fact that you have Isabella's head in a box." She stared down at me with those mirrored glasses now back over her eyes, hiding the dangerous gazed just on the other side. I could feel what little blood I still had left turn to ice water. If Inderia knew about the ominous delivery it meant that others could know as well, making my assumptions of Asa being alive a bit more farfetched. I looked to Kasey. It also meant they had been working together a lot longer than tonight. "That is right sweetheart. I know who killed your little princess, and it's not Asa. He *is* dead." I didn't like that. My whole nightmare hung on the hopes that he still walked the earth. "I happened to be there the night that Asa tried to kill you in the hospital."

"Why?"

"Picking up blood samples," she joked.

Kasey paced in front of me, filling with rage by the second. He would glance to the mouth of the alley from time to time as if waiting on something. He continued to ball and release his fists in repetition. I knew at any moment they could be used against me. Not a pleasant thought for me.

Finally, Inderia stopped and looked back at me. Mirrored eyes glared at me like fresh meat. "I had waited two hundred years for someone to kill Asa. He had grown complacent in his age and position. But at the time, he was far too powerful for me to kill and our society looks down on assassination. You gave me opportunity. I could kill you and remain a prominent member of the coven. I would be looked up to, not down upon for saving our kind. And as you have said, the human laws would try and hunt me down. But I now have a way of making everyone's dreams come true."

Kasey continued to stare at me for what seemed to be forever. Those large fists continued to threaten me with further bodily harm. I glanced at my hands hoping to see fingers. With fingers I could even up this fight a little more. The scales tipped back toward human, but not enough that I could effectively pull the trigger or even hold the Magnum or 9mm. I would have to be a patient grasshopper for the time being and allow Inderia to continue her spewing speech.

"You may be the most despicable, vile creature in this city to me, but to the coven as a whole, Sasha was the bigger threat with Asa's death. I knew that you were too stupid to figure it out that if you killed Asa, you would become the new *Dracul Sang*. When I found him, he was still alive but dying. I knew that Sasha wanted to be the next master vampire. I saw him as a psychopath that would crush us all into tyrannical submission. If he had found Asa while still alive and killed him, he would have been the new master, not you."

"Why not just kill Asa yourself?"

Her body moved like fluid as she strolled to me again. A quick shrug of the shoulders followed. "The timing was not right. If I had killed him then, Sasha would have challenged me. He would have killed me. But if he thought you were the *Dracul Sang*, I knew it would only be a matter of time before he came looking for you. I had faith in you, Avenger. I took a great chance that you would be good enough to kill him. And when you did, it left me as the most powerful pure blood vampire in the city. Killing you at a later time seemed to be the easier choice to make. You are far more predictable and have many more tangibles that compromise what you do and how you do them."

I wanted to strangle her now. Again, I thought only of myself. The blood licker before me had been responsible for putting me in harm's way and making me a reluctant master roach. "How did you keep Sasha from finding him?" I knew that coffin sleepers had some sort of homing device that helps them find their master, so I had to ask the question.

Inderia stopped pacing. "I played cat and mouse with Sasha until

Asa was dead. I knew it would only be a matter of minutes based on what you did to him. He was an incredibly powerful vampire, but without a beating heart, even he could no longer cheat death. I did not have to come up with anything too elaborate. Plus, if you remember on that night, the hospital was crawling with police ready to kill anything with fangs. That slowed Sasha's pursuit enough that he could not get to him in time." Inderia looked back toward the mouth of the alleyway as if something might be there listening. "And I had the help of Kasey in keeping Sasha at bay."

I looked back into the werewolf's smirk. I felt my own blood boil. "Kasey wanted me to be the master vein weasel?"

Inderia gave a slow nod of her head. "Makes sense when you are in lust with a woman, Avenger. Kasey knew that if you were to become the *Dracul Sang*, sooner or later one of us would kill you. With you dead, he has Angie all to himself. Lust is an incredible motivator." She looked at my hands. "Not to mention, now that you are showing signs of the were-virus, you could be a threat to his status as well. Simply didn't plan on Quinn picking up the pieces. Now that Angie has made herself less than valuable"

"So you kill me and everybody gets what they want," I answered.

Inderia shook her head slowly. "I do not plan to kill you, Avenger. You will confess to the Council that you are responsible for the attack at the Crowne Plaza. I shall be the beneficiary of the actions that follow. No need to risk my life in a battle with you. I will allow the Council to do my dirty work. All you need to do is sign the papers and we will be out of your life, ever how short that may be."

"You think I will confess to making maggot walkers?" I had to laugh in spite of the pain. It sounded so farfetched. I was already making myself grow stubborn. "Kill me, eat me, whatever, but I'm not going to go before the Council, confess I'm a master dirt humper and tell them I raised the dead heads." I threw the papers to the ground next to me. "And I won't sign your papers. Game over, Inderia."

"Oh, I think you will." I followed her eyes back to the mouth of the alley, where the she-wolf now led Angie toward us. Her hands had been bound behind her, mouth gagged and a lot more blood dripped from her than I would like to have seen. Inderia had fed from her.

"You psycho bitch!" I yelled. I struggled to make my way to the Magnum only to feel the pain shock me back into submission. My muscles refused to act on my commands. I rolled along the ground like an injured worm.

Inderia turned to me. I looked over to the alpha male. How could he have allowed this to happen to her? "Was killing me worth this, Kasey?"

"Do not blame the wolf, Avenger. He, unlike you the other night, is willing to do whatever is necessary to keep his kind safe and alive. Now, I am giving you the choice to do the same." Inderia took the leash from the wolf and led Angie to me. I expected to see terror in those beautiful eyes, but instead I saw the power of a woman ready to come undone. I wanted to save her, but at the moment I couldn't even save my own life.

Inderia pushed Angie away from me and grabbed my chin in her hand. Her free hand gathered the papers and placed them gently on my lap again. I felt the snap of power light up my skin. "I am not into games any more, Avenger. This is what you will say and do. Any deviation and your wolf will die very slowly. You will confess to the Council that you are the true *Dracul Sang* of the city and that you are responsible for raising the dead and killing all those at the reception. By doing so will keep your precious wolf from dying for something she did not do. Right now, you will sign the papers or watch the wolf die."

"And what if the Council doesn't believe my story?" I meant it as much of a threat as I could.

Inderia turned and slapped Angie hard enough that her knees buckled under her. If it hadn't been for the leash holding her, she would have dropped to the ground. "Then I suggest you find a way to convince them." Inderia moved within an inch of me. "Now sign the paperwork." I felt the sharp pain hit my stomach as if I had been set on fire. I couldn't contain the screams that fought to get out. My knees gave way and crashed to the pavement below. Burning. I burned from the inside out. Hands reached for the pain just below my sternum. Blisters formed as my paw-like hands touched the silver knife wedged in my abdomen. I could hear the laughter from Inderia above me and in my head at the same time. Screams from undead souls rattled my bones. Convulsions moved through my muscles like a puppet on strings. *"Die for me, Avenger. Die for me!"* Inderia chanted in my thoughts.

24

I WOKE COLD, naked and disoriented. Which with my line of work and bad habits shouldn't have seemed all that strange, but the flashes of memory that ran through my head made this awakening a bit more stressful if not all out scary.

I expected to wake up to a board of evil roaches looking at me with hungry eyes. Thoughts of being bound to a chair and gagged to keep the twisted sounds of screaming down clogged my head. Perhaps all of it had been nothing more than a shape shifting dream or out of body experience. Never shifting before, I didn't find it surprising that I would have more questions than answers.

I carefully searched for any signs of haunting things but found everything eerily familiar. I remained in the alleyway where all the little monsters had taken me. Sirens wailed in the distance as I scanned the horizon. Nothing moved. Nothing exposed itself from the dark. I had lived too long to think I could be alone.

A sting of fresh pain hit me. My hand reached for the wound just below my rib cage. Warm blood painted my skin in gloss red. Okay, so not all of it had been a dream or out of body experience. I had to get to somewhere safe. And fast.

In a jolt of hope, I looked at my hand again and saw just that. A hand. A human hand. Not some cross hybrid form somewhere between man and beast. Only an honest to God hand. Bloody and shaking, but a human hand all the same.

I allowed the endorphins to rush through me as I lay on my back and looked up at the stars and started to laugh. Somehow, I had returned human and alive. I still didn't know how long I had been out, but as I studied the full moon, it gave me reason to believe that not a lot of time had passed.

But the presence of darkness and the pool of blood under me led me to a sobering fact. The coffin munchers would be back. Dodging a bullet with Inderia and Kasey didn't mean a safe haven for me by any means. It only meant that something else would have the opportunity to find me and eat me. And some call me a pessimist.

With slow, methodical moves, I rolled onto my stomach. I fought against the biting pain that shot through my body from the silver induced wound. My mind raced as I tried to find the strength to go vertical. Something had to have scared my attackers off. I couldn't see any of them having me on the ropes and then simply losing interest. It became miserably clear that I could be worth far more alive than dead to both the roaches and the fur balls.

I had come to the realization that the world of bloodsuckers and shape changers wasn't all that different from the human side of things. We all coveted two things and two things only in the most raw of forms. Sex and power. Everything from happiness to death could be achieved from those two things. Both would take their toll and eat us alive far worse than the zombies that roamed the streets. Yet no matter how many times the trap had been set and the neck snapped, we go right back and take another chance.

Ahead of me, I saw the leather trench coat wadded up on the ground like day old laundry. My shredded clothing unsalvageable, leaving me with the uncertain prospect of having to go to the emergency room practically nude.

A little further toward the opening of the alley, I saw the holster with the Magnum as well as the one holding the 9mm. It gave me enough motivation to try once again to drag my body from the ground, lick my wounds and thank baby Jesus that I had survived the night. Even if that changed somewhere between here and the 'Cuda.

"Either you took after your mother or you are not my son after all."

I felt my entire body convulse with magnified trepidation. My mind simply came to a much simpler point. *Who the hell was that?*

I turned in spite of the pain that shot from the wound. In the circus of confusion, the thought of grabbing the Magnum or any weapon for that matter never had time to sprout in my pea-sized brain. I no longer had any doubt that something still waited on me. A terrible thing had been watching me from behind, draped in the shadows of the blackness.

What I saw proved to be far worse than any monster I had ever seen before. Far more hideous than any victim dismembered or decaying. I tried to scream, but couldn't. Tried to move, but couldn't. I simply stared back into the eyes of true death.

Albert Kincaid sat on a wooden box no more than fifteen feet from me. Or better put, what remained of him. His skin appeared decayed and gray, eroding into a network of pot holes, exposing the bone underneath. Eyeballs that stared into my soul dangled inside sockets. Teeth jutted out of the side of his cheeks where the flesh had been torn away.

His skull rested not on his shoulders, but in his hands. Dirt, mud and decayed flesh had stained his suit. Maggots wiggled along most of the remaining skin, which gave it the illusion of movement. Real cock roaches darted in and out of the holes in his body in such quantity that I could hear them crawling.

The breeze brought me the first whiff of death and I felt my stomach start to convulse. My muscles tensed with the action, which in turn caused the wound from the silver blade to react with enough pain that I stopped the retching almost immediately. I found myself in a fetal position, doubled in pain and horror.

If that had been all I had seen, it would have been enough, but tonight, nearly turning into a werewolf, being stabbed by a blood sucker and seeing Albert Kincaid in dead form proved only the beginning.

Out of the dark shadows came another figure and I felt my heart pound with such intensity it drove my chest into full on implode mode. My mother stood and stared back at me with carbon copy dead eyes as those I saw in Kincaid. Her skin, which I remembered to be soft and light, now nothing more than decaying mush, dry from age. Her once golden hair replaced with long strands of oily matter that clung to the side of her head in several clumps. Most of her scalp nothing more than bone and stained dark red from blood that had dried decades earlier.

Behind her, I experienced another nightmare. I pushed against the pavement with all the strength I had, trying to reach the Magnum only a few feet away. I had a real good feeling it wouldn't do me any good physically, but mentally, it would be the only sanctuary I would find.

Father Garcia, like the other two, stared at me with eyes absent of any emotions. Simply two orbs in his skull. Unlike the other two, his skin looked more life-like. Or better put, less decayed. Time hadn't taken its toll on his body yet. His presence hurt the most, which I found odd, when compared to my mother. Inside, I knew the answer, but tried to find a way to re-justify it. Time hadn't healed the wounds of losing my mother. No amount of time would do that. It was the blatant fact that I had been the one that killed Father Garcia. I had been the one that had to drive the stake through his heart and remove his head from his shoulders. I could still see his dead eyes open and look at me. I remember the anger that stared back.

Inch by inch I moved away from them and closer to my weapons, all the time keeping my eyes focused. My senses alert. Power wrapped around me like a warm soothing blanket. I tried to brush it from my skin as if I had just run into a spider web. I had never experienced cockroach power so warm and soothing. It had always been as cuddly as a live wire.

I tried to convince myself of the illusion. That the three things I saw represented nothing more than demonic bat power. I tried to blame it all on Inderia and her ability to twist the reality in me from the inside out.

But I couldn't take that chance. My hand continued to work behind me, searching for the Magnum as I inched away from the creatures. I had already convinced myself that the gun wouldn't stop them from getting to me, but I also knew sitting in the middle of an abandoned alley didn't offer me much safe haven either.

"Once you reach the gun, what do you plan to do? Shoot us? How do you plan on killing something that is already dead?" Kincaid called out. My mother and Father Garcia joined in the moment of laughter.

"After all I had done for you, this is what I receive in return? Betrayal?" Father Garcia added. His voice laced with anger. Anger I had known growing up in the orphanage at his church. Old habits die hard with me. I instantly started to panic. My heart beat faster. My mouth bone dry.

I looked back at them, all my sins, demons and losses had combined. Given the choice, the bullet in the Magnum would go into my head, not theirs. But I experienced horror like nothing I had ever known before. I couldn't move. My thoughts never materialized. Time stopped.

"Is there something you wish to tell us?" my mother asked. I hate saying it that way. The thing before me no longer my mother. An animated corpse, brought to life by some sort of cockroach magic. I couldn't take my eyes off of the hideous creature that represented her. That grotesque head still rested in the arms of the female body. But her voice drew me in the most. While the face and body represented the mother I once had, the voice far more real. If I could have closed my eyes, I wouldn't have been able to tell the difference.

As I tried to break free from the voice, the smell of rotten flesh gave way to something far more evil. Blood. Inside, I could feel things changing. My human instincts attacked by something that flowed through me from the beginning of time, but had just now made their presence known. Power rose from under my skin. Muscles charged with ancient power. Just as it had when I looked into Inderia's eyes, my mouth began to water. My fear now replaced with hunger. I needed to feed. I needed to gorge myself on the warm vein of the living to satisfy my thirst.

My mother spoke. "You left me that night. Left me to die by the hands of the vampires and the assassins. You could have saved me, but you ran."

Her words sent me back to the night she died. Eight years old. Small. Scared. As if I had been transported, I could feel, smell and hear the things I did on that night. I tried to speak, but couldn't. I watched as she approached me, exposing me of the things that had haunted me since that night.

"How could my only son do such a thing as leave his mother to die on the floor? So ashamed."

I shook my head. "So sorry," the only thing that escaped my mouth.

Dead eyes looked to me with resentment. "Sorry? Do you know what they did to me and all you can say is sorry? Where were you while they tortured and killed me?"

Choking on my own fear, "Hiding in the woods. Under a palmetto bush."

"Hiding? Didn't you hear me scream for you, for help? All you ever thought about was yourself. I am so ashamed of you."

"No," I begged.

"I loved and protected you and this is what I get in return? I am dead because of you. They poured holy water down my throat while another raped me. No one came to my rescue. The only person that could have saved me was you. Hiding under a bush." Only inches from me now. "You are no son of mine. Not worthy of the things you are on trial for." She walked around me. I knew better than to move. "We have been summoned here because you have claimed to turn a woman into a wolf and to be the *Dracul Sang* of the city. Is this true." By the time she finished, we were face to face again.

"Because of you, yes."

An answer she hadn't expected. "Me? I never told you to pull the wolf out of a woman and kill anyone. Do not place this blame on me."

"But I am what I am because of you." My voice quivered with uncertainty. One thing to be on trial, but when your mother represented the prosecution, it changed everything.

Our faces touched. My skin stung. "You may carry my virus through your veins, but you are not my son and you will not be *Dracul*

Sang. You are nothing but a coward and should die for the things you have done three nights ago and for what you did to me." Her hand touched my shoulder. Again, I refused to move. "As for the wolf, I say she dies for her involvement. A clean slate."

"Kill me if you want, but let Angie go. She didn't do anything."

I could see her processing my answer. "This is not about innocent or guilty. I hope you didn't think so. It is about what is best for all vampires of the city. Many vampires, far more worthy than you, have met far worse circumstances. You and the wolf will both die. Not because of the things you are accused of, but for being weak and unworthy of title of *Dracul Sang*."

I shook the thought free as the Kincaid thing spoke. "Guilty or innocent?" His words seemed to slip out of his mouth like invisible serpents, slithering inside my brain. I knew it was in my head, but I tried to shake them free all the same.

The words seemed hollow and distant. My hunger for blood over-rode everything. My senses focused in on every heartbeat around me. Each pulse throbbed in my bones. I did my best to speak. "About what?"

"Raising the dead and killing two of your own kind," the Father Garcia thing answered. "Because of you, I live in this hell for all eternity. Never allowed to find heaven. All I did for you after you ran away that night, you allowed those things to invade my soul. I agree with your mother. You are not worthy of living past tonight much less being *Dracul Sang*."

Fingers wrapped around the Magnum and I pulled it to me. I had to get it to my temple. Everything in my body wanted to run wild and feed. I couldn't let that happen. I'd put the barrel to my own head before allowing it. I had to stop it. I had no clear way of knowing if the three things before me were raising the power in me, but I couldn't take the chance of stopping my actions on my own. Again, I tried to speak, this time I couldn't.

Another figure appeared from the blackness. The young boy I had killed the night before my wedding. Emotionless. He stood there in the suit he had been buried in, faded and stained. "Remember me?"

I looked down. Never answering him.

"Look at me."

His shadow moved toward me. Against my better judgment, I raised my head.

The damage I had impaled on him, still visible. Dried blood along the cut line of his neck. "Killed me in front of my own mother and family. Your anger killed an innocent man and yet you did nothing to face your responsibility. You allowed my name to be victimized, while you hid behind authority for your actions. What happened to my little brother?"

I didn't know. Simply shook my head.

"Committed suicide five years later by eating rat poison. My mother died of a broken heart. Your actions have led to the deaths of so many and now you unleash your anger on innocent people."

"I didn't do it."

"Your past contradict your words. Now I am in charge of your fate. Not only yours but someone that I know you love. I don't give a damn about being *Dracul Sang*. You will not live through the night. I hold your life in my hands now and I will show you the same mercy you showed me."

I remained silent at first, allowing it to sink in. Nothing he said had been untrue. I deserved to die by my actions to him alone. "I beg you to leave Angie alone. I'm sorry for what I did to you."

He laughed. Blood oozed from the cut in his neck. I had to look away. "You beg me? Sorry for what you've done?" He shook his head. "No, you are only sorry that you are here tonight. Sorry that the wolf will die because of who you are and what you did. Anyone other than you would have been rotting in a jail cell at this point. I find you guilty as charged."

"You have been accused of the deaths of two vampires as well as raising the dead. You now stand before the Vampire Council. Do you plead innocent or guilty?" I felt my body ache with power as another figure moved from the shadows. His low, deep Jamaican accent resonated in my bones. Asa stood before me with a gaping hole in his chest. A trail of wet blood reflected light. Unlike the others, his head had not been severed. Which was a bummer since I only came up to his neck as it was.

Asa walked toward me. I pulled the Magnum up. He stopped and looked at the gun with those dead eyes that rolled around inside the skull. "Put that thing away. It will not help your cause."

"It's not for you, it's for me."

Kincaid stood next to Asa. He placed his head in his left hand and with the right, patted the former *Dracul Sang* on the back. The eyes in the skull remained on me. A half grin formed on the decayed skin. "I assume you know of the gift I left you." A large beetle scrambled out from behind the left eye socket. I shivered in disgust. "Tell me, can you truly raise the dead? In our guidelines it is not a death sentence to hold the power, only if you use that power. We have your confession to such things, why should we show you mercy?"

"I'm not here for mercy. I only want the safety of Angie. She's innocent. But for the record, I didn't raise the zombies."

"Who did?" Kincaid asked.

"I don't know yet. My guess is Inderia or Quinn. They have the most to gain by killing Peavey."

"And you are willing to die for their power?"

"No, I told you. I'm here to save the life of the wolf."

Kincaid grinned. "Ah, yes, the wolf. I know of her well. Tell me of the things that would make a vampire want to die for a lowly wolf? Perhaps she does things?"

I knew where this line of questions would end up. "I only ask that she be spared."

"Innocent or guilty?" the Father Garcia thing asked again.

I had always pictured the Council as ancient creatures of the night. Powerful beings that even dwarfed the energy in the blood maggots. This made no sense to me at all. My mother's voice remained emotionless and far too matter-of-fact. I thought about Angie. I didn't want to confess to something I didn't do, but I knew her life hung in the balance. I weighed the options in my head. I could confess and hope that Inderia kept her part of the deal, or I could claim my innocence and take the chance on getting to Angie before the bitch roach did something I would regret.

I looked over to Kincaid and grew so angry I wanted nothing more than to drop kick his head out of those boney hands. For now, I would have to tolerate this freak show. In my mind I tried to convince myself that none of this could be real. It had to be Inderia messing with my mind, or what remained of it. And clinging to that kind of hope, showed me just how twisted and low my life had gotten.

My mouth filled with saliva as the scent of blood rose in the air. The sound of throbbing heart beats thumped against my temple. I could almost taste it. Metallic and warm. I dug my fingernails into the palms of my hands to keep some sort of reality within me. Stomach muscles twisted in need.

The hunger continued to grow inside me. Being before a Vampire Council seemed more of a nuisance than anything. They were taking my time. Time I could be using to feed. At this point, I would confess to anything just to sink my teeth into warm skin. Maybe it accumulated into all the twisted things involved with these monsters. Make the accused hungry beyond thought, and they will confess to anything.

My eyes shot back to Asa as he shifted his weight from his left foot to his right. He had been dead for months and still his black skin shined under the moonlight as if still alive. Killing him had cost me the most. His death had left me tangled in vampire politics and accolades I didn't wish upon my worst enemy. My finger begged to pull the trigger, but I remained still.

Another form emerged from the darkness and I caught myself hyperventilating. A tall lanky man, early twenties, bathed in the light. Bright red hair waved in the night air, big green eyes that never blinked. Freckled skin still visible on decayed skin.

My reaction never materialized in the form of fear or vengeance, but of guilt. Instead of blazing a trail with the Magnum and hoping for the best, I found myself lowering the gun and staring into those dead eyes. I couldn't explain it. Yes, he had been a fang head. Yes, I had killed him. He stood there with wild emotions running across his face. It wouldn't surprise me if I found him at my throat at any moment.

"Joshua Price." I immediately thought of his grandfather Frank Price and hated myself.

"So we meet again, Avenger," he said. A large hole in his chest reminded me of what I had done. I shook my head in the irony of it all. I had been his judge and jury all those years ago, and now it seemed as if he would be mine.

"Your grandfather and I had to do it, Josh. We had no choice."

"If you had admitted to what you were, this wouldn't have happened to me. I blame you."

"They would have killed you either way. Nothing I or Frank did would have saved your life. I just couldn't tell him that."

"I find you guilty as charged. You deserve your fate."

"Any other surprises?" I said to no one in particular. With what little strength I still had, I slowly stood. The wound below my ribs throbbed as the blood rushed to it. Being nude, I shivered in the winter night air.

"Paul Isaac, you are accused of raising the dead and killing two vampires at the Crowne Plaza Hotel along with the wolf named Angela. How do you plead? Innocent or guilty," the mother thing asked.

"Guilty." The words fell from my lips with a finality that I hadn't expected. I threatened Inderia from my future grave.

My words fell off the deep end of the earth. Five pairs of dead eyes stared back at me. None with any form of compassion. "Why should we believe you?" the Father Garcia thing asked.

"Come again?" I found it to be a rather odd response.

"Three of the Council have been killed by your hands. Give us a reason why you may find mercy in our judgment," the young man added. "To allow you death by us seems a bit too lenient."

"You and Asa deserved to die. Nothing more than cold blooded killers." I looked back at him and tried to stand my ground. I had made up my mind that I would not be bullied by the creatures before me. My eyes wondered over to Father Garcia and my mother. No longer could I or would I look at them and see the humans that they once were. The people that I remembered them being were dead and gone. The things standing before me were nothing more than physical evil animated by the living dead. I knew if I could convince myself of that fact, I stood a better chance of making it out alive. "You may not have killed those people in the house that night, but you were still a vampire and no laws protected you at the time. Given the chance, I would do it differently, away from your mother, but I would still have killed you. I have no remorse in that."

"So you do not take responsibility for the deaths?" Asa asked.

"Responsibility yes, remorse, no."

He stepped toward me. I wanted to take one back, but I stood still. "You do recognize the fact that you are not only a vampire but *Dracul Sang* do you not?"

I gave a weak shrug. "Cut the crap Asa, you know as well as I do that I'm not a cockroach, much less their new leader, but if it gets us through this a lot quicker I'll agree to that part." Funny how even in animated death, Asa seemed to get under my skin. He had always been as aggravating as a fly that continues to buzz around your face. Swat it all you want, but it keeps coming back.

"You are a necromancer are you not?" the Father Garcia thing asked.

I studied the man that had raised me since the age of eight, for a few seconds, trying to convince myself that the Father Garcia I knew, no longer existed. I looked at a ghost or some sort of roach magic. The thing looked back at me from a skull in the hands of a dead body. No longer the gentle God fearing man that I knew. He had been resurrected as something far more dangerous and sinister. "I'm not a blood sucker, I'm not a necromancer, none of those things. Stop asking questions you already know the answers to." I grew distracted as I saw another beetle run across Father Garcia's face. His jaws opened like a trap and snapped down on the bug with a disturbing crunch.

"With what I witnesses at the church that night would contradict your statement. Did you or did you not channel the power of the living dead even in the house of God?" the father asked. I started to answer, but he continued before the denial left my mouth. "If you could not, Olivia would not have been able to ride on your power and enter the church. If not for that power, Paul Isaac, I would not be standing before you with my head in my hands. Your power channeled the living dead and the living vampires that led you to putting a stake through my heart. Do not deny what you have become."

I felt sick to my stomach. "Even if I do possess those powers, it proves nothing. I don't drink blood, I can walk in the sunlight and I don't turn into a bat." I continued to keep close tabs on Asa. Out of all the oddities before me, he, for some reason, was giving me the worst of all the vibes.

"As you know, Isabella's brother was killed in one of the necro films by Sanguine. A lustful woman that could not control her bite. And I am sure you know by now that Peavey's daughter was in a sex film by NecroPussy."

"I knew Isabella's brother had been killed by a vampire, but I didn't know it had been in a necro film. Are you going to get to a point, Asa?"

He continued as if I had never interrupted him. "It is this film that has caused the deaths of two vampires at the Crowne Plaza. Question is, if you are guilty, then what is your motivation for wanting this film? One woman saw the film as revenge, the other as a way to save her brother. Now they both lie in a state of death."

I shrugged. "I don't give a damn about some film of a politician's daughter doing the horizontal dance with a cockroach." I tried to catch my breath. "As for Isabella, getting her head in a box wasn't all that big of a surprise. I told her that spending money trying to keep her brother alive was just waste of time."

Asa smiled wide, allowing those ancient fangs to show through. "Spoken like a true *Dracul Sang*." He stood in the moonlight and basked in the glow. "The film in question was stolen by your sweet Isabella Dunlawton shortly before she was fired from NecroPussy." Asa turned to Kincaid. "She planned on trading it for her brother's freedom by blackmailing Peavey."

I opened and shut my mouth a few times before collecting enough thought to complete a sentence. "So you're telling me that Isabella had the sex tapes Peavey was so hell bent on finding?"

Kincaid paced behind Asa. The young man that I had killed continued to simply stare at me as if he would strike at any moment. I would glance between him and the Magnum from time to time, hoping that he would figure out that I would kill him again if it was possible. So far it worked or he hadn't found the right moment to kill me yet. "For a short period of time, yes. Seems as though she contacted Mr. Peavey about having the tapes and wished to do business with him in exchange to keep them from surfacing during the upcoming elections. She was to meet with him shortly afterwards, but I am sure you can figure out the rest."

I felt the muscles around the wound in my side cramp as it began to heal. The more human I became, the less the silver blade remained lethal. Down side to it all was the more human I became, the more the pain became unbearable. I felt my strength leaving me. My legs urged me back to the ground. I refused. If I went to the ground, I knew I'd never get back up. I'd be dinner before I could even twitch.

The young man next to Asa now spoke. "Word among the vampires is that Peavey hired Inderia to hunt Ms. Dunlawton down, kill her, and retrieve the tape but never followed through on payment. Never double cross a vampire you are sleeping with." He moved toward me in a quick motion. My finger refused to back off this time and I fired. An ultra violet bullet blew through his right shoulder, but the man still stood before me as if nothing had happened. I made a quick move. Backwards. I saw the monsters before me starting to circle me. I tried to move, but couldn't. Too much power to overcome.

I continued to try and back myself out of the alley. In my heart, I knew I had no escape, but I didn't plan to just stand and allow them to be judge and jury and do nothing about it. "Being the all-seeing eyes and ears of the cockroach community, I have a feeling you know who the real killer is. Why not take your heads and find the fang head you're really after?"

The young man moved closer to me. My steps grew smaller as the circle around me closed. "But you are the *Dracul Sang* of the city and the burden of proof is on you."

I tried to speak in desperation, but they ignored me. I couldn't make rhyme or reason out of cockroach logic. I had pleaded guilty and still Angie's life remained on the line.

The smell of rotting meat filled my nostrils as the bodies around me decayed before my eyes. A slab of flesh slide from Albert Kincaid's cheek and fell to the ground inches from my feet. "It is time to call upon the Council of Paul Isaac. Innocent or guilty." I could see the white maggots dancing on his skin and suit jacket. I swallowed hard but remained stubborn as I looked at the skull's eyes. "I find you guilty."

The mother thing spoke up. "Guilty."

That was followed by the young man that I had killed. "Guilty."

Father Garcia was next. "Guilty as charged."

I heard Josh and Kincaid answer the same.

I looked to Asa with my Magnum flashing in all directions. I knew it would be about as effective as a water pistol, but I planned to go out in a blaze of glory. The former master looked at me with inquisitive eyes and that patented smirk. At seven foot tall, he practically blocked out the full moon on his own, reflecting the heavenly light across his bald head. He looked around at the others before landing back on me. "I can think of nothing more pleasant that to watch you die, Avenger. You are nothing. You are not a man, not a beast, not a vampire, but somehow you have become valuable to all three. Killing you would be the easy way out of your dilemma." His smirk turned into a grin. Those large fangs jutted out, inches from my throat. "But I owe you a favor."

I caught myself as I jumped in surprise. This big, overbearing, oaf owed me something? So many things ran through my mind, but I remained silent, which I think surprised Asa as much as it did me.

"When the police tried to frame me, you stood by my side. Reluctantly, I agree, but you did. Now I stand, reluctantly by you. I will find it far more amusing watching you live your life as a living master vampire than to throw it all away with a swift death." His eyes sparkled with mischief. A stronger man would have put the barrel of the Magnum against his own head, but I simply stood there like death's doormat. "Innocent. Like you, I do it with great reluctance. The vampire responsible must be stopped. The future of all vampires is written on the wall."

I could literally feel the power around me twist. I was able to shove it back in the direction it came. Unconvinced eyes looked at me and then to Asa. I couldn't tell which of us they hated more. Being new at all this, I stood there waiting for the next evil thing to happen. Had I survived? Or had I just stepped into something far worse than death?

25

An explosion of power knocked me to the ground. Mixed with the fatigue and pain from the wound, my body felt limp and unresponsive. Sweat poured from my eyes. My mouth so dry my tongue stuck to the roof of my mouth. I simply wanted to die in peace. But my better judgment told me that I couldn't just lie there and wait for the creatures to eat me. With all my might I turned over onto my back and stared back down the alleyway where the Council had been. That's right, had been.

I scanned the darkness in quick darts. I jumped each time I saw or heard anything move or rattle, but found nothing more menacing than old papers and hamburger wrappers. A soft wind blew. I could hear cars just out of sight as they moved along the grid of streets around me. I had no intentions of letting my guard down. If these things could somehow cheat death and return from the grave even after their hearts had been cut out and their heads removed, anything remained possible.

Even though my eyes only saw darkness and shadows I could feel it. Something still remained, watching and waiting. I did everything I could to convince myself of my own paranoia, but if I've said it once, I've said it a thousand times, being paranoid in my line of work keeps you alive a lot longer.

It's those in this profession that drop their guards and turn their backs that end up getting headstones carved out for them. I might be repulsive, hateful and a manic depressant, but in spite of it all, I didn't think of death as an alternative.

I ran my hand along the wound on my side. Tender to the tough, but at least it had stopped bleeding. Not being able to turn completely furry had probably saved my life. It started me thinking about my life and the things I took for granted. Being something between wolf and fang head left me with questions about my vulnerability. Silver and crucifixes could turn out to be deadly to me if I became too complacent. I hoped somewhere in the monster cocktail that made up my DNA I could find enough human to hang on to.

The more I thought about it, the more I wanted to rip my skin from my bones and get away from all the things that made me this way. And even that grew harder to define. I had become a lot of things and none of them all at the same time. A year ago, I hated to look in the mirror and see the reflection. Now, I wished to God I could become him again with no strings attached.

I could feel my strength trying to make a comeback. With well thought out movement, I began to sit up. My head spun, which caused me to think that even slow movements needed to be better choreographed. I did little more than drag myself along the ground as I gathered my clothing and weapons along the pavement around me.

"You're alive?" I heard the voice say.

I knew the voice all too well. I never looked up. Kansas stood at the mouth of the alley dressed in a long gray wool trench coat. His black dress shirt peeked from the opening. His faded jeans looked dirty and stained. To his credit, he looked better than I had seen him in months. Not good, not himself, just better.

His eyes looked at me with a mix of horror and disgust. Being naked in front of Kansas gave me a whole new set of icks. I cursed at myself as I reached for the leather trench coat to my right. In a quick hustle, I gathered my own jeans and put them on. "And just when I thought this night couldn't get any worse."

Kansas smiled as he meandered toward me. He looked up for a moment. "I thought the only full moon I would see tonight shined above us." He took another step toward me. The grin on his face evaporated. "Tell me it's all lies, Paul."

I grabbed hold of the building wall next to me and pulled myself vertical and pulled the jeans over my behind. My shirt looked like it had been through a shredder. I thought about not even putting it back on. My muscles remained lethargic and weaker than I hoped. Kansas seemed to always give me the incentive to find the inner strength needed to put as much distance between us as possible.

I leaned against the wall with my left shoulder. With my right foot, I scooted the 9mm closer. Bending down to pick it up wasn't an option yet. I found myself out of breath. Old age, smoking, out of shape, take your pick. "What lies, Zeke?"

My breathing came in gasps as I pulled the coat around me. Moonlight glowed on top of Kansas' balding head. Deep eyes looked back at me under well-manicured brows. Couldn't figure out why, but he almost appeared borderline sober.

"Rumor has it that you confessed to the murders at the Crowne that night. That you confessed to Quinn and the police of being the master vampire of the city. Things you conveniently forgot to tell me the night at the bar. Tell me it's a lie."

It took a while for me to really let it sink in as to what had happened to me in the last few hours, much less three days ago. The reality of it all hadn't hit me yet. Dreamlike visions of things my mind couldn't grasp. "It's true. Members of my Council met with me tonight, I guess you could say."

With apprehensive steps, he moved toward me. His pale skin, a beet red. Eyes wide and glassy. Fists balled with tension. Without warning or saying a word, he hit me so hard I nearly went down to my knees. The sting moved through my nose and across my face. My eyes watered. "Jesus, Zeke, what's that for?"

"With everything that me and my wife are going through right now and you do this to me? Become a vampire! I should kill you right here."

I wiped away the trickle of blood from my nose and put my hands out in defense. "You got it all wrong, Zeke. I did it to save Angie.

None of it is true. I didn't do anything to harm those people. You should know that."

His body language didn't change. "Why would I know that? We both know you're capable of it."

"Not that. I'm still on your side of things."

"Really?" He pulled out his Glock and pointed it at me. Nervous pacing began. "Talked to your ex tonight. Seems as though you've been hanging out with the blood suckers a lot lately. Tells me you're the Dracula whatever of the city."

I pushed myself away from the wall. Moving around was still not on the table. "*Dracul Sang.*"

Kansas stopped and stared at me. I made sure I stayed just outside of his aim. We stood roughly ten feet from one another. Far too close for my comfort. "Do you really think I care what you're called? Tell me it's all a lie, Paul. I swear if you're one of them, I'll kill you where you stand. I've lost everything because of those things. I won't cut you any slack on this."

"Put the gun down, Zeke. Let's talk about this. I told Quinn what I told him in order to keep them from killing Angie. That's all." My back pressed against the wall so hard my spine popped.

Tears began to roll down his cheeks. The Glock moved far more random than I liked. I tried to dodge it, but it seemed to follow my every step. "I came here to ask for your help on this case, but now that you're one of them, I can't think of anything I'd rather do than just watch you bleed out right here."

I had overestimated Kansas and his sobriety. He pulled out a small flask and took a drink with his free hand and returning it to the inside pocket of his coat. "If you only knew where I just came from. Now that you're one of them, I can't take you there."

I pulled my cheeks wide allowing him to see the inside of my mouth. "Do you see any fangs?" I pulled out a crucifix and held it out toward him. "If I were a roach, could I do this? Come on, you know better than to listen to vampires and ex's. Neither have any credibility."

The Glock pressed against my forehead. "I'll blow your head off right here!" he screamed.

Perhaps this is the way it should end. I never had the guts to do it myself. My way out. I could accept the consequences. "Do it," I said as I grabbed the barrel of the Glock. "You'll be doing me a favor."

His hands shook with anger, not fear. I could see it in his eyes, this would be no bluff. He could do it. His hatred for vampires had grown to such a level that I felt optimistic that he would do the dirty deed for me. "Don't push me, Paul." His words slithered between his gritted teeth.

"I don't have the guts to do it myself, Kansas. I'm begging you to put me out of my misery. I am the *Dracul Sang*. Do it!"

"Tell me you will kill them all if I tell you what I know." The barrel still against my forehead. I could feel him pressing harder and harder with each passing moment.

I thought about what I was doing. Selfish and stupid. If Zeke pulled the trigger and killed me, he stood a good chance of dying in prison for it. At the moment I didn't know where the law saw me. Human? Vampire? I couldn't let him do it. "Put the gun down. If for no one else, do it for Stephanie. You know me, I'll help you anyway I can."

It seemed to be working. I could see the wheels turning in his head. "Met some guys like us."

Like us? That could be a loaded statement. "Meaning?"

"Hate vampires as much as we do." He began to laugh hysterically. The barrel left my forehead. He began knocking the butt of the Glock against his own skull. Signs of stress, possibly. The Kansas I once knew didn't live here anymore. "You're going to laugh, but I've been seeing a shrink just like you. Joined a group."

"Good?" Didn't know what else to say to that.

His attention refocused on me. "The more we try to be different, the more we're alike I guess. You see a therapist, now I see one. Maybe it's the job, Paul. You used to be the one that hated the vampires and I tried to talk you down. Now look at us. Just the opposite. Had to find friends that felt about them like I do."

"She's going to pull through, Zeke. You have to believe that."

I don't think he heard a word I said. "They may have taken me off of the case, but that doesn't mean I can't snoop around and find things on my own. Talked to the people with Peavey's campaign, did some leg work and found out that a certain business has been financing his climb to the top."

"NecroPussy."

He looked surprised. "Yeah, how'd you know?"

"Been doing a little investigation on my own." Let's leave it at that for now.

"Seems Peavey had a thing for vampire porn stars. He had been seeing Inderia. I think she raised the zombies to kill him. He planned to stop her line of work if he made it to D.C." Began to pace again. "Two vampires have been discovered on video surveillance at the Crowne with her. From what I found out, I had been close but no cigar. Names are Dominic and Z. The other night when the zombies attacked, we found the body of Dominic. Chewed up." He put the Glock back in his holster. "After this, I'm going to get a search warrant for NecroPussy and see who's running that place these days. Seem to be hiding a lot more than just a few dirty movies."

Instant nausea. "Let's not jump to conclusions." I hesitated for a moment to gather my thoughts. "What do you mean you found Dominic chewed up?"

"Those in charge seem to think that's what the attack had been about. Looking for something at NecroPussy and killing Dominic, which as fate would have it, worked there as an actor, or whatever they're called."

"And Z?"

An evil grin hit his face. "We are interrogating him now."

"The police?"

He shook his head. "Not exactly. My new friends and I found him."

"What do you mean you found him?"

"He's going to tell us who the killer is. Like it or not."

"Where is he?"

"Not far from here."

Energy charged through me as I thought it through. My strength filled me so fast that it felt like mini explosions just under the skin. I moved past him. "You kidnapped a vampire? Are you really insane?"

The thought of catching and killing the roach responsible for raising the dead far outweighed my physical condition or possessions, but now, I found myself toying with the Magnum. The little voice in my head told me not to get involved, but I stood there like the idiot I am.

Kansas' hand reached into his front coat pocket. I pulled the Magnum up just enough to catch his attention. The look of surprise painted his face. "Got something I think you might want to see."

I lowered the gun again and took a step back. My form of compromise. His hand returned from the pocket and held two white fangs, stained red with dried blood. I felt my shoulder hit the wall to my left as I stared at the prize. "Fangs," was all I could get out. Pulling fangs from a cockroach about guaranteed a death sentence and a slow torturous one at that. For a vein head to feed it had to bite into a human vein and form the enzymes. Without its little hole pokers, the dirt napper would starve to death.

"Z's teeth."

I looked at the fangs for a long time. "What the hell have you done, Zeke?"

"Plan on getting him to confess that Inderia is our killer."

I grew more skeptical with each answer. "I want to see him."

Kansas stood stoic and lifeless as he studied me. "Perhaps I can arrange something."

26

LUCKILY, I had another set of clothes in the trunk of the 'Cuda. Something I had done for some time now. With as much blood as I got on me, and not all of it mine, I preferred to put as many layers between myself and it as I could. Not to mention the urban myth that if you get vein sucker blood on you, you can catch the virus. Science has proven this false, but still, I can't help but think about it. Thanks to heredity, I no longer had to fear catching the virus. I got mine naturally.

After re-dressing, I followed Kansas' Explorer across town. I tried to dismiss the gnawing feeling that we would both end up dead. Yeah, he had someone's fangs, but I had no way of knowing whose.

We ended up at a small meat processing building off of Kaley Street. To the naked eye, the place looked locked up for the night, but I could already feel the power coming from it. The hairs on my arms stood on end as if I had walked into a pocket of arctic air. It's a lesser known fact, but roaches are not fond of being around pigs or pork. Kind of like silver, it won't kill them, but it will keep them from wanting to put holes in your neck.

I got out and turned in circles and looked for anything that might be out of the ordinary. I trusted no one, especially when they had already threatened my life earlier in the night. Other than the occasional car driving by, there were no signs of life anywhere. I hadn't made up my mind if I found that to be a good thing or not.

Across the street, I stared at the hospital that illuminated the sky behind the large trees. I shook my head at the irony. If things didn't go well here in the next few minutes, the hospital would be one of two places I might end up. The other being the funeral home.

Kansas got out of his Explorer and motioned me to follow him. Like a lamb being led to slaughter I did. But unlike that fated animal, I had everything on me that I needed to level the playing field.

We walked up the loading ramp and Kansas unlocked the door. I could instantly smell the blood that slithered out of the opening. I found myself repelled and drawn in by the scent at the same time. My mouth watered to the point that I needed to spit, but I refrained for now.

Kansas stood about ten feet inside the doorway and looked back at me. Behind him, I could only see blackness, which made me more than just a little apprehensive. He grinned as he walked back toward me and turned on the light. "Thought you blood suckers could see in the dark." Something told me it hadn't been said in jest. I let it slide.

"Can you see this, Kansas?" I gave him the middle finger and stepped inside. I found the warehouse cold and death moved in many forms around me. My arms tingled with life that still gathered here. Sounds were amplified in the hollow room. The buzz of the overhead lights made me think I might have just walked into a hornet's nest for real. Each step I took produced loud echoes off of the distant wall.

Sides of beef hung in neat rows all around me. I came across a large container of cow heads, eyes staring into nothingness. I tensed. So many places to hide I hesitated to move. Only the sound of large refrigerator engines broke the silence. My mouth watered from the smell of both meat and blood. I constantly looked at my hands to make sure the were-virus remained in control. The last thing I needed right now would be another episode of the furry kind.

Glaring light fell mercilessly on the area. White painted walls and stainless steel equipment gave it about as much personality as a surgery room. Looking around, I grew impressed with how immaculate everything appeared to be. Large machines, designed to slice and dice watched over everything. Toothy blades grinned back at me, stained in dark red.

Ahead of me, I saw a figure hanging from meat hooks that had ripped through his shoulders. His head hung low as if passed out. A small pool of blood formed at his feet. I patted myself, taking an inventory of weapons. Even with the frosty breath that came from my mouth, I could feel sweat forming on my head.

"You do this, Kansas?"

His eyes remained fixed on the man at the far end. "With the help of a few of my friends. About time we pushed back." He continued to walk ahead of me, not waiting to see my reaction or hear my retort.

I gave it anyway. "Would have thought you had learned your lesson by now. Never feed the animals." I could feel his power move along my skin and I began to look through the maze of meat. I stopped to gather my thoughts and listened. My hand grabbed the Magnum and I tried to prepare myself for the violence that my mind created. I slunk low in search of feet. Nothing.

Kansas stopped just short of the figure that hung from the hooks and I joined him. From my right, another man appeared, dressed only in a pair of over-alls. "Paul Isaac." He held out his hand and gave a genuine smile. "Dave Bridgeford. Big fan." His grip nearly broke my hand. I guessed he weighed near three hundred pounds, middle age, mullet and beard. I had no doubt he had a Confederate flag on him somewhere.

"Who is this?" I asked as I waited for the feeling to return to my hand.

"I take it Kansas showed you enough to know this ain't no game?" He stopped in front of me, spitting tobacco juice on the floor next to me. "Seems as though we got a genuine zombie raiser here. Don't worry, we done took out his fangs. He can't hurt you none."

I could now see the vampire's face as he swung slightly from the hooks. Pale skin, painted in dark red around the lips from the impromptu dental work no doubt. Tips of the metal hooks broke through flesh and left it splintered in a number of directions. Trails of wet blood still oozed from the exit wounds. The undead piñata's eyes remained closed, but not dead. His power appeared weak. Didn't matter. Killing him only put him out of his misery. Shame. *"Dracul Sang,"* he whispered as he looked me up and down.

"I take it that you're the one that pulled his fangs."

Dave stepped to the side and admired his work. "Yep. Thought you'd find that more to your speed. Killed one or twelve before the laws. Damn liberals done let these things crawl all over us." Another spit. "Can't have prayer in school, but these things are allowed to kill as many of us as they want and nobody does a damn thing about it."

I looked to Kansas, "Not that I care, but you know that the police can still arrest you for his murder. Human law looks down on this type of interrogation." Honestly, I didn't care, but I wanted to plant as much doubt in Kansas' head as I could. Something told me I didn't hold the advantage.

"Don't go gettin' soft on us now, Isaac. Went to a lot of trouble to flush this one out." Dave's laughter echoed through the high ceilings. "I guess we got somethin' else in common. We both vampire executioners. Between you and me, I've killed my share of these things since the laws came to be. Ain't gonna let no politician tell me these things deserve any protection. What about our protection?"

I continued to survey the warehouse, ignoring Dave's attempt at bonding. "Do you have a license?"

Dave looked at me funny. "No." Splat. "Don't need no license to know what's morally right."

"Then you're looking at some big fines. 'And no, we aren't anything alike."

Kansas turned and looked up, absent of any emotions. "He's the porn star known as Z. One of Inderia's henchmen."

I looked at him in a much different light now. The man that hung from the hooks nearly got me killed and he didn't even know it. My attention returned to Kansas again, this time more careful of where I looked. "What makes you think he's the one that raised the zombies?"

Kansas moved to Z. He placed his hand on the hanging blood leech's chest. Z screamed with pain and danced in the air. As his mouth opened I could see that indeed, he missed a set of upper fangs. Dried blood decorated his mouth. He looked back at Kansas with wild eyes. "Z, so good to see you're still alive. Didn't want you to spoil all the fun."

Z shook his head frantically as he looked over to me. "Help me."

Kansas grabbed a large metal rod from the table behind him and smiled at me. "Know what this is?"

"No."

"Cow prod. They use it to move the cattle. Gives one hell of a shock, right, Z?"

Z looked back to me, "Please, *Dracul Sang*, mercy."

"Confess to Paul and I'll see to it that your death will be quick. If you don't cooperate with me, you'll hang here and slowly die of hunger as the rats eat your flesh." A different side to Kansas than I had been used to. He took the prod and jammed it against Z's rib cage. I saw the blue flame, heard the electrical charge. I cringed in disgust.

A bit harsh, I thought. I raised an eyebrow to Kansas as I moved to where I could look Z in the face. "Detective Kansas says he has you on video the night of the murders. Is that true?" I looked at his bare pale chest. I saw the points of the meat hooks peeking through the skin just under his collar bone. I now had all the confirmation I needed. The two men next to me had become vigilantes.

"I'll tell you anything you want to know. Just please let me go." Z's attention darted among the three of us. Somehow I had to convince Zeke and his new friend not to do anything stupid. Or at least not to dig their hole any deeper.

"Tell him what you have confessed to me," Kansas commanded.

"Peavey found out about a video his daughter and I made. Seems she wanted to get back at him for some real disgusting things he had done. At first, I planned on killing him, but after talking, realized he was worth more to both of us alive than dead. We planned on black-mailing him. He came into the studio and threatened to expose me and have me arrested and charged with false charges if I didn't give him the file. Inderia was furious when she found out and threatened to kill Peavey. I took the original file so that I had some sort of leverage.

Inderia and I went to the Crowne that night to talk money for the file. Peavey's daughter was already there. The plan was supposed to be, either he gave us what we wanted or we exposed him in front of his biggest donors. The way we saw it, he had no choice. Inderia drugged Angie and left her at the hotel, hoping everyone would think she had killed Peavey. We planned to plant evidence on her." He continued to lose his concentration each time Dave moved. Couldn't really blame him. I did the same thing.

"Peavey called your bluff. Inderia raised the zombies to kill him. Why didn't you plant the evidence on Angie?"

"That's just it. We didn't raise the zombies. Happened to show up at the same time we did. Neither of us had time to kill Peavey or plant anything on the wolf. We left her there thinking if she got eaten, it covered our tracks a little more. You have to believe me. We didn't do it. We were running for our lives just like everybody else."

"Where's the jump drive?"

Z looked at me with fear. "Dude, you don't want to know. Planted it for a later time. Told everyone that Peavey had it. End of story."

"Well Z, I hate to say it, but I don't buy your story." I lit a cigar to calm my nerves. A light breeze blew through the warehouse that made the sides of beef sway ever-so-slightly. But through my peripheral vision, the swinging carcasses looked like vein divers sneaking up on me.

"Your ex-girlfriend was in on it too."

I looked back to Z. "Ashley?"

The vampire shook his head. "No, the other one."

"Angie?"

Another shake. "The other one."

I drew a blank. For someone that didn't date, Z happened to come up with a lot of names. "Just tell me."

"Isabella."

More of a sexual encounter than a girlfriend, but I didn't challenge it. Her head still sat in a box in my attic. She had stolen valuable vampire art in order to save her brother's life, not to mention, tried to have me killed when I got to close to the truth. Having her involved didn't surprise me, but the details had me curious. "Talk."

Z licked the blood from his lips. "Isabella convinced Peavey that she had the original file. She wanted to cash in on his dilemma as well. They had planned to meet that night and exchange the video for money." He lowered his head. "See her and Inderia had a little scam going. Isabella's brother was killed and turned into a vampire in one of Inderia's necro movies. Isabella wanted money from NecroPussy Inc. to keep her brother alive. Inderia had laundered most of the money through her boyfriend Mr. Peavey and his campaign. Isabella appeared to be on the payroll of his staff, but in reality it was nothing more than bribery money. When that gravy train ran dry, Isabella planned to turn Inderia in. Those chicks were making things very complicated for everyone on the set."

"Inderia has the video?" I ignored the head comment completely.

Another shake of the head. "No. Or at least I don't think so. If she does, you'd know it by now. I had it when I went to the hotel that night. I lost my balls after the zombies showed up and I hid it where I thought no one would think to look."

Kansas moved in on him. "You're a lying little blood sucker. You know you and Inderia killed those people. We have you on video. Now confess and I'll make this painless." Again, Kansas' Glock rested against someone's head. "I want to hear it spew from your dead mouth."

Z started to scream. "I'm telling you the truth. We didn't kill anybody! Please, you have to believe me! We went there to strong arm him, blackmail him, but not to kill him."

"Kansas calm down," I added. I did my best to make my words as calm as I could. He could explode at any moment. "Don't do anything you'll regret." My attention went back to Z. "Where's the file now?"

Kansas had zoned out on me. "Do I look like I'm going to regret this?"

"Maybe not now, not tomorrow, but you will. Stephanie needs you." I tried to ease him back a step, but he remained solid. Intense stare, shaking hands.

"Talk or we'll splatter your brains all to hell," Dave added. His gun present in his hand.

I stepped between the two men and the vampire. "I need to know where the file is. You kill him and we have nothing on Inderia."

I knew I had to get Dave away from the situation. Kansas, I could talk down, but Dave happened to be a ticking time bomb. He hadn't come here for answers. He planned on making something bleed tonight. I knew his type. Macho man that wanted to have the head hanging above his fireplace.

"Kansas, guilty or not, this will be murder if you kill him. Let's let Ashley in on this and walk away." As bad as I hated to admit it, my head had already thought of ways to blame all of this on Dave. I just didn't like him.

Zeke looked to me. "You're pathetic you know. I bring you here to kill the vampire responsible for all those people's deaths and you want to let him go. Afraid I might kill him. You're a vampire aren't you? The Paul Isaac I once knew wouldn't think twice about this. The day they tell me you're a real vampire, I'll be calling on you. You can take that to the bank. You're not one of us anymore."

"Maybe not, but you can't do this. Let's get Inderia tonight. It will be all over. She's the one that raised those things, not this one. You're not revenging anyone's death by killing him. He's our only lead right now. Kill him and we have nothing on Inderia."

"We will if we kill them both. Kill them all."

I agreed on the inside, but needed Kansas to walk away with some sort of opportunity of staying out of prison. "Please, Zeke. It's not worth it. You're not thinking straight right now."

"They all deserve to die for what they did to my son and wife." He screamed loud. Gasping for air, saliva rolled out of his mouth. Shivering. "They all deserve to die! Hate to admit it to you, but this won't be the first one I've killed since they took my son."

Inside, I tried to convince myself that I hadn't heard that part. I grabbed the barrel of the Glock for the second time in the same night and slowly pulled it away from Z's chest. "I'll call Ashley. Walk away. Think it through."

He looked at me and the pain poured out. "I can't do this anymore, Paul. It's eating me alive." He collapsed to the floor. My body deflated as the intensity in the room evaporated. God what a night it has been. I crumbled next to Kansas and started to breathe again.

Above me, I heard a gunshot. Droplets of blood rained down on me. I spun out from under Z's shadow only to see Dave holding a gun against what remained of the vampire's skull.

27

I HAD A HUNCH.

Nothing more, nothing less. As fate would have it, the hospital we needed sat across from the meat packing plant. I could already feel the bile biting at the back of my throat. My fingers shook with fear, with anger and with the unknown. I had a gut feeling about something very dark and disgusting and it ate me from the inside out like some sort of paranormal cancer.

I brought Kansas along, but left the red necked idiot across the street to his own demise.

We crashed through the doors of the emergency room as I had always done in the past when headed to the morgue. Being a creature of habit, it had been my comfort zone and most here were so self-absorbed with their own issues, seeing a six foot six man with a leather trench coat running by barely registered.

My knees buckled as I caught sight of Frank Price. A man that I admired most among those still living. But also a man that I had the most guilt associated with.

Price stared back at me. Neither of us knew what to say. I had helped kill his grandson not long ago. Given better circumstances, I would probably have let the young man go because of his grandfather, but it became a life or death situation. Price retired shortly after that and we hadn't talked since.

With apprehension, I held out my hand to him. "What the hell do you want?"

I retracted the hand. Kansas stood next to me and acknowledged Price. "You look good."

Price shook with anger. I knew him well enough to know when he had reached the point of no return. "You too killed my grandson and now you think you can come in here and everything's going to be okay?" He pushed me backwards. "You killed him!"

Anyone that hadn't seen us come through the emergency room before, knew we were there now. Sets of eyes drilled into us. I turned to face Price again. "We had no choice, Frank. You know that."

"I hope they kill you slow." His large body shook. The words didn't offend me. I deserved them.

"I am sorry, Frank."

His lips quivered as he fought against the tears. "Sorry. You're sorry. Well, that's comforting. I'll let my wife know that the man responsible for killing her grandson know that you're sorry. I'll be sure to let Josh's mother and father know that shit happens from time to time." He moved closer to me. I expected a fist to be in my future. "The day gathered his ashes, I remember looking at my wife and knowing there was nothing I could do that would console her. Even now, she sits in her chair at home and holds a picture of Josh and rocks and cries. It's only days until Christmas…" It took a while for him to gather his thoughts. "It's only days until Christmas and the thought of putting up a tree or lights on the house or even buying gifts have never entered our minds. You took all of that away from us. Not the vampires, you."

"They had already turned him. It was either you or him that night. You have to believe that."

"You should have killed me!" He beat his chest. "You should have killed me! Josh had his whole life ahead of him. Taken just as he became a man." He wiped his eyes. "You didn't even have the guts to come to the funeral and say you were sorry to us."

"I've been thinking about you. I know I should have called by now."

"Call? You think I want to talk to you. Ever? You killed my grandson."

It became clear, nothing I said would make a difference. I didn't blame him. What had happened to him had been the reason I turned out the way I did. I thought of my own parents and how I felt. I thought about Father Garcia and Ashley. I had walked away from my fiancé for the same fears. I thought about Angie.

I remembered Price coming to my house that night. How I reluctantly told him I would help him. Could I have done more? Done it faster, better more efficient? One thing for sure, it didn't matter now. All the things I had done wrong had come back to haunt me. "You came to my house that night remember?"

"Yeah, to save his life."

"He was already dead, Frank. Paul did everything he could to save Josh's life. You know that." Unlike me, Zeke's tone rang out very matter-of-fact.

"How's your wife?" Price asked.

"The same." Now his voice fell defeated and thin.

Price's glare returned to me. "Keep an eye on him, Zeke. I'm not convinced he didn't have anything to do with your wife and son's kidnapping. If he can kill an innocent boy, he's capable of just about anything."

"Frank..." I started.

Price ignored me. "Watch out for this one. He'll go up there and kill her too." Without more words, he pushed through us and walked away. I wanted to go after him. Talk to him, but I had nothing to change his mind, I couldn't take it back, and time didn't allow it.

Kansas and I watched him disappear through the sliding doors. He looked back to me. "Why are we here again?"

"Call it a hunch."

Zeke shook his head. "No. You don't do hunches. You torture things until they tell you give you answers. I don't care where your 'hunch' is bleeding to death right now, but I do want to know what you think you know."

I weighed my options. "I think our zombie puppet left us something with Peavey."

Kansas rubbed his eyes and took in a deep breath. "Care to elaborate?"

Again, I weighed my options. I could look stupid now, or stupid later and I hoped for a free pass to make it later. "We need to take a look at Peavey's body. I'm probably barking up the wrong tree, but it's the only thing I have to go on right now."

"So you want to tamper with evidence," Kansas finished. "Good to see the Paul Isaac I know has made a mild comeback. You had me worried back at the packing plant."

"Zeke, you know I wouldn't ask for this if I didn't think I was on to something."

He looked at me and rolled his eyes. "What you're on, Isaac, is thin ice." Without further agreement, Kansas turned and strolled down the long hallway that would lead to something sick and twisted. And that was if we were lucky. "I can't get you clearance into that room on this one."

I pulled out my cell phone. "I know who can."

28

THE MORGUE HAD GONE through quite a few changes in protocol and personnel since Dr. Montgomery worked here, but it still had the eeriness of death. It never took sides or made exceptions, no matter how rich, evil or perfect we were. This room had a lot of ghosts for me. Memories of wooden stakes going through the hearts of unfortunate souls declared to be undead. Above it all, this room represented what I had become and what I dealt with.

Through a series of informal negotiations and badge flashing, Ashley had retrieved the body of Dennis Peavey. I stood there trying to build up enough courage to go through with my hunch. My mouth watered as I tried to swallow the bile in my throat.

"Well?" Ashley finally asked. She had the patience of a gnat. It shook me back into reality. And I wasn't totally happy about it.

I unzipped the bag and carefully removed the head, doing my best not to shake with disgust. The body rocked back and forth a few times before coming to a stop. My focus darted to his pale gray face. The eye lids were closed as if he had fallen into a deep sleep. I took another deep breath as I convinced myself that those same lids were not going to suddenly open and stare back at me.

I unzipped a little farther as sweat formed on my brow. In front of me, I saw mangled meat held in form by the bones. Practically no skin remained. Large bite marks that isolated islands of flesh. Ripped muscle twisted and strained against the violent act of days earlier.

My heart began to pound harder. I wanted to be wrong, but in order to track down my killer, it had to be done. I swallowed hard and vowed to push through.

With great planning, I turned the head to look at the large gash in his neck. Strings of flesh and muscle refused to give way at first. Applying a little more pressure, I could here and feel the popping and tearing of rigor mortis defeat.

I grabbed a pair of latex gloves and put them on. I looked up to Kansas and Ashley Vaccarro and saw the horror on their faces. In some twisted way, it made me smile. Agents that had seen every twisted thing man and monster could do, but now looked at me as if I had become Dr. Frankenstein.

My hands moved closer to the opening of the severed head. Fingers twitched with the anticipation of touching dead cold flesh. It hit too close to vampire flesh in my opinion. I took a deep breath and held it. Throwing up became a real possibility. I grew lightheaded as I wiped my brow with my forearm.

The cold flesh reached my fingertips before they actually touched it, but I couldn't turn back now. I tilted the head to get a better angle at the opening and worked my hand inside the muscle and flesh. I tried to keep my mind free from what my hands were doing. I shivered, not from the cold abyss I searched, but from pure disgust.

"What the hell are you doing, Paul?" Ashley asked. I wondered if my face reflected the shock and awe I saw on her mug. "Please tell me you haven't gone off the deep end."

"Making new nightmares," I replied as I continued the cavity search. My fingers forced together in a tight knot as they inched along the cold throat. I watched as my forearm disappeared inside Peavey's head. I had to push with all my strength to move forward in the narrow passageway. With each force, I could feel muscle pop against the strain as I pulled it away from tendons and bone.

Kansas continued to watch the door, then shot a glare back at me. I knew there wasn't much time. Not from the hospital staff by any means, but from the two officers before me. I had given them no more information than that I had a hunch about the killer. Kansas' patience began to show stress cracks.

"I hope you have a reason for this," Kansas said as he choked.

"Go back up and sit with Stephanie. I'll stay here with Paul and help with…whatever the hell he's doing," Ashley looked to me for answers. I simply shrugged and nodded to Kansas in agreement.

"I know this time tomorrow that would have been great advice, but I can't wait to see just how far this circus goes." Kansas cleared his throat in an attempt to keep from vomiting.

I withdrew my hand from Peavey's throat and placed the skull back on the gurney along with the pieces of flesh that had broken off and clung to the latex gloves. My gut feeling grew more distant. "I thought that it would be hidden in the head somewhere. Like with Isabella, the blood munchers seemed to like to use the heads of their victims as trophies." In tandem, I thought it might be in Isabella's head as well. After all, it had been sent to me personally.

But I shook away the thoughts of doubt. This attack had been one of revenge not simple violence or feeding. The monster had attacked all those at the reception had real issues with the Peaveys. Ms. Dunlawton had simply bit off more than she could chew and it had caught up with her.

"I'm afraid to ask if you found what you're looking for?" Ashley added.

I looked at Peavey's body and took another deep breath. The thoughts of going in again made me sick to my stomach. It would have been easier for me to stick my hand inside a meat grinder than the man's abdomen if given the choice, but I knew that to leave with nothing now would give Kansas and Ashley proof that I was certifiably insane.

"What the hell are you looking for?" Kansas asked again. I could tell by his voice that my time was running out. Unlike Ashley

Vaccarro, the game had grown old and tiring. "You've lost it this time, Isaac."

I never answered and pulled away a large flap of flesh from Peavey's side that allowed me access to the gut work. Not a lot of the vital organs remained. Inside, were nothing more than a loose fitting network of muscles and tissue mixed with secretions of blood and bile. I coughed as I took in an unappealing odor.

My fingers hit something slick as they worked through the stomach. I could tell without seeing that it wasn't flesh or bone. Something foreign hidden inside the muscle walls. As I grasped the object, I grew scared and relieved. With my other hand I pulled away more of the tattered stomach wall and freed my prize.

It wouldn't prove my sanity, but it would prove my hunch to be correct. I looked at Kansas as I held the flash drive. Wrapped in a sandwich bag, I began clearing away the dried debris from around it.

"I'm afraid to ask," Kansas said as he gawked at the shiny object. He looked at me as if I had just preformed some sort of twisted magic trick.

"It's a flash drive," I added.

"I know what it is, but how…?" The words just seemed to have been caught in his throat. I had no doubt that I would have reacted exactly the same. No I take that back. I would not have been close to as calm as Kansas was.

"I told you. It was a hunch. Dennis Peavey's body was the only one that wasn't torn into pieces too small to measure. The zombies weren't full. His death was supposed to be this way. Our night crawler had something special in mind for him." I held the flash drive in my hands as if I had just found the Arc of the Convenient. As I looked at it, I thought about the twisted truth. Hundreds of people died because of it. And most of them had no idea that it existed. Simply a case of being in the wrong place at the wrong time. With great care, I removed the latex gloves and threw them away. In my mind, I had blocked the next two hours dedicated to washing and scrubbing my hands with as many bars of soap as I could find. "Question now is, why did the daisy pusher kill Peavey like this and why did he leave this flash drive for us to find."

"I don't know whether to arrest you, have you committed, or thank you." Ashley said, moving closer to take a look at the treasure before us.

29

"I suppose you're going to tell us what we don't know," Ashley Vaccarro finally said as she looked back toward Kansas. She looked at what had been Peavey's body. "Now that we are all accomplices and doing something outside the boundaries of ethical behavior." With a slow, methodical glare, she turned his attention to the baggie in my hands.

Her fingers reached out to take the baggie. I held tight. If anyone else died because of this jump drive, I wanted it to be me.

Ashley spoke. "You know withholding or tampering with evidence is against the law. I don't have to negotiate with any of you in order to get the flash drive if I wish."

"Are you sure you're willing to die for the evidence?"

"I have been going through the things of Dennis Peavey. His finances, reports, phone calls and messages. I'm sure it is no surprise to any of you that whoever raised the zombies and killed Peavey and the party guests had a personal vendetta against him. This attack was not a random killing." She gave a toothy grin. "I know you'll find it hard to believe, but I'm glad you have it. Hopefully it will answer many of the questions we all seek." She looked down at Peavey's body. "A lot of people died for it."

"Like with any politician it comes down to votes and sex," Kansas added.

"Question for all of us is, how did it get inside Peavey?" I looked to Kansas. Neither of us said a word. I didn't think Ashley would be as accommodating with our method of interrogation.

Ashley shook her head. "Let's play What I Know, What you Know." Ashley glanced at the thumb drive again. "I talked with those that knew Peavey the best and found out that he had been having an affair with a porn star by the name of Inderia. Familiar, huh? Anyway, come to find out Peavey's daughter had been threatening him over money. Rumor is that there's a tape of Peavey and possibly Inderia in compromising positions and Peavey's daughter knew about it. At first I thought she might be involved, but she's dead too, which kind of stomps out that theory. If the thumb in your hands is indeed the one of Peavey and Inderia, we might be able to bring Inderia in for questioning and get a search warrant for the Risen Sins strip club where she works."

I did my best to make light of the ugly situation in front of us. "I call checking out the strip club. You know, for evidence."

Ashley rolled her eyes. "My informant says Peavey was offering half a million dollars for the evidence. But in order to hide his tracks, he wanted a few people gone. Including his daughter and another vampire. My guess is that they were blackmailing him over the video."

"So you found a paper trail and cash leading to someone?" I asked. "Who?"

"Peavey never planned to pay for the killings. Instead, he simply planned to distance himself from the killer, knowing the chances of anyone going to authorities were slim to none. After negotiations fell through, our killer sent a message to all those involved that reneging on a deal leads to unfavorable results. In an act of rage, the vampire raised the dead and attacked the party. Like I told you, we already have Inderia on surveillance. "

"Let's go kill a very bad little stripper," Kansas said as he opened the morgue door. Ashley started to follow.

"Wait!" Knowing what Z had told me and what Ashley had said, I knew something didn't fit. I looked at the baggie and opened it, pulling out the thumb drive. "Before we go out all guns blazing, aren't any of you curious as to what's on this thing?"

"It's a stripper polishing off a politician," Ashley answered. It took me by surprise. She never used to talk like that. It must have shown on my face. "What? It's true."

"Go get your stripper, I want to take a look and see if there might be more. If I find something, I'll call you." The talk with Z played in my head. Time to find out who's been lying to me to save their ass.

30

I THANKED God Kansas and Ashley Vaccarro had decided to go without me. I worked better alone. Opportunities sometimes get compromised when you have to stay within the limits of the law. But more times than not, I had found that my tactics worked much better than theirs. I never worried about minor things like cockroach rights or probable cause. I found probable cause very simple. If I found fang marks, a neck biter had *probably* caused it.

I held the flash drive close to my chest as if some phantom figure might emerge from the hallways of the hospital and take them from me. I kept my body on high alert for any signs of hidden power.

My eyes scanned the office areas for any unused computer. It wouldn't take a long look at me to tell that I wasn't staff material. Add in the fact that I would potentially be looking at a necro-porn and I had set myself up for explanations that I knew no one would buy.

My luck held out. I spotted a small, vacant room to the right. One desk, one computer, no peeping eyes. My plan would be simple, as most of them are. I'd lock myself in the office and hope to Baby Jesus that I figured this all out without having to watch the whole thing.

According to Feelgood, I had issues with sex before all of this, add on watching what might be on the flash drive and I multiplied my sessions by infinity. I shook my head as I thought about what my life had become.

My mind raced with the infinite possibilities of how I would get caught and what I would say. My heart raced and my stomach grew queasy as I stared at the thumb drive again. Could there really be secrets on this thing worth people's lives. What would I see that some twisted monster would be willing to kill in order to protect.

I sat in the no frills blue office chair and tried to catch my breath. I listened to the various noises and voices just on the other side of the door, knowing at any moment a hand could reach for the handle.

My obsessive compulsive behavior had me locking and re-locking the door several times only to return to the chair and repeat the act all over again. I procrastinated as long as I could. Sweat poured from my brow. Every nerve jumped just under my skin.

Sitting back down for the final time, I placed the thumb drive in the computer. To give myself added privacy, I muted the sound. Blaring orgasmic pleasure just might draw the wrong attention.

As the movie started, I saw a young woman standing in front of the camera, still dressed. Peavey's daughter, I assumed. I had never seen a picture of her. She looked to be about twenty or so and even though it had probably been the power of suggestion, looked like Peavey in a way.

Looking closer, I could see a certain sadness in her face. She looked tired and almost sick. By looking at her, I could tell, at one time, she had been a very beautiful woman. Only a shell of that person still existed.

As the camera zoomed closer, I could see bite marks along her shoulder. Roach bite marks. I grew sick. Not only did the woman have signs of drug use, but also had been feeding the monster I would have to hunt down and kill. My stomach turned as I watched her. Flashes of what I had seen at the Crowne rushed back into my memory. The woman I looked at, now rested in a morgue.

Her lips moved as she looked into the camera. More sounds of people walking by, just feet away from me. I watched the door as I did the unthinkable. My hand reached for the mouse and clicked on the sound icon, pulling the level low, then unclicking the mute button.

"...I'm a dirty girl, but tonight, I will make sure that you never get away with it again. You can kiss your political dreams goodbye." Rebecca Peavey's words were filled with anger and hatred as she spoke to the camera. She wore a white mini-skirt, already revealing more than it should. She appeared high on something.

"You got away with molesting me for all those years, now I'm about to show you what it will do to you. I'm sure all of your political supporters are going to love seeing this as they realize what a piece of scum you are." She licked the camera and gave it the middle finger, before taking a few steps backwards. Rebecca stared into the lens for a few seconds before doing a strip tease. First, she removed her white blouse, one button at a time in as titillating a fashion as possible. Milk white breasts now sat inside a lacey white bra. Light reflected across her young stomach as the top was tossed to the floor.

"Nice and slow, just the way you liked it, right daddy?" I sat back in the chair as I felt the repulsed feeling grow in me like vines. She had planned on destroying him though a sex tape and confession to the world all at the same time. My mind jumped from place to place as I thought about it. If what Becky said about her father rang true, it served him right that he had been eaten alive by zombies. Two wrongs don't make a right, but if it eliminates a scum bag, I'm willing to look the other way.

I shook the thoughts from my head. Dennis Peavey might have deserved what he got in the end, but there were others that didn't deserve to check out the way they did. And even if they had deserved it, it didn't take away the fact that there was a daisy pusher out there with not only a vendetta, but also raising zombies.

Rebecca continued her strip tease act, now in nothing but bra and dental floss playing the part of panties and stiletto heels. I watched as shadows moved against the wall behind her against the over exaggerated light on her. My pulse began to race. Even on film, I could feel the evil. Something dark and sinister lurked just out of the eye of the camera.

Her hands reached behind her back to unsnap the bra as she smiled and looked at something to her left. Those sultry eyes shot back to the camera. "And now for you, lover, something special. You've told me your darkest fantasies, now you shall have them on film for all eternity." With that said, she stepped out of her remaining attire and moved to one of the make shift sets and crawled on the bed, where a male figure already rested. "Thought I would keep it in the family. It's the least I could do after you broke my heart." Again her voice filled with rage.

I found myself bent as close to the monitor as I could. "Dominic," I said to myself out loud. My first thought was that he was the one raising the dead, but something told me there was more to it than that. I could see a roach revenging the honor of his human lover, but that didn't fit Dominic. He looked to be nothing more than a prop being used for sex. Revenge sex.

The two began their escapades in the bed. Lips formed against the other's. Tongues exploring part of the body that no man should ever go. Heavy breathing turned into purrs and then into screams of passion. I found myself reaching for the control to lower the volume again. I felt dirty and voyeuristic as I continued to watch under the mask of twisted detective work.

I cringed as he worked down the front of her body. Unlike most that would view this type of filth, I knew that at any moment those kisses could turn deadly. In the back of my mind, I continued to reassure myself that she lived. Hell, she had to.

Rebecca continued to moan with escalating pleasure as I sat back in the chair and tried to breathe. I stared at the ceiling, afraid to watch Dominic feed from her. My eyes glanced down from time to time as the heat of pleasure distracted me. "Brotherly love?" Again I said it as I thought out loud. Was it possible that Peavey had a vein sucker as a son that had also molested Becky? Anything could be possible at this point and I knew I had a whole new level to the word *shock* about to slap me in the face.

I pictured Dennis Peavey's gnarled body. Bits of flesh and bone loosely formed in the shape of a body. His face red with stained blood, most of the skin sliced and removed. Only the muscle gave shape to the human form it had been. A large pool of blood spread out along his form, gathering reflected light.

More audible pleasure oozed from the speakers. It distracted me back to my dirty reality. I looked at the woman on the screen performing oral acts on not only Dominic but now another fang head that had joined them. Hands moved across bodies and each indulged in the pleasures of the others.

My mind returned to the memories of the crime scene. Gratuitous violence and death. I wiped away the beading sweat on my forehead. The room felt a hundred degrees. More voices just out of reach of my perverted world. I stopped and held my breath again and again, convinced that I heard a hand touch the handle.

I stuck on the word VICTORY written on the wall. *Why would the killer write that word?* I thought. Victory from what, or for whom? I studied it until my vision grew blurry. I refused to allow the groans and screams coming from the speakers to distract me.

My mind zoomed in on the word. Frantically written. Smeared with desperation. I hit pause on the movie as I sat up in the chair. Trails of blood tracked from the 'Y' in four small grooves.

More to be written.

Unfinished.

I hadn't been looking at the words of the killer, but letters Peavey had written himself with his own blood. My hands shook with denial. I shook my head. My fingers gripped the desk so tight, it began to break.

The room that had felt like a hundred degrees moments ago, now plummeted. I could feel the cold sweat move down my spine. Not only had the answer hit me like a dump truck, but the coffin sleeper I would have to face, I knew would be a bitch to kill.

31

WITH DEMANDING SPEED, I ejected the thumb drive from the computer. My mind grew distracted with the visions of slaughter as they mingled with the certain death that I knew would still come.

After placing the thumb drive in the front pocket of my jeans, I made as quick of a getaway as I could. I feared I would pass out as I made my way through the sea of doctors, nurses and patients walking against my run. Sounds and vision became nothing more than blurred sensations, people became nothing more than faceless barriers. I took an inventory of the weapons I had on me. I called Ashley and Kansas and told them where to find me.

Next, my hands locked on the cell phone and called the next piece of the puzzle. As I looked down, my fingers felt three times as wide as they should have been. Thought moved at an agonizing pace. It felt as though I had been captured in a dream, unable to navigate with any speed. I trembled so badly, I nearly dropped the phone.

All my effort and strength relied on me finding Feelgood on speed dial. I moved across the lobby of the hospital and shoved the automatic doors open. I hit the cool December air. Around me, I could see the festive signs of the holidays and simply shook my head in a terror that only I knew. I nearly threw the phone as I got her voicemail for the third time in a row. She had the answer to a few of my questions before I started my assault on the cockroach in question.

I never stopped dialing the number until I reached her office. Before the 'Cuda's muscle could come to a stop, I bailed out the door and ran at full throttle toward the door. I felt numb. My mouth became so dry I couldn't swallow. What if's ran through my mind at breakneck speed. Still, I had gaps in my theory that if I remembered right, Feelgood would have the answers to.

My chest squeezed so tight I expected me heart to burst at any moment. I thought about what I had seen on the thumb drive. A part of me hoped I had jumped to conclusions. By being wrong would allow me to have the smallest of slivers of not having to come face to face with one mean son-of-a-bitch.

I opened the door to the lobby of Feelgood's office on the first floor. It appeared she learned her lesson. Jumping out of a second story window with fur balls on your trail isn't as much fun as you're led to believe. A row of chairs outlined the room much like any other doctor's office. A table sat in the middle with a pile of magazines for anyone that wanted to know who had been caught sleeping with whom. Soft classical music played in the background, soothing enough that you almost forgot she represented blood drinkers.

The receptionist looked up with eyes wide and full of questions from behind a glass window. Around me, patients began to scramble, not knowing if I had arrived for a kill or not. It kind of made me wonder what they might be guilty of. I gave the room a quick sweep and made sure that the monster I had to come face to face with was nowhere to be found. The traces of power in the room were nothing out of the ordinary, but tonight, they would all get a free pass if they behaved themselves.

"Where's Feelgood?" I asked. I never waited for an answer. I didn't have time.

"She's in a meeting," the thin, woman said as she started for the door between me and the inner rooms. She grew a brain, thought better of it and sat back down. I heard her scream and yell something about not being allowed beyond this point, but nothing she had to say would stop me.

There had been just enough commotion that the good doctor opened the door her office. I could tell by the strange look on her face my presence had not been expected. Especially like this. Usually when I came here, I kicked and screamed, but not today.

"What the hell are you doing?" she yelled in a hushed voice.

She started to take a step towards me, but with the inertia I had already built, I crashed into her, knocking her back a few steps. "We need to talk," I said as I pushed her back through the door.

Inside, I found two patients, one male, one female. They looked at me, not sure what to do. They exchanged looks at one another, to Feelgood, then landed back on me. "You can't just barge in here like this, Paul!" the doctor said. This time with a bit more balls.

"Get out," I said to the two fang heads. Needless to say, they did as told, glad to make it out alive. Something told me they wouldn't be back or cause me any trouble tonight. Relieved to know when they had received a free pass.

"This better be…" Feelgood started.

"Important?" I finished. I shook my head. "Don't worry, it's about as important as anything you can imagine." I saw the controlled rage in her eyes, but she kept a safe distance. We had had enough therapy for her to know when to talk and when to shut up. "The other night when I changed the tire for you, you said something and I want to make sure I have it right."

"What's this about?"

I moved in on her. She sat down in her chair and leaned as far away from me as she could. I leaned across the desk, my arms rigid against the dark wood and stared into her eyes. "We were talking about some roaches having certain gifts."

"Paul, please refer to them properly." She placed her hand up to her temple as if fighting off a headache. Coincidence I'm sure. Her long hair covered her face like the Great Oz behind the curtain.

"Do you remember!" I shouted.

Her head darted up, revealing that face I had come to love to hate.

Pupils wide with hate. For a second, I had been distracted by eyebrows plucked and replaced with ones made by some sort of magic marker, I was guessing. Strange. "Yes, of course. What's this all about?"

"You said Victor had a certain gift."

Feelgood's attitude began to change. Agitation grew in her body language. I could see those impregnable walls being built before my eyes. Not a good sign in order to get the information I needed.

I stepped around the desk to gain a closer look at her. I saw it in her eyes that she wanted to move away, but held still for the time being. "You said that he had the ability to raise the dead, and you referred to him as Dr. Yancey. Am I right so far? Victor's last name is Yancey?"

"Paul, this is ridiculous." She started to move around the corner of the desk. I pulled the arm of the chair and drug her back to me. "Does he have a brother?"

"A what?" Now the look was confused. "Have you lost what little mind you have?"

"Does he?" I yelled.

"I can't tell you that. Not without a…"

"Court's order?" I looked behind me and saw Kansas standing there holding a piece of paper.Feelgood turned to meet Kansas. "What's this really about, Detective Kansas?" Her tone grew softer, but full of apprehension. I could already read it on her face. She began to come to the same conclusion I had. A no win situation for the shrink. Feelgood turned to me. "I honestly think your soul purpose in life is to ruin my reputation and practice."

"Answer Paul's questions, please." Ashley added as she moved into the door frame. Just her being here led me to believe I was on the right track. I saw the flamethrower on her hip holster and made note of it.

Feelgood looked at the paperwork in his hand and reluctantly dropped her guard. "Yes, his name is Dr. Yancey and yes he has a brother. What has he done?"

"Was he a fang head too?" I already knew the answer, but needed to hear it for myself.

She closed her eyes and shook her head. "Yes, he has a brother that is a vampire. Is Dominic in some sort of trouble?"

"You could say that. He's dead," Kansas said as he moved deeper into the room.

I looked at Zeke Kansas. The questions rested on my lips, but I still had trouble spitting them out. I needed the answers, but feared the answers. I begged myself for a different conclusion. "It wasn't VICTORY written on the wall. It was VICTOR Y."

I felt myself getting sick as I said it. Ashley shook her head. "Dennis Peavey was trying to tell us who made the mess. He wrote Victor's name on the wall before he died."

I couldn't get the thoughts and images of the necro movie out of my head. The questions poured out of me like water. "Inderia didn't set up the murders. Rebecca did."

Another quick smile from Kansas. "Dennis Peavey was far from being an innocent man in the privacy of his own home. Rebecca tried to blackmail her father before the elections with accusations of molestation. Seems our little angel had quite a large cocaine habit and needed to pay off some mounting debts to some very dangerous characters. She told her father she would go public with the story unless he paid her the money she needed. Unfortunately, Rebecca had a dirty little secret of her own. She and Dr. Victor Yates were secretly having an affair and her father found out about it. He called her bluff. Threatened to tell her fiancée about everything from the affair, the cocaine habit, the movie, the debt. Victor broke off the love fest on the orders of Quinn, who saw the scandal detrimental to the vampire community. Even bigger problem was Peavey thought Isabella had the movie file, not Rebecca. Becky only had empty threats."

"Everyone had a smoking gun," I said more to myself than anything.

Ashley continued, "Rebecca had been out of control at the end. To get back at daddy and Victor at the same time, she made the movie with his brother, Dominic. Victor found out and killed Dominic. That's why we had the second attack of zombies the other night. Meant to kill Dominic and continue the heat on Paul as the true killer. Victor thought the thumb drive might still be at NecroPussy and trashed the place that night while everyone was focused on the zombie attacks."

"Victor raised the zombies?" Feelgood mumbled.

Kansas turned his attention to her. "Yes. Now the only way to bring this all to an end is to kill Victor." He hesitated for a moment.

Feelgood bolted toward Kansas. I had a feeling that fact might just put a large dent in her, You Can Rehabilitate a Cockroach therapy. "You can't really be serious about killing Victor can you? Sounds like everyone got what they deserved." It fell out of her mouth before she had time to stop it. She looked at me with a horrific look.

Ashley opened her mouth to say something, but I beat her to the punch. "Can't save them all, Feelgood." I pulled a wooden stake from my trench coat and looked at it. For no other reason than to get a rise out of the doctor. "Do you know where Victor is?" I asked Kansas.

Ashley gave a single nod. "Getting ready to kill Mayor Lopes I would assume." She said it with about as emotion as a kid asking for a second helping of broccoli.

Feelgood and I both snapped to attention with a synchronized, "What?"

A shrug. "Ms. Peavey having no other way out, contracted Victor to kill her father and planned to cash in on the insurance money. Victor wanted money upfront. Seeing that Rebecca wasn't of the most upstanding type, he wanted a down payment. To make the arrangement complete she contacted Mayor Lopes. She offered sexual favors, shall we say, in exchange for the money needed to pay Victor. Lopes secretly saw Peavey as a soon-to-be rival for his position and agreed to secure the payment. But things, as you know, went wrong. Victor raised the dead in order to kill Peavey. Now Lopes wants to distance himself from the deaths and refuses to pay Victor the money he still owes." Ashley gathered her thoughts. "My personal opinion is that Victor intended for the zombies to kill everyone, including our little starlet. He had a lot of hatred for Rebecca after seeing the movie. I think he wanted them all dead for a variety of reasons."

I replaced the stake in its holster. Checked the Magnum for bullets. I had already done it once, but old habits die hard. In my head, I said a little prayer knowing that my chances of survival against Victor weren't as favorable as I would have liked. I knew killing him would take everything I had. I had tried to kill him several times, only to find myself with most of the bruises and broken parts.

"You won't need that," Kansas said nonchalantly. I looked at him and waited for an answer. "We will find the zombies before we find the vampire." He pulled up one of the flame throwers that he carried and handed it over to me. "You're going to need one of these to burn your way through to Victor. I have larger ones in my car."

I took hold of it and tried to control my breathing. "How are we going to find Victor?"

Kansas smiled wide enough that his large fangs showed. "We follow the screams."

32

I HAD FOLLOWED the taillights of Ashley's BMW from Feelgood's office on Orange Avenue to the lower end of Bat Town, and parallel parked just a block from Church Street. My mind played out so many scenarios that would leave me dead. Distraction the only thing I had going for me.

Ahead, I could see the massive amount of police vehicles and crowds of people so thick that they almost sucked the lights out of the night. As I got out, I became surprised and shocked that I didn't hear sirens wailing or people screaming. With this amount of police activity, I assumed Victor and his zombie army had already struck. I grabbed the Magnum and started to move in the direction of the mob. But the nothingness I saw and heard left me confused. Oh, there were plenty of sounds, but nothing that indicated death and mayhem. Instead, I could hear the sounds of what sounded like marching bands and Christmas carols, laughter and excitement. My vision picked up on the thousands of strands of lights glittering in the darkness like diamonds.

I placed the Magnum back in the shoulder holster for now. "What's going on?" I asked Kansas as he moved toward me. In his hands, he had a larger flame thrower that seemed to have all the bells and whistles one would need to kill things that rose from graves. I looked down at the smaller flame thrower he had given me earlier and had weapon envy. I had seen firsthand what those things could do and I was convinced that the bigger the weapon, the better. "You don't happen to have another one of those do you?"

He smiled as he looked over the weapon in his hand. "The Christmas parade. And no." Like a spoiled little brat, I thought about pouting, but held it in for now.

Finally, the light bulb went on. In all the gory details going on inside my head, I had forgotten about the annual Christmas parade on Church Street. I just didn't get it. Undead things with no souls celebrating the birth of the Messiah and none of the humans seemed to pick up on it. A simple lapse of judgment all in the name of the holiday spirit. Throw out a few candy canes, dress up a few roaches like elves and everybody buys into the whole peace on earth crap. I shook my head in confusion. "With what we need to do, do you really think now is a good time to watch a parade?"

"Mayor Lopes and Quinn are going to be on the last float. Victor will try to kill him once the parade rounds Garland Avenue."

I watched as he checked his arsenal. He didn't seem to have a sense of urgency, which in turn made me very nervous. "Victor is going to kill Lopes right out in the open? Either he had giant balls or a very small brain."

This made Ashley laugh. "Any good vampire can make enough of a distraction that he can get away with murder." She began to walk toward the large crowd at the corner of Orange and Church streets. Hiding the large flame thrower didn't seem to be top priority. She carried it across her chest with the barrel resting on her right shoulder like a bag of groceries.

"Speaking from experience I'm guessing?" I followed, still distracted by the growing crowds. I could feel power close by and lots of it. Nothing abnormal this close to Bat Town, but when you know there is a crazed killer lurking nearby, the large population of people gave him plenty of places to hide. I grabbed the butt of the Magnum as

I heard a scream, only to see it was a couple of teenage girls horse playing with their dates. I had already convinced myself that I wouldn't prepared for the battle ahead.

"I've never killed a vampire that didn't deserve to die," she added as she continued to walk.

I stepped next to her and could see the outline of her face in the glow of the lights. She had a different look about her. One of great seriousness and concern, which did wonders for my own paranoia. "What's that supposed to mean?"

Ashley didn't answer. Instead she began to weave her way through the thickening crowd. I expected someone at some point to make a comment about the elephant gun on her shoulder, but everyone seemed oblivious to it. I guess if you spend Christmas in Bat Town a flamethrower isn't all that out of place.

As we turned the corner and onto Church Street, it appeared as if someone opened a door to another world. Fake snow, nothing more than soap bubbles, blew in the light breeze from machines high above the buildings. Music as loud as a rock concert belted out Jingle Bell Rock. Floats decorated with vivid colors and flashing lights inched their way down the narrow street. In the air the smell of cotton candy and corn dogs, along with a faint smell of human blood. I doubted that I really smelled the blood, but I had convinced myself of the fact years ago and couldn't break the habit.

Across the street, the Sun Bank building glowed with a larger than life wreath. Banners and smaller wreaths hung from light poles with sayings such as "Season Greetings" and "Happy Holidays" gave the area a festive flavor. From behind the float I could hear a high school band playing an out of tune version of Silent Night.

We snaked our way through the abyss of faceless potential meals so consumed in the parade and celebration that we were able to pass without any questions.

To my right, the smell of perfectly prepared steaks oozed from The Coffin, Quinn's restaurant for the rich and famous. I stopped for a second at the door and tried to peer in. A lot of death had come from inside that hell hole, and I couldn't convince myself that it wouldn't happen again.

"He's not there," Kansas said. I jerked back to reality and found him stopped and looking back at me. "Come on."

I followed without questioning it. Far be it from me to know what I might be about to face. I thought about Angie and knew that she was either cuddled up with the other furballs or naked on Quinn's bed. Either way, I didn't like it. Though I'd never admit it, I found myself jealous to the point of distraction. I shook off the disgust. Love had been a pain in the ass on its own. Throw in a sexy shape shifter to boot and life got complicated fast.

With all my being, I tried to clear my head of sexy monsters and flesh eating zombies when a tattered man who appeared to be homeless jumped out of the crowd and faced me. "Is your soul saved, my friend?"

I stared into his eyes and grew cold. Underneath the dirt and grime I saw Father Garcia. Be careful when asking a higher power for some sort of distraction, you just might get it. "Father?" I felt my knees buckle under me. Before I knew it, I had slammed into another man watching the parade.

"Heathens and devil's toys. That's all they are, son. Get right with God before they take your soul." He seemed to be looking right through me. I couldn't take my eyes off of him. I lost my visual on Kansas and Ashley. Time had come to a complete stop.

He moved around me as if I would bite him. Close but keeping his distance at the same time. I watched, not knowing what to say or do. All the sounds around me seemed to disappear. All accept his voice.

The man stopped. His face grew with a look of confusion. A long boney finger pointed at me as he became far more animated. "You're one of them, aren't you?"

"What?" I asked.

"A vampire. A no good son of a bitch, vampire." His body language started to show hostility. I wanted to take a step backwards but couldn't. I wanted to move past him but was unable. Like a fly caught in a spider's web, I became tangled and immobile. "Look at you. You're a no good, son of a bitch, vampire," he repeated. He looked ahead to Ashley. "Told you she would be trouble for you. Should have listened to me."

Another homeless man appeared from the crowd. A large black man also dressed in rags. The smell of body odor and alcohol hit me hard. But as I took it in, I realized it was the smell of rotten meat. I coughed as I tried to catch my breath. "Asa?" I asked.

The large man looked down at me and shook his head. A baritone voice filled the air. "Yeah, he's a vampire. Trying to hide it, but I can see through." His attention moved to the first man. "What was it he called things like him? Cockroaches?" As he asked the question, his face squinted up as if confused.

I tried to speak but couldn't. I shook my head in denial to what I saw and to the accusations they were making. *Dracul Sang* or not, I hadn't come to terms with being anything other than a simple human being. Nothing more than a mutt that was caught in the crosshairs of genetic defects. "No," I simply replied.

Others began to turn and look at me. I recognized my mother, Albert Kincaid, and countless other roaches I had killed. All looked at me as if I were the monster. Each spat out their interpretation of what I had become.

I put my hands over my ears and hoped it would stop, but it didn't. The voices crawled inside my head in the form of demonic whispers. Others in the crowd began to turn and look at me. Each with hollow eyes. Beams of bright light exited the sockets. Screams of lost souls howled from their bodies.

"Stop it!" I shouted, but the chants continued. The screams remained a constant.

I pulled my hands from my ears and tried to move again, only to find myself unable to do so. Under the skin of my palms I could see something slither. Not like a worm or serpent, but a face. My face. My very soul tried to rip through my skin. Pain hit me as it grew. Claws dug from the inside out. Pressure built to the point that I was sure I was about to lose consciousness. I screamed so loud that I could feel my vocal chords snap.

My chest bulged with the movement. From inside my own body, I heard my sternum crack under the mounting pressure. Skin split in a single jagged path from my throat to my groin. I tried to move to the ground, but some unseen entity held me in place. Blood shot out of my mouth and nose with such a force that my teeth became loose.

The thing inside me, continued to claw and eat its way out of my body. Instead of wanting and trying to set it free, I found myself holding it in. I knew that if my soul escaped, I would have nothing else.

A head popped from between the muscle and skin and looked up at me. It smiled with a devilish grin. Two small horns on either side of its temple dripped with my own blood. I tried to push it back in me. Razor sharp teeth snapped at my hands. Tiny fingers wrestled with me. "Oh, God!" I shouted.

"We've eaten your God!" the thing shouted back.

All the figures, those I knew and the ones with the empty eye sockets, circled me and echoed my screams in patronizing sounds.

"Paul!" they shouted.

I refused to answer. My hands still firmly on the soul as it tried to get out. Large holes marked where the thing had bitten me. I held tight to it as the pain mounted.

"Paul," they all shouted again.

A leg broke free of my body now. The thing was strong. Simply playing with me. Prolonging the inevitable. "Paul," it shouted as it bit my wrist.

"Paul!"

It vanished.

Kansas stood there looking at me with eyes filled with questions. "Are you alright?"

Good question. I looked around as the sounds of the parade came back to life. The lights of the floats and street returned to my sight. Sweat dripped from my body as if I had just stepped out of a pool. I looked at Kansas and Ashley and tried to recollect the things that I had just seen. My hands felt my chest and found nothing out of the ordinary. Still dazed, I shook my head.

"Let's go." Ashley's attention remained on me for a lingering few seconds before adding, "You look like you've just seen a ghost."

33

I HAD no time to dwell on the nightmare that I had. Distractions came at me from everywhere, and as I looked down the line of parade floats, my heart began to beat a little faster. Coming at us like a march on death's door, the final float. High above, I could see the mayor along with Quinn Rubio and Santa Claus, waving at the crowd and throwing some sort of candy in shiny wrappers. Before I could stop it, I caught myself rolling my eyes. It seemed like such a calamity of characters to see together. A dirty politician, a blood sucker, and an elf that likes children to sit on his lap for candy. Oh, by the way, happy holidays!

When I turned to Kansas, he already looked at the approaching float of death as well. We glanced at one another, knowing that this is where things were going to start to go bad. I tried to take in as many faces as I could. If everything Ashley had told me turned out to be true, Victor had to be close by.

I looked to my right and could see the intersection of Church and Garland. Again, I scanned the sea of people and hoped to find the monster before it found us. Inside, I screamed to all of them to run. Here they were, hoping to have a few minutes of holiday cheer and had no clue that they stood in the middle of a death trap.

I started to move toward the float, when Ashley grabbed my arm.

"You go after Victor, I'll arrest Mayor Lopes." In her eyes I saw something I had never seen before. An emptiness. Hopelessness. I started to speak when I thought better of it. As the float moved closer, she smiled and added, "Good luck."

Unlike the human side of things, Quinn would see the situation very differently. This would never be about justice or getting a psychotic killer off of the streets. The master roach only saw it in dollars and cents and how it would affect his power on Church Street. Arresting the mayor from a Christmas parade float in public would look worse than him being killed in the darkness a few feet further down the path.

Quinn didn't oppose to killing by any means. In fact, according to information I had, he had set Mayor Lopes up for the big end of life. Not for what he did at the Crowne Plaza, but because he knew too much on too many blood heads.

I looked back at Quinn as I took in what Ashley had said. I had no doubt I would get the short end of the stick, but in the bat world, I understood why. With a great deal of reluctance and paranoia, I nodded and took a step toward Garland.

I had no more than taken a step when I heard the first scream. Like a rogue wave washing over the crowd, it grew with intensity and chaos. Even before I pivoted and started my run, I knew and that scared the hell out of me.

Three zombies crashed through a group of people, not far from the float with Lopes and Quinn. One of them already had an arm in its mouth. A shower of blood colored the street and more fell victim to the monsters. Bodies with gaping holes rested along the edge of the street. I pulled up the small flamethrower and looked over to Kansas, who already began a defensive attack. Glancing at my weapon and comparing it to his all I could do is shake my head and pray that little things really did come in big packages.

A massive wall of people began to rush toward us. I dove in front of one of the floats in an attempt to keep from being trampled. I felt the vehicle rock as hundreds of runners plowed into it. It heaved to one side, threatening to turn over before coming back on all fours. Several fell to the pavement and were unable to regain their footing as hundreds more behind them crushed them back to the ground.

Screaming. Crying. Panic. Running. It all meshed together like a Thanksgiving dinner from hell. I peeked around the float to see if I could get closer to the zombies and hopefully save a life or two, but found the impregnable wall of endless people, nonstop.

If you can't go around something, you might have to go over it. I climbed up on top of the float and scanned my situation. From here, I stood high enough that I could see the zombies as they ate their way through the dispersing crowd. Kansas moved on the far sidewalk as he tried to inch his way through the mob.

Lopes, Santa Claus and Quinn Rubio stood on the float, watching the events unfold. The mayor desperately tried to find sanctuary, while Quinn stared at Santa with confusion and what resembled anger. There was something about the jolly ole elf that made me believe that he was a roach.

As I continued to watch the zombies work the crowd, I sensed something wrong. The monsters could have easily gotten to the float by now, but instead continued to push them towards the float I stood on. Then I remembered what Ashley had said about a good coffin sleeper always making a distraction in a crowd in order to get to its prey.

Through the fleeing crowds below I noticed a shadow along the sidewalk that did something very peculiar. It didn't run like the others. It moved towards the float with great ease as if on a Sunday stroll.

I sat the flamethrower on a make-shift present and pulled out the Magnum. I didn't know a lot about zombies, but I banked on the fact that if you kill the daisy pusher that raised them, they all die with it.

But getting a good shot off wouldn't be that easy. Hundreds of people still rushed by my float. Each crashed into it as the ones behind them pushed forward. With each growing scream the panic increased and the float rocked a little harder. I could feel it lift and drift along the street much like a raft on a river.

I second guessed myself and the intentions of the roaches. Victor in particular. I couldn't believe that Quinn would want something like this to happen right out in the public. Bad for business, you know. Which led me to even darker thoughts. Either the zombies were out of Victor's control or something far worse pulled their strings.

Each time I tried to get a decent aim, I would be knocked off balance by the next wave of dinner with legs. I searched along the ground for another place to go, but knew I had the best vantage point I could get. If I went back to the ground I would not only have to contend with the people, but I wouldn't be able to see Victor, much less get off a shot. Worse yet, I would lose sight of the zombies that continued to kill those that weren't fast enough to get out of the way.

I continued to be amazed at the strength and speed they had. Unlike Hollywood's version, the real zombies moved with unnatural grace and velocity. In a few more minutes, the monsters would be biting distance from my float. I laid a hand on the flamethrower just as a precaution.

Victor continued to move through the lights and shadows of the street. I lost him from time to time from the combination of flickering lights and clumps of falling "snow". So much movement around me. I found it impossible to focus on anything. I had sensory overload. Lights. Colors. Movement. Speed. Blood. Death.

My eyes volleyed between Ashley and Lopes. The detective worked her way through the crowd, clinging to the side of the buildings. Victor didn't seem to notice her. His attention seemed to be on the zombies and getting to Lopes.

Kansas had the flamethrower ready to fire as he pushed his way toward his targets, but like me, he had problems getting into a position where he could get a clean shot. Some might say catching the public on fire might be counterproductive in saving their lives. I, on-the-other-hand, hadn't made up my mind.

Lopes panicked. He jumped from the float and began to run in the opposite direction of the crowd and zombies. I spun in a concoction of horror and anger as I saw it happen. With all the strength I had, I kicked the large Christmas present on the float with me. Pain shot through me. I liked it. It proved that I still remained human deep down inside, no matter what the blood gluttons thought.

"No!" I shouted as I jumped back to the ground in an attempt to run. I was immediately knocked on my ass by the stampede. With all the human strength I had, I pushed myself back up, but found I had been rolled nearly twenty feet further back than what I had started. I pulled the Magnum up and shot in the air, in an attempt to part the escapees. When you have a big gun, people tend to move out of your way.

As I forced my way forward I noticed Kansas. He had worked his way from the sidewalk to the opening just shy of the parade float where Quinn and Santa still stood. I had lost sight of Victor and Lopes and could feel the adrenalin in me starting to kick in.

Dead eyes turned to me. Quinn felt my presence. He stood above us all like a buzzard waiting for death to finish the deed. No look of remorse in his eyes, no sympathy for the innocent that were dying. He simply stood there as if not sure what to do.

Another body crashed into me. The force knocked me back on my heels, but I remained vertical. I grew tired just trying to stand my ground. Having a weapon in either hand didn't help either. I found my balance uncertain at best. By the time I got to Victor, I would be too fatigued to do anything about it. The crowd around me attempted to clear a path, but there were so many of them, no one could successfully get out of the way.

I replaced my Magnum and pulled the flamethrower up. With all those that still ran by, it made it difficult to get a clean look at the target. People packed so tightly, I found it almost impossible to simply raise my arm enough to attempt a shot.

The first zombie drew within twenty feet or so from me. His rotten skin a blue-gray with areas on his face where the flesh had completely fallen off and exposed the dull white bone underneath. Even from this distance I could smell the death and see the crawling maggots on its skin.

Its mouth opened wide and took out a woman's throat. Strings of flesh dangled from putrid lips. Jaws worked like a hungry beast. Blood dripped from its chin. The victim already on the ground dead, but still twitching as more crimson liquid gushed from the large wound.

Animated corpse eyes turned to me with hunger. No time to think.

Reaction the only thing that kept me alive. I pulled the trigger on the flamethrower. The monster rushed forward. Dead hands clung to me. A blackened mouth wide with fresh kill. Fire. Heat. More screams. Most mine. Along its skin I saw the inferno starting to take hold. Burning dead skin filled the air. Smoke took away most of my vision.

Those hands remained tight on my wrist. I had to get away. If I failed in only a few more seconds it would either eat its way through me or I'd also be an overgrown tiki torch. I beat the dead hand with the butt of the flamethrower. Teeth snapped at my wrist. Bugs and maggots jumped from the burning corpse to me.

I began to hit it in the face with the flamethrower as panic set in. Even if this thing didn't eat me, I'd be burned alive. Flame lit on my shirt then burnt out, but the pain and terror of it remained. As the jaws opened again, I stuck the barrel of the weapon in its mouth and nearly pulled the trigger when Kansas moved behind it and sliced its neck clean from the shoulders.

Unlike with roaches, decapitation didn't stop zombies. It simply created two monsters instead of one. Before I could convey that message to Zeke, he sprayed it the head with more flame as it sat on the pavement biting its way toward me.

The body remained attached to me. With the large knife, he stabbed it in the heart as it lay on the ground burning. I flung the hand, still attached to me several times before it set me free.

He never said a word as I watched what remained of the zombie burn lifelessly. I stood there as I tried to gather my thoughts on what to do. My gut told me to go after Lopes, but I couldn't leave Kansas alone with the zombies that continued to pour onto the street.

In a quick scan, I counted ten of the things as they ate their way through the stampede of people. Two moved to my right. I pulled the flamethrower up and blasted them with everything I had. This time I became wise enough to burn and move. Catching them on fire proved easy, killing them took time. I found out the hard way that they could easily eat you alive while they burned to death.

Another monster attacked a woman next to Ashley. Saliva and blood dripped from the dead flesh that had at one time been a chin.

Muscle and bone worked in harmony as they bit into his back. I knew, like with humans, fire and roaches didn't mix, but I had no choice. Either I torched the earth worm or it would eat its way through to me.

I held my breath and pulled the trigger. I felt the heat as it blasted into the back of the zombie. It screamed in pain. My muscles stiffened as it turned to face me. Ashley fell to the ground like a rag doll. I pulled the trigger one more time and watched him light up the night and fall before me like a burned marshmallow.

When I turned, I ran into Santa Claus. I could feel the power race along my skin. Hollow vibes shot through me as I glanced into those demon eyes. "Victor?"

34

RAZOR-LIKE CLAWS STRUCK me across the face. Four rivers of blood filled wounds where skin and meat had been. I hit the ground and reached for the Magnum. But in doing so, I knew I'd have to sacrifice the flamethrower, which would leave me vulnerable to the zombies.

One thing I had learned in my years in the freak district, take care of the monster closest to you first. Before I could get a hold on the Magnum, I felt Victor's weight on me. It drove me further into the pavement then lifted me back into the air. For what seemed to be forever, I became suspended above the street, looking down at the miserable creature that had started all of this. The flamethrower ripped from my fingers and spun into the darkness.

I swung with everything I had. My fist connected with the side of his face. Unimaginable things squirted from the wound. Slime dripped from my knuckles as I pulled them back. I did my best not to think about it.

Deadly fangs revealed themselves from the lethal mouth. I braced myself for the attack. I wanted to reach for the Magnum again, but knew I'd never make it in time. Those menacing jaws would be on my jugular too soon. I stiffened my arms and tried to hold off the bite.

Victor smiled as he played the game. Never the kill that gave him the thrill, but the torture that came before it. Fangs bit into my left shoulder, tearing away muscle. I screamed as I felt the tingles of pain rip through my body.

He slammed me forward, through a glass window of one of the clubs that lined the street. Pieces danced around me as I tried to catch my balance. I could feel the warm blood from the bite cascading down my back and along my collar bone, but none of it washed away the torment of the wound.

The club would have been wall to wall people on any ordinary night when the local zombies didn't have the munchies. But tonight, not even a vein hijacker to be found. Unlike on the other side of the window, I found no life other than me.

Victor stood with my blood dripping from his jaws and chin. The red Santa suit now wet with my fluids. He floated through the window in a way that all roaches do. It seemed so graceful, yet instant. I watched him move in on me, but found it impossible to break away from his magic. "Do not worry, *Dracul Sang*. I do not plan to use magic on you. I want you to enjoy every bit of the pain I have in store for you."

He twisted my head and neck around. Impossible to look anywhere but in his eyes. I did the only thing a defenseless man in my position could do. I closed my eyes as if my life depended on it. If he could gain control of me through his gaze, there would be nothing I could do. I had been in the gaze of a powerful daisy pusher before and knew that even if he didn't plan on using magic on me, there would still be some twisted shit behind those things.

The vein weasel shook me so hard that I became disoriented. "Look at me, *Dracul Sang*!" His words were filled with the uncontrollable anger.

I had to rely on my ears now. And unlike my eyes, I couldn't block out the sounds that echoed inside my head. I could still hear the screams and the pandemonium that existed just feet away. Somewhere close by, zombies still lurked, ready for a hot meal. I had no reason to believe that they wouldn't come looking for me.

From time to time I could hear the growl of Ashley's and Kansas' flamethrowers. The only indication I had that they were alive. Out of the speakers, I could still hear the jolly sounds of the season, unaware of the death and mayhem below.

Boney fingers pulled at my cheeks, as Victor tried to pry my eyes open. My hands wrapped around his wrists in an attempt to stop him. It felt as though he would peel the skin right off of my face. I grunted in defeat as eye lids were separated and I stared into the face of death. "Open them and look at me or I will cut your eye lids off."

I tried to turn my head, but his grip held like a vice. My own blood still dripped in slow, methodical amounts from his chin and mouth. More infectious slime slithered from the wet wound on his cheek. Pale skin seemed to almost disappear behind the brightness of those hypnotic orbs. Dark, endless and ageless, they coiled around me like a serpent.

"Tonight, you die like a real vampire," he said as he forced me back to my feet and hung me in the air. The bite in my shoulder came to life like nothing I had ever felt before. My vision blurred with unforgiving pain. From here, I could see the remains of the nightmare that had taken place in the street. Dead bodies scattered along the pavement, sidewalk and some even on the floats that had been abruptly abandoned. I scanned for Ashley and Kansas as best I could, but found nothing. I could see the float Quinn and Victor were on, with no sign of the master blood bank. To keep what little sanity I still had, I turned away from the window in total denial of what I had witnessed.

Victor shoved me forward, over several tables, still decorated with various drinks in pretty little glasses. I felt the table that met my back, break under the collision as it sent me to the floor. Within seconds, I became doused with the alcoholic debris. The wound in my shoulder burned as if set on fire.

Large amounts of power entered the room. I grunted with pain as it ate away the skin on my arms and along my back. On the far end of the room I saw three figures standing as if at attention. Camuel de Belatucadros , Aelfric and Ella Selene. Oversized black eyes watched with lifeless curiosity. I had no way of know if they had come here to kill me or simply watch me be killed. Didn't matter, my fate ended the same.

"I was beginning to worry you weren't going to figure it all out," he said as he bounced a table leg in his hand. I didn't have to guess or wait long to find out what he planned to do with it. "I only wish you were stronger so I could make the pain last longer."

The force of the blow caught me in the upper right leg, followed by a repeat visit before it had time to swell. I reached for the Magnum just as he stepped on top of me. Above me, I could see the sharp splintered end of the table leg.

"You made me what I am, Avenger." He pointed to his heart. "Deformed misery as a reminder of what you are." His mouth moved against my ear. I could smell the blood that spewed from the hole in his face. "My zombies and I will eat our way through your humans and pure blood vampires as well. The deaths of those at the Crowne Plaza only the beginning. Think about that as I drive this stake through your heart."

"Help me," I shouted to the three in the back of the room.

Ella Selene spoke. "It is not for us to decide, *Dracul Sang*."

Well shit…

Victor raised the table leg high in the air and with all the force he had brought it down on me. I twisted just enough that the stake missed all of my prized organs and lodged between my ribs. Vital organ or not, I was in indescribable agony.

At nearly the same time I had brought the Magnum up and drove it in his crotch. I pulled the trigger and closed my eyes. Internal organs and blood splattered on and around me.

The monster stepped away, dazed and staggered to one of the tables. A hollow look replaced that evil façade. If he was in pain he kept it to himself. More glassware crashed to the floor as demon eyes shined back at me. I pulled myself as upright as I could to get a better aim at my target. I didn't plan on taking a chance that he wouldn't be able to come back on me again. He leaned on the table leg that had been used to impale me. Everything around me seemed to drip with my blood. Not happy about that.

Those dead black eyes now crimson red. He threw up blood and ash as he faltered to the floor just out of my reach. His right hand still gripped the piece of wood and he gagged on more blood and ash. I could smell the cinders coming from him and knew it would only be a matter of time before he caught fire.

Aelfric spoke, "You must end him now, *Dracul Sang.*"

Victor pulled the stake above his own heart and started down with it toward Ella Selene. She never moved a muscle.

"No!" I screamed as I pulled the trigger. A large hole opened between Victor's eyes. Staring back at me as life left them. I could hear the hissing and burning inside him as if sitting by a camp fire. He smiled one last time with a grunt of laughter. Moments later his head exploded. Dead matter littered the walls and floor of the abandoned night club.

I took as deep of a breath as I could, which wasn't much. As gingerly as I could, I patted the wound in my side. To my relief it was only blood. Nothing dark to suggest that the stake had punctured my liver. I stood in spite of myself and walked to Victor's remains and kicked them. Like a well burned log, it lit up with firework sparks. The form that had only moments ago been a cockroach now fell under its own weight into a pile of ash.

All three of the roaches in the room with me turned toward the broken window in synchronized motion.

I raised my head as I listened in the not so distant night.

Werewolves!

35

I COULD BARELY STAND. In the last few minutes of my life, I had been bitten, punched and stabbed and I had no reason to believe that my night would get any easier. I leaned against one of the tables that hadn't been broken stared at the ashes in front of me. The end of an era. Victor and I had been bitter enemies long before the cockroach laws made it illegal to kill them. We had had debts to settle with one another, but we were both too stubborn to die. It didn't seem real that he lay dead below me. I never thought I'd live to see the day.

I patted the wound with my right hand, only to have it return red, but already I could feel things at work inside me. Thanks to the monster viruses, I healed much quicker than the normal human. Normal? What the hell did that mean anymore?

As I started to take a step forward, the doors crashed open. Kansas slid into more chairs and tables to my right. Quinn followed. I could tell by the look on the master blood head's face, it had been no accident that Kansas flew in like an undead Frisbee.

Before I could react Quinn jumped on top of Kansas. He grabbed Kansas and pulled him up, only to slam him against the wall. The detective let out a painful yell. His face swollen and bloody. The power I felt around me nearly forced me backwards.

Quinn looked over to me. By the look I got, I don't think he knew I had been in the room. His jet black hair dripped in his face, fangs jutted out of that gapping mouth. "You." That word alone made me take another step backwards. Said with as much animosity as possible. While still staring at me, he threw Kansas to the other side of the room with little effort. That alone made me reach for the Magnum again. The monster before me began to walk my way. Shit. "It could have all been so perfect if you two had just left it alone. Now you have both broken vampire code and for what? The lives of a few pathetic humans?"

"I *am* one of those pathetic humans," I answered, the Magnum aimed at his dead heart.

Kansas rested along the wall, blood pouring from his head. By the looks of him, it hadn't all been applied by Quinn. I guessed he had had a chunk taken out of him by our zombie friends. Quinn looked at the gun, but his anger out thought his brain. He took a step towards me. "Oh, but you are not one of them, *Dracul Sang*? You have given your word to the Vampire Council stating that you were indeed a master vampire." He stopped as he looked at three vampires behind me. I didn't have to guess. He looked like he had seen a ghost.

"Take another step and I'll ash you like I did Victor."

"Welcome *Dracul Morte*," Aelfric said in his solemn voice. It didn't take much to figure out, the three were here to watch more death and dismemberment.

"Your blood says you are afraid, *Dracul Morte*. Why is this?"

Quinn looked back to me. "Things would have ended so much better if you and your detective had just stayed away. We would have handled Lopes quietly. For the detectives' participation in the act, it will cost both of them their lives. For you, my actions may be a bit more complicated due to your status, but I am willing to take my chances with the Council." The vein weasel moved on me before I had time to react. My finger pulled the trigger but didn't hit its mark.

For the second time on this night, I found myself on my back, staring up at a cockroach. His power shifted me violently. Brutal punches rammed my jaw and nose. Blood poured so quickly I thought I might drown. My vision nothing more than blurred images of Quinn's fist. God, this would work to my advantage if the three stooges would help out just a little, but they remained like granite statues with shiny black eyes.

More howls moved in on us. I could feel them. Not something I needed right now. Shifters had a very different type of power, but I was finding out that when they were near, it was changing things in me. I felt a throaty growl come into my throat. I swallowed it back down for now.

Quinn twisted the flesh of my shoulders into a handle and threw me back across the room. I had no choice but to hold onto the Magnum and hope that I got an opportunity to kill him. Losing it could mean an instant obituary for me. He moved on me with paranormal speed. I kicked an overturned chair in his way. For a moment he had been thrown off balance. I pulled the Magnum up again and fired only to find Quinn not there by the time the bullet left.

He reappeared on the other side of me as if by some sort of magic. Kansas moved in on him from the other side. Quinn turned and kicked him as he advanced. I heard his collar bone snap as Kansas twisted back to the floor. I used the time to grab a wooden stake and use it as a baseball bat against Quinn's head. Pieces of flesh splintered away with each violent blow, but I was still far from being in control.

Kansas stood again and battle rammed his way toward Quinn with a table. They rolled across the floor as the table disintegrated into nothing more than splinters. I moved on them both, still holding the wooden stake in one hand and the Magnum in the other.

Ashley entered through the window, her Glock drawn. Screaming in fear and anger at the same time.

Quinn moved back to his feet before my eyes adjusted and he grabbed the wrist with the stake. Long fingernails drove into my flesh. The smell of death rolled from under his expensive cologne. I was driven forward just as Kansas tried to stand.

Ashley shot twice, hitting Quinn in the chest. It didn't take long to realize they were regular bullets. The master vampire rushed through me toward Kansas.

The wooden stake pierced through Kansas' chest, just below the neck. But we weren't done yet. Our inertia pushed us to the far wall where the stake lodged itself. My weight hit against him and continued to cut through Kansas' body. Blood and other things spewed from the hole. His eyes now dark with death. Real death. He opened his mouth as if to breathe or speak. Impossible for him to do one and was unable to do the other.

I felt my own bones beginning to break and reform. Terror and questions filled Ashley's eyes as I was slammed against the wall. Quinn rushed forward again, his shirt red with blood. His laid back personality nothing more than a cold blooded frenzy. He grabbed me by the throat and pushed the Magnum away from him. "How dare you bring zombies here!"

Now I was confused. The last thing I would be bringing to this fight is zombies. "You know Victor raised the zombies." I did my best to lower the gun, but he remained just too strong.

"The zombies Victor raised are dead. They have been for some time." He began to lower the arm with the Magnum. I tried to resist, but I could still feel too much pain from the puncture wound in my ribs. Like with Victor, he liked to play with his food before he killed it. He looked back to the three stooges. "One of them sent the zombies here."

Outside, I saw the first flash of something move by the broken window. I didn't have to wait long to find out what it was. Two zombies crashed through the doorway and stared at Quinn and myself. At this point, I had no idea where I had dropped off my flamethrower.

The two dead things moved in on us. Quinn evaporated into thin air. I pulled the Magnum back down as the resistance released. I knew from experience it wouldn't kill them, but it did a hell of a job of slowing them down.

I looked back to Kansas, who continued to be pinned to the wall and nearly truly dead. "Where's your flamethrower?"

Gray eyes looked up at me, drained of any animated life. "Gone." His head lowered and never moved again.

The first zombie landed at my feet as it tripped over the debris that littered the floor. I pulled the trigger and placed a nice big hole in the back of his head. Maggots and dead flesh scattered along the blood and ash already below.

I ran back and forth, trying to outmaneuver the one zombie and stay clear of the other that popped back on its feet. With my left hand, I pulled out the 9mm and began blazing a trail to the door. Who knew if more zombies waited in the street, but I knew two were in the bar ready to eat me. I was more than willing to take my chances outside.

Power hit me hard enough that I stumbled. Not roach power, but fur ball power. My muscles tensed again. "Not now!" I screamed as I looked at my hands. They were already beginning to change, which made holding the guns almost impossible. Bones began to break inside me again. I felt my strength increasing, but my mobility becoming less. By the time I became furry, I had a bad feeling I'd already be eaten. Before I lost all control of my hands, I placed the two guns back in their holsters and hoped for the best. In a twisted way, it seemed better to have them and not be able to use them than not have them at all.

Moving between me and the two zombies, I saw a flash of speed. The werewolf caught the monster by the throat and rolled it back inside. Their momentum pushed the second worm taxi with it. I could tell by its size that it was Kasey, which really didn't improve my situation much.

Behind me were two more wolves. They moved with unnatural speed through the street and attacked another zombie as it was pulled from the shadows.

On the ground another twenty yards, I saw the flamethrower that Kansas had had. With all the power I still possessed, I worked my way to it. I had a very good chance it would be the only thing that saved my life tonight. Of all things on this happy little earth, fire is the one consistent thing that could kill coffin munchers, fur balls and zombies. My plan remained simple. Kill as many of both as I could and let things sort themselves out once it ended. At this moment, I knew beyond a shadow of a doubt that the zombies were willing to kill me and I had no proof that the wolves wouldn't do the same.

Just as I reached the flamethrower, another cramp brought me to the ground. More bones moved and broke. Muscles twisted. Claws broke skin.

My hands no longer hands that I could use. Somewhere in between human and animal, but nowhere close to what I needed to hold and shoot the flamethrower. Instead, I lingered in the middle of Church Street twisting like a fish out of water. Worse yet, I knew that I couldn't complete the act, which left me nothing more than zombie bait.

One of the zombies came back out of the bar with Kasey on its back. The thing swatted him as if he was a fly. The second emerged from the shadows with the right side of its face now missing. Again, I reached for the flamethrower and tried to somehow grasp it, but it only made me more frustrated. The pain inside me probably would have stopped me even if I could hold it, but my mind told me I had to do something if I wanted to see the sun rise.

Angie moved from the street and attacked the second zombie. As primal as it sounded, I knew her from the scent. She moved in full on wolf form and drug the thing to the ground. I cursed everything I could think of as I watched her in the battle of her life. From deep inside myself I pushed the change back like gorge in my throat. Muscle and bones unsure of what to do. I concentrated on my hands. If I could get them back, I could level the playing field. How could she save Kasey's life with all she knew about him?

Skin started to replace fur. Fingers replaced paws. My hands gripped the flamethrower and I moved with as much speed as I could. Still being in the middle of the change kept me from being all that quick.

Angie saw my advancement and shoved her zombie towards me. I lit it up with heat and flame and prayed to God that it worked. Kasey and the other zombie continued to fight along the street. He had ripped most of its dead flesh from the skeletal frame, but still it moved towards me.

Ashley fired a second lethal shot on it and watched as the orange flame engulfed the thing. Heat and fire gave the otherwise cool

December night a change. Shadows became more predominant. Dark hiding places now visible.

The two zombies fell to the ground and never moved again. Kasey and Angie panted with exhaustion. I shook with cold sweat despite the heat of the fires and fell to my knees.

I had forgotten about the third zombie until it hit my vision. Two wolves were on it, but it continued to move against their will. I took a deep breath, came back to my feet and met it in the middle of the street. I looked it in the eyes and pulled the trigger. Illuminated death flickered. The thing fell face down and the stench of death filled the air.

36

I MUST HAVE PASSED out for a few seconds, because when I opened my eyes, I found myself looking at the black night and faces of Kasey and Angie, along with a few other fur balls. They, like me, were now back in human form. I remained quiet for a few seconds and tried to take it all in. I weighed my options and cursed at my results. Behind them stood Ashley, flamethrower still smoking.

The alpha male held out his hand to me. I looked at it, still not sure whether to move or not. "I'm not going to bite you."

With a great deal of reluctance, I took his hand and he pulled me back to my feet. I ached all over. The beating and the changes had taken their toll on my body. Which throbbed more at the moment I hadn't decided. It didn't matter. Pain is pain, no matter the source. "Thank you."

"Consider it an olive branch," Kasey added. I started to speak, but he continued before I could get the words out. "My job is to protect the pack, even if that means making questionable alliances. I can make that alliance with you or with Quinn." I started to open my mouth again, only to be stopped a second time. "We are here to kill Inderia. She's the one that has brought the zombies here tonight. Her infatuation with power nearly got members of my pack killed. I plan on hunting her down and killing her for that but it presents a problem."

I shook my head. "Somehow I'm guessing that involves me."

Angie spoke up. I could tell by the tone of her voice that things were changing between her and me. "If Kasey kills Inderia, it technically results in a death warrant by you. My alliance is with Quinn and the commercial vampires, so if Kasey makes an alliance with him, it will make us enemies. If he kills Inderia, it technically makes us enemies."

I had to laugh in disbelief. "You people are nuts. I don't give a damn about Inderia or Quinn." I looked to Kasey. "Kill them both for all I care." I looked back at Angie but continued to talk to Kasey, "You have my blessing." I started to walk away, then came back to Angie. I couldn't win. "You mean to tell me that if Kasey kills Inderia and I do nothing about it that makes you and me enemies even if I give him my blessing?"

The three pure bloods walked to my side. "Do you trust this one, *Dracul Sang?*" Ella Selene asked.

"No further than I can throw him, but I trust him more than Inderia."

"And the female?"

"Out of all of them, she's the one I trust..." I stopped myself from saying more.

Ella Selene looked to Angie. "You look for the *Dracul Sang's* blessing?"

"So to speak," Angie said. I could tell by the coldness in her voice she tried to distance herself from me. I hadn't encountered that with her before. My emotional attachment to her seemed out of place. As if something had ripped a hole in me.

"What about your alliance to Kasey and the pack? You plan on turning your back on them?"

I got madder by the second. It all seemed so irrational. I didn't know where to land emotionally with her. Friend. Ally. Lover? None seemed to fit at the moment.

"My alliance with the pack is the same as it always has been." I looked at her nude body and lust filled my mind. All of this alliance stuff seemed too much to talk about in our current state. Still I tried to grasp hold of the conversation at hand. "I also have an alliance with Quinn, like it or not. If Kasey sides with Quinn it makes things far less complicated for me. If he sides with you, it makes things complicated for you."

"I claimed to be the *Dracul Sang* to save your life from the Council and now you're going to use it against me?" I walked in a circle holding my head and screaming in my made up language. "You self-absorbed bitch!"

Her demeanor never changed. A cold stare stayed on me. "If you kill Inderia yourself, it would at least help you with Kasey and the rest of the pack."

"But for you and me, there is nothing?" I said it as if finding out that Santa Claus wasn't real. I couldn't imagine having her as an enemy. She drove me crazy, borderline insane, possessive and still I found it devastating to hear. It cut deep and I hadn't prepared for it. Sleeping with that maggot mouth proved disgusting enough, but to use it to build a wall between us made no sense. I knew Quinn had to be somewhere laughing at my demise.

37

I NEVER GOT to hear her answer. From our left, Inderia walked out of the bar that had been the focal point of a lot of ash and blood. She pulled Kansas' lifeless body by the wrist, the stake still in his chest. If he was alive I couldn't tell. I looked over to Kasey and begged him with my eyes not to move. Angie followed my eyes to Kasey and seemed to be telling him the same thing.

Mayor Lopes stalked just behind Inderia. I placed my hand on the Magnum once again, knowing that death had become the special on the menu tonight. Inderia stopped and stared at me. She made Angie's affections seem right down erotic. *"Dracul Sang*, I have been waiting for you." Inderia gave a show of her fangs as she dropped Kansas to the pavement.

With methodical care, I pulled the Magnum up. "Goodbye, Inderia."

As I started to pull the trigger and end all the drama, Inderia jerked Lopes in front of her. With her index finger raised she spoke, "To kill me, you will have to kill him. You are *Dracul Sang*. Which Council do you wish to address, human or vampire?" Lopes eyes shined wide with fear and I didn't blame him. "Are you willing to kill one of your precious humans to stop me?" We both knew she could and would kill him without thinking about it. Inderia looked down at Dieter who had rolled over onto his back

"Let them both go, Inderia. It's me that you want." The Magnum stared into her face. If she moved just an inch I'd take her down. Inside, I grew far more nervous with what Kasey or Angie might do than what Inderia had planned. We walked a very thin line and at any moment any of us could snap.

Inderia held Lopes with her left arm, covering as much of herself as she could. With the right, she reached down and pulled the stake out of Kansas' chest. He let out a loud cry of pain. His body tensed, but he remained flat on his back as if paralyzed.

Inderia's razor-like nails dug into Lopes' throat. "What will you chose? An innocent vampire or a corrupt human that can be linked to a lot of deaths."

"None of us are innocent, Inderia. We all deserved to die here. But in the end, we both know what you're after. You want to be *Dracul Sang*, so let Lopes go and kill me. Time to end this twisted game."

Things had changed for me tonight, but it had nothing to do with being a master cockroach or a pathetic human. I had no words to truly describe it, but I was willing to sacrifice Lopes in order to save Kansas. I began to doubt who or what I was. A year ago, take that back, a day ago, I'm not sure I'd have thought the same way.

Inderia moved her attention to Angie. "Perhaps it is not your loyalty to the human race that will make you sacrifice, but instead the lust of something far more monsterous. Killing the wolf would bring about so many more consequences. Both, you and Quinn are willing to die for her. Such a shame to vanquish so much love and lust at the same time."

Angie took a step toward Inderia just as Quinn appeared from the darkness. "Angela, stay where you are." I rolled my eyes in some many forms of disgust. First of all, he was about to make a complex situation even more complicated. But the real bitch of it was that he was walking in here like a hero on a white horse to save the lady in distress.

The jealous monster in me returned. Quinn gave me that knowing grin as he spoke. "Unlike the *Dracul Sang*, Inderia, I will destroy you before you can blink. You shared my bed only because I wanted to keep you close. Not because I loved or trusted you. Now your thirst for power will get you killed." He stared down at Kansas. "And the Council will find me innocent if destroy you." He looked at me. "I find it odd that of all those before you, it is my vampire that you seem most loyal to. Perhaps there is hope for you after all."

Damn it, he had forced me to make choices that I didn't want to have to make. I wanted to keep things cut and dry. Kill Inderia, arrest Lopes, walk away. But now Quinn stirred the pot. He knew I would have to sacrifice one or more of those options. He closed in on Inderia. "*Dracul Sang*, upon the common curtesy of the vampire code, I request your permission to kill Inderia for the crimes she has committed upon both our covens."

I knew he hadn't really asked for my permission. I just needed to know what he was really up to. "No," I simply said.

He gave me a sinister smile. I had somehow fallen into his trap. "Very well then. I will uphold your request." He looked back to Angie. "Then she will kill Inderia and Lopes, but please keep in mind that in doing so, she will put her own life at risk, not from Inderia alone, but also from the Council that may not see this as cut and dry as you and I see it. Not to mention human law will not be as lenient."

"You both talk as though you have a choice in who lives and dies. Do not underestimate what I am willing to sacrifice in order to take my rightful place in the coven." Inderia's nails cut through his throat like butter. The mayor's hands reached for his throat, his eyes bulged with horror as blood spewed between his fingers. He fell to the pavement.

Angie ran toward Inderia. I screamed in anger more than anything. Her caramel skin nothing more than a blur as she reached the blood sucker. Angie hit Inderia like a locomotive. I shifted the Magnum back in their direction, but with all the speed of the attack I was just as likely to hit Angie as I was Inderia.

Power filled the street again as Kasey returned to animal form. He joined Angie in the assault. Canine jaws and teeth ripped at Inderia's throat, but the fang banger created a comeback of her own. She ripped into Kasey and had him in a headlock. Kasey yelped out in pain.

Angie moved in on Inderia and Kasey. I wasn't sure which she was going to attack. The rational side of me said she would be loyal to her pack, but after tonight's conversations, I wasn't sure what I believed.

Angie bit into Inderia's back and ripped a large piece of pasty white skin free. The cockroach turned and held Kasey by the throat and shoved both of them backwards. Her jaws snapped at Angie, but unable to connect. With the alpha wolf in her grasp, she was unable to maneuver as well as she would have liked.

Ashley and I moved in on the three, still being very cautious of Quinn nearby. If I hadn't been so distracted, I would have gone ahead and added one bullet to his head.

Inderia spun Kasey around as she tried to break his neck. Angie continued to attack from behind. Quinn was being typical Quinn. He stood in the distance being undead coward of the year. Getting his own hands dirty, whether it was matters of the heart or life and death, he seemed to shy away.

Kasey grew limp as his airway tightened. With no resistance, Inderia would be able to finish him off with no problem at all. My fingers readied on the trigger. I had to take the shot. Even if I killed Kasey in the process I had to get to Inderia.

My Magnum rested against Inderia's temple as she released Kasey. Angie fell backwards on top of Dieter. A large gash on her right shoulder matted fur along her back. I couldn't tell how serious the wound had been, only that I presumed the worst.

Inderia turned slowly toward the Magnum and smiled in spite of her demise. "I would have done anything for you *Dracul Sang*. Together we could own this city. Do not let the loss of the wolf dictate your actions. She is not worth it. Unlike her, I only want you."

"Angie, are you alright?"

Nothing. Out of the corner of my vision, I could still see her lying on the pavement.

"Do you think killing me will make all your demons go away? Make you any less of a *Dracul Sang*?" Inderia taunted.

I could feel her power growing. My life flashed before my eyes. These things had taken everything from me. My mind grew clear, my body light. With little effort or concern, I pulled the trigger, sending the ultra violet bullet into her dark skull.

Ella Selene clapped and giggled. "Oh, the blood is fantastic, *Dracul Sang*."

38

INDERIA'S BODY lay at my feet, already turning to orange ash. How long I had been standing in the middle of the street, I couldn't remember. Nothing seemed real. Nothing mattered.

The sound of bones breaking and reforming snapped me out of my funk. Angie and Kasey took on human form again. They were covered in slime and sweat, but alive. Kasey limped his way to the sidewalk and sat down with great care. Large cuts along his face and neck bled down his chest. I could see his skin already binding back together. In a few hours, he would be as good as new.

Kansas lay in the darkness of a nearby alley. Ashley hugged me and gave me a quick kiss on the neck. "I'm glad you're alive." I didn't answer.

Angie's naked body made its way to Quinn's arms. Like with Kasey, her wounds would heal in time. Torn delicate skin exposed muscle underneath. I grimaced at the sight.

"I bid you farewell, *Dracul Sang*," Quinn said as he kissed Angie's head lightly.

"I'm not done," I replied.

Quinn stopped and looked back at me with a puzzled stare. Angie rested her head against his chest. She looked so innocent and fragile. I couldn't take in enough of her. The sight of her was addictive. My heart raced with jealousy. I loved and hated her at the same time.

I moved toward Quinn, checking my Magnum for bullets. By the time the sun rose, I planned to be free of all my enemies. Quinn, Kasey, and anything else that crossed my path. If it was a *Dracul Sang* they wanted, it was a *Dracul Sang* they were going to get.

"Excuse me?" Quinn asked.

My momentum stopped only when the Magnum hit Quinn's temple. If I had to live by cockroach law, I would use it to my advantage. My finger hooked the trigger. Everything I hated about myself, rose to the top. This monster before me had become the symbol for everything I hated and had lost.

Strong fingers grabbed my wrist and threatened to crush my bones. "Don't do this," Angie said with controlled anger. I could tell by her voice, it wasn't my best interest she had at heart.

"Step aside, Angie. I plan to kill Quinn and Kasey, don't add to my list." Quinn remained perfectly still. A crack of a smile curled in the corners of his mouth. Power began to prick my skin and cramp my muscles.

Angie's fingers gripped tighter. "I will break every bone in your body, Paul. Don't let your new title go to your head. I can still kill you."

Ella Selene moved toward Angie and held out her hand. "No!" I shouted.

The roach looked to me, no expression on her face. "Death is the answer, *Dracul Sang*."

"As *Dracul Sang*, I'm telling you not to harm her." I hoped in some twisted way it would work. For now, it did.

Angie stood there in front of me. Beautiful and alive. I took her in with all of my senses. Smells of vanilla filled my nostrils, sights of flawless caramel skin. I bit my tongue, trying not to confess my feelings. Beautiful eyes and full lips only an inch away, yet off limits. Even in her current condition of slime and sweat and blood, she made me weak. "But I'm a vampire now, Angie. Thought that would turn you on considering your low standards now."

I shouldn't have said that. In retrospect, I should have simply pulled the trigger. Angie slammed me to the ground. Her bare foot rested against my windpipe. Quinn's fine leather shoe only an inch from my bleeding head. He looked down at me with pity. The Magnum still in my hand, but now I simply lay there, loathing in my losses.

I looked in the eyes of Quinn Rubio. I didn't give a damn about getting caught. My hand shook with hatred. My fingers ached to pull the trigger. Angie continued to put pressure on my neck. If I shot, I knew I would lose her forever. Was she worth it? Was it worth her killing me? Time stopped. Sound evaporated as I weighed my options. Angie became invisible to me. Dead to me. I would have to kill them both.

Fingers released the Magnum in defeat. "Get out of here," I spat.

Quinn nodded and smiled. He pulled a handkerchief from his pocket and dropped it on my chest. "Farewell, *Dracul Sang*."

I watched as a great killer and a beautiful woman slipped out of my hands.

39

It was just after New Year's and I still hadn't come to grips with the nights that happened. I had thought about it again and again and made no sense out of any of it. I had become and enemy to myself. For now, willing to simply walk away from it all. I represented everything that slithered in the night and nothing at all, all at the same time.

I stood at the entrance of the hospital where Stephanie Kansas remained in a coma. Ashley appeared behind me and smiled. In her hands, I could see a small pot of daisies, complete with a small balloon with "Get Well Soon" on it. Now I looked bad. I didn't even have a card. After the month I had, details on things like this got lost in the shuffle rather easily. It showed how out of touch I had become. The thought of flowers had never entered my mind. I looked at the woman before me and it all came into focus. The little details had been the reason I could never make relationships work no matter how hard I tried.

I regrouped and tried to combine small talk and apologies together. A dangerous concoction for the average person, but right down lethal for me. "I am sorry for everything, Ashley. I hope one day you can believe me."

I honestly don't think she heard a word I said. Questions she had

had bottled up over the last few days could no longer be contained. She needed answers. Deserved answers. "Paul, tell me what you really are? Vampire, man, more, less."

I shrugged. "A monster, Ashley. I always have been. It's just that now I have an official title."

"I'm leaving for Jacksonville in the morning. Just wanted to say thank you for everything you did." She extended the hand with the small pot of daisies toward me. "Here, would you mind giving these to Stephanie for me."

I didn't take the bait. In fact, I retracted even more by placing my hands in my jeans pockets. "You did it, I just...I don't know. Forgive me, Ashley. I will always..."

She closed her eyes and huffed in aggravation. "Don't say it, Paul. Things will never be the same. I don't know who you are, what you are now, but know I'm here for you if you ever need me." She opened her eyes and adjusted the collar on my leather vest. "I know you're too much of a tough guy to ever open up to me, but I'm extending the offer just the same."

I opened my mouth to speak when alarms went off. Machine alarms. From inside Stephanie's room. Both Ashely and I started to move toward the room when we were flanked by an army of white coated blurs that pushed past us. Their eyes showed the fear and urgency of the alarms and I felt my body start to sink.

I could hear Kansas inside the room shouting out questions. His voice high and trembling. The other voices from inside the room commanding him to exit. More shouting. More questions.

Ashley and I met Kansas face to face at the entrance of the room. Kansas' frame crashed with Ashley. The daisies spilled across the gloss floor. Black dirt and white flowers danced in pure chaos.

Inside the room, I could see four bodies moving around the bed where Stephanie lay. One man in his mid-thirties and three, what I assumed to be nurses.

Stephanie's pale skin and sunken eyes synchronized with the high pitched sounds of the machines. Tubes ran from her arms and chest giving her the appearance of a macabre puppet.

Kansas crashed to the floor behind me. I could hear Ashley's voice, but couldn't make out the words. Everything in my world had suddenly shrunk to the body on the bed. Something I had seen before. Way too many times. It didn't make sense. It was too early. Impossible, yet the signs were all there.

I felt the cold rush of fear run through me. My muscles shook with anticipation of something strong and evil around me. Death had lay dormant here, but now awoke in full bloom.

"Get out!" I shouted as I reached for the Magnum.

"Paul!" Ashley screamed.

"NO!" Kansas added.

Eight eyes looked back at me as if I had lost it. I couldn't blame them not deny their conclusion. Each looked at the Magnum that shook in my hand, wanting to move. Unable to move. The first seed of a scream entered the room when the unimaginable happened.

Stephanie rose from the bed. Pale and light gray skin hid the lively woman I once knew. Undead orbs looked through me. Stephanie howled and clutched her chest.

"Stephanie!" Kansas shouted.

"Kansas, get back!" I answered. My weapon still aimed at Kansas' wife's head. "God don't make me do this. Not now. Not here." I prayed.

"Quinn!" Stephanie screamed as she turned and grabbed the small woman next to her by the throat. I could hear a distinct crunching sound as Stephanie's fangs pierced the skin. The room filled with shouting that matched the machines in pitch. Blood splattered across white sheets as Stephanie released the woman's throat minus a large section of flesh.

Smells of copper crawled through my nose. Saliva filled my mouth. My heart raced with both fear and excitement. Kill or feed? My thoughts fought with themselves. Fingers urged me to pull the trigger. Three white blurs slammed me against the wall as they escaped the fury of madness before me.

The young nurse grabbed what remained of her throat as she hit the wall behind her and slid to the floor. Fingers turned glossy red in a matter of seconds. Her eyes grabbed me as if I could do something to stop it.

Kansas' hands grabbed my wrist. More screaming filled my head as I wrestled with him to keep control of the weapon. More sirens and flashing lights added to the soundtrack of death around me.

I could see Ashley out of the corner of my eyes as I brought my attention back to Stephanie. "Run Ashley!"

Stephanie sat on her knees on top of the hospital bed. She looked right at me through the blood coated smile. A gray tongue licked more blood from her chin. A deep growl gurgled in her throat.

I had seen this all too many times. The awakening of a vampire is the most dangerous thing I've ever encountered. Hungry, confused and wild. The only thing motivating them is blood. But this remained a shock to me. Stephanie couldn't have been dead more than a few seconds, a minute at most. The events before me were impossible. And the cherry on top. Stephanie had shouted out Quinn's name. What the hell?

Kansas pushed past me shouting his wife's name. Life suddenly moved in slow motion. I could see the actions happening as if in a dream. Methodical and deliberate, yet I seemed unable to stop it.

The Magnum weighed heavy in my hand as I watched the scene unfold. Ashley started past me and toward Kansas. I did my best to block her momentum.

My anger rushed to my tongue. Having Ashley here only complicated things for me. "I told you to get the hell out of here. Go!" The words spewed from my throat with such force I instantly grew hoarse.

At the same time I saw it happen and could do nothing to stop it. The roach that used to be Stephanie grabbed Kansas. His body twisted across the bed rail. Now in the clutches of the monster, his face shown back at me. Pink skin glowed under his blond thin hair. Eyes bulging, his throat covered by the forearm of the blood licker.

"Quinn!" the thing hissed again.

"Let him go." From behind me, Ashely had returned. Her weapon moved past my right shoulder and pointed at Stephanie. "Do anything else and I'll shoot."

"No!" Kansas shouted. "Please, she's my wife. We can help her!"

It caught me funny. He didn't appear to be afraid of the thing that held him prisoner. Even now, in the clutches of this thing, he only cared about protecting her. "Is this what love is all about?" I thought. If so, it made perfect sense why I remained single. It made me think about the woman behind me. Yeah, we had had some very good times but if she turned all nasty like this, blowing her ass away would not be all that hard to do.

The creature grasped hold of Kansas and looked right at me as if piercing my soul. Inside those eyes I could tell she was daring me and begging me to kill her at the same time. Like me, she was trapped inside a body riddled with the virus that fed on its host as well as those that loved it.

As I looked at Stephanie, my rage burned. I hated Quinn for so many things in my life and now I had one more. He had led me to believe it had been Judas that had done these things to Kansas' wife, when the real rat had been only feet from me. I made a note of it. Underlined it. Highlighted it.

It also made things easier for me. The last thing I wanted to do was pull the trigger on my friend's wife while he watched me do it. I had no choice in the matter. I couldn't just let Kansas be killed by this monster. I tried to reason with all the scenarios that could play out in this and none of them ended well for me or for Kansas.

My Magnum pointed at the new roach's head. Ashley's Glock aimed at the same target over my shoulder. Like me, she pleaded with the evil before us to let Kansas go. Behind me, I could hear the screams and chaos that bloomed over our dire situation. One thing remained constant. I couldn't let Stephanie escape the room. This gave me very little time to play with. I had to end this and end it quickly or things were about to get very messy.

"Please Paul, no. She can be saved. God no!" Kansas bellowed. "My God, it's my wife."

"Not anymore," Ashley added. "You need to pull away now."

Kansas' attention darted to Ashley. "Either of you shoot her..."

"Kill Quinn," Stephanie growled. "Please. Kill me and kill Quinn."

With the Magnum still pointed at my target I methodically made my way around to the entrance of the room. Again, I couldn't let it get out. My mind raced with the thoughts of what Stephanie said. I could see Quinn's smiling face. Getting to him after everything that had happened over the last few weeks suddenly became a hunger. I wanted to kill Stephanie quick simply so I could go hunting. My hands shook with rage. Sweat beaded on my forehead. Cotton mouth chocked me.

Stephanie looked back to Kansas. "Goodbye." With that, the creature on the bed threw her husband against the wall across from me. IV bottles crashed to the floor. Alarms sounded. More screams from behind me. How many stood there I don't know. Why they were there had always been a bigger mystery to me. Humans always loved to see the blood and guts and elaborate the story as it gets told through time I guess. "Do it!"

In a blur of speed the thing lurched from the bed towards me. My finger pulled back on the trigger. I heard a combination of explosions as both Ashley and I shot. Kansas screamed from the floor as he tried to stand and move, but it had been too late.

Stephanie's body draped across the near side railing of the hospital bed and slithered to the floor. Rotten egg smells mixed with the gunpowder as the woman turned to ash like a well smoked cigar. Orange flashes sparked against dead flesh. I took a deep breath and shook with disgust.

Who shot first, who got the credit for killing the thing, didn't matter. What we had done would be unforgivable in Kansas' eyes. If he turned and did the same to us, I don't think I could blame him. There could be no hero in this. Nothing but a room full of victims. Damaged goods. I hated me for what I had become.

I watched as Kansas held handfuls of ashes in his hands. Deep gut wrenching heaves of sorrow filled the room now. Reasoning with him not an option. My life imploded. Hollow, yet vengeful. Nothing will ever be the same. His mouth wide open in shock. Silent screaming. He shook with tremors.

Ashley put her body against mine. She shook for a thousand reasons. I wanted to console her. I wanted to console Kansas, but the truth remained far more simple. I needed to go. Far away. I needed time to digest it all. I backed out of the room as a flood of doctors and other bodies entered. Beyond that, everything blurred into nothingness.

In the hallway I let the stress and the anger out. Hard screams echoed around me. I put the barrel of the Magnum in my mouth and did everything I could to pull the trigger but couldn't. I had so much more to do before I died. I thought about my life, who I wanted to be and compared it to who I became. Blood would be my calling card. Bloodshed would be the end of it all.

Again, I whispered to myself, *"Nothing will ever be the same."*

ABOUT THE AUTHOR

James Gillen is the award winning author of the Paul Isaac Vampire Series. His love for the macabre started with Edgar Allan Poe short stories and vampire comics his grandmother would sneak and buy. He lives in Central Florida and has worked for a major theme park for 33 years. Besides his passion for writing, he enjoys graphic art, riding motorcycles, collecting Batman memorabilia and cheering on the L.A. Chargers. He also plays bass in a couple of big band jazz groups in the area.

ALSO BY JAMES GILLEN

The Paul Isaac Vampire Series

Tortured Skin

Crimson Madness

Sins of Retribution